Devlin's Angel
Bad Boys Book Ten

Christine Young

Chapter One

Late spring 1828
Scotland

Merry Stewart walked from the kitchen in Daryl's bakery with a tray of her newest accomplishment, sticky buns. Justine, Donal's cook and Daryl's helper in the bakery, had been teaching her to bake with great success. Merry could list the string of conquests, as it seemed she had an aptitude for baking.

She set the tray on the huge round table where her sister-in-law's sisters sat chatting and letting their children run around the empty tables. It was after closing time. They all made it a habit of meeting in the bakery once a week, mostly on Saturdays. Their men would join them in a few hours to walk them home.

Five boys ages a few months to five years were gathered around the table. The newest addition to the family was Lacie and Leslie's little boy who would grow up to be the next Duke of Southcliff. Except for the littlest one, each was given a sticky bun. Each little boy managed to get the melted sugar and cinnamon butter everywhere but in his mouth.

Before too many minutes they would be sticky from head to toe and need to be dumped into a bath before dinner. Merry knew from experience growing up with her brothers, little boys just found ways to get dirtier than little girls.

"Auntie Merry, can I have two," Grant asked, tugging on her apron.

"If he can have two, so can I," Garret's little voice followed. "Wouldn't be fair otherwise."

Bliss cleared her throat ruffling both boys' heads, "Neither of you can have two so do stop asking. Your begging is grating on my frazzled nerves."

Merry laughed at the boys, wishing she could have one of her own, but that opportunity was taken away from her nearly three years ago when her brother, the Duke of Southcliff, ended her elopement with Douglas simply by informing the man she was fifteen years old. Well, she understood her lie would be uncovered but she'd hoped that Douglas wouldn't find out before they were married and had consummated the vows.

He did end the hasty engagement and immediately cried off. In less than a year, he was wed to another heiress. Now he had two sons. Well, he wasn't worth her time anyway. All he wanted was her money. She'd been brought low by his beautiful body coupled with the twinkle in his sky-blue eyes. In any case, she returned to her original idea. She intended to wed the Duke of Weston.

She set her sights back to the man who stole her heart when she first saw him in a coach in Paris then on a horse in the streets of Glasgow. It had to be love at first sight. At the time, she didn't know who he was. She often wondered if she would ever find out the man's name, the man who stole her heart.

Two months ago, at a masquerade ball in Glasgow given by some earl, she couldn't remember his name, she discovered he was there. At a distance, she'd seen him, standing so tall and broad shouldered, his dark black hair falling rakishly over his forehead. She couldn't quite make out his features as a mask covered them but she knew it was him. His introduction cemented her opinion. By the time she pushed her way through the throngs of people to ask for a dance or at least to introduce herself, he was gone.

Vanished. Her early eagerness changed to despair then caught at her heart, moisture filling her eyes. Still, she didn't intend to lose this man of her dreams.

Despite the fact she searched every room in the mansion, disrupting several liaisons, she failed to find him. For a minute or two she slumped to the floor, sitting with her dress splayed out all around her and fought the tears. At the time she was two weeks from turning eighteen. While she didn't have any illusions he would fall in love with her the very moment he saw her, she still needed to find a way to meet him. She couldn't do that unless she could manage an introduction. Despondent once more, she slowly made her way back to the ball and asked permission to leave. She couldn't bear to be there one more second, knowing he left.

It was just her luck as her carriage began to draw away from the mansion that he stepped from another carriage, striding up the steps to return to the festivities. She would have turned the carriage around but Lacie pleaded exhaustion along with the ever present need to feed her baby and was accompanying her home.

Now, back at the bakery, "Your mind is in the clouds." Lacie sat down beside her holding the young heir on her lap. "Are you thinking of the Duke of Weston again? Glad you finally managed an introduction. I've met him before and he's very handsome, but boring if you ask me."

"Didn't get an introduction. Besides, he is just stoic like my brother. Believe it goes along with the title as well as the responsibilities. You changed my brother though."

"Perhaps he's really a bad boy at heart. He could be just like our husbands," Chelsea said with a smirk as she wiped her son's fingers after he smeared the sweet mess over his chubby little cheeks.

"I am and just how I'm going to go about meeting him I haven't the vaguest idea." She sipped the tea in front of her as she placed a sticky bun on her plate. "How do you think I can do that?"

"Well," Lacie paused to adjust the baby sleeping in her arms, "I did hear he might be in Glasgow for the summer. Seems there was some scandal he was involved in. Also heard he's escaped London to a quieter place."

"Probably to avoid a duel. I heard that too," Daryl said. "Your duke got himself in a fine fix. He must have a temper. If you do meet him, you need to be careful."

"I heard he's gone to ground it was so bad," Merry muttered. "Nobody is going to see him, least of all me." She swiped her finger across the icing on the sticky bun then licked the sweet stuff. Think I'll spend the summer at Southcliff. At least I've free reign of the countryside, with no one there to tell me what I can and cannot do. You and Leslie will be stuck in town most of the summer, so I won't have to explain to anyone what I'm doing or where I'm going."

"No nightly rides," Bliss pointed out shaking her finger for emphasis. "You know it's not safe. Promise us."

Merry avoided Bliss' eyes, staring at her hands resting in her lap. She would do as she pleased. There was no danger in the nightly rides that she could see. After all, she never saw anyone when she chose to indulge in one.

"Yes, you will have the house pretty much to yourself. However, if we hear of any exploits, Leslie will be the first to drag you back to the city so he can keep a brotherly eye on you," Lacie said, apparently recognizing the simmering need to do her own thing in her eyes.

She lifted her shoulders in a deceptive shrug, "What would I do? There is absolutely nothing for me to get into trouble with. Besides, I'm eighteen now and very capable of making my own decisions. I don't need a guardian or a chaperone, thank you."

"While I don't doubt that for one instant, we both understand certain things." Lacie winked at her. "A girl doesn't have to do much to get into trouble, especially with their men folk."

"I've no men folk," Merry pointed out with a wistful smile as her thoughts flew to the Duke of Weston.

"There is the river and the pond," Chelsea said as she wiped the mess from the mouth of her little boy. "All of us know you have some kind of attraction to the water and swimming."

"Well, if I do go swimming, it won't be naked," she muttered as she looked from one lady to the other, heat creeping up her face.

Last time she swam that was exactly what she did. That was only two weeks ago.

Garret and Grant took that moment to run yelling around the table, their younger cousins chasing after them. Bliss grabbed one of the twins around the waist then stalked after the other, her intentions clear.

"Believe it's time to take these little hellions to the park so they can run off some of this extra energy before they see their doting papas,"

Bliss said with a determined air. "Of course, if I took them home, I would tell Broc it was time for him to do his duty with the boys and play with them."

All the little boys except Daryl's and Lacie's were herded out of the bakery to run off steam. Daryl and Lacie were left with Merry who was still moping, mostly for effect. Yet there was a certain depression that had settled around her, weighing down her shoulders. She needed a diversion. Wished for something to take her mind off the Duke of Weston.

"You're set on marrying this Duke of Weston then," Daryl said watching Merry closely. "Perhaps you should go to a few more balls coupled with an open mind. It might lead to something. You don't know who you might meet. There could be another man for you."

"Just as there was another Donal for you," Merry shot back clearly angry and unwilling to compromise in this. She did know her heart better than anyone.

"Promise me you won't wed him if you don't love him. He could be awful, you know, a real bounder. With the scandal hanging over his head, there is a hint of that," Lacie told her.

She let out a long dramatic breath of air as she tilted her head thinking about the man she wanted so desperately to meet that she could just barely inhale air. "I'll promise. Just because he's devilishly handsome and owns a magnificent stable doesn't mean he's a nice person."

Lacie laughed, obviously amused by the stable part. "There is more to a man than his stables."

"It's all true. I could meet someone and fall madly in love at some ball, but..." She drew in a deep breath of air feeling as if her eyes were crossing. "I've been to five balls in the last three months. All the men I've seen are boring and simpering fops. I want a real man. One whose body is like Leslie's and Donal's, all muscle and hard. Believe it or not, I want him to challenge me, give as good as he gets. I don't want a man who will cow tow to my every whim."

"Be careful what you wish for," Daryl murmured slanting Lacie an all-knowing glance before she laughed softly. "You might get more than you've bargained for, especially if you like your freedom."

"That is hardly giving the men a chance if you've already made up your mind," Daryl pointed out.

"Why was it so easy for you? I'm certainly not going to settle for a simpering dandy. None of you did." She had thought so long on this she was sure mazes of confusion were forming in her head, labyrinths she would never decipher. "I would rather never marry than settle."

She sighed then, envisioning the Duke of Weston, his long well muscled legs to his broad shoulders and strong chin. She wondered what color his eyes were. Merry just knew she would melt when he looked at her with desire in his eyes. She knew what that looked like. She'd seen the passion in Leslie's eyes often enough when he stared at Lacie.

"Of course, you won't have to settle. When you're least expecting it, you will look up and the man of your dreams will be standing in front of you," Daryl said thoughtfully. "That's what happened to all of us."

"I will not hold my breath," Merry murmured. "I plan on having fun until then. If pining away would get me what I want, that's exactly what would happen." She was thinking of riding her little mare every day and perhaps even at night since Leslie would not be there to chastise her for her behavior. Come hell or high water she was going to make the most of this summer. Even if she didn't meet the duke, there would always be another day, another ball, another chance.

"Perhaps Cam can find some nice man at the university to court you. There are nice men there, perhaps a student and not a professor," Lacie said thoughtfully.

Immature. Was the one word that came to Merry's mind when she thought on the students at the University of Glasgow. She promised herself she would not settle even while she closed her eyes and saw the Duke of Weston's masked image standing in front of her, holding his hand out to her, asking for this dance.

She would never settle.

Daryl left the table to finish closing the kitchen for the weekend. Tomorrow was Sunday. The Sabbath was the only day the bakery was not open. Justine poked her head out the door to say goodnight and Emilia, the other lady who helped Daryl, was right behind her.

Lacie set the heir apparent in the stroller before giving him a quick kiss to the forehead. "I'm going to the townhouse. Do you care to come with me or do you want to stay here for a while?"

Merry let out a long breath of air, pushing her hair from her face. "I'll walk with you then I think I'll get a carriage ready to send to Southcliff with my maid. I'm so restless and out of sorts I can barely stand myself. Fresh air coupled with the freedom of being alone is what I need. Then and only then will I feel better."

Once inside the townhouse, Merry called for her maid. Lucy appeared so quickly it seemed to her she must have been waiting for the summons. "Get my trunk packed, yours as well. We're going to Southcliff for the summer. We're just getting started a little early. I'm riding Sir Alistair. You can take the carriage as soon as everything is ready."

With the directions given, Merry quickly changed into her riding habit. Less than fifteen minutes later she was astride her mare and headed out of town. While the sun peeked its way from behind clouds, the day was relatively cool. A soft breeze blew from the west and even though it was not a hot day, within the hour Merry's forehead was covered in a fine sheen of perspiration. She longed for the cooling waters of her pond and to laze the rest of the day away.

As she drew closer to Southcliff, more intense ideas of veering off the road in order to head to the small pond near their home captured her thoughts. Mayhap she would give in to her inhibitions later this evening. This time of year, the water would be nearly frigid but would also be invigorating.

No, she decided, now would be the best time. She would rid herself of the dust and sweat accumulated from the ride, rendering herself refreshed and ready for whatever would come next. Turning her horse off the road, she headed for the pond, sweet relief from the scattered workings of her mind.

When she arrived at the pond, the water rippled a soft silver hue capturing its beauty. She slipped from her mare leaving her where she could graze. As she walked toward the water, she noticed a huge black stallion tethered nearby. Perhaps she should leave. In this case curiosity drove her, needing to see who dared invade private property, her very own pond. Well, the pond was Leslie's, but what difference did that make?

The stallion was amazing; tall, sleek and well muscled, his

hindquarters strong, made for running. He nickered when she stepped close, stroking his nose, murmuring sweet nonsense words to him. She couldn't help staring at the magnificent animal's sleek clean lines, the beauty of his coat.

"Now, who has left you here. I've a mind to ride you, you sweet guy. I bet you're the gentlest male in all of Scotland." She continued caressing the horse, her mind lost in images of her on top the stallion, racing the wind.

For minutes her gaze was focused on one animal. As if sensing something, she turned to see a man rising from her pond, his shoulders broad, his body lean and muscular. His dark wet hair fell rakishly long around his head before dipping to nearly his bronzed shoulders. His chest was broad, his stomach muscles hard. A tiny gasp parted her lips as she could not stop her unruly eyes from lingering on him. From the top of his head to the point where the water hid the rest of him, she liked everything about the man.

She drew in a quick ragged breath of air even while she walked to the edge of the pond. Her gaze having switched from the stallion to the man, she could not force herself to look away. Her stomach somersaulted again and again. Heat flushed her cheeks

Merry's parched throat made it difficult to swallow.

The man stopped, wiping droplets of water from his face as he stared at her, his gaze almost as penetrating as hers. With a bit of laughter to his voice, he spoke, "You might want to turn around."

"Why would I want to do that? You are trespassing, sir. This is Stewart land. You should understand that is my pond where you're swimming. Did you ask anyone's permission? I should send for the magistrate."

She knew she was all bluster. No way in hell would she have this man tossed off her land.

His brows drew together, eyes narrowing. His hands were placed on his slender hips. "You could join me. That might prove interesting, lass."

A gasp of air filled the silence before she stepped back, thinking it might be prudent to walk away while she still could, having noticed a pile of clothing near his horse.

"You're naked." Her words were a bit strangled. She wasn't sure he heard, wasn't sure she wanted him to hear. Didn't think her statement warranted a reply since his lack of clothing was blatantly obvious.

"Would not be swimming in my clothes, sweetheart. At the moment though I'd like to leave the water behind me. Your pond is a bit cold. Unfortunately, right now, not cold enough."

"I'm not your sweetheart," she grit out suddenly angry yet she didn't know if she was angry with herself as well as her wayward thoughts or with the man who dared swim in her pond.

Now you know good manners should have you turning away and riding on home.

If I did that, I wouldn't see him naked, now would I? As you well know, except for my brothers when they were young boys I've never seen a man with no clothes. I'm sure he's a fine specimen of a man.

You would regret it. He doesn't look like a man who would let you see him, without there being repercussions.

Do be quiet. I'm going to go in just a minute.

"Ah, but you could be my sweetheart."

More curious than she had any right to be impulsively ignoring the voice of reason in her head, she crossed her arms in front of her, thinking perhaps if she could soak up the beauty of the man for a few more minutes she would leave. Merry truly did want to see what he was hiding beneath the water. This man was no simpering dandy. She could tell by the arrogant tilt of his head, along with the way the lighthearted note of his first words changed tone when she confronted him.

"Turn around now or leave. I care not but I'm coming out."

His voice rang out, loud and clear. Threatening.

She was far too curious.

Merry gasped as he started walking again, the water covering less and less of him. Her gaze followed the water line as it dipped downward. She saw the dark hair on his chest narrow. "How dare you?"

Not as curious as she thought she was she turned tail, mounting her horse and racing toward home.

From behind her she heard his laughter along with the ensuing comment, "For some reason I thought you had more courage."

She almost turned the mare around, the need to confront the arrogant man foremost in her mind. Prudently, she thought better of it.

Merry felt the heat of the encounter on her cheeks. Even the light wind caressing her face did little to cool her flaming face. An eternity seemed to pass before she was in the safety of the stables. For at least a minute, she leaned against her mare's neck trying to calm her racing heart.

The man was an arrogant cad of the worst sort, playing with her emotions with his nakedness. Finally, feeling more in control of her shaking body, she slipped from her horse. She saw to the mare, taking the saddle off, feeding and watering the horse. After that she brushed her, stroking her, thinking of the man as well as the way he stared at her, remembering his rudeness as he threatened to show himself to her.

A noise from the front of the stables caught her attention. She stepped from the stall only to find the man of her thoughts standing at the large door, the reins of his stallion in hand, a dark wicked smile gracing his arrogant features.

Her breath caught in her throat as she fearlessly strode toward the man. "What are you doing here?" She was pointing a finger at him. Had every intention of poking him in the chest before she thought better of it, dropping her hand.

"Nice to meet you again." His gaze raked over her just as hers did when he stood naked in her pond. He settled on her bosom before lifting his eyes upward to her mouth. She couldn't help herself. She ran her tongue along her lips, leaving a trail of moisture.

"I will thank you to answer my question."

She endeavored for all the authority in her voice she could gather. Stiffening her spine, her chin tilted high while she waited.

He quirked a dark eyebrow upward before turning her question back on her. "Then don't thank me. What are you doing here?"

"Of all the..."

Merry was at an obvious loss for words, something that never happened. Her verbal aptitude was well known. She could spar as well as hold her own with anyone. After all, she practiced with her brothers. She wasn't sure if she liked him staring at her or not. Heat throbbed in strange places, while butterflies danced in her stomach. His gaze seemed appreciative. That gave her a bit of a thrill, thinking he might like what he was looking at. Not even Douglas looked at her that way.

"Nerve?" He supplied the single word for her, a half smile tilting the corner of his mouth.

Thoughts of him kissing her came to mind, his lips touching hers. He had the most beautiful mouth she'd ever seen on a man, full lips that beckoned. "I would appreciate an answer," she told him as her anger with this man simmered deep in her belly and her confusion about how she felt about that raged. "Why are you standing here?"

He strode closer, his stallion following behind. "I'm the duke's new horse breeder."

Insolently, his gaze locked with hers, challenging her in a way no one had ever done before.

"Kelly O'Brian is our horse breeder." She spoke with a confidence she didn't feel.

Surely Leslie would have told her if he hired someone to work at the stables. Surely... but Leslie was out of town for a while, ensconced in London with Drake Montgomery. If Lacie had known of this, she would have told her.

"Horse trainer," he corrected, "and he's away on his honeymoon. The duke told me he had mares coming. Also told me he wanted to breed them. I'm in charge of that. Breeding. You do *ken* what that is? Don't you?"

With his gaze focused on her mouth then dropping to her bosom more heat flooded her, warmed her as well as her face once again, felt the fire as if he stroked her. She placed her hands on her hot cheeks in a feeble attempt to cool herself off.

It seemed he realized the effect the direction of his attentions had on her, his grin widening for a moment before he sobered.

He crossed his arms on his chest still staring and frowning, his dark blue eyes simmering with heated emotions.

"How do I know you speak true?"

"Why should I not toss you from the stables. You've yet to explain your presence here," the man said, his voice filled with confidence.

"Leslie Stewart did put me in charge here."

She clamped her hand over her mouth, stopping herself from giving him a few choice words. "You've no right to speak to me that way as well as in that impudent tone of voice. You're hired help and a commoner at that."

"Ah, now we have part of the truth. A commoner who dares to return a noble's rude gaze or should I say stare? You were more than gazing at me now. Also when I was naked. Had no choice except to allow the insolence. I know you found me quite to your liking. Didn't you? Tit for tat, why not?"

He stepped even closer, his presence overpowering, stripping her of what sanity might remain.

She moved back, her heart in her throat as she tried to look anywhere except at him. She found she could not stop staring at him, all of him, and remembering the Adonis rising from the water, his muscles, the sleekness of his flesh as water sluiced from his form.

"I trust you should apologize. I'll go to my brother. When I tell him about your impudence, he will fire you for your brazenness."

She stepped back again, bumping into her mare, groping for words. With nowhere to go she tried to step around him, but he blocked her way from the stall.

His arms still crossed over his well-muscled chest, "You can try." This time he smiled, an all-knowing smile, an arrogant smile as if he knew she would get nowhere if she went to Leslie with any type of complaint. "Didn't you say he's in London? Was that my imagination?"

He set the challenge. She meant to win. "He will be home soon. If he won't dismiss you, I'll have his wife fire you."

"Ah, so you do agree I work here." He extended a hand. "I'm Devlin Mathews. Would you mind telling me exactly who you are along with what you are doing at Southcliff? Perhaps even why you believe you can have me fired with the snap of your fingers."

He bent closer, his breath whispering so close she could scent mint on his breath.

She sipped air, unable to get a real breath into her lungs. Heat flooded her body, an inferno, smoldered from her toes to her head, "I'm

Merry Stewart, the duke's sister."

"Ah, the youngest of the tribe, Angelica. I've heard so much about you."

Nobody calls me Angelica.
Seems this man does.

"How?"

She had her hands placed on her hips in defiance. Now his words were a set back for her. She couldn't think of a single reason why her brother would talk about her to a man such as this, a commoner. "Leslie would not have spoken about me to the likes of you."

"Here we are again, this commoner-noble thing you have going. Doesn't your older brother have several very good friends who are minus a title?"

He implied so many things by his comments, least of all was the notion that she was the baby of the family. She had this incessant urge to prove to him she was no child, least of all a baby. Yet she could think of no way to do such a thing.

"I'll show you to your room."

This time he didn't block her way when she marched past him. He didn't follow either. Instead, the odious man continued to watch, making her feel self-conscious without saying a word.

"Should take care of Windwalker first."

He set to work on his horse, ignoring her as well as the firestorm building inside which he was singlehandedly responsible for.

She stood nearby unable to leave, unwilling to stop looking at him while beneath his fine white lawn shirt his muscles moved and bulged with his work. After his dip in her pond, he had failed to fasten his shirt.

When he finished and with that same rakish, devilishly handsome smirk on his face, he said, "Now you can show me where I'm to bed down."

The way he said the words seemed to take on a different meaning, almost as if he was asking her to join him. That couldn't be. He couldn't be. No, it wasn't possible for a commoner to imply that.

Was it?

Her breath caught in her throat, as she was sure he meant more

13

than what he said. There were subtle innuendos in his words and tone. She wasn't sure she understood. However, she'd been around the bad boys long enough to make significant guesses. Curiously, she wanted to ask him what he meant but prudence, something she rarely had, stopped her.

~ * ~

Devlin Mathews enjoyed the brisk cold water as he swam beneath, surfacing then diving deeper. It had been his intention to wash the dust and sweat from the road before he walked into the Stewart stables. Leslie Stewart told him many things. Nevertheless, the foremost was that even though Angelica was expected to summer in Glasgow, she could always be a surprise. She changed her mind often. Could invariably turn up unexpected. Leslie also told him she could be a very real thorn in his side.

Doing the unanticipated had long been her agenda. As Leslie told him, she improved with age but still, if he was to live in the stables and breed the new mares that would be sent within the week, he would have to learn to deal gently with his unpredictable but lovely sister. Merry would be under his step and in his way most nearly all of the time.

Because Angelica could not be trusted to stay in the city despite her promise. Because she would do as she wished. Leslie had not entrusted him with the need to make sure she did nothing to risk herself, nonetheless he implied that if he needed to do just that, he had free reign to handle her in a way he deemed appropriate. In short, she was his to discipline if necessary.

The week traveling here he enjoyed the Scottish countryside, enjoyed the playing of the pipes and everything Scottish. Half way he stopped at his great aunt's home letting her pamper him with an amazing meal and soft bed, understanding that until he was able to purchase a bed as well as have it delivered, the pallet in the stable boy's room was not worth sleeping on. So, he remained in Glasgow longer than he intended and despite everyone's wishes until the bed was delivered.

Well, it had been delivered this morning. He would be there in less than an hour, as soon as he was fatigued enough and was able to drink enough brandy to fall asleep. Nights were an impossibility for him, drifting into the depth of Morpheus eluding him. His best friend called him out over the most ludicrous of stories. He didn't even like Teddy's sister, Emma. There was no way in hell he would get her pregnant so he would have to marry her.

His lungs near to bursting, he surfaced. Wiping water mixed with hair from his face, he looked up. What was left of his breath caught in his throat. While she wasn't the most beautiful woman he'd ever seen, she was intriguing. He very much liked what he was gazing at. When he looked again, he found she was staring at his horse, stroking him, murmuring soft words that only Windwalker and she could hear. More intrigued than ever he strode to shore only to stop short recalling he was buck-naked and his clothing was piled near his stallion.

When she focused her attention on him, her smile was devastating. Now she was staring at him, at his mouth to be exact, her gaze drifting lower to remain at the waterline as if she wanted to see him intimately. When he told her to leave, she remained feet firmly planted in one spot for the longest time, challenging him with her blatant perusal of his body. By the time she finally left, he was aroused beyond anything he'd felt in his life. He was ready to ride after her and throttle her.

She told him this was her pond. That led him to believe the girl must be Angelica Stewart, the unpredictable lass Leslie warned him about. If she was going to be a handful, she would be his handful, at least for the duration of his stay here at Southcliff. He began to whistle, thinking he might come to enjoy the summer here in the country outside Glasgow. Leslie also told him she would use the argument that she'd come of age to justify any ridiculous and dangerous behavior she was inclined to perpetrate.

He would see her again soon. Just how he would handle this delicate situation without getting into hot water with the Duke of Southcliff eluded him. However, he would figure something out. During the ride from the pond to the stables, he went over various possible scenarios in his mind, all of which ended up with him in bed with her.

Well hell, that just wouldn't do. Angelica Stewart was not just a skirt to be tossed and enjoyed for the summer. She deserved better. Better was not something he could do. So, he would have to find a very real way to leave her alone, which might be a nearly impossible task given the fact he was still aroused.

When he strode into the stables on the Stewart property, he wasn't surprised to see the woman of his tangled thoughts in the stable once again staring at him. She was stroking a horse, her horse this time while murmuring sweet nothings to the beast. What he wouldn't give to be on the end of her whispers. Wrestling with his thoughts of her murmuring in his ear while she caressed him, he cleared his throat, pushing everything from his mind except the present along with how he would deal with this willful and thoroughly spoiled woman-child who burned him with a smile.

He stared at her, waiting for her to notice him. Several seconds ticked by. She did notice. The coming confrontation was heated, simmering with soul-penetrating passion between them, hunger he could not, should not touch. If he caved to his desire, the heat would flame.

When he was finished grooming the big stallion, he followed her through the stables to the back room. She told him she would show him where he would sleep. With her so nearby and untouchable, his nights would most likely be restless.

"Your room," she said, bending over to peek inside. "There's a new bed. I didn't know Leslie ordered one."

"Thank god," he said laughing before offering, "Care to try it out with me?"

He leaned over her; his hand splayed across her back as she was bent slightly peering into the room. Playing with fire would be the death of him, pure torture. This time, he didn't think he could stop.

She stood up so quickly she nearly knocked him over, her head hitting his chin. "What? What did you say?" Her deep blue eyes flashed, seemed to touch upon his soul as she turned to confront him.

His grin deepened even as he regretted his next words. He looked to the bed then back to her, "Care to try it out?" he repeated, needing a way to get her to leave.

The blatant invitation might do the trick.

If she didn't go soon, by the way she stimulated him, he would have her skirts tossed. He'd be deep inside her before she could tell him what she thought of him. He would tease and flirt. Nevertheless, he drew the line at blatant seduction. Her brother was a friend after all. If anything did happen between them, he would be honor bound to wed. He wasn't ready for marriage. Not to Angelica, not to anyone and especially not to Teddy, his best friend's little sister, Emma.

She was standing now, in the middle of the doorway, stepping backward again. This time, it was to move further inside his bedroom. He grinned as he watched the play of emotions across her lovely face. Her eyes shimmered and darkened with what he knew to be desire, a passion he longed to test and explore. Even though he understood the consequences, he couldn't help himself. He stepped forward watching her once again move in the opposite direction, ever closer to the big bed occupying most of the room.

"You didn't answer my question," he told her, his voice softening, tempting her to run he hoped. If she didn't, he wasn't sure he could be responsible for himself.

Suddenly, her arms whirled. It seemed she was losing her balance. "I..."

He moved quickly, holding on to her then falling with her he turned them so he caught the brunt of the fall as they landed on his bed. He grinned at her, "Guess I've your answer, Brat."

He laughed as she fell across his chest, her slight weight settling down on top of him. This was not the outcome he wanted from his teasing. For now, he meant to enjoy the few seconds he would have her in this position.

Her hands on his chest, she pushed, "Let me go," she said, but there was neither command in her voice nor any realization of the situation she was in now. She was sprawled on top of him, her breasts pushing against his chest. Until he rolled with her, presenting his body atop hers, she could have gone anywhere she pleased. Now she was tucked nicely in his arms. She was beneath him.

"Not yet," he said, resting on his forearms, staring at her lips then the valley between her breasts, wondering about the size and texture of the twin morsels on either side. "Not until you answer me. Well, I guess you decided it would be a good idea to try out the bed. What do you think? Should we crawl under the covers and see what happens next?"

The invitation was blatant as well as another attempt to frighten her to remain far from him.

She glared at him as if he was a mad man. Perhaps he was a bit crazy challenging her in this way. He meant to provoke her to get her to leave when in truth he was enjoying her company far too much. She would leave soon enough then he'd be left to tamp down his lust. A powerful lust that if she cared to look was quite obvious.

"I didn't answer as well you know it. Did you push me?" She hit him on the shoulder. He grunted simply because he thought it was most likely what she wanted.

"I would never push a lady."

He fiddled with flyaway strands of hair moving them away from her face, wishing he dared kiss her. A commoner kissing the sister of a duke just wasn't done.

Well hell.

This wasn't at all what he thought would be happening tonight. At this point in time, he was enjoying the feeling of her breasts pressed against him. Turning her again, he ran his hands down her back until he reached her nicely rounded bottom.

"Sir." The single word sounded breathy while at the same time filled with passion.

"Devlin," he reminded her.

He was amusing himself with ungrounded hope. Moving away from her he held out his hand.

She blinked a few times before she accepted the offered hand, her cheeks flaming with color. Quickly, he pulled her to a sitting position then off the bed and into his arms again. Pressed close to him he held her for a few more seconds. His arms dropped to his sides.

"I should go." She smoothed her skirts, looking to the floor.

"You should." He agreed with her even though he would have liked her to stay. Damn the consequences.

Merry wiped her hands on her dress, plucking at the fabric as she looked around him. "You might step aside." Her voice was breathy as she finally lifted her chin high enough so she could see him. High enough he had no doubt she was the sister of a duke.

"Perhaps I should require a token from you," he said, sliding a finger along her chin before letting it travel down her neck to the rapidly beating pulse. "A small token before I let you pass."

"What would that be?" she asked, her voice gaining strength as he allowed her more distance between them.

"A kiss, only then will I let you pass."

Where did that come from? He just spent a considerable amount of time convincing himself a kiss was not possible. Now he asked for one. Damn, but everything he was doing with the girl was out of character.

"You are no gentleman." Anger tingeing her words, she pushed past him as he let her stomp by.

"True. I never said or implied I was."

He laughed, watching the provocative swing of her hips as she marched from the small bedroom he was going to call home until the end of the summer. At least he managed to get her out of the stables for now, yet he was anxiously awaiting his next encounter with Angelica Stewart.

His angel.

Now that he was alone, he managed to look around the room. His valet had been here ahead of him with a trunk where he would find the clothing he would wear. His secretary had also been here. A small desk sat in the corner with papers on top he assumed would be the correspondence he needed to examine before the end of the day.

While his grandmother thought he needed to rusticate for a while, he still had work that could not be left undone. Finding a bottle of brandy on the desk, he made a quick note to ask for a case. If the following days were going to proceed anything like this one, he would need to drink himself into oblivion just to fall asleep at night as well as keep Angelica a virgin.

Sitting against the headboard before stretching his legs out in front of him, he sifted through the papers he held in his hand. Really, there was nothing that needed his immediate attention. He sipped the strong drink, finishing the glass then pouring another. With his eyes closed, he let his imagination take over his thoughts. Inadvertently, they all sped directly to the little brat who had felt so comfortable and appealing in his arms. To Devlin it seemed she was made for him.

The second glass finished, he decided to take a look at the stables. The mares would arrive tomorrow or the next day. While he was sure Leslie had seen to the accommodations for the mares, he had a pressing need to make sure they were kept safely away from his stallion. Even though it was a distraction for him, the breeding of these horses was important to the livelihood of both stables, his as well as Leslie's.

As he wandered the stable, he realized Leslie was most competent. The wandering changed to pacing until his restlessness took over his body. It wouldn't do to finish off the bottle of brandy so he decided a midnight ride might be in order. Perhaps it was now closer to dawn, he couldn't be sure. His pocket watch was in his jacket. While he was curious, he couldn't be bothered to discover the time. Somehow, in the country with so little to occupy his days and nights the hour of the day just no longer seemed to matter.

He wondered then when Angelica would make her next appearance. The sooner the better he decided. Her very demeanor challenged him, kept him on his toes. He realized he couldn't wait to see her. He decided that perhaps sleep would do him well in this circumstance. A midnight ride could be had any time. Perhaps he could convince her to go with him.

You're playing with fire. If you don't watch yourself, you're going to get burned. Aye, he might. In this case the pleasure would well be worth the ensuing inferno.

Or would it?

He would have to leave that question unanswered for the moment.

He disrobed, eyeing the bed and remembering her splayed on top of him then his body over hers. The groan leaving his lungs surprised him for a moment. She would never agree to bed him, a commoner coupled with a noble lady. No, but this situation intrigued him to see just how far she would go. Perhaps he would push her a bit farther today. The sun might shine upon them. He fell asleep with thoughts of Angelica filling his dreams.

The scent of strong coffee wafted in through the slightly open door to his room. The hinge didn't work; was one of the things on his list to improve before he left at the end of the summer. He was surprised to smell coffee. Unlike most in the British Isles, he preferred coffee to the tea that was most often served.

With one eye open, he saw that light filtered in through the one window, the day giving a promise of warmth.

"Devlin? Devlin are you up?"

So, she was back and bringing coffee as an offering of sorts. Was it a peace offering or did she want something from him? Perhaps she thought the strong brew would replace the kiss he asked for last night and didn't receive. If it was strong enough, it would at least for the time being replace thoughts of the kiss. Perhaps not.

He pulled on his soft doeskins before striding shirtless into the main area of the stables. She'd set up a table and two chairs, the coffee and something else on the table.

"Would you like a sticky bun? I just learned how to make them a few days ago." She held out a cup of coffee.

"A sticky bun." He grinned accepting the coffee, his mind taking a different route all together than what she would expect. *Yes, I would definitely like to try her buns.* As he sat down, her stare travelled along his chest, lower then lower until it stopped at his unfastened pants. Heat flamed inside him at her blatant perusal. What had he expected? He chose not to wear a shirt for his own purposes, wanting to see if the heat from the night before still existed between them.

It did. Now it flamed brighter and hotter.

"Daryl taught me. I made some for the bakery. Some of the customers told me they are really quite good." She sat down on one of the chairs, sipping the hot liquid she held in front of her, watching him expectantly, a hesitant smile.

"I bet your buns are very tasty." He bit into one, chewing thoughtfully, studying her, realizing she had no idea what he meant.

Her brows drew together, chewing over his words. "They are," she agreed with him. "As is the coffee."

"How did you know, Brat?" he asked.

"Know what?"

21

"That I preferred coffee over tea."

"Do you? I always thought coffee tasted better with my buns," she said straight faced. "Link, my youngest brother brought a lot back from Virginia."

The liquid in his mouth spewed out with a cough. "What did you say?"

"You heard me. Coffee tastes better with my buns," she told him so much indignation in her voice.

Keeping his laughter behind his teeth, "That's what I thought you said."

He'd like to try that particular combination as he wondered how much of what she said was feigned innocence or if she knew exactly what he was talking about. He'd like to discover that too. Did she have any clue what he referred to?

"So, what do you think?" She leaned forward, her eyes sparkling with anticipation of his response.

His heart twisted, lightened, changed from his usual jaded thoughts. With his mouth full of sticky buns, his eyes catching her gaze, he said. "They are really very good with your coffee. Or is it your buns with the coffee? Maybe it's the cinnamon and sugar with the melted butter that makes your buns so delicious."

She smiled, her twin dimples changing her face, so much he gasped, "Thank you. I can make them for you every morning if you like. You can taste my buns every morning along with all the cinnamon, sugar and butter you want."

He inhaled then very slowly he said, "I would like to taste your sticky buns every morning, thank you."

She beamed even more. "Ask and you will receive," Her eyes were alight, her smile beautiful, overpowering.

Inwardly, he groaned. *Ask and you will receive.* There were a lot of things he could think of that he might want to ask of her. Trying to stick his wayward thoughts to the farthest recesses of his brain, he finished eating.

"Are you wanting to ride this morning? I'd be happy to go with you since the mares aren't here yet."

Her face fell, her lips turning downward in a small pout. "Of course, if that is what you'd like."

After such a good beginning he didn't understand her reticence. Didn't understand why she appeared disappointed by his invitation. "Why don't you want me to go with you?"

She pursed her lips together, stiffening. "Yesterday you were in my pond. If you remember correctly, I couldn't swim. I was..."

"Wanting to swim today. Do you think that is wise? Swimming all by yourself?"

He would go with her. If he did, he would never be able to keep his eyes from her. To save his soul, he couldn't help uttering the next question. "Do you swim in the buff?"

Her lips quirked, her eyes smoldering with defiance, "Yes."

If she kept this up, he wasn't going to be responsible for himself. Trying to keep his body in check was increasingly impossible as every word from her moist pink lips provoked and inflamed his senses. "You don't want me to go with you then."

He wasn't sure if he should allow her to go by herself. Leslie implied he might want to keep her from doing something stupid. In his mind, what she planned was indeed stupid. "Perhaps you could swim in your shift."

"What good would that do?" she asked him with more defiance. "As soon as the fabric got wet it would be like swimming in nothing at all. My shift would be soaked through."

She was right of course. "Can't let you go by yourself."

His voice was harsh when he spoke. The thought of anyone coming along and finding her as good as naked sent his gut rolling as anger built within. His imagination sped to what might happen.

"It's really quite safe. However, just to be certain that's why I usually go at night. Even if someone would ride by, the night would be too dark to see anything. They wouldn't even know I was in the water."

His gut tightened even more. He stood so quickly his chair fell over hitting the floor with a loud bang. "No. You are not to go riding at night, Brat."

While Leslie had mentioned keeping an eye on her, he didn't think she would ever do anything quite this reckless or stupid.

"I'll thank you to keep your orders to yourself."

She stood also, striding, back stiff to the stall where her little mare was housed.

"Don't thank me then." He raced after her, grabbing her arm, swinging her around. "I'm coming with you, Brat. You've obviously no idea just how dangerous this endeavor could be."

"Then I can't swim. You would keep me from one of my few pleasures?" Her voice was incredulous as if her intentions were not something other than absurd and dangerous as hell.

"You can swim as long as I am there to guard your buns."

He grimaced as her face flamed, regretting his words and undermining the few minutes of peace they shared this morning.

Well hell.

"It's the only way you are going to get wet as well as get what you're thinking. Choose what you want. Don't leave without me."

He strode to the stallion deciding he should saddle Windwalker before he saddled her horse. If he didn't, she would most assuredly take off without him. In truth, he thought he was being very diplomatic. In his way of thinking, this was the only solution. He would simply not look at her.

When he finished saddling his stallion, he heard the hooves of her horse pounding behind him. His heart caught in his throat. By the time he turned, she was out the doors. Bloody hell. The frustration and anger simmering deep in his belly caught him by surprise. If anyone was going to see her wearing what would be nothing, it was him.

He swung onto his horse, racing out behind her. She was incorrigible, didn't take to reasonable commands at all. What he asked of her, he believed was extremely sensible. He didn't understand how Leslie assumed he could ever keep track of her. By the time he was out the door, she was disappearing behind a hill.

When he caught up with her, he'd tan her backside.

He'd rather kiss her senseless until neither could breathe.

~ * ~

Lacie looked up, startled from her musings about her husband when Leslie walked into the drawing room. "You're home sooner than I thought you would be. I missed you."

"Montgomery finally took no for an answer. The man surprised me," he said, placing a kiss on his son's forehead then Lacie's. "I missed you also. Kept thinking of you so, couldn't wait to get back. Did the horse breeder show up, Devlin Mathews?"

"I believe he did, a few days ago. He stopped by to say he was going out to Southcliff after he spent a few days here in town. Mumbled something about needing a new bed, among other things." She laughed, remembering the lumpy pallet that was in the room. Leslie had made love to her there. "He didn't seem too worried about the sparse accommodations. Said he would take care of whatever he might need."

"Thought as much. The man is resourceful."

"Why, is there something you're not telling me?" she asked, cocking her head a bit sideways to study him.

She was sure there was more to Devlin Mathews than he was willing to share with her. That didn't sit well with her. Since Merry was at Southcliff, she felt it only right that both understood exactly who the man was. Horse breeder, that wasn't all Devlin Mathews was. She was sure of that fact.

"So, you haven't heard anything from Merry." It seemed he didn't want to talk about the horse breeder.

"It's been strangely as well as eerily quiet around here. Not real sure what to think about it. Beginning to wonder if she is sick or if I should be alarmed. From time to time, I've thought to send someone out to check on her. Didn't think she'd stay in isolation for more than a day or two."

Lacie still watched him closely even though she knew he would never give his thoughts away. His time as a spy trained him well.

Leslie held out his hands for his child swinging him into the air. "Missed the little tyke." Then changed the subject back to his sister including the horse breeder. "We should wait a while before we send out the troops. I'm trying to keep in mind that Merry is an adult. Now that she's attained that status, don't want to worry about her. Besides, I've the utmost faith in Mathews' integrity. Nothing will happen between them simply because of who I am."

"He's still a man," Lacie logically pointed out while she watched the play of emotions over her husband's face.

She remembered the times when he kissed and coaxed her to his way. He was always successful in his seductions. If Mathews had it in his mind to kiss Merry or do more than just kiss, the deed would be done.

After a lengthy pause, he said, "Perhaps I should pay a call to see if the mares have arrived. Wouldn't hurt to give them a surprise visit in order to see what they're up too. It would be interesting to hear Devlin's version of my sister involving of course, her antics, because there would be antics."

"Merry won't be suspicious if you show up unannounced?"

Lacie was now more concerned than ever if Leslie thought his sister and the horse breeder might be up to something that would only serve to get Merry into trouble. Even with all her considerable knowledge garnered from listening to her two older brothers, she was an innocent. If she guessed correctly, except for a few shared kisses three years ago with her bodyguard, Douglas, she was totally untried.

"If I have my way, Merry won't even know I'm there."

"You know that would be impossible. The black stallion you ride is unmistakable. As you well know Merry spends several hours every day in the stables."

Lacie wondered now if Merry might not spend more time there. Devlin was a handsome young man, arrogant to boot, although Leslie would most likely call it confidence.

When Lacie first saw the man, she wondered if possibly Merry could lose her heart to him, suspecting he was more than just a horse breeder. He had a way about him that spoke of complete confidence—of nobility. She stared at her husband, playing with the young lad in his arms who would eventually have so much responsibility. It might be nice for Merry to find someone who could be carefree, be able take a moment to play rather than spend most hours working.

Leslie seemed to read her mind. Defending himself he began, "I'm much better than I used to be. I've made snow angels with you every time the sky has brought snow our way. Playing with my son has become an essential part of my life. I've emitted a few choo, choos when we brought out the toy train."

"Yes, but you had to be coerced each and every snowfall. It's time for his nap." She took the boy from Leslie, heading up the stairs.

"When you put him down, we can play. More than willing." He was behind her on the stairs, his hand resting on the small of her back before drifting lower. "Need to play with my wife. Been away too long without her in my bed."

"It's almost dinner time. You will have to wait." She set the boy in his bed, covering him with a blanket.

"I've waited weeks." His lips caressed her neck then slid across her shoulders. He moved up her neck, playing with her delicate earlobe with his teeth and tongue then travelling to her lips where he could nibble his way across her mouth.

She shivered with the desire she always felt with his touch. "I suppose I'll let you have whatever you want. I've missed you too much to deny either of us."

Chapter Two

Devlin caught up with her before she traveled very far from the house. His annoyance and frustration over her blatant disobedience inflamed his actions, anger smoldering just below the surface. Reaching over, he tugged on the reins pulling her to an abrupt stop before lifting her from her mare and onto his lap. He needed to teach her a much-needed lesson. In this situation he wasn't quite sure how to go about it.

"I told you to wait for me, Brat."

His hands upon her were determined, his annoyance at her willfulness tangible. In short, he was seething with emotions he'd never felt before. He wasn't used to having his wishes ignored let alone his commands, distinctly remembering that he told her to wait for him, to not leave without him. He never expected her to saddle her horse.

She shoved at his hand, nearly knocking herself from the stallion before clutching his arm to keep herself stable. "I don't take orders from you." Having ridden off in irritation at his highhandedness, it seemed she felt no different now. "I'll thank you to stop ordering me around."

"Don't thank me then but you will obey me. Hold still before I let you go and you land on your arse or your delectable buns and hurt yourself. I should tan your backside." He gritted the words out between clenched teeth, his pulse racing.

"You arrogant, bastard. You're the one who is hurting me." She paused a moment as if thinking over what he just said. "How dare you threaten me with bodily harm."

~ * ~

My delectable buns? What the devil. How dare he talk about me that way? I made those especially for him. What do I know? This is how he thanks me.

You didn't realize he was talking about your buns before when you were talking sticky buns this morning. In addition to making matters worse, the way they taste with cinnamon, sugar as well as melted butter on them? Didn't take you for being stupid. What did you think when he was grinning at you like a besotted fool? That he was speaking of his breakfast. The man wanted you for breakfast.

Why would I think he was talking about my posterior? I'm not a fool, just trustworthy. It's not my fault the horse breeder thinks he is above reproach.

As well as too innocent to be trading barbs with that man. If you continue in that vein, you will always come out on the losing end.

Can't be innocent considering that I've grown up with two of the worst bad boys ever.

Of course you're naïve. What would you call the conversation just a little while ago?

I'm not naïve.

Yes, you are otherwise you wouldn't have let the conversation go on as you did.

Just be quiet. I'm not going to listen to you any longer.

Only because you ken *I'm right.*

She ignored the voice in her head then beat on his chest. Didn't seem he liked what she did, he grabbed her hands. She was now in his arms, pulled up tight against him.

"There is no reason for me to obey you. You've no authority over me."

She remained still then, waiting until he would let her go.

He urged the big stallion to a walk as he grabbed the reins of her mare and with his other hand wrapped his arm around her. "We're going to your pond together. I'm going to let you swim until you turn blue if that's what you would like."

"I can't do that with you watching," she protested to no avail.

"I won't watch."

~ * ~

Yet he understood he would eventually have to look at her. He had no idea if she could even swim. Making sure she remained safe was a task this morning he would enjoy.

"I'm not foolish enough to believe that." She looked at him with startling wide blue eyes, eyes that seemed to shimmer as well as hold a wealth of disbelief. "Now that I'm here, safe and sound, you can leave. You've done your job." She waved her hand in the air in a feeble attempt to shoo him away.

Tossing his head back, he roared with laughter, his amazement at her antics giving him good reason to chortle. "You cannot get rid of me that easily. He set her on the ground. "Go swim. I'll wait right here." He dismounted then finding a rock he relaxed, his gaze roaming the landscape away from the pond. He listened to her shoes hit the ground, imagined each article of clothing whispering across her body as she shimmied out of them.

Keeping a wary eye, she watched him then with her back to him she tried to wriggle from her dress. He heard her heavy sigh of exasperation, had a pretty good idea of her problems. He wondered if she'd thought at all about this expedition to her swimming pond, appropriate clothing being imperative. He would have to help, he thought as he moved away from his perch on the boulder.

She jumped, startled when his fingers brushed her long hair from her neck. "Were you planning on swimming in the dress or do you always act so impulsively you don't think of any of the problem that could occur."

As the buttons slid open, the backs of his fingers brushed across her warm silken skin. He hissed in a breath of air more determined than ever to look but not touch.

"I didn't think," she said.

"You just wanted to swim and could think of nothing but your pond or did you want me to come with you. Did you know I would undress you?" He finished for her, his lips hovering so close to her ear;

she shivered when she felt his hot breath brush her skin.

"I..."

"Cat got your tongue?"

He finished with the buttons. With a great effort not to run his fingertip down her spine, he turned and walked back to his rock. He wondered if there were twin dimples at the base of her spine. While he didn't mean to keep his gaze away from the pond, he did allow her time to get herself into the water.

When he did look, she was only knee deep as she tried to get used to the frigid water, splashing mini droplets of water down her back. She was dressed in her pantaloons and camisole the fabric clinging to her well shaped butt. If she would turn, he would see even more. He grit down hard on his teeth. The clothing would be plastered to every sweet curve when she walked from the water. His over stimulated body heated with need, the bulge in his doeskins growing as he watched her slow and very gradual descent into the pond. He couldn't ever remember being so tempted to consume something that wasn't his to devour.

She swam, every few seconds disappearing beneath the surface then reappearing. He was getting used to watching her bob up then down. Suddenly, she didn't surface when he thought she should have. His breath caught in his lungs, his heart stopped. He leapt to his feet, watching as he raced to the pond's edge, shedding clothes as he ran. Hopping on one foot then the other, he pulled off his boots. In just his underwear he dove into the pond, stroking to the last spot he saw her.

Her head appeared above the water then she stroked to the other side. He waited for her to notice.

Well hell.

Relief and anger swept through him as he tried to come to terms with his real fears for her life. Putting the blame on her for swimming, as she liked to do was not appropriate. However, his terror sent his raw emotions to the surface. His meager control vanished. She should have told him what she was about. Should have prepared him for this. He should tan her backside.

Or kiss her lips as well as her softly rounded buns until she agreed to be his mistress.

Where the hell did that thought come from?

Treading water, he waited for her to turn and swim back to this side of the pond. He knew the moment she realized he was in the pond with her. She froze. Her eyes were wide. A few strokes brought him to her side. Crystal clear water surrounded them. Her breasts were well shaped, the rosebud tips hardened by the cold liquid. At the sight of her, startled ribbons of heat surged straight to his loins. He grit down on his teeth.

"You said you weren't going to watch." Her accusation took him by surprise for a second before he shrugged it off.

"You, milady, disappeared for way too long. I was afraid you drowned. That wasn't something I could allow."

"I didn't."

"Can see that," he laughed, trying to hide his chagrin at breaking the promise he made to her even though he'd been watching her for quite some time. "It was in your best interest, however, to make sure you remained alive."

"You can go back to your rock," she paused, "or better yet, you swim. I'll go to the rock and dry off. Do I have your permission?" her escalating cynicism evident with each word out of her dainty mouth.

Devlin didn't miss her sarcasm, still he nodded. "It seems I'm in need of more time in cold water."

He didn't wait to see what she would do but ducked under water, swimming as far as he could before he had to surface for air. When he imagined her breasts as he saw them, the coldness did nothing to alleviate his awakened condition.

He swam two pond lengths submerged then half way back on the third length he ran out of air and burst to the surface. He gasped in a long drink of air then he looked to the rock. She was stretched out one knee bent heavenward, her hands behind her pressing against the rock, her back arched toward the sky. He was close enough to see the dark outlines of her nipples, the rounded curves of her breasts as well. Unsure why he tormented himself, he slowly swam to the shore before wading out. He turned, casting off his wet underwear then slipped on his pants. The short walk to the boulder she adopted took an eternity, yet he enjoyed the unencumbered view of Angelica.

Either she heard him and deliberately meant to entice or she had no idea he was approaching, watching her with avid interest. He went with the latter thought. When she saw him, she sucked in her breath with a harsh sound then looked for something to cover herself. Every article of clothing sat on the ground below the rock.

He bent down and picked up her gown, holding it up to her. "You looking for this?"

With her arms crossed in front of her, she nodded, her eyes wide blue pools, her cheeks a warm pink. Flushed with excitement or embarrassment he wasn't' sure, either way the color enhanced her charms. He enjoyed baiting her almost as much as he would enjoy making love to her.

He tossed it to her. "Put it on. You should be just about dry. I'll help you with the buttons when you're ready."

She clung to the fabric, holding it as if it was a shield to her modesty. He was sure she didn't have an ounce of decorum in her entire body. In any case she was just far too curious about him to suggest shyness. If she continued in this vein, he would lose all patience and show her what she was not so subtly asking for.

"You are no gentleman."

"You are far from a lady proper."

He liked her just the way she was though, would like her better if she wasn't off limits to him.

He smiled at her words. In other circles he was considered stuffy and the personification of appropriateness. He didn't like to think of himself as stuffy or too proper. That was one of the reasons his grandmother sent him to rusticate in Scotland. Rest as well as sleep would not be his bed partner anytime soon, neither would Angelica Louise Stewart. She was a handful of woman, a lady who needed taming. He wasn't the man for the job, even though he wanted to be.

"Perhaps you want to ride home in your underwear?" he asked after waiting for her to move from her perch and dress.

She shot him a disgusted look before slipping the dress over her head and jumping down from the rock. In a second her back was turned to him and she was lifting her wet hair. "My hair hasn't dried yet. It can do so while I'm dressed."

"Good, I'm glad to see you're thinking sensibly as an adult and not a spoiled child." As if her skin burned him with each accidental touch, he had the dress fastened in record time. "Now what?"

"I'm no more spoiled than you are. You're so used to getting your way in everything, you have no idea how to compromise." she shot back at him.

He let her words digest before he finished dressing. He half expected her to take off without him while he was still in the process of tugging on his boots. She didn't though. With an air of indifference, she sat atop her mare and watched, her gaze riveted on him when he began to fasten his pants.

Where she was concerned, his mouth had no filter. "Would you like to do the honors?" he asked, the stain on her cheeks turning from the soft pink to a brilliant red. He grinned. "It's only fair since I fastened your gown."

She turned then urged the horse forward, racing away from him before he could finish dressing.

Well hell.

This temporary babysitting job wasn't at all to his liking. The hands-off situation he found himself in was going to be the death of him by summer's end if she didn't get so furious with him then flee back to the city leaving him in relative peace and quiet. Somehow, he didn't think he'd ever find peace again. Thoughts of riding into Glasgow in order to find a willing woman for a night passed through his head.

If his guess was accurate, she was heading home so he decided not to rush. With any luck she would be out of the stable and ensconced in the main house by the time he returned. Tomorrow would be soon enough for another encounter with the lovely Stewart lass. Perhaps he would get used to her provocative antics along with the need to taste her sweetness vanishing.

Luck was not on his side. When he lazily rode Windwalker into the stable, she was still brushing down her mare. By the look she slanted him, he wasn't going to get away without an ear full of pleasantries from her. She slid her small pink tongue across her lips, gearing up for what he assumed would be a lecture. Her brows were drawn together in a delicate little frown, her breasts heaving with feigned indignation.

"My brother is here," she began as the brush made several forays down her horse. "He will see to your dismissal."

"You never told me what her name is." He stared pointedly at the little mare she was stroking as he'd like to be caressed by her.

"What?" She appeared taken off guard with his statement and now at a loss for words.

"The mare's name. Your horse. What is it?"

"Oh." She smiled at him seemingly forgetting then her intention to lambast him as well as the threat of dismissal she just uttered.

He didn't think it would take her long to remember. However, he meant to enjoy this moment.

"Sir Alistair," she said, her voice soft, the tone caressing.

He felt the stroke of her words almost as if the whisper was against his lips.

He was sure her mind just veered off on another tangent. Then the name as well as the significance hit him square in the gut. "That's a man's name."

"I know," she said, appearing sheepish then bolstering herself, "What if it is?"

"It's a stupid name for a mare."

Lord, his first name was Alistair. This just wasn't something he could accept. In this he didn't have a choice.

"I named her after the Duke of Weston."

He choked when he heard that tidbit of news. "Why?"

"I fell in love with his stables when Leslie brought me there three years ago to pick out a mare. I decided I would honor him by naming my horse after him."

"Bloody hell," he muttered. "That's the stupidest thing I've ever heard. Would have been more of an honor if your mare had been a stallion."

"No more stupid than a lot of other things I can think of. In any case, as I just told you my brother is home."

"So what, Brat?"

"As I told you earlier, I'm going to ask him to dismiss you after that tell him all about your impertinence as well as the way you order me around, thinking it's your duty along with your right."

She set the brush aside, turning to him her hands on her hips, her expression filled with triumph.

"Ah, I see, his stallion is here. Perhaps you should see to his grooming before you confront the duke. It will give him a few more minutes to relax from his journey as well as cool your temper."

He meant to make it impossible for her to enlist the stable boy, although knowing Leslie as he did the duke would have taken care of his horse before leaving the stable. "Timmy," he called out. "Would you see to my horse? I've a few things to talk over with the duke."

"You can't go talk to him." She stepped toward him a defiant tilt to her delicately feminine shoulders. "I'm going."

"We have business to discuss. The mares should be here tomorrow, perhaps as soon as this evening. I want to know if he's going to stay to watch the first breeding."

He now had a plan that just might stem some of her avid curiosity about sex. Perhaps she'd stop staring at his crotch. His grin widened as he strode to the house to tell Leslie just what he thought about babysitting his spoiled little sister.

"You can't go there."

She ran after him, tugging on his arm to stop his advance.

"Of course, I can. You can come along too or you can wait for a private meeting. I don't care. Don't have a thing to hide from the duke, your brother."

He smiled when she let her hand fall away, cursing a blue streak. He imagined her stomping her tiny foot in protest. No, his brat wouldn't resort to stomping feet. He suspected she would find some way to get even. His grin widened at the thought of discovering what she considered revenge. The following games could be enjoyable and far from boring. What had started out to be an uneventful sojourn in the country was beginning to turn quite pleasant. He whistled feeling pleased. Since he had to stay, he might as well find some pleasure. Angelica didn't know it yet but she would be the diversion he so thoroughly needed.

The butler let him inside. He discovered Leslie in his office amidst a stack of paperwork. He looked up, shoveling the work aside, "Brandy? Don't suppose you've come to talk about the mares or is it Merry you'd rather discuss? Been expecting a few complaints. She tends to be impetuous and hot headed at times."

"Don't want to talk about Angelica. She is a handful but..." There wasn't anything he wanted to say to her big brother concerning her. For the summer this little brat was going to remain his challenge. His challenge with the emphasis on his. He wasn't going to burden Leslie with gossip. "Are you staying?"

Leslie shook his head leaning back while he stretched his long legs out in front of him, eyeing him critically. "No, Lacie thought I should see how things were going between the two of you. She was worried about Merry. Quite frankly, I was worried about you."

"Just Lacie was worried?" He arched one eyebrow.

"As I said, I was more concerned about you. Mother allowed Merry to run all over the French countryside with no restrictions. Didn't think she could get into too much trouble. There weren't a lot of people. She always did exactly as she pleased. Wouldn't expect anything different from her now."

"Just like here." Devlin sat down with the brandy in hand, wondering what the young lady would do next. He would have to be ready for it. "Mares still supposed to be here tomorrow?"

"Haven't heard anything different. You're going to oversee everything I presume. So, I don't need to be in attendance. Rather spend the days with my wife. I've been away awhile on business. You understand."

No, he truly didn't understand missing a wife. He'd been engaged. That state ended when he caught her with another man. "Have to. Windwalker's the stud. I'm not letting anything go wrong with the breeding of the mares. Too much is at stake." He anticipated this, looked forward to the new foals. Their bloodlines would be impeccable. He meant to look for just that kind of thing in a wife when he got around to settling down. That was a long way off. Christ, he was only twenty-seven.

He had a lot of good years in front of him. Still, he didn't like the direction of his thoughts as they drifted to Angelica. Marriage to Angelica would be hell on earth, he paused thinking, or perhaps heaven.

If she loved him.

"So," Leslie made a steeple of his hands, seeming to study him, "Merry hasn't been a problem."

He kept his grin behind his teeth, not wanting to let on what a delightfully infuriating woman his sister could be. Thoughts of tasting her sticky buns waffled through his head. If he told the duke what happened so far, Leslie was bound to spend more time here. Truth be told, he wanted more private time with the little minx. He wanted to be able to deal with her exactly as he chose. "None, she's been quite enjoyable, a perfect angel. She brought me coffee and homemade sticky buns this morning."

Leslie's brows drew together as if concentrating. "She brought you sticky buns. The two of you had a conversation and that was that? An angel, just doesn't sound like my sister."

He didn't tell the truth. It didn't matter.

Somehow, he didn't think Leslie believed him but he wasn't going to say anything that might get her sent back to the city. If he did that, the rest of his time here would drag by, an endless summer. He waited in expectation of the next crazy thing she came up with. The thought spurred several ideas to his mind as to her punishment. Perhaps he should call what he would do discipline. This afternoon went very well, if he didn't mind saying so. He enjoyed the swim and watching her sputter for words to defend her actions when there was nothing that could be said in her defense.

The conversation continued for another hour or so, Leslie continuing his questions about Angelica coupled with how he was dealing with her. The way Devlin painted the picture of their relationship, she was an angel. Yes, she was. She was his angel and he wasn't about to disparage her to anyone, even the all-knowing Duke of Southcliff her big brother. What happened between them would stay between them. How they dealt with each other was no one's concern but theirs.

Sipping his second glass of brandy, he could hear the topic of his thoughts pacing outside the room. He grinned. She was probably trying to figure out what he told Leslie about her behavior along with what she was going to say to justify all her wild and irresponsible actions. If all went well, she would learn his dismissal was not in the cards. When that occurred, she would need to figure out a way to deal with him.

He stood, finished with the conversation, saying his goodbyes, anticipating the arrival of the mares tomorrow morning. "I believe your sister is waiting to speak with you. She has something she is determined to ask you, perhaps demand is more apropos."

"That she is. I don't, however, have time for a lengthy conversation. Need to get home before dark."

Devlin left the room. He smiled at her, "Your turn, Brat."

He whistled as he left the house.

~ * ~

Two days later as she entered the stables for the first time since the horrific meeting with her brother, she held her breath. She remembered everything she would rather forget. The humiliation devastated her. Leslie gave her an adamant no to her dismissal request. Despite all her arguments, he continued in the same vein. He would not dismiss the egotistical man. The mares arrived. She'd been too afraid of seeing Devlin to go see the horses.

Looking back, Merry cringed when she saw Devlin's smile after his meeting with her brother then heard the happy whistling as if he didn't have a care in the world. When he left her brother's office, he knew what the answer would be. She clasped her hands tightly as she stalked into the office to see Leslie, relaxed and grinning, sipping his fine French brandy.

"Brat? You want something?" He didn't even look up from the notes he was writing, didn't give her a second look. If he noticed her, he wasn't giving any indication that he did so.

"You know damn well why I'm here."

"Do I?" One elegant eyebrow arched upward as he took a second to regard her before returning to his work.

She'd poured herself a glass of brandy before she plopped down in the wing chair opposite his desk, no longer confident that her demand would be fulfilled. She meant to confront her brother anyway. Leaning forward, she said, "You have to dismiss him."

"Not possible."

He wasn't even paying attention to her but staring out the window. There was absolutely nothing outside to look at except a tree that had been there for more years than anyone could possibly remember.

She'd gasped at the quick response, devastated that he was so adamant. So, she switched tactics. "What did he say about me?"

She watched her brother's dark eyebrow as he lifted it once more into a perfect arch. Heat flooded her face at the realization there was so much he could say, all would embarrass and humiliate her. Perhaps she should have left her inquiry unsaid. This was too much to bear.

Leslie smiled not removing his gaze from her then tapping one finger. He was finally acknowledging her presence. "What do you think he said?"

A small simmering rage grew in the pit of her stomach. Fear she'd be sent back to Glasgow suddenly prevalent in her thoughts. "Don't play with me, Leslie. He must have told you how difficult I've been. He's the one who's been difficult, hard to please. He's arrogant and presumptive. Has spent his time here ordering me around. I won't have it from a commoner. He thinks way too highly of himself and his abilities."

"With good reason. He comes with the best recommendations of any man I've met. If he wasn't a commoner, I might be thinking of a betrothal. He would make you a fine husband, not that lineage should make that much difference. Perhaps the two of you should wed. I would no longer need worry about you."

"Never!" In her lap, her hands fisted, appalled by her brother's hurtful words.

"That being said, all he alleged about you was that you made him sticky buns and brought him coffee. He was quite pleased with your endeavor. Said they were very good. Also told me he was shocked you could bake."

"Oh."

Heat encompassed her, flaming on her cheeks. She downed her brandy then poured another one, furious with the situation he placed her in. How was she to know he didn't talk about her? She would have thought...

You would have thought he would have told your brother all the outrageous things you did.

Yes.

Just as you tried to tell him certain things then stopped yourself because it was none of your brother's business.

True.

Then mayhap you should adjust your impression of him.

My first impression was really quite good.

Your second?

I find him to be too controlling.

You still want him to kiss you.

Yes.

Slowly, Leslie drummed his fingers on the desk, showing her a quirky half smile. "What did you think he said?"

"Nothing." She turned her head, hoping he wouldn't catch the distress she felt or the embarrassment. She didn't dare regale him with the swimming episode or even the way he taunted her with those very same sticky buns. Both men could make innocent words into something else entirely.

"If there is something to be said, say it now, Brat," Leslie encouraged. "I'll be leaving within the hour. I doubt if I'll be back for at least a week, maybe longer. Might bring Lacie with me next time so I have a pleasant diversion when the work is done."

Merry gritted her teeth together, her pulse pounding. Knowing the answer ahead of time. "You won't dismiss the arrogant man."

"No, he comes with the stud. I've no other man who can handle that horse while he's doing what he's supposed to do."

"Impregnate the mares."

"Yes."

That did catch her brother's attention. With the look on his face, Merry felt a tiny bit of vindication. Perhaps she should try using the word with Devlin. She wanted to embarrass him as much as he did her.

He'd probably turn it back on you.

How the hell do you think he could do that?

How would I know? In this case I'm sure he could think of some way. Do you truly want to risk finding out then afterward have him lord it over you?

Nothing would probably embarrass the odious man. He would most likely think what she had to say was funny. Well, she was going to try her best not to give him something to laugh at about her. Why, Leslie was just as bad. Merry spent a few more minutes in an attempt to convince her brother to dismiss Devlin even knowing how useless it was. If she was true to herself, deep inside, she didn't want to see him go. She supposed it was a good thing Leslie didn't back down. Her summer would be so boring without Devlin Mathews. She was going to make another batch of sticky buns and turn the table on him.

When she walked into the stable early the next morning, she carried with her pieces of apple. She meant to make friends with Windwalker, meaning to ride him as soon as she could garner permission from the king of the stables.

At Windwalker's stall, she stopped, slipping inside. She murmured nonsense to the big stallion before offering him pieces of apple in the palm of her hand.

"You are so handsome," she purred, stroking his nose. "Sir Alistair likes to be caressed just like this. Yes, she likes it too. I see that you do. Perhaps the king would let you mount, Sir Alistair."

She continued in this way then turned her attentions to the mare. "You should insist that Windwalker impregnate you. I'd like to have one of his babies." Her words hummed softly while Sir Alistair nuzzled her hands and she thought of having a baby, Devlin's baby.

"Not going to happen."

She whirled at the sound of his voice, her heart in her throat. Even though she expected him, he surprised her. Had purposely spoken to the horses to get Devlin's attention. It seemed she had it now. He was standing a few feet from her, very nearly naked, clad only in his unfastened doeskins. "I could ask Leslie."

"Believe you understand now just how far that will get you. The stud is mine. I'll decide what mares he covers. Your mare, not being part of the contract I have with your brother, won't be impregnated."

His mocking eyes slanted down upon her, infuriating her beyond anything she'd ever known before.

"I don't see what it would hurt."

Unable to help herself, her gaze swept down his chest, following the dark hair to the top of his pants, which he left unlaced. He didn't seem at all concerned that she was ogling him. She was, blatantly and thoroughly drinking in every part of him, committing his body to memory, devouring him. She wanted to touch him just to see if he was as hard and unyielding as he looked.

She wanted him to kiss her.

"I woke to the soft sounds you were making. Thought you and a lover were going at it in the hay," he said, returning her blatant regard of his body, fastening his stare on her lips then her bosom. "Didn't take long. I figured out it was you sweet talking my horse. Perhaps you'd like to say sweet things to me. I certainly wouldn't mind."

"You sound jealous," she muttered tossing out the accusation before she thought clearly about doing so.

He stepped closer, his muscles rippling as he moved, fascinating her. She reached a hand out to touch him then quickly drew it back. "No reason for jealousy when I could have you right now if I wanted. Would you like me to cover you?"

Heat flamed and pooled in her stomach. Indignation filled her at the assumption she was easy even while warmth flushed her face. "You're wrong."

She did want to know what it would feel like to be in his arms again, remembering the first time.

"Care to give it a try? I'm sure I could coax you into sweet submission; a little nip on your neck, a stroke to your hindquarters. If I nuzzled your body, bit in a few strategic places, would that gentle you? That's what Windwalker would do if he covered Sir Alistair. Perhaps I could tame you."

He reached out to her, touching her, provocatively running his finger along the side of her face. Her shiver of desire did not go unnoticed by him as she watched his eyes darken the blue changing to silver.

"No."

She turned away from him, stroking Windwalker in an attempt to make Devlin vanish, realizing she was venturing into dangerous territory. If she ignored him long enough, maybe he would go away.

"No?"

His lips and teeth grazed across her neck, nipped and sucked on tender sensitive flesh, finding purchase at the base of her throat. She shuddered in response to him, unable to stop herself.

He would prove to her she could not resist him. She could. With a shaking voice, she uttered a weak, "Stop."

She whirled to speak to him only to find him too close for comfort, his face so near she felt the fire. She swallowed, setting her hands on his naked chest, pushing him away. He did not give up ground to her.

"For now. We can pursue the promise of the kiss. Your eyes are telling me how much you want that kiss. Truly though, I'm wondering about my breakfast. Did you bring more sticky buns for me and coffee?"

"You cad." She pushed his chest again as he grabbed her hands pulling her close once more. "I'm not getting in a conversation about sticky buns with you."

"You figured out we were having two different conversations, did you?" He laughed, pure male laughter at her expense.

"I did and it was not well done of you. In compensation I want to ride Windwalker."

"No."

"Is that the only word you know? You and my brother." She wanted to throttle him, pummel him with her fists. "There is absolutely no reason for you to be so negative. I'm an accomplished horsewoman. I would have no difficulty..."

His dark brows narrowing, "Windwalker is not a lady's mount. You are not strong enough to handle him in case of a crisis. I would never put you in that type of jeopardy." After a short pause, he went on to say, "You can ride him with me."

She felt her eyes start to cross, her voice a barely audible squeak. "With you?"

That will mean you can wrap your arms around him or more likely he can wrap his arms around you.

I know that's stupid. Only he will be wrapping his arms around me. He would never put me behind him.

It will also mean...

Well, go on.

I think that will be putting you too close for your best interest.

What do you know about my best interest?

Everything.

"If you like we can take him out this morning. I'll finish dressing. Would you like to watch?" Then he turned, calling, "Timmy." When the boy appeared from the back of the stables. "Get Windwalker ready to ride but don't saddle him."

"Yes, Sir."

She watched in fascination as he strode back to his room. They would not repeat the ride to the pond, she was sure. She could show him to the creek where she liked to wade. It was a beautiful secluded spot bordering on MacTavish land. Maybe he would teach her how to kiss. Lacie showed the spot to her awhile back when they were riding.

He returned, his shirt only partially buttoned but at least his pants were fastened she noticed, feeling a tiny bit of relief. Every part of him spoke of arrogance and privilege, pure masculine pride and power. She wondered about his heritage.

"Are you ready?" He was smiling at her, extending a hand. It was the first time this morning. When he wasn't taunting her, his was a nice smile, one that reached all the way to her toes.

She nodded. He helped her mount before settling behind her, controlling the reins. His arms were around her. She felt them as they brushed against her breasts. Felt the soft rumble of his breathing, the steady beat of his heart. Suddenly, it seemed her heart was thumping at the same pace. Because she wanted to ride Windwalker, she had dressed in pants and a cool shirt instead of her usual riding habit. One of his large hands rested on her upper thigh. The inferno he created grew. Seemed to billow with increasing urgency.

"Where to and don't say the pond. I want to see a bit more of the countryside surrounding Southcliff." She felt the whisper of his breath caress her ear as he leaned close to speak.

She nodded, inhaling a wobbly breath, deciding she would do a little coaxing of her own and see just how far she could push him. Once more she thought a kiss would be nice. Since the first moment she saw him walking into the stables, she wanted a kiss. Perhaps today. If she ever figured out how to meet the Duke of Weston, she wanted to know how to kiss, didn't want him to be disappointed in her.

At the moment the horse was walking as Devlin waited for directions. "Head south. We'll come upon a creek and a tiny waterfall. It's a pleasant morning. We can wade in the creek."

He set the horse to a faster pace, racing the powerful stallion. She clung to his arms, her breasts moving against the long, muscled length of his arms, her body nestled close to his in an evocative way. Her eyes closed while she listened to the wind as it rushed past her ears, reveled in the feeling of the powerful horse beneath her along with the powerful man behind her. Laughing, he seemed to enjoy the thrill of the ride as much as she did. By the time they rode only a few miles, she was breathless, excited and stimulated beyond anything she'd ever known before.

After a while he slowed the pace. He didn't speak and neither did she. She didn't want to mar the beauty of the moment with words either, but the little voice inside her head didn't want to stay quiet. As usual she argued with herself.

You should not act so blatant around him. He'll think you're a tart and show no respect for you. If he kisses you then, it will be because he believes you to be easy.

He doesn't show any respect as it is. Why do you think he is always telling me what to do? He looks at me as if I'm a child. Even calls me brat.

Sometimes that is the way you act. You of all people can agree with him you are spoiled.

That's not my fault. Mother let me do whatever I pleased and Leslie was never around to tell me no. Not that he did when he was home.

That doesn't mean anything. You're acting like a tart still, pushing against the man when he can go nowhere.

He insisted we ride together. He could have let me ride by myself.

What are you going to do to make him kiss you? Ask him?

That's probably the best idea you've had yet. When we stop, I'll do just that. A gentleman wouldn't refuse a request such as that. I can tell him why too.

A gentleman would refuse, would never take your question seriously. He won't like it if you tell him you want to learn how to kiss because you've already picked out your husband, the Duke of Weston.

We both know he's no gentleman. Why should that matter? He's a horse breeder. By that fact alone he's not marriage material. Besides, it wouldn't be prudent to tell him about the duke and my marriage plans. A man doesn't like to hear things like that.

She adjusted her position as they slowed a little more, heard his groan from behind and smiled. She thought perhaps the sound was one of desire on his part. Her plan was coming along nicely.

"What's wrong?" she asked hoping he would be honest with her, turning slightly when she asked.

"You aren't wearing anything beneath that shirt, are you?" he asked, as she moved again, knowing her breasts were pushing against him and realizing the friction made the tips harden. Surely, he would feel that.

You should be feeling wanton as hell. He's not just going to kiss you. He's also going to rip your clothes off and do whatever. You might want that kiss but you don't want to be ruined before you even meet the Duke of Weston.

I can say no. He'll stop if I tell him to.

In your dreams, doubt if you could tell him no.

I will.

What if you are so curious and delighted with the kiss, you don't notice anything else?

That's not going to happen.

"Here we are."

She slipped from Windwalker's back before he could help her, feeling she needed distance from him to regain her equilibrium. The little conversation she had with herself left her feeling unnerved and confused. What if she did ruin herself? What if she didn't? What if she never met the duke?

With a bit more finesse he dismounted, letting the reins dangle. "You in a hurry to get away from me?"

He sauntered toward her, a smoldering gleam in his eyes.

She fell silent, watching him, her breasts rising and falling with each fragile sip of air she managed to inhale. She turned to talk to him. "Thank you. The ride was...was. I'm at a loss for words. Breathtaking. Feeling his powerful muscles move beneath me left me breathless."

"I feel it too, the power of the stallion. That's why he isn't a lady's mount. A lady has to be careful as to where she sits."

He slanted her that quirky half smile of his as if she said something funny. It was the same look he graced her with when they were talking about her sticky buns. She stiffened, believing he was mocking her again.

"I could ride him."

"Possibly. This is a beautiful place. Do you wade in the creek often?" He changed the subject as he turned to look over the water, his hands clasped behind his back.

Before the words left his lips, she was taking off her shoes and rolling up the pants she wore so they would reach her knees. She felt his gaze on her back. Didn't turn. The heat on her cheeks was embarrassing. She didn't want him to see that he'd made her uncomfortable again.

Her toes on the edge, the water was colder than the pond, much colder. She fought back the urge to cry out at the frigid cold liquid passing across her skin. She thought for a moment before going farther. She was already half way, might as well go all the way. That also meant asking for that kiss. She just had to get up the nerve.

"Do you always show a man so much of your anatomy? I almost think you would like me to make love to you. The other day, I saw you in just your underwear. Today, I see most of your legs. If you ask my opinion, you're a little hoyden."

She stiffened listening to his words, angry with him as well as the insinuation. At least he didn't call her a tart. He just wasn't the kind of man a lady could reason with. "I'm not a tart or a hoyden. I just like my simple pleasures," she told him as she moved farther into the creek, shivering, her arms wrapped tightly around her as if that gesture could ward off the numbing cold to her toes.

It was higher than usual and faster. She gasped in a tight lung full of air, continuing to wade, refusing to admit even to herself the water was too cold for wading. The prudently wise thing to do would be to leave.

Water splashed against her as she managed to get all the way to her knees. The front of her shirt was now plastered in spots to her bare skin. It seemed she was having a repeat of a few days before. She didn't like it. He would condemn her again, call her a tart, a brat, a hoyden. If she were a man, there would be nothing wrong with this little and very innocent escapade.

You aren't a man.

Shut up, I'm not talking to you.

"Never mentioned anything of the sort," he told her, his voice closer than before. "You really need to come out of there. It's not safe. You're going to slip then I'll have to come in after you. I don't relish the thought of a water rescue."

"Not a whore either," she muttered.

You're going to make his thoughts run in that direction. When you ask him to kiss you, he'll confirm your words.

What should I do?

Get out of the water before you slip and manage to soak yourself. It will be a cold ride back home. You won't get your kiss either.

I hate it when you're right.

Reluctantly, she strode from the creek, slipping once but catching herself with her hands, elbow deep in the water. Her shirt was wet now, soaked in the front where the water caught the fabric. When she straitened, she looked down only to see her nipples, tight dark buds against the fine white material. He cursed a blue streak. She inhaled a sharp breath of air, her hands coming up to hide herself from him. Stepping on to solid dry ground, she pulled the shirt away from her body, hoping he didn't see.

His eyes gave him away. He saw everything. She could have worn more, covered herself better but she wanted to entice him, tempt him to kiss her.

"You really do need a keeper." He set his hands on her shoulders, his face inches from hers.

She thought perhaps she would get that kiss. Instead, he stepped away from her. Her eyes were wide in wonder. She knew she should ask him now, ask now or forever hold her peace. He was glowering at her, his expression so angry she didn't dare.

Pointedly, he looked at her bosom before he looked away.

She ran her tongue across her lips, staring at his, wishing she could taste him. What did a man taste like? She'd been kissed before, years ago but that was a boy not a man. Nevil kissed her but she despised his taste. He made her skin crawl, meant to rape her. That had been three years ago. There was Douglas, a mistake from the first meeting. All he wanted was her inheritance, just as Nevil had.

She'd forgotten about Nevil and Douglas until now. Turning from Devlin, she tried to readjust her clothing. "I didn't think," she said, wishing he wasn't always right. "I knew I wanted to wade. I forgot you would be here. Not used to having a man following me around."

"You should learn not to tempt a man so."

It was either now or never, so inhaling a lungful of air, she whirled to face him before saying, "Will you kiss me?"

"Why?"

She could not find the courage to tell him why, knowing he would mock her again. If he knew the truth, he would never kiss her. "Never mind."

~ * ~

That afternoon Merry needed to get away for a few hours. Devlin was a constant in her mind from one second to the next. Asking him to kiss her, she made a fool of herself, humiliating herself one more time. If anything, she needed to talk to someone, not Lacie though. Lacie would tell everything to Leslie then she would be sent back to Bordeaux. She didn't want to go home simply because she needed to figure out how she was going to meet the Duke of Weston as well as how she was going to get a proposal from him. Then she needed to figure out just how she was going to go about learning how to kiss. Devlin didn't seem receptive to the idea of instructing her. He didn't even want to kiss her.

In the stable, Devlin was beside her almost as soon as she walked through the doors. Blasted man never left her alone. He'd become her shadow. Why he felt it necessary to keep a constant eye on her comings and goings was beyond her.

"What are you up to now, Brat?"

He stopped her from entering Sir Alistair's stall, his hand on the door, his eyes focused on her.

"Not your business." She tried to brush past him. He continued to block her way. She understood he wasn't going to let her go until she told him what he wanted to know. Merry stiffened, her chin held high more determined than ever to get her way this time.

"Unless you want me by your side," he paused, staring at her, his eyes dark pools of suspicion and mistrust, "you will answer my question."

With a long, exasperated sigh, she looked at him, her heart in her throat as the inferno he always created within her began to simmer, never quite sure if the seething, churning emotions she felt was anger at him or just pure frustration. She was mortified, devastated, truly wishing for him to vanish into thin air as she recalled his refusal to kiss her earlier today. Asking him had been her biggest mistake. She didn't want to be anywhere near him. Couldn't be anywhere near him.

"I'm going into town," she replied unable to look at him or acknowledge his presence in any other way.

"Why?"

"I need to talk to someone."

His grin widened before changing. She was sure he mocked her now. He knew what she wanted to talk about.

That damn kiss.

"I'm here. Talk to me." He leaned against the pole holding the stable door latched. His arms crossed against his chest, his well-muscled forearms the focus of her gaze for a brief time before she settled on his mouth again.

"Don't want to talk to you. Now let me go."

He relaxed his pose before stepping to the side, leaving her room to enter Sir Alistair's stall. Keeping her back to him, she saddled the horse, wishing he would leave and quit staring at her back. She knew he stared at her back.

"Are you staying the night or coming home?"

She wanted to tell him that was none of his business either. If she didn't tell him, he would most likely follow her. Begrudgingly, "Home," she muttered.

Quickly, she led the horse from the stall to the mounting block. She was astride her mare now, watching and finally feeling a bit of safety even though she knew if he wanted, he could race after her on Windwalker. He would catch her and demand answers or he could follow her.

"Be back before dark."

When she looked over her shoulder on the way out the stable doors, she saw him. His face was grim, his body taut. Tempted to defy him, she raced out the door. What would he do if she were late? Surely, he didn't have the power over her to punish her if she disobeyed him.

Do you want to put it to the test?

No.

Then you best be back before it's dark.

When she entered the bakery an hour or so later, the little bell on the door chimed, welcoming her. She smiled finally feeling relaxed. Over the last few minutes of the ride, she kept a constant vigil over her shoulder, expecting Devlin to suddenly appear by her side. Daryl stood behind the counter, an openhearted grin on her face and Lacie sat at a table with ledgers in front of her. It was the beginning of the month when the books were kept. She shouldn't have been surprised to see her sister-in-law at the bakery.

"May I get a cup of tea, a scone with strawberry preserves?" she asked, setting her hat on the table.

She wasn't sure if Lacie was the right person to talk to but it was only the two sisters at the moment. Just being away from Devlin gave her a tiny bit more confidence. She'd been questioning everything, every action she made, everything she said or thought. Devlin Mathews was worse than any parent or guardian ever could be when it came to ordering her around.

"Why are you here?" Lacie asked, looking up from her work. "Are you staying the night?"

"No," she said as Daryl set her order on the table. "I'm here to get away from Southcliff." *To get away from Devlin Mathews.*

"Oh?"

A frown marred Lacie's features. She appeared to be muddling over Merry's statement as well as what she didn't say.

Merry understood the expression was there because of her curt reply. It wouldn't do to be rude to the wife of her brother. As it was, Devlin had far too much control at Southcliff. For some reason she didn't understand, she didn't want the duke and duchess interfering. This was her battle to fight as well as win. She already knew, they, or at least Leslie, would side with Devlin in just about any decision if not every decision. Leslie might even decide to bring her into the city for the remainder of the summer if she wasn't careful. He didn't have that right though. She was no longer a child. She did have a say in what she wanted in her life. Leslie always tried to let her make up her mind. That was why this was so hard. Devlin didn't want to give her any say in her present or her future. He was an autocrat.

She sipped the tea. For a few seconds, she closed her eyes, relishing the silence as well as the peace of the moment. With her family, her in-laws, she could relax, knowing she wouldn't be judged. "I needed to get away from Mr. Mathews." Merry finally said. "We are constantly at odds. He orders me about as if he has the authority to do so."

"Is he being...?" Lacie didn't finish. "Is he a gentleman around you? I just have never quite understood why Leslie let him stay out there with you unchaperoned. Perhaps I should go to Southcliff for the summer."

Merry couldn't help the gasp nor could she help scowling. More interference in her life was nothing she wanted to contemplate. "No."

"Who would understand what Leslie does?" Daryl said while she sat down next to Merry with a cup of tea, studying her carefully.

"I don't care about that. I'd just like to understand why Mr. Mathews thinks he can tell me what I can and cannot do."

Merry was shocked when an eyebrow rose in an arch on both Daryl's and Lacie's faces.

What did they know?

"Did you tell Leslie? He is the only person who can do anything about Mr. Mathews' behavior," Lacie said thoughtfully as she scribbled a few things on a piece of paper. "Would you like me to talk to Leslie? I can, you know."

"Already did when he was at Southcliff the other day. He sided with Devlin, left me feeling like an utter fool, humiliated," Merry muttered, grimacing when she swallowed too much hot tea. She felt the steaming liquid burn while the heat slid down her throat. It seemed Devlin left her feeling that way with every encounter.

"Do you know what they agreed about?" Daryl asked.

"Well," Merry began, "I asked Leslie to dismiss the man. Leslie told me no. He didn't even think about or reflect on my proposal for one second."

"His work with these horses is truly important. Windwalker will be the basis for the next line of racing horses for the stable. With Kelly O'Brian as the trainer, well, they'll do well. Leslie's not going to do anything that will harm the chance of having the best racers in this part of the country; England and Ireland as well. The only stable that will be able to compete with his will be the Duke of Weston's Which is why he didn't need to think about your request. Dismissing that man, with his skill, is out of the question. Besides, he comes with the stud. If he goes, the stud goes."

"Oh." Merry had to muddle through Lacie's evaluation of this situation. She understood the stallion was valuable but... "Just because the horse is important does that give the man the right to order me around, verbally abuse me? Just maybe I'm not as important as the damn horses."

Lacie smiled, "Of course not. What has he ordered you to do?" She was leaning forward, listening intently. "How has he abused you?"

Suddenly, Merry felt a bit sheepish. Most of his orders if not all of them were well founded in common sense as well as logic. "Well, he did tell me to be home before dark." She held up her hands to stop the two women from responding before she could finish, knowing she was foolish to ride at night. She didn't do it very often, just when she was restless or out of sorts. Which seemed to be all the time now that Devlin lived at

Southcliff. "I would have been home before dark without his command. I know better than to ride at night. He thinks he can punish me if I disobey. Said he would tan my backside. If he lays a hand on me, I'll, I'll..."

She didn't know what she'd do. There would be repercussions. She would make sure of it.

"Do you?" Daryl asked, chuckling. "Seems to me, if you want to ride at night, you should be able to. It's safe enough around Southcliff as long as you're not planning on riding to the Firth. I would not have let Donal dictate to me that way."

"He follows me."

"So, you did ride out at night."

"No, he followed me during the day."

"But you have ridden at night."

"Yes," she reluctantly admitted. "Not since he's been here though. I've a mind to do just that and defy him."

You just want to see what he'll do.

I think I know what he'll do.

Then you should be willing to accept the punishment you know will be forthcoming.

Perhaps you're right. It doesn't mean I won't complain about his highhandedness.

The conversation had been nice, lasting well into the afternoon. Merry liked the fact the sisters agreed with her about Devlin. A man shouldn't have the say in everything a woman did, especially not a man who had no familial connection to her. She stayed too late at the bakery though. The girls insisted she remain in town. She told Devlin she would be home. If she raced Sir Alistair, she might make it home by dusk. She wasn't going to run a horse into the ground just because it might cause Devlin Mathew a bit of inconvenience. In any case, the hour would not be that late when she reached Southcliff. She should be fine, she told herself over and over again during the long ride home.

Still, when she finally reached the manor, her entire body shook with fear of the upcoming encounter with the tyrant of Southcliff. Sir Alistair simply balked at keeping up the grueling pace that would have resulted in a timely arrival. Now, the moon was shining, the stars twinkling as well as the fact dusk disappeared at least an hour ago. Perhaps if she were lucky, he'd be asleep.

The damn crickets were even chirping.

No chance of that, she mused angrily. He was sure to be counting down the seconds while he decided on her punishment. After dismounting outside the doors, she rubbed her sweaty palms on her riding habit before she inhaled a deep ragged breath, trying to prolong the inevitable. She thought of giving the little mare a swat on her rump then running to the safety of the house. If she thought for even one second he wouldn't follow her, catch her as well she would do it. She knew better. There wasn't anything she could do to avoid a lecture along with the possible chastisement he had no right to deliver.

He told you he would tan your backside. You should have paid more attention to the time when you were in town.

Well pardon me, I'm not used to watching the clock. I was enjoying my visit with my sisters-in-law. Besides he's no right to touch me.

You know better now. Besides, I think you were late just to see what he would do, how he would react.

Of course, I didn't do any such thing.

You wanted to see if you could goad him into that kiss you asked for earlier in the day.

Of course not.

But she did. She still wanted him to kiss her, needed a lesson so she wouldn't seem so naïve as well as inexperienced when she finally met her duke and he kissed her.

Well, she needed to get this over with if she was going to get any sleep tonight.

Inside the stable, all was dark except the light shining from his room in the back. Merry thought if she could just walk without making a noise, she might not have to encounter the autocrat. Nothing, not even the stable door meant to cooperate with her. As she pushed it open the usually well-oiled hinges creaked, making a noise that would wake the dead. She stopped, holding her breath, waiting for the encounter.

Good lord, but her heart pounded nearly out of her chest. He wasn't coming out of the bedroom. So, perhaps she had a chance of escaping unscathed. She led Sir Alistair into her stall, thinking she could claim she'd been here the last thirty minutes grooming her mare while making sure the horse had water along with her feed. The hair on the back of her neck stiffened. She froze.

He was behind her. She could tell, feel his presence as well as the fire of his anger surging toward her. Swallowing the dryness in her throat she turned slowly.

Chapter Three

"You're late."

He stood beside her now as he set his feet apart before crossing his arms over his chest. Of all the childish things he thought her capable of this wasn't one of them. He supposed he learned a lesson tonight even while he meant to teach her one. "Little fool."

Battle raged in her eyes, as she looked ready to fight him. She turned her back to him as if she tried to ignore him. Her back stiffened. "I didn't mean to be late. I couldn't ride Sir Alistair into the ground."

"You do not act—not one tiny bit—like the daughter of a duke nor do you tell the truth. You could have left earlier." His voice was harsh.

He grit his teeth together just as he kept his fingers clasped tightly in fists so they wouldn't wrap around her beautiful white neck. She was not going to goad him into acting less than a gentleman. In this instance, she was close, damn close.

"Well, do you know what Mr. Mathews? You are a horse breeder in the employ of my brother, a duke. No matter what you think you cannot dictate to me. I will come and go as I please."

Her words further infuriated him; not that she defied a command but because she put herself in danger. "As long as I am here and my sleep is at the mercy of the hours you come and go from the stable, I will dictate anything I damn well please."

He reached out to her, not sure what he meant to accomplish. At the same time, he had to make her understand riding at night was hazardous. He was in charge here. She was going to behave.

She ducked away from him, attempting to distance herself. He was too fast, stepping in front of her. Her skirt caught on the door to the stall.

Tugging at the fabric she wrenched it free. He heard the cloth ripping. His arms closed around her as she fell into him, keeping her from ending up on the floor.

"What I do is not your concern." She braced her hand against his chest, pushing at him.

He felt the frantic trembling of her body. Saw the blaze of her eyes. Her intentions clear, "It is when I'm the only man on the premises. If your brother were here right now, I would happily give over your keeping to him. I'm afraid he doesn't want it though. He's made it abundantly clear to me you're a woman grown and will make your own decisions. He also gave me carte blanch where your behavior is concerned."

"Oh, just let me go!" she cried furiously, trying again in earnest to wrench herself free from him. "That's what I've been trying to tell you all along. I'm a woman grown. I'm responsible for myself."

"Stop. You're caught. It's night, dark. The stars are out. The moon is full. You said you would be back before all that happened. You weren't. There were promises made that were not kept." His hands closed around her arms.

Silent echoes gathered in the stable as she pulled away from him. The second loud rending sound caught both of their attentions. Her skirt caught further on the stall door. She swore, spinning around to assess the damage. Her movement ripped it even further. He allowed her distance even as the remains her skirt seemed to all but disappear to land in a heap on the floor.

"Oh...hell!" she cried out.

She was standing in front of him in her pantalets, a raging ball of fury, eyes blazing. Desperately, she looked around, cheeks flushing brilliantly as she searched for something to cover herself. There was nothing nearby.

"Horse breeder," she muttered, pushing him angrily as if he might stumble in the process then make good an escape.

What she didn't understand was there was no escape for her, at least not until he had his say. He meant to teach her a lesson she wouldn't forget. Just how he was going to go about such a thing he wasn't sure as yet. He'd told her he would thrash her soundly. He couldn't hurt her. Hell, she was too good at doing that herself. What he needed was to figure out a way to keep her from harm at the same time convince her riding at night was foolish.

He reached behind her to grab a blanket that had been left on one of the stalls. Gently, he draped it over her shoulders, watching her, hoping to second-guess her next act of childish defiance before she could hurt herself. What he couldn't understand was why she wouldn't confess she was wrong.

And he was right.

"Brat," he returned before grabbing hold of her wrist, tugging her.

She stumbled into him, her body flush against his. He started walking, taking her with him. Determined now.

"Where are you going?"

She sounded desperate, breathless, her deep blue eyes widening in seeming alarm as they approached his room. She dug in her heels, resisting.

He wasn't sure what exactly she was resisting, him or the possible chastisement. "To mete out your punishment. Discipline is important. You do remember your promise to me as well as the fact you broke it. I'm sure you could have found someone to carry the message that you were late and staying the night."

She was struggling against him, trying to pry his fingers lose from her arm. He continued forward in single-minded determination to make her understand the importance of behaving as a rational adult woman. Still, she pushed against him dragging her feet, resisting further the unavoidable.

"Well hell." He picked her up before slinging her over his shoulder. She wasn't docile or biddable. Her fists pummeled his back even while she tried to kick him. He understood this wouldn't be the last misunderstanding between them. When finished here, she would know he was not about to roll over and concede defeat.

No, she would concede, she would surrender.

"Put me down!"

She continued, pummeling his back, trying to rear off his

shoulder, risking a fall even while she tried to escape his wrath. He suddenly realized he was no longer angry but determined.

He did just that, tossing her on his bed, straddling her, his hands placed on either side of her head.

"Brat!" His voice was harsh deep turning husky.

"Horse breeder!" she whispered, closing her eyes for a moment.

She fell silent, her breasts rising and falling with each desperate breath as she stared at him. He grinned. She was exactly where he wanted her, needed her beneath him since the moment he saw her at the pond. The feel of her body against his excited every male sinew and muscle he possessed.

He reached out, touched her face. His knuckles brushed her cheek. She inhaled sharply at his caress. He could afford a gentle smile for her. After all, she was lying on his bed, half dressed. It would not take much effort on his part to finish what she started when she tried to run from him. She defied him, in the process jeopardizing her safety.

He drew in a ragged breath of his own, understanding the strength that would be needed to get his point across without falling victim to his desire or hurting her. "You will take heed as well as great care with your life, Angelica. I won't allow anything else. Won't allow you to hurt your tiny woman's body."

Unable to help himself, he leaned down, kissed her, touched her lips with his own. It was brief and gentle but blinding in its intensity. He sucked in a breath of air, amazed at the streak of fire that seemed to sear through him at the simple stroke.

Such heat.

It was the anger. He told himself. It was the brandy he consumed while he waited for her, counting backward, smoldering with fear. It was something that had to do with this striking intriguing woman who infuriated him one moment seducing him with the exotic slant of her crystal-clear eyes the next. She enthralled him.

The fire burned with a blinding heat.

Unable to stop with the brief meeting of their lips, his mouth molded over hers, hard, persuasive, demanding as well. He needed to feel her response, the sweet pleasure he knew she could give him. Now, parting her lips to the thrust and play of his tongue, passionate, determined to wrest emotions from her. His fingers cupped her cheek, then moved...soft and mercurial as they brushed her throat, collarbone, the rise of her breast...

He should not be doing this, had sworn to keep his hands off the lovely brat who haunted his nights before tormenting him throughout the daylight hours. His dreams so real they woke him nightly in a hard sweat, needing to feel her beneath him, stroke her, learn the magic only she possessed.

Well, she was beneath him now. She responded sweetly to him. He felt the fire of her passion. His mouth continued to ply hers, taste and stroke. He pulled away, swearing at himself, hearing her tiny cry of dismay as he wrenched her to a sitting position, telling him she wanted this as much if not more than he did.

"Damn you."

He could not, would not give into her seductive, innocent charms. She was everything he'd spent the last year avoiding. Involvement with another female was not part of his plans. He would not fall victim, especially not to this woman who inundated his dreams as well as his days. Hell, he was isolated here at Southcliff miles away from London and the problems plaguing his existence. It seemed now he was hell bent on creating new issues he would have to deal with. He swore at himself, cursed her beauty as well as the innocence drawing him. She was wild and untamed, everything he didn't want in a mate. Why couldn't she be biddable?

He stared at her hard, his gaze fixed on the shimmering anger in the depth of her eyes. Just what the hell did she have to be angry about? She seduced him.

"Damn you," she murmured softly her eyes blazing. "Let me go. I'll never darken your door again."

"Liar, you can't help but darken this door since I live in the stables. You can't resist me. I do believe half of what you do is on purpose just to aggravate me. He swung his legs to the side of the bed, pulling her so she landed face down across his thighs. "I told you I would tan your backside if you arrived late, in the middle of the night." His hand rested on her buttocks, his fingers tightening on the soft rounded curve. He inhaled a sharp shallow breath. She quivered beneath his touch. "You arrived late."

"Don't you dare," she cried out wriggling, swinging her hands, trying desperately to dislodge herself from him.

Suddenly, he let her go, watching as she landed on all fours, turning to look at him, her dark black hair in wild disarray around her lovely face. He wished there was more than lantern light in the room. Truly, he wanted to see her more closely, gage her reaction to him, see the wondrous shimmer of passion in her eyes.

"Where you are concerned, I will dare anything," he spoke softly even though he couldn't keep the edge of frustration coupled with very real fear for her from his voice. The emotions were tangible, distinct.

She rose on her knees, her breasts heaving, eyes wild with fury or passion. He couldn't be sure. Only moments ago, he felt her response to his kiss, knew he could have taken the moment as far as he wanted. She would not have stopped him if his intention was to make love to her. He smiled.

"What now?"

She didn't move, seemed to wait, gauging his reaction.

He knew she wanted to run. If she did, he would go after her. This would be settled tonight.

"What now?" he asked her in return. "What should I do to make sure a wayward little hellion does not do something to endanger her life?"

"My life is no concern of yours." Her words uttered in a flurry of anger. "You've no say here, no rights at all where I'm concerned. I will never bow down to your wishes, horse breeder."

"We are back to that again?"

"Yes."

"Ah, but it is my concern when I'm the only one around to pick up the pieces of your stupidity." He smiled at her again, reaching out to brush a lock of hair from her face, wishing he could convince her she would play by his rules or not at all. What would it take to put that notion in her female mind?

"There are no pieces to pick up," she gritted out, still furious, still fighting him. "See, I am all here. All of me. I'm just fine. Never better."

"Not tonight," he gentled his voice. "Tonight, there are no pieces. If I have my way, there will be none in your future."

Yes, he could see more of her than he was sure she intended, more than he knew he should.

"Let me go."

Her back straightened, her chin rising with her words and the hope.

"Never."

She was kneeling, her hands fisted at her sides. He was sure in the next second or two she would flee. When he placed a hand on her shoulder, to give her an indication she should remain where she was, he felt the fine shuddering of her body. Fearing him was not something he wished for.

"What? What are you going to do? Remaining on my knees the rest of the night could not possibly be the penance you are claiming from me."

"No, no it's not." He patted the bed beside him. "Come sit."

"You've got to be joking."

Perhaps he was, "Remaining on your knees while we exchange verbal pleasantries is not to my liking."

"Tell me."

"Come sit," he insisted as he extended a hand to assist her from the floor. This situation turned delicate. He realized what he would do, his idea brilliant. His actions would cause her no harm or humiliation, just a very real warning she would not do as she wished in defiance of his decisions.

She rose without help, pressing her hands along her pantalets before sitting as he wished. "What do you want now?"

She sounded resigned. He was pleased. This would go better than planned or rehearsed in his mind. "Your punishment. I've decided what it should be."

"You will not tan my backside as if I was a small child."

Once again, she spoke with gritted teeth, her hands fisted at her sides.

He turned to her, tracing the line of her face before gently touching his knuckles upon her cheek. Kissing her would be so much more enjoyable than giving her the news of the discipline he was about to inform her of.

"Just this morning you asked me to kiss you. Was it what you expected?"

He easily changed the subject thinking his words would have more impact if she was forced to wait and brood about what was coming.

She drug in a sharp breath, her cheeks flaming red. "You cad."

"Me?" He feigned innocence, smiling inside since his words had the desired result. "You made the request. Don't deny it."

Merry looked away with seeming fascination on what wasn't happening outside his door. "If you don't have anything else to say besides reminding me of the stupidest question I've ever asked, I'll leave."

Placing his hand on her shoulder, "Not until I give you permission."

She turned on him. What he could see of her eyes blazed with deep-seated fury. He was frustrated, angry as well. She was a tease as well as a flirt, a beautiful flirt, a woman used to getting her way in all things. Leslie should have disciplined her a long time ago.

"Permission? How dare you!"

"You've mentioned my daring before. You will learn. I dare anything."

"I'll thank you to give me leave to go back to the house. I'm exhausted. Would like to go to bed." Her gaze shifted to his bed.

He almost let the laughter out before he schooled himself for more control than he ever thought possible. "Don't thank me. There is always my bed. It's big enough for two if you ever care to join me." The moment the words left his lips and he saw the flash of hurt in her eyes, he knew he should have said nothing.

"Bastard."

"No, concerned horse breeder."

"Just tell me."

"Then quit teasing me," he gritted out knowing full well her intentions.

She was used to getting her way in everything. Now she just didn't know what her less than subtle hints could lead to. He would enjoy another kiss, something a bit more thorough than the last one. If that happened though, he didn't know if he could stop.

"I'm not, as you well know."

"You asked me to kiss you. There must have been a reason. Care to tell me what that is?"

"Not really but if you must know, I need to learn how to kiss. It's important." Her voice turned prim even though what she was saying was far from proper.

"Why?" If she was going to kiss anyone, it would be him.

Wide-eyed and a bit hesitant she stared at him as if he must already know the answer to his question. "Why I want to learn isn't your concern," she muttered looking away again unable to meet his gaze.

"It is if you mean to practice on me."

Never before had he felt such a rise of anger over a woman wanting to kiss him. Well hell, she wanted him to teach her so she could kiss another man. "Who is he?"

Merry was shaking her head while she scooted away from him on the bed. He reached out, grabbing her wrist, pulling her toward him. "N-no one."

"Little liar," he said, his finger beneath her chin, lifting it so he could read the expression in her eyes. "Who?" He meant to stay with this until she decided to answer him. The question for him was whether or not she would tell him the truth. "Who is it you want to impress with your kisses? Why should I help?" Helping her learn how to kiss another man was ridiculous.

The rapid rise and fall of her breasts intrigued and provoked. She had no idea what she unleashed in him with her words. He wanted to shake her, shake a tiny bit of sense into her. In more ways than one, she was playing with fire.

She ran her sweet pink tongue across her lips before it vanished inside her mouth, a mouth he would like nothing better than to plunder and explore. Teach her for some other man, not a chance in hell.

"You must know how to kiss," she finally said. "It wouldn't be so hard for you to kiss me, would it? To show me what a man likes as well as what he doesn't."

"Brat, there is nothing a man doesn't like."

"Devlin, please..."

No, not hard at all. It was what he wanted since he first saw her and now he wondered why the restraint over the past days. He could take what he wanted. It would not have been difficult at all. His hands were wrapped around her arms as he was bringing her closer, his body taut with need to put an end to this self-inflicted torture. Still, he could not let his question dissolve unanswered. "Who is it you want to learn to kiss for?"

He watched her swallow, the pulse at her neck beating a rapid staccato, as it seemed she tried to figure out if she should answer him. He placed his lips on the pulse, touched and stroked with his tongue before pulling away.

"You're hurting me," she whispered.

Immediately his hands dropped from the tops of her arms to hold her wrists. Letting her go now was out of the question. He'd yet to tell her what her punishment was. She'd yet to tell him who the object of her desire was. "Who is he?"

"Truly, Devlin, what does it matter? You wouldn't know him. Even if you did, I can't see why it would make a difference."

She was most likely right about some of what she said. At the moment her words made a hell of an impression on him that if he kissed her, she would use what he taught her to win the affections of another man. It just wasn't to be done. "Doesn't matter whether or not I know the man. Who is it?" he gritted out, furious she could make him so frustrated.

For a moment she looked down, her dark sooty lashes falling against her soft white skin. When she looked up, he thought he saw moisture in her eyes then she blinked. The tears vanished replaced by tenacity coupled with determination.

"The Duke of Weston," she ground out in a fury. "Are you satisfied?"

He choked. His breath quit even as his heart wrenched to a complete halt. He tried to calm himself, attempted to school his features. Finally, after several seconds he could breathe again, "Why him?"

"I'm going to marry him." Her chin lifted in defiance.

"You think so, Brat?" he queried, suddenly more amused than angry. "Why him? Do you even know him? Oh, that's right. Leslie purchased your mare at Weston's stables." He paused for a few heated seconds. "You like the stables. That's why you want to wed the man. Because of his horses."

"No, I don't know him. I saw him in Paris a few years ago, once more in Glasgow and..." She looked up slipping her tongue along her bottom lip. "I liked what I saw. My stomach did a little somersault both times I saw him. I knew then I was in love."

"I see." *A little somersault*? "Did your stomach somersault when you first saw me?"

She hesitated a moment seeming to think about his question before answering. "I suppose it did."

"By your reasoning you should want to marry me. You're in love with me, a horse breeder. Are you sure your insides don't somersault when you look at any man?"

He was pleased with her answer even knowing he was pushing her too hard.

"No, I'm not sure of anything except that I intend to marry the duke."

"Because he has a title?" he grit out.

"No, I don't care a fig about titles."

Her petite shoulders lifted to put emphasis on her statement.

"Then why?"

"Because I think I will fall in love with the man."

"You think you will love him, do you? Very interesting but you don't know because you've never spoken to him yet you want to learn how to kiss him."

He wanted to laugh at her convoluted line of thinking. She was putting all her hopes into marriage to a man she'd yet to meet. "He could be a bounder, a cad, a reprobate of the worst sort. He could have a paunch."

His voice turned soft as he watched her with a tenderness he never felt before for another living being.

"If he is, well then, I'll not marry him. I have to be in love. I promised my sisters."

Well hell, she told her sisters about this crazy scheme of hers. Now he knew. Who else knew? Supposedly, everyone but the man of her dreams. This was truly beyond the scope of anything he'd ever thought about before. He would have to take extreme care, more so than before if she ever discovered the truth about him.

"I told you my secret now I need to go to bed. I want to ride in the morning."

She started to get up. He pulled her back down.

"Not so fast. You're not riding in the morning or the afternoon."

"What?" Once more she tried to stand.

He tugged her back to the sitting position on his bed. "You may not ride for the next week. Your punishment for disobeying me, Brat."

~ * ~

She wanted to lash out and hit him, needed to tell him exactly what she thought about his horrible discipline. It was the worst possible punishment. He had no right, no right at all. She knew she couldn't fight him. Apparently, his word was law. "Don't call me that."

Turning to run from him, she didn't look back, at least not until she reached the stable doors. She stopped, swirling around, her fury unleashed now at the words he'd only a few minutes before uttered. They were absurd. He was ludicrous. If he thought he could get away with anything so preposterous, he didn't know her. Never would she let him dictate to her. Somehow, she would find a way to get past his orders and ride her mare.

With fists clenched tight, she stomped back to the room surprised for the first time Devlin didn't follow her. Going back, she must certainly have cobwebs for brains.

She reached the door to the room he occupied, unsure now what to say, her legs wobbling so badly she wasn't positive if she could stand. He was still relaxed, standing by his trunk. His grin was smug, supremely arrogant. She wanted to wipe it from his face.

"Back so soon, Brat?" he asked, no longer holding the smirk or the laughter back.

You should not have come back.

Need to tell him what I think.

Don't need to do that. He will only rub your face in his decision.

He can't keep me from riding.

Of course, he can.

I'll fight him every step of the way.

Just how do you expect to do that? Talk to your brother?

"You can't keep me from riding." Was all she could think of to say. "I..."

"Believe what you will." He shrugged his haughtily broad shoulders. "For now, though, either join me in bed or go back to the house. I've had enough conversation for one day. I need to go to sleep."

Her eyes widened at the preposterous invitation as she stared from him to the bed then back. So furious a few seconds ago, she never noticed he was now half dressed. He didn't seem to mind her looking at him. Good lord, but his shoulders were tanned and broad, his muscles tight and hard. Her breath caught in her throat as her gaze traveled the length of him, from his chest to the well-muscled thighs back to the bulge in his pants. She swallowed hard thinking escape was necessary and prudent.

When had she ever been prudent?

Lazily, he returned the perusal, his gaze resting on her bosom then lower just as hers had done the same. She realized again she was barely dressed. Now her focus was riveted on the bed. He sauntered to it, sitting down before patting the area beside him. Well, they were back to the bed.

"You cannot stop me from riding."

She understood this was not going to get her anywhere, knew he would find a way to stop her. He was bigger and stronger. She would just have to find a way to outsmart him.

"I believe we've already had this conversation. Now, as I said a few seconds ago, join me or leave. It's been a long day."

She turned once more, muttering and stomping from his room. Looking over her shoulder to find him, she was surprised anew that he wasn't following. Lord but she should be embarrassed, mortified with everything she revealed to him. There had to be a way to get him to change his mind. Somehow, she knew he was impervious to anything she could do. She wasn't going to sleep with him.

He hasn't asked. Didn't even want to kiss you it seems.

He did kiss me.

You call that a kiss? He stopped as soon as you brought up the reason for allowing him to kiss you.

He did, didn't he?

He didn't like the idea of teaching you how to kiss so another man would reap the benefits.

Now that's just ridiculous. He's a horse breeder. Why would he want to kiss me?

He's a man first and why wouldn't he want to kiss you?

A few minutes later, she found herself inside the manor, slamming and locking the door before she stomped up the stairs to her room. This wasn't going to do. It just wasn't. When she peered in the mirror hanging in her bedroom, she gasped. Her hair fell in disarray down her back. The pantalets revealed more than they hid and somehow the bodice of her riding habit was halfway unfastened, leaving a clear, unobstructed view of the valley between her breasts. She inhaled sharply devastated by what she saw looking back at her.

You didn't realize how much you were tempting the poor man. He's a saint for resisting your blatant overtures.

Trust me, he's no saint.

He could have kissed you a second time, kept you there for the night, in the process ruining you for the duke. You would have never found the strength to object.

He could have tried. I wouldn't have let him.

Do you really think you've the power to stop him from seducing you?

I can say, no.

Dream on.

Merry went to bed, dreaming of the man then waking furious with herself. The next day the sun was shining, the weather not too hot. A ride would be glorious this morning. She picked up the pieces of what was left of her riding habit before dropping them to the floor again. Lucy would be appalled at what she saw. Merry didn't have any way of explaining the clothing to her without being judged. She didn't need to explain anything.

She stood at the window, staring at the closed stable doors and wondering if Devlin truly meant to keep her from riding for a day let alone a week. He hadn't known her for very long, didn't understand how determined she was. What he would know about her was that she loved her horse and riding. She wouldn't let a simple dictate stop her from what she wanted.

This just wouldn't do. Perhaps she could offer him something to change his mind, a bribe perhaps.

The man couldn't or wouldn't be enticed. He must enjoy torturing her. She couldn't even go to Leslie and have him fired. Devlin knew his power over her. That knowledge wasn't going to stop her from trying.

She dressed carefully in a split skirt and blouse. Something between a gown and a riding habit just in case he did change his mind before she wandered into the kitchen.

To her surprise, she found him sitting at the kitchen table eating. His grin seemed to stretch from one ear to the other. "Join me?" He motioned to one of the chairs not bothering to rise and seat her.

He was acting suspicious as if he was privy to something important to her. She didn't reply as she watched him. What was he up to now? He'd never eaten this late or with her unless she brought food to the stables. Never been in the kitchen when she came down for breakfast. Of course, she usually rose earlier in the morning and was riding by now. She supposed he ate after she left.

Dishing up eggs and bacon, she sat down across from him. "What are you up to?" She pointed her fork at him wishing she had the nerve to stab him. "I don't like that grin."

"Eating. I see you've dressed as if you plan on going for a quick ride or a long one. The stables are closed to you," he reminded her. "There is nothing you can do about it. No ride today or tomorrow or..."

"You're right. I am dressed for riding. As soon as I finish eating that's what I'm going to do." She thought perhaps a bit of bravado would help accomplish her mission.

"Suit yourself."

That wasn't what she expected. There should have been further argument or manly dictates. He should have reinforced his tyranny. Should have been a denial. Something was very wrong here. She sipped her coffee watching him studying her. He was just waiting to pounce, waiting for her to try something then he would assert himself into her life.

"Suit yourself. What does that mean?"

He looked toward the stables before focusing his attention on her, lifting his shoulders insolently. "You can try to ride but the stable is locked to you unless I'm with you. I don't have time to ride this morning. In any case you would have to ride with me on Windwalker. That won't happen this week either."

"No."

In a flurry she rose, stomping from the kitchen to the stable doors. The heat of his gaze seared her back. She knew he watched, could imagine the smirk on her face when she tried to open them. They were locked to her. Bloody eyes but she didn't even know there was a lock.

He was behind her, so close she felt the heat of his body. "You may not ride for the week," he reiterated. "The discipline is your penance for disobeying me, for doing something childishly foolish, for putting your life at risk."

She leaned against the wood, closing her eyes, wishing him into oblivion or beyond where ever that might be. Seconds ticked by as she inhaled air, listened to the rapid beating of her heart. Sunshine warmed her skin, heating her from the inside out. Well, she wasn't going to stay here. If she couldn't ride, she would walk.

Pushing herself from the door, Merry strode away from the stables, away from Devlin Mathews as well. If she didn't see him again for another week, that would be just dandy.

"Where are you going?" His question was curt, demanding an answer.

She heard the voice, chose not to tell him what he wanted to know. Let him worry and wonder where she was. Telling him she was going to the lake was the last thing she meant to do. Inwardly, she groaned. It was at least four miles to the lake, a good hour's walk. Well, she didn't have anything else to do. She'd make a day of it, enjoy the coolness of the water as well as the fact she was escaping his hold over her.

He was beside her, wrenching her around by one arm. Her breath caught in the back of her throat, the desperate beat of her heart pounding in her ears.

"Where are you going?" he asked glaring at her, his expression hard unyielding. She could not deny the power he held.

"I don't have to tell you."

She knew she was being petulant. Why should she tell the tyrant anything? This was her life not his. She could spend it as she pleased.

"I will lock you in your house."

She heaved a huge sigh realizing it was best to tell him so she could get on with her life. "To the pond. Don't try to stop me."

He dropped his hands. "Have a nice walk, Brat. Be back before dark."

"Or what?"

"You don't want to find out."

She started walking again, knowing he was watching her, understanding he wasn't going to give in and bring out a horse.

See what you've gone and done?"

What I've done?

You thought if he knew he would give into you. If he knew you would walk, he would offer a horse. Admit it.

No.

I'm right.

My feet hurt.

What did you expect?

Half way to the pond, sweat dripped from Merry's forehead while she regretted her hasty decision, a decision made with little thought spurred by anger. What breeze there had been when she started vanished now as the time edged toward noon. She stopped, her hands at the small of her back stretching in an attempt to ease the pain. It would do her no good to turn around, at least she could think of nothing good. She wanted to cool off in the pond.

She would have to walk home.

Thinking about that would best be put off until later.

He told her she had to be back before dark. It would be much more pleasant to walk once the sun went down. The sun's heat would not be unbearable. She was certain an evening breeze would cool the land.

There was nothing else to do but keep walking. She was too stubborn to give in now and prove to the tyrant she was foolish and stupid. Over an hour later closing in on two hours, she reached the pond, limping. Both feet hurt like the very devil. She made it the last quarter mile by sheer determination. Now had no idea how she was going to walk the four miles home. A frantic wobbly breath raced from her lips. She looked toward Southcliff wishing he would appear on the horizon, even if he would goad her mercilessly. Indeed, sometimes she was her own worst enemy.

Sitting on the boulder near the pond she carefully rid herself of her boots, grimacing in pain as each one left her foot. On each foot there were more blisters crusted with blood than she cared to count. She rolled her stockings down, gritting her teeth as the fabric pulled away from each blister.

Tears streamed down her cheeks. She didn't know if the tears were from the pain or her frustration. Swimming would make her feel better as well as wash the blood away. She wondered if she didn't show up tonight, if Devlin would come after her. Wondered too what his lecture would entail. If she didn't have to walk home, she wouldn't mind his lecture.

Nothing else to do, she slipped from her clothing, wearing just her shift, before wading into the water. She knew the thin fabric did little to nothing to conceal but she didn't give a damn right now.

It's Devlin's fault.

Of course, it is. He's the one who made you walk to the pond so you could swim.

He wouldn't let me ride.

You broke the rules.

His rules.

His rules.

He will call me a fool.

Well, this time you are a little fool. He has every right to call you names. He should shake some sense into you.

Doubt if a little shake would do something like that.

Merry's stomach growled as she watched the sun as it began to settle behind the hills. She knew she would need to start back. If she began right now, she would make it before the sky turned ink black.

As soon as her shoes were on her feet, the pain so intense tears began anew. There was nothing to do except put one foot in front of the other; after that try to ignore the agony of it all. This journey home was going to take a hell of a lot longer than the two plus hours it took to get here. The sky would be dark by the time she reached Southcliff.

Good Lord, what if he didn't miss her? She never felt fear when she was riding. Now, shivers of terror rifled through her. The manor house was so far away. Not so far, just four miles, an eternity when one can't walk.

She sat down to rest. The pond was still in clear view. How far had she gone? Two hundred feet? Her gut tightened, her resolve wavering. She grit down on her teeth, standing again. How the devil did a person limp when both feet hurt?

She didn't know how far she'd gone. The sun was behind the hills while a crescent moon hovered on the horizon. She pushed tears off her cheeks with the backs of her hands. "Won't do you a bit of good to cry. If anyone can do this, you can."

Standing, she inhaled a long deep breath as she pushed herself to move one foot at a time no matter how long it took her. Devlin would have to miss her soon. He knew she was on foot. If he was involved with the breeding, he might not know she wasn't in the house. Every shadow sent a debilitating ripple of fear through her.

He might not know she wasn't stranded halfway between the pond and Southcliff. Despair sent more tears to her eyes. By now he should have missed her. She should hear hoof beats. He should have been here by now to rescue her before telling her how stupid she was, call her a little fool. She would agree with him this time. Her walking to the pond had been pure perversity on her part a way to show him he couldn't keep her from doing what she wanted. Evidently, he couldn't. In this instance, she paid the price.

More stars littered the dark sky. An owl hooted swooping close to her as if chasing some nocturnal animal. She stubbed her toe on a rock, crying out before sinking to the ground, landing on her hands and knees. Random streaks of tears turned to sobs. Over and over again she told herself there was nothing dangerous out here. Stand up and keep walking. You can't stop now. All she wanted was to curl up and fall asleep.

That was when you were riding.

I know, I know.

What was that noise?

As long as it's not going to eat me, I don't care.

You need to get up and start walking. You know you can't count on Devlin to rescue you. Obviously, he doesn't even know you are out here. He would have come for you if he did know, just to say 'I told you so'.

She pushed upward on hands and knees, slowly getting her feet beneath her. With each step she was closer to home. What seemed like hours ticked by before she finally saw Southcliff. She was spent, exhausted as well as in pain.

He had not come for her. What had she expected?

By the time she reached the porch, she could go no farther. She slipped off her shoes and stockings. Her feet now were decorated with old and new blisters. Managing to reach the swing as well as the quilt that was always kept there, she curled up, falling asleep within seconds.

"What the devil do you think you're doing now? Don't think I've ever seen anything so ridiculous. Did you sleep there all night?"

Merry didn't want to open her eyes. She pulled the cover over her shoulders and head only to find the quilt yanked away. Her lashes fluttered against her cheeks a few times trying to close out the brilliant sunshine.

She groaned, "Go away."

"No."

He should have discovered her missing yesterday. She had nothing to answer for. She was here unscathed. Well, almost unscathed. He stared at her for the absolute longest time before pulling her from the porch swing and into his arms.

"Bastard!" she cried out as her feet hit the wood of the porch while she crumpled downward.

"Did you sleep out here?" He picked her up before placing her on the swing. "You look like hell."

"I'll thank you to keep your thoughts about my appearance to yourself." Her voice wavered even though she tried to put a stern edge to it.

She was so very close to tears. She didn't want him to see her cry.

"Don't thank me, Brat. Did you sleep out here?"

"What does it look like?" she retaliated, wishing him to perdition.

She pushed her tangled hair from her eyes, glaring at him now, more furious than ever he didn't come for her last night. Since he didn't, he had no right to insult her now.

He was bending over her, holding onto her foot then the other one. "It looks as if you walked to the pond and back. What time did you get home?"

His eyebrows were drawn together in what appeared to be intense concentration. He looked fierce, angry as well.

"I don't know."

"Little fool."

He picked her up in his arms; carried her into the house then on into the kitchen. With a foot he kicked a chair away from the table so he could set her on it. Then he was pumping water into a basin.

"I can take care of myself."

At this moment she didn't believe it. Neither did he.

"I can see that."

When he finished getting the salt bath ready, he brought it to her, putting her feet in the bath.

She shrieked. "It stings."

"Will also help keep the raw blisters from getting infected. When these are clean, I'll pour some whiskey on your feet and wrap them."

He stood up, raking both hands through his hair. "I should tan your backside."

"Seems to be your answer to everything."

"Perhaps I should carry through on the threat."

"As if that would help. You should let me ride."

"If you did this so you could get your way...?" he swore before heading out the door which banged shut behind him.

He was gone, vanished. Thank God. Too soon, he was back again.

After finding a towel, he knelt beside her gently drying her feet whiskey bottle in hand. "This is going to hurt like hell."

~ * ~

The day before, Devlin watched as she walked away, thinking she would be back in a matter of seconds complaining of sore feet. For several minutes, he stood outside the stable doors anticipating her timely return. She would not be foolish enough to walk all the way to the pond. Would she?

"Devlin, the mare is ready."

Timmy stood just inside the doors waiting for him. There was so much to do today. He turned his attention away from Merry telling himself he would check in on her later when he had more time. She certainly wouldn't walk the four miles to the pond. This was just a show of bravado.

The first mare was ready. Windwalker was more than willing. He observed critically as Timmy secured the mare before bringing his stallion into position.

The breeding went off without a hitch. Devlin saw to his horse as well as the mare before retiring to his room to work on correspondence. The hours sped by. He lit the lantern on his desk. Grabbing a bottle of brandy, he strode into the stable to check in on the two horses. The cook seeing to his needs brought him a basket of food for dinner. He leaned on the stall, content, watching the horses.

All seemed fine. He took a long pull from the brandy bottle, trying to forget the night before and the encounter with Angelica. She was slowly burrowing into his heart. It seemed he couldn't stop thinking about her. About the way she would feel beneath him, naked. Last night he came pretty close to discovering exactly how that felt.

Well hell, he should check on her. He strode from the stables intent on seeing her, even resuming their argument over her riding. If she would only show some sign of remorse or capitulation, he might give in. Night had fallen. The silence surrounding him seemed eerie. When he looked at the house, it was dark, not a solitary light from any window. He pulled out his pocket watch, nine o'clock. Would she go to bed this early?

The night before had been a trying night. He was exhausted from the encounter with her as well as the inbred tension from the breeding. Surely, she returned home. Most likely in a snit and with sore feet. He chuckled softly, thinking of how far she must have walked before she decided to return. She might have gone an extra hundred yards just in childish spite but all the way to the pond? He thought on that for a moment.

Never.

His soft sigh of exhaustion whispered into the sultry spring night. Thoughts of Teddy and his little sister, Emma, whirled in his head. She told his best friend she was pregnant with his child. Hell, he didn't even like Teddy's sister. Would have never bedded her.

He had more control than that.

Of course he did, except where his brat was involved. Control seemed to have slipped away where she was concerned. He sighed again, deciding Angelica must be asleep in the house before turning back to the stables and his room.

Once inside, he opened a new bottle. It seemed he lived on brandy just so he wouldn't attack Angelica. He was hard just thinking about her while he remembered exactly how she felt beneath him. Last night she displayed just about every inch of her. Last night he tasted her, felt the soft curves of her body nestled against him.

This was not the relaxing peaceful sojourn in the country his grandmother thought would happen. He was supposed to breed a few horses, sleep when he wanted, perhaps enjoy a few moments of solitude.

Truth be told, he didn't like seclusion, didn't enjoy a peaceful existence. What he did enjoy now was provoking Angelica.

When he wandered into the kitchen the next morning, he was surprised not to see her eating her breakfast or the plate left in the sink. Of course, she usually rose early so she could ride. He took that pleasure away from her. He didn't like robbing her of something she loved.

Perhaps she would learn her lesson.

He poured himself a cup of coffee before wandering through the house. Stopping at the staircase, he turned his attention to the stairs and the second floor. Unusual for him and with a bit of hesitancy, he strode up the steps looking into her bedroom.

She wasn't there.

The bed had not been slept in.

Fear coursed through him. Where the devil was she? He set the cup on a table before racing down the steps then out the front door. She was there, sound asleep on the porch swing. His heart caught in his throat.

She was curled up on the swing. Her shoes were on the porch as well as her bloody stockings.

Well hell.

Obviously, she had walked farther than a few hundred yards. Could she have gone all the way to the pond? When did she get home? He inhaled a long-ragged breath wishing he had paid more attention to where she was yesterday. He knew how impetuous she was, how angry she was. She would have done things just to spite him or prove she could do it. Lord, but the most beautiful woman he'd ever known wanted to be a man, or play at being a man.

What to do?

Chapter Four

Two more days of her seven-day punishment passed before she could walk again. Devlin stayed away from her as well as the house for much of the time, unwilling to rub salt into her wounds even though that process might have been the most prudent.

When she slowly limped into the stable on the third day, she was wearing men's pants along with a loose shirt. Her hair was pulled back in a tight bun, her lips a soft pink, her brows dark, pulled together forming a frown. The long white column of her throat, more prevalent now with her ebony hair pulled away. A lump caught in his throat.

Perhaps today was the day.

He grinned as he walked toward her, smiling at her, pleased she wasn't limping too badly. "I'm glad to see you can walk again."

"No thanks to you," she muttered as she made her way to Sir Alistair. She did falter a bit.

"Very well, continue to blame me for your stupidity. I don't mind as long as you learned a much-needed lesson."

Goading her seemed the right thing to do at the moment. Either that or he would pull her into his arms. If that happened, nothing would get done.

She glared at him crystal blue eyes blazing, "It would not have happened if you let me ride."

"So, you didn't learn anything. You still think you're a man."

He tossed that out to make way for his next outrageous suggestion, one he meant to enjoy immensely. She would learn another valuable lesson. She couldn't compete with a man in a man's world.

"Of course I don't think I'm a man."

Her back turned rigid while her chin rose at least two notches.

"Then why do you believe you should be able to do everything a man does? You're not making sense." The question was logical, meant to elicit a response he might come to understand.

"I don't. I don't believe I should be able to do anything a man does. What makes you say that?"

"You ride at night with no thought of the repercussions, of the very real dangers to your person. Your strength is not great enough to control a stallion if trouble might arise but you don't see it that way. The list could go on. Am I making my point?"

She was shaking her head, clearly disagreeing with what he said. "The countryside surrounding Southcliff is safe. As to riding Windwalker, I'm an excellent horsewoman. I could handle him with ease."

"With barely any muscle in those arms and legs of yours," he told her judging her body. "If he were to take it into his head to disagree with his master, you could never hold him on course."

"I could prove my ability to you. Let me ride him," she challenged stepping closer to him.

"Never. At the moment the only stallion in here is Windwalker. You won't ride him without me. I won't take a chance with your life or his."

She was pushing too far. He would not let her ride for a week, Windwalker not at all.

She opened the gate to Sir Alistair's stall. He grit his teeth ready to stop her before she could mount. She would not ride out of here. He didn't have the time to go after her. However, he would if she persisted. Instead, she merely began brushing the mare all the while cooing to Sir Alistair. When he listened, he realized she was talking about him and how horrible he was.

"You can't stay awake twenty-four hours a day." She was talking to him but she wasn't looking at him. "I will find a way to ride. Just you wait. I'll show you," she challenged him.

When she bent over, the rounded curve of her bottom caught his attention, reminding him of what he was going to test and confront her with. "I'm breeding Windwalker to one of the mares today. If you believe you should be part of a man's world, I want you to watch. In time if you would like, you can help."

He watched the interesting play of emotions contort her face. She pursed her lips for a moment, her eyes wide, questioning in disbelief.

She stood up so quickly the movement freighted her mare. "You want me to do what?"

He shrugged, his brows drawing together, his smile widening in anticipation of the next few hours with her. "I want you to watch with me."

"That's a man's domain."

"So is riding at night. That hasn't stopped you."

He liked the way her lips compressed, as she thought over his outrageous proposal.

"Is that a command?" she asked, a bit hesitant.

He saw the light in her eyes, the curiosity as well. He had her right where he wanted her. "Yes, if you want to take it that way. You need to stay and decide for yourself."

Her eyes nearly crossed. Still, he could tell she wasn't averse to this intoxicating notion of his. She wanted to see, curiosity winning over propriety and decorum. She was acting true to form. "Alright."

"Good."

He turned his attention toward the back of the stable, searching for his helper. "Timmy, bring the mare in the fourth stall, set her up in the breeding stand."

He strode toward Windwalker, taking the big stallion's reins in hand, carefully guiding him. "I want you to stand back there, behind the wall I built. It will suffice as a place to view the affair. The barrier will also keep you safe."

Her eyes wide blue spheres in a face gone suddenly very pale, she walked to the place he indicated. He saw the tension in her shoulders and spine, the lift of her chin as well. It seemed she would brazen this out. Understood this was not easy for her. She would do this just to prove a point.

"Timmy, this is the mare's third time. She knows what is going to happen. I expect you to give just a bit of guidance. Make sure Windwalker doesn't hurt her."

He looked over to Angelica, watching her for a response other than her pale face and wide eyes. It didn't seem she meant to say anything. "I'll be behind the viewing screen if you need anything. When they are finished, you may put the horses in the stalls and go home." Lord, but he wanted privacy.

This scene was just too damn perfect. After this, she would understand the way of things, what she could and couldn't do. He strode to Angelica, standing behind her, his hands on her waist. He flexed his fingers. "What are you doing?" she asked in response, her voice a quiver of tension.

"Watching."

Actually, he was more interested in watching her than the mating in front of him.

"Oh dear."

"The mare likes what the stallion is doing. Don't you think? See, he is nipping her neck. She's making noises to show the stud how she feels. He wants her to enjoy the mating."

Cautiously, he bent closer, his teeth grazing the long white column of her neck then her ear, stroking with teeth and tongue as they observed the breeding of the horses.

He was sure she would stiffen further. Instead, she leaned into him, pushing against him before turning her head so he had better access. He ran his hands up then down her sides, loosening her shirt as he did so. The stallion nipped the mare's hindquarters. He would have liked to parrot that movement.

Not today.

With his teeth, he grazed the other side of her neck, listened to the soft sweet sound of pleasure ripple through her. Windwalker mounted the mare, plunging into her.

"Oh dear."

"What is it?" he whispered, his breath fanning across her ear. He was rewarded with a tiny shiver and more sounds.

"It's so big."

"Yes, it is."

He nearly laughed wondering if she thought he would be as large. "Do you think she likes what he is doing?"

"Hear the sounds she makes, the high-pitched whinny?" The mating continued for another few minutes. "Yes, she likes what he is doing, thrusting into her giving her pleasure."

He nodded at Timmy and watched as the stable hand lead the horses back to their stalls. Good, they were by themselves. During the process, he pulled her shirt from the man's britches she wore. His hands settled on her soft flesh, rising only a small amount to cup her breasts. Her waist was small, her skin soft, her nipples hardening more with each caress.

She inhaled swiftly, realizing suddenly he was stroking her, relishing the soft smooth skin beneath her shirt. His thumbs stroked her nipples bringing them to tight hard buds. He wanted to taste them. Not today. He caressed and explored while he continued to bathe her neck with kisses, stopping to spend more time at the base where he felt the rapid beating of her heart.

"Perhaps we should leave now."

Her voice squeaked. Was barely audible as he dipped one hand between her pants and her belly.

He found the nest of soft curls there, touched, explored, stroked until he parted the feminine petals between her legs. He spread them further, giving him more access. Her breath was ragged as her body began to tremble; a quivering need seemed to encompass her. She pushed against him, begging him, seemingly unable to tell him to stop. With his feet, he pushed her legs farther apart.

"That's it, come closer, come as close as you can get."

Her folds were hot and wet, dripping with moisture telling him she was ready for him. She moved her hips pushing nearer to him. She was shaking, desperate in her need.

Well hell, but he wanted to be deep inside her. This was meant to coax responses from her, meant to teach her she could not assume a man's role in any context. The sight of Windwalker mounting the mare while Angelica stood so close to him sent him over the edge. He was hard, growing harder. Control for him was vanishing more quickly than he would have ever expected. He wasn't going to make love to her, not today, not ever, especially not until she wanted to learn how to kiss for his enjoyment instead of the Duke of Weston's. Not until he could no longer deny himself, so, in reality, when hell froze over.

This moment, this lesson was over, now while he could still put her aside, now while he could keep himself from carrying her to his bed and stripping her. He released her, turning her to face him, his emotions blazing, raw, savage with his need. He stroked his knuckles down her cheek, across her jawline as well. "You should not wear men's clothing, Brat."

She stepped back. Briefly he saw a stunned, hurt look in her eyes. She turned from him then, whirled, hitting him squarely on the cheek. He did not except that show of indignation. "How dare you!" she cried out before she raced from the stables.

He supposed he deserved that. He wasn't going to apologize. He'd never let a woman slap him. The act quite took him by surprise. He grinned. Perhaps she did learn the lesson he intended.

Beyond aroused, Devlin walked to his room, contemplating a quick trip into Glasgow to find a willing woman in order to ease his swollen problem. Instead, he decided against it, afraid that even with the stable doors locked, Angelica would find a way to get inside in order to steal a horse. She, still had several days left of her punishment. He meant to make sure she didn't ride until the time was up.

During the remaining days, she stayed in the house, keeping her distance. He was more than a little disappointed, having come to enjoy her company as well as the ensuing confrontations. All he saw of her were the plates left in the sink after each meal. She was moping, pouting in her upstairs bedroom. Either that or she thought she was punishing him by not showing herself.

During this time, he made two trips into Glasgow to speak with her brother about the breeding, keeping him apprised of the situation, leaving out any information about Angelica.

"How is Merry? Still an Angel?" Leslie queried thoughtfully at their last meeting, seeming to need information. "Wouldn't ask except

Lacie is chomping at the bit to visit. My wife does not like the fact Merry is alone with you without a chaperone as well."

"Everything is fine. Angelica is acting her normal self. We certainly have no need of a chaperone. In fact, I haven't seen much of her the last few days. She's been keeping to the house."

He remembered the feel of her soft breasts cupped in his hands, the way her belly quivered as he stroked her, parted her. A chaperone would never stop him if he meant to make love to her. He didn't. So, there was no need of supervision.

"She's pouting? Did you take away some privilege or two, perhaps three?"

Leslie laughed as if he knew or understood more of what was going on than Devlin wanted him to know.

"Angelica doesn't pout." Devlin said, as he watched the myriad of expressions crossing Leslie's face all shouting, he thought him a liar. "She gets even."

No, his brat took action. Even now he was worried she would find some way into the stables. If she did, the punishment would last another week. If she did, he might indeed make it damn uncomfortable for her to sit.

"Very well, she is incorrigible. Don't know why she would act differently around you than everyone else. If you say she's an angel again, I'll believe you. Suppose I don't have any other choice."

Leslie's laughter told Devlin he understood the lie as well as the damming information the fib concealed.

"Didn't say she was an angel, at least not this time."

Devlin remembered the way she felt against him, her breasts, her sultry, so very hot feminine petals. In his arms she was his angel anyway.

"No, you didn't. So, what did you discipline her for?" One dark eyebrow lifted in a perfect arch when he asked the question.

"What makes you think I disciplined her?"

He didn't like the fact someone was telling the duke tales even if they were true.

"Don't have to be a seer to know you must have done what any respectable man would do. I know for a fact she didn't leave here last

Sunday soon enough to reach Southcliff before dark. Lacie came home from the bakery that evening, pacing, wringing her hands while she feared you would hurt her. Naturally, I assured her you wouldn't."

"You know me better than that, although I did contemplate a thrashing on her backside. It was only a thought."

"I do. My Lacie doesn't. She was worried about her sister-in-law. Thinks of her as a real sister these days."

Devlin's hands were steepled in front of him as he sat back slowly in the wing chair in Leslie's office. "If you must be reassured, I took away her riding privileges for a week. I deemed that more appropriate than tanning her backside. It wasn't like she was a few minutes past dark. There was almost an hour of darkness before she walked into the stables. No, she sneaked. Anything could have happened to her. I was ready to mount Windwalker and ride out after her. If she knew she was going to be late, she could have sent a message. I would have been happy to ride into town in order to escort her home."

"You were afraid for her safety? It isn't like Merry to think far enough ahead to send a message."

"Mayhap, she should learn to think. No woman should be out by herself after dark. It seems that some of the things that have happened to her sister's-in-law, she would be more careful with her person. She's seen firsthand the dangers. Still, she ignores them."

"It does seem that way. I did give you carte blanch as far as disciplining my sister since you are in a position to see what she is capable of. Never did have the taste for discipline myself. Lacie handles our son with ease, leaving me with the joy of playing with him. It is as it should be. Seems to know just what to do to set him on the straight and narrow path."

"You think I do?" *I'd rather kiss her senseless than keep her from enjoying herself.* "No, punishment for misdeeds is not my forte either. Took me several hours to come up with a suitable form of discipline."

"Well, I do trust you to keep the mares safe as well as my sister." He rose, walking to his desk pulling out a sealed envelope. Then with a conspiratorial wink, "This is for Merry. I trust you to give it to her. It might be the appropriate time to introduce yourself to her."

Ignoring Leslie's suggestion, "What is it?"

Devlin accepted the letter, turning it over in his hand, having a bad feeling about the contents. He wasn't ready for proper introductions he couldn't explain. If she knew the truth, their relationship would change. He was sure it would not change for the better. While he hadn't lied to her, he also didn't tell her the entire truth.

Leslie was chuckling softly. "This will take some decision making on your part. I trust you will figure it out."

Once more Devlin felt his gut constrict. "What is it?"

"An invitation to a ball. One the Duke of Weston is supposedly attending. Lacie discovered this and immediately got invitations for all of us even though my wife is not particularly fond of balls. She knows how much Merry wants to meet the duke."

His gut tightened. "Weston is supposed to be there," he mused with a slight grimace. "Angelica is going to attend, meet him as well as immediately fall in love. What a ridiculous notion. It puts all the other foolish things she has done to the background."

"I'm afraid the duke must fall in love too," Leslie said, watching him with a great deal of intensity. "Do you think that is possible?"

"First, he has to be there." Devlin stuffed the invitation in his pocket trying to decide if he would give it to her. If he didn't, she might never meet Weston. That fact would suit him just fine. He didn't want her to meet the duke. If she didn't, however, he would never know how she felt about him. She didn't need to fall in love with a duke when there was a perfectly acceptable horse breeder willing to seduce her. Too bad he already decided, promised himself that wasn't going to happen.

"You don't think he will attend?" Leslie asked, a smirk on his face twirling the crystal glass between his hands, watching the liquid.

"Who would know?" *I'll be there and I'll make sure she doesn't fall in love with the duke, the cad. She'll believe him to be the bounder I told her he was.*

Leslie sat back, sipping what was left of his brandy, studying the man in front of him. "I believe you've firsthand knowledge. You would keep her from meeting the man of her dreams? Seems pretty selfish to me, petty as well."

"Never pretended to be anything but selfish." Devlin said, knowing exactly what he would do. "I'll take my leave. Hopefully, I'll see you in another few days with updated information. It will take some time to know what mares are breeding and if we want to try again. I'm assuming we'll have good results."

Devlin left the Stewart townhouse with a great deal on his mind. When he reached Southcliff, he fully intended to see Angelica. She would cease her pouting and talk to him today, this instant. He would give her the invitation, even go with her to select the dress for the ball. He had exceptional taste where women's clothing was concerned. Knew exactly what he would like to see her wearing.

This might give him the desired results, much more quickly than if he had to wait the entire summer. In truth, he was becoming bored with this isolation in the backwoods of Glasgow.

The sun had nearly dropped below the horizon when he unlocked the door of the stable at Southcliff. He dismounted, leading Windwalker to his stall. Timmy was there, asking to help but he sent him away wanting more time to think. Taking care of his horse was cathartic, tending to the animal would give him the time he needed to put his plans in motion.

Devlin no sooner dismissed Timmy than Angelica showed up behind him, hands on her hips, fire blazing in her eyes.

"You were almost late," she accused him, anger in her voice as she stood behind him.

"I wasn't. Besides..." He turned toward her his grin stretching wider as he studied her, read the indignation in her pose. "I'm a man therefore not in jeopardy."

"So you say."

"You doubt I'm a man?" he asked, laughing, stepping closer as she moved in the opposite direction. "Perhaps you need more proof. Would you like me to show you?"

"No, you might have been in danger. One never knows, now do they. Highwaymen with guns, asking for money. Accidents." She tried to hold her ground.

As he closed the distance, she reacted by stepping back.

"It wasn't dark and there was no danger. Besides, as you well know I've nothing of value save my person. I am, after all a horse breeder."

"I could say the same a thousand, no, a million times and you would remain just as pig headed."

He released a long draft of air. "I don't want to argue this point with you, Brat. You won't change my mind. Obviously, you won't change yours either. I have something for you. News of sorts. You might even like it." He handed over the invitation.

"What is it?" She looked up at him, her eyes wide in question.

"You should look. I don't open other's mail or invites."

His eyes narrowed as she ripped the envelope letting the scraps fall to the stable floor.

"But you know what it is." She opened the ornate card.

"Leslie told me what it was also that I was to hand it over to you." *At the time, against my better judgment.*

"It's for a ball."

"Are you going?" he asked, his hands flexing on the railing to Windwalker's stall.

"I don't know. I'm thinking there was something else, some piece of information you're neglecting to tell me, something to go with this. Why don't you tell me what Leslie told you? Everything."

"If you insist," he said reluctantly, yet his plan was continuing to form, to take shape.

He would have his way in this. Convince her this duke of hers was the bounder he was reported to be. When that happened, she would have no qualms about a horse breeder courting her. Now, he even knew exactly how he was going to go about convincing her. He would have a special mask made for him, one that would completely conceal his identity. Also, he would have to change the timbre of his voice.

"Well?" Impatiently she was tapping her foot, waiting for him.

He meant to let her wait, relished the upcoming ball now more than when Leslie told him. "Well, what?"

He kept his laughter behind his teeth, yet the urge to tease her was strong and uppermost in his mind. He loved to watch her eyes flash with anger and passion.

"What did Leslie tell you?"

He drew in a long deep draught of air. "If you must know, Lacie lobbied for an invitation even though she doesn't particularly like the affairs. It is a masquerade ball, isn't it?"

She stepped closer to him, closer than she'd been since the horse breeding. Of course, it would take a hell of a lot to get any closer than they'd been that afternoon. She poked him hard in the chest, her eyes narrowing. "Lacie would have to have a good reason for doing what you just told me. She detests balls."

He caught her wrist in one hand, pulling her closer before placing a hand at her waist. Would she return his kiss, he wondered? His lips brushed hers, lightly at first, coaxing, enticing. Her body melted into his just for a second.

She pulled away, attempting to distance herself with no success, "Don't you dare. Don't. Tell me what I want to know."

"I forgot. What was it you were asking?"

He still held her; her hips pressed tightly to his belly. She would feel him, realize what was pulsing against her, remember the mating they watched. He wasn't sure why he damned himself this way. It just didn't seem he had any control where his little brat was concerned.

She did push away from him, leaving ample distance. "Why did Lacie seek out this invitation?"

Running his hands through his hair. "If you must know, it's because the Duke of Weston is reported to be in attendance."

~ * ~

Merry clapped her hands together, unable to subdue the wide grin forming. Her heart was happy. This was her chance, "Really. Really! I can't believe I finally will meet the Duke of Weston. It's a miracle. Whatever is he doing in Glasgow?"

She whirled around in a tight circle, her skirt and frothy petticoats billowing out around her.

"Really," he parroted dryly for a moment obviously regretting handing over the coveted invitation. "Don't you think your reaction is a bit over the top?"

"I have to get a new dress. How am I going to get into Glasgow?" she asked looking from Sir Alistair to Devlin, hoping, no wishing he would lift her punishment so she could ride to the dressmakers. Unless she paid extra it would take nearly the two weeks left before the ball for the dress to be finished. While she knew her brother would do that, she didn't want to ask.

"No, you can't ride into Glasgow," he told her his tone dry.

"How?"

She felt close to tears, hated him for the audacity of his that led him to believe he could dictate to her. This just wasn't conscionable. Without access to her horse, she had no way to get what she wanted. He was unfeeling a monster of the worst sort.

"This is important to you?" he queried, looking smug then resigned. "I'm sure you have closets full of gowns you could wear for just this occasion. Why don't you pick one of those?"

"You know it is important. I don't have closets full of gowns either," she said exasperated with the bloody man and the situation she found herself in now all because she was late coming home one night. He was acting perverse once again.

Negligently, he leaned against the stall, his thick arms crossed in front of him as if he didn't have a care in the world, watching, studying, almost as if he was waiting for her to explode with indignation. Letting out a long drawn-out breath, "If it's that important to you, I'll take you in the buggy. What else have I got to do with my spare moments?"

Her heart stopped shortly, thinking about that. When it started beating again and she could suck in a deep breath of air, "And what would you do all the hours I'm at the dressmakers?"

She backed up disliking the arrogant grin on his face. The way his negligent pose always disturbed her in unfathomable ways. "I don't mind helping out. In some circles, I'm known for my remarkable taste in women's fashion."

"What would you, a horse breeder, know about fashion?" The last thing she wanted or needed were his comments about the dress she would choose. "Lacie will be there. She can be the eyes as to how it will look."

"Leslie says she has horrible taste. She might be there, but Leslie has already picked out her gown. For Lacie it's just a matter of the fitting. Truly, you don't want Lacie to give advice. She might have you wearing something in puce and with too many god-awful ruffles. You would look horrible."

She sucked in air at his audacity. She liked ruffles. Why did his words surprise her though? Merry knew he was right. Leslie never allowed Lacie anywhere near the dress shop without him or unless he already gave the dressmaker the exact directions for his wife's new gowns. She stuck her nose in the air. "I don't need you. I've got impeccable taste."

"You do, do you? Not even for a second opinion?" he asked a hint of skepticism in his voice as he perused what she was wearing at this moment as if she had cobwebs for brains.

This morning she'd donned her oldest and most ragged gown not wanting to entice him in anyway. She didn't want him to notice her. Truth be told the events during the horse breeding took her by surprise. She was having a devil of a time dealing with them along with the way his touch made her feel.

"I do."

She wasn't going to give him the satisfaction of an explanation for the clothing she was wearing at the moment. She wanted to walk away even though she still had to come to terms with his offer and accept graciously. If she didn't, he might just take his offer to drive her back and she would be stuck with wearing something made for her when she was a little girl. She wanted to look sophisticated and womanly.

He waited, unmoving, smiling at her. The answer would come soon enough. She had no choice.

"Very well, you can take me," she capitulated begrudgingly.

"Well, if you don't want me..." He started for his room at the back of the stables. "I'll find something else to do. Perhaps you can find the duke and have him go with you."

To her he was just being ornery, perverse, making her sweat. She didn't like the way he was acting, but it seemed she didn't have a choice if she was going to get a new gown.

"First thing in the morning then?" she asked before he could reach his room.

"Don't be late," he told her over his shoulder as he sauntered away and she was left with the view of his back.

Well, she wondered, looking around the stables, would he know if she quietly slipped out with Sir Alistair and went for a midnight ride?

Of course, he would know. The punishment if he caught you riding at night would be worse than the first time. He might not even let you attend the ball.

He wouldn't?

He might.

What more could he do? How could it be worse?

He could actually thrash you until you couldn't sit for a week.

No, he wouldn't do that. Not Devlin.

You don't think so?

No, he'd keep me from riding for two weeks this time. If I don't behave, I might not ride the rest of the summer.

You want to take that chance? The man sleeps with one eye open. Besides, I think he's just lying in wait expecting you to do something stupid.

I know.

Remember, he might even refuse to let you go to the ball.

No!

Resigned and knowing she only had two days of her restriction left to endure, Merry wandered back to the manor. The sun just set. She wasn't ready to lock up the house nor did she feel like eating. She wandered into the drawing room, bringing her feet around her as she sat on a wing chair. Sighing softly, she stared out the window at the twinkling stars. The moon shone brightly, a half crescent in the dark sky.

Doubts about the duke assailed her, giving her second and even third thoughts about believing in the fact he might fall in love with her. Devlin told her he was a bounder, a cad of the worst sort. What if he wasn't the man of her dreams? What would she do then? Lacie told her she would eventually find the right man. Devlin would never let her live it down. She wanted to fall in love with the Duke of Weston, spend her life with him. What did she really know about him?

Nothing.

Even without the annoying voice in her head telling her so, she understood the chances of making a lasting impression on the man in such a short time was nil. Restlessness took over, standing she found the bottle of brandy Leslie always kept in the sideboard. Instead of two fingers of the potent stuff, she poured herself half a glass, staring at the amber liquid for the longest time before she finally sipped letting the fire burn down her throat.

She settled on the sofa this time, stretching her legs out in front of her. With her eyes closed she imagined dancing with the Duke of Weston, his hand on the small of her back, her hand in his other one as he guided her around the dance floor. He was tall and broad shouldered. His hair was dark, midnight black. She knew he loved horses because his stable was so magnificent.

"If you drink too much of that stuff, you'll have a headache in the morning. If that happens, I'll have to do all the work when it comes to picking out your dress." Devlin strode haughtily into the room.

Her hand on her throat she jumped at Devlin's voice, a tiny gasp escaping her throat. "What are you doing here? You scared me near to death."

He poured himself a glass of what she was having, grinning. "You dreaming of dancing with the duke? We could practice here," he taunted her, an all-knowing smirk on his face.

"Of course not."

She downed a liberal portion of her drink, knowing he was right about both the liquor as well as the dance. He didn't like playing second to the duke, didn't like her practicing with him in order to impress the duke.

"Your eyes tell a different story. You either want to practice or you would like nothing better than to have my arms around you. Tell the truth. Which is it?"

"They were closed. No, I don't want to practice with you nor do I want you to hold me in your arms." Her breath caught at the notion of being in his arms, something that happened all too often.

"Are you sure, Brat? We could do other things, practice those kisses. You almost know how I like them."

"Positive."

Almost know how who likes them?

You want to know how the duke likes them.

Suspiciously, Merry watched as he sat down on the sofa next to her, lifting her legs so he held them on his lap. He didn't say anything, just stared at her as if he could read her mind. She chose to try to ignore him. He wasn't supposed to invade her space and private thoughts this way. She came here to be alone. His hands unnerved her, always did.

He ran his fingers along her legs. She had neglected to put stockings on so they touched flesh. They rose higher, stroked, teased the sensitive skin. Her breath held in her chest, letting it out impossible when she didn't know what he would do next.

"You still want kissing lessons?" he asked as his hand continued to stroke and explore places they shouldn't be, intimate places she should tell him he had no right to be.

She swallowed unable to say the words she should.

"I'd rather dance."

She wanted both, kissing lessons because she knew she was lacking in experience as well as dancing simply because it had been a while since she attended a ball.

The duke had been there too. Much to her disappointment, she never received an introduction, never got a chance to talk to him. This one would be different. This time she would not keep her mask on. She would make sure he danced with her before time came to leave. They would have a chance to talk.

He rose then, extending his hand. She accepted a bit nervously. Before she knew what was happening, she was in his arms. Now, he was guiding her around the small room. He was humming softly as they danced. She found herself mesmerized by his voice, drawn to him by the sheer romance of the moment, the power and size of him, realized suddenly she didn't want this moment to end.

Devin stopped near the couch, his hand cupping her chin, lifting it until his lips settled softly on hers. The warmth and the tenderness stole all her senses, left her wishing for more. His tongue slid slowly then oh so provocatively across her lower lip bringing forth tiny sounds from her throat. He pulled away to look at her, to touch her cheek with his knuckles, run them lightly down her neck. His eyes seemed to burn everywhere he looked.

She didn't know what he was thinking, wasn't sure if she wanted to know. His eyes were dark, brooding, his expression almost angry. He bathed her neck in kisses, stroking with his fingers, nipping with his teeth before he returned to her lips tugging the bottom one with his teeth.

"The duke would expect to taste you," he murmured while he turned his attention to her ear, worrying the lobe with his lips, twirling his tongue around it.

He stroked her back, pulled her hair lose from its pins. His hands ran up and down her sides before one covered her breast. "You taste like brandy and sweetness."

She gasped now wanting to pull away, knowing that was what she should do. "He would not touch me there or where you touched me the other day. The duke is a gentleman."

"I doubt it."

"What do you know?"

"Maybe he would take liberties or perhaps not. He is a bounder as well as a reprobate, of the worst sort so I've heard."

His thumb rubbed across her nipple while his lips and tongue invaded her mouth.

For a few seconds, she wondered if the duke was a worse reprobate than Devlin Mathews. Probably not, she decided, giving into the sensation he aroused so easily, shivering, desperate to learn more, desire running unchecked. She stroked his lips with her tongue, pushing inside when he opened his mouth to allow her access. He seemed more than willing to take this as far as she would allow.

"You taste like brandy and cigars," she murmured, speaking now in a daze and with little thought. "Would the duke taste like that too?"

Suddenly, she felt emptiness, distanced from his arms, nearly thrust away. His curses practically leveled her as he strode to the chair he'd been sitting on previously, leaving her to gape open mouthed at him.

Silence echoed in the room, silence surrounding her as she watched him, the frown lines etched clearly in his face. His brooding countenance unnerved her even though she knew what brought it on. She understood what angered him. The fact of the matter was she never pretended, never lied to him about what she wanted no, hoped for where the duke was concerned, had always been honest with him. She had no regrets nor did she have any apologies for him.

Pouring herself more brandy she sat in a chair opposite him.

"I saw him for the first time when I was twelve. My mother and I were in Paris. Don't remember why or even if it was important in any way. It was just my mother and me. The day was cold, rainy, exceptionally so. We were walking, shopping, trying to stay warm. We stopped for a pastry and a cup of coffee. People were sightseeing but we weren't. Paris was almost as familiar to us as the small town of Bordeaux near our vineyards."

She suddenly missed the rolling hills along with the small ageless villages, missed the rows and rows of grapes as they ripened in the summer sun. She had not been back. Perhaps it was time for a trip to France and to see her mother.

He's not going to want to hear your explanations.

I know. He's angry. Probably has every right to be.

What man would want to be practice for the real man of your dreams?

He's a horse breeder. He can't be the man of my dreams.

You're a fool. You know you want him. Your curiosity is going to get you into trouble. Damn, but it won't.

He didn't say anything. She'd give just about anything if he'd ask a question or two. Instead, the frown lines increased as he sipped the brandy, his gaze remaining fixed on her. She hoped he was trying to understand how she felt.

"That was when I saw him. He was drenched, his hair hung in rivulets around his face, drips falling down behind his collar. His carriage waited for him, you know. He didn't have to get out of it but he did to rescue a dog."

"A bounder would rescue a dog?"

"That's why I don't believe you about him. You don't really know the duke. You're just making up stories so I won't fall in love with him." She wondered if that could be true.

"Perhaps I am, Brat." He spoke through clenched teeth.

"Why?"

"Don't want to see you hurt. The duke is too old for you."

Well, that didn't hold any water as far as she was concerned. "No, he's no older than Leslie was when he married Lacie. That can't be too old. In any case, my stomach told me the truth. I knew from that moment on he was going to be my husband. That is if I could grow up soon enough, before he fell in love and married someone else. Everyone laughed at me. I saw him again three years ago riding a horse in Glasgow."

"Your heart did a flip flop?" he asked her dryly.

"No, my stomach felt as it was filled with butterflies." Her romance with the duke, albeit one sided, for her at least it was love at first sight.

"Then again at that ball a couple of months ago. No one falls in love that way. Just proves how immature and young you are. You don't fall in love unless you get to know that person."

"I'm old enough to know what I want. Your words can't stop me." She didn't understand why she was arguing with him. He would never understand.

"Old enough to get hurt, your heart stomped on when he doesn't return your sentiments. I suppose you are. Don't expect me to pick up the pieces when that happens."

"That might be true. The reality is that I have to try. I could never live the rest of my life if I didn't at least get to judge the man for myself." She knew that to be true. He would have to dash her hopes, break her heart. She would never give up on him.

Never.

He sipped his brandy thoughtfully, watching her still just as intensely as he had a few minutes before. "Is Leslie escorting the two of you to the ball?" he asked the question.

At this moment, he didn't seem too interested in the answer. The man was staring into the distance and drumming his fingers on the armrest.

"I don't know. Lacie never said if her husband was going to attend. He might just to humor us."

"The Duke of Weston is known for accepting invitations then never showing up," Devlin mused as he watched the liquid in his glass. "It's been rumored that he gets so many of them he forgets what he has accepted or even if there are conflicts."

"Why are you telling me that? Just to dash my hopes?" She felt ready to toss her drink in his face. He deserved it for being so moody.

"No, would never do that. It's true though. Just relating the truth so you won't be overly disappointed when the man is a no show." He finished the brandy setting the glass on a table. "Time for me to go before you kick me out. Did enjoy the conversation."

She watched him stride from the room only to stop at the front door. "Don't forget to lock up before you go to bed, Brat."

Merry heard the screen door bang shut behind him. She stood, inhaling deep breaths of air, trying to calm her nerves while she remembered the kiss, the way he touched her, how she melted in his arms. With Devlin her stomach did more than a few flip-flops. There were more than a few butterflies as well.

There was just no way she would allow herself to fall in love with a horse breeder.

~ * ~

Angelica thought he would be bored at the dressmakers and leave soon after they arrived. He was far from uninterested. No, he was enjoying the disagreements between them on the choices, even understanding he had no say in what she was going to wear. He knew exactly what he wanted to see her wearing and that was that. Except for the shrill shriek of Madame Chantel, the dressmaker, he was going to poke his nose into her dressing room.

Then, when they perused the fabrics he voiced his opinion, drowning out her voice. "No, no, Angelica, pastels will look hideous on you. You must wear a vibrant color. This royal blue will bring out the color of your eyes. You do not want to look like a child."

He was sure she disagreed with him, just to be ornery. In this he was right. He would not allow her to choose something foolish.

"I like the burgundy."

"The burgundy is nice he conceded. Why don't you go with the white tulle over a blue satin slip? Don't put those gaudy roses down the center though. He was studying the fashion plate. Simple is better don't you think?"

Angelica looked as if she wanted to toss him from the shop, as did the dressmaker. "I do like that idea," Angelica finally said.

"It is very nice," Lacie agreed, the corsage can be cut a bit lower. "You do want..."

"She doesn't want to give an unobstructed view of her bosom," Devlin cut in with a wave of his hand.

Lord but he'd seen her breasts, touched and stroked them. He didn't want anyone else having that opportunity. If she showed too much, the duke would not be able to stop himself from sampling.

"It is perfectly modest and in the height of fashion." Lacie slanted him a penetrating stare as if to say who are you to act as if you are her father or a jealous husband.

Apparently, the duke had not bothered to apprise his wife of who he was. Perhaps this will prove even more interesting. He was beginning to look forward to this ball along with the effect he would have on Angelica's feelings for the duke.

Several hours passed before all the matching frothy and frilly undergarments were also purchased. A mask was also designed to go with the ball gown. Angelica was supposed to return for a final fitting next week. That shouldn't be a problem for her since barring any more disciplinary situations, she should be able to ride again.

Leslie picked up Lacie an hour before Angelica was finished. When the seamstress was finally through, the day seemed to have passed in a whirlwind of fabrics and laces. Devlin could honestly say he enjoyed this excursion with her.

"I'm famished. Would you like to go somewhere for dinner before we return to Southcliff?" he asked wondering if she would accept an outing of this sort with him.

Seemed a lot like courting. This evening he didn't care. He just wanted to enjoy a few unguarded moments with her. In addition, he hoped they wouldn't argue.

Surprising him, she beamed, her smile sending ripples of pleasure all the way to his toes. "I think I would like that." She paused in thought a few seconds. "We won't be getting back after dark, will we?"

"Even if we do, Brat, I won't consider it your fault. If you're with me, you won't be in any danger."

"No punishment?"

"Or discipline."

He agreed wholeheartedly with her grinning as he thought about returning after dark. They could stop at the pond, the moon shining in the night sky, stars twinkling on the velvet background. He groaned, taking his mind from kissing her. Giving her practice before meeting the duke was not part of his plans for her.

She learned too damn well.

"Where should we go?" she asked eagerly, her eyes alight and sparkling with what appeared to be pleasure.

He couldn't help but grin, watching her. Lord but when she smiled, she was beautiful, ripping out a part of his heart. He clenched his teeth, resigned to keeping his hands to himself.

"The Prince Street Hostelry?" he asked.

She nodded, innocently slipping her hand through his as they left the shop and headed for the buggy. She held his hand with both of hers, turning to him, her smile wide. He couldn't help but fall under her enchanting spell.

They dined, they ordered several dishes to share, and they drank wine. Angelica spoke of the wines they sold from their vineyard. He listened attentively. More than an hour later, he was helping her into the buggy, his hands on her waist, his thoughts elsewhere.

He didn't stop at the pond or anywhere else to gaze at the moon with her. He clamped his teeth together, reigning in his raging emotions.

"It's dark," she said. "I suppose I should tell you that you cannot ride for a week since you got me home late," she teased, a pretty smile on her face. "I would have been on time if it had been up to me."

"I suppose you should," he said softly as her body slid the length of his.

Needing to do this all day as well as all night, he slipped a finger beneath her chin. Gently, he sipped her lips, stroked her mouth, felt the soft brush of her tongue against his as he parted his lips to receive her gift. As she opened for him, he explored inside the sultry warm recesses she presented to him. She tasted of the Bordeaux, sweetness as well. "If he can't kiss you like this, Angel, don't marry him."

A tiny sound of pleasure escaped her as she leaned into him, melting against him. He supported her, one arm around her, still kissing her, touching her. He stroked her arms then her back. Stopping was out of the question. He ran his hands down her back again, cupping her buttocks pulling her close to him. She pressed against his sex, warm and soft so very willing even through her layers of clothing.

"You taste like wine tonight. Would you like to go into the house with me?" Her soft murmurs did little to ease his condition. "I like the way you taste."

He groaned, "That sounds like an invitation to something you don't intend. You wouldn't want to ruin yourself for your duke, would you? If you ask me into your house, I might end up in your bedroom."

If he made love to her before she met that man, she would never find out the duke wasn't marriage material for her. She would always blame him. He wouldn't allow that to happen.

"I didn't mean it that way and you know it. I would never...just thought you might want a drink. Don't come if you don't want to."

She pushed herself away from him, striding to the house. Her back was stiff even while her hips swayed provocatively. His grin widened as he watched her.

"I'll be right in after I've brushed down the horse." He laughed softly, understanding more than he wanted to admit.

It would be so easy for him to seduce her tonight, coax her into his bed. She wouldn't even know what was happening to her until the deed was done.

He couldn't do that to her. Not when there was so much anticipation simmering inside her, finally the meeting of her duke. She held on to her dreams for years now, ever since she was twelve. Her future was hers to win or lose. The duke was reputed to be a terrible bounder. He knew first hand he wasn't. Actually, he was better known to be the stuffiest duke in all of England

Well hell.

Unable to stay away from her, he finished up in about ten minutes before making his way to the front door of the manor. If Angelica had any sense at all, she would have the house locked up tight just to keep him out, just to protect her virginity.

It wasn't to be.

When he rounded the corner, she was sitting on the swing, a glass of wine in her hand a bottle on the tabletop next to her. There was also a tray of food on the side of the swing where she wasn't sitting.

"You should have gone to bed," he said, sitting down and accepting the glass of wine she poured for him, unsure where this would lead. All he knew was where it shouldn't lead.

"This is a Sauterne from one of our vineyards. They pick the grapes after they're dried. It's very sweet. That's why the crackers and cheese. Needs something to go with it." She watched him sip the wine. "Do you like it?"

He drank again enjoying the taste. "You're right, this is sweet."

He ate a few of the crackers and cheese she set out, leaning back, relaxing, one arm spread wide, across the back.

She was gently pushing the swing with one bare foot, gazing off into the distance. "I love it, the sweetness. What are you going to do at the end of the summer when the mares are bred? Will you move on to some other place, another stable?"

"That's a good question. Go home I suppose."

She had never asked probing questions. He'd never had to lie to her.

"Where is home?"

Chapter Five

Merry and Lacie stood on a balcony searching the area below for any sign the Duke of Weston had arrived. It was early still yet Merry couldn't stop thinking about the things Devlin told her. He accepted so many invitations he couldn't keep them straight. The duke was a cad and reprobate of the worst sort. Rather than fall in love, he would more than likely make an indecent proposal. She certainly didn't want to believe any of his comments.

"Stop wringing your hands. You're making me nervous," Lacie said, placing one of her gloved ones over hers. "It will do you no good to fret. We should go downstairs so you can fill your dance card. If nothing else, you will meet a few eligible bachelors who you perhaps could fall in love with. It doesn't have to be the duke, you *ken*."

"I'm already in love with the Duke of Weston. As you well know, I'm not interested in anyone else." She was afraid it wasn't true. Devlin had this way of burrowing under skin.

You're half in love with Devlin and you know it.

Can't be, he's a horse breeder.

Where a heart is concerned it doesn't make a bit of difference what the man's profession is.

Leslie would never approve of him for a husband.

And why not?

Because he's a horse breeder.

You've come full circle.

I hate it when you're right. I still don't love him.

Lord, but she knew his profession wouldn't matter to her brother. She had enough money to live in fine style for the rest of her life, probably enough she would never spend it all. Leslie would let her make her own decision when it came to marriage. So, if she wanted to marry Devlin she could. Only Devlin thought of her as a brat. The other night he did call her Angel.

Devlin doesn't strike me as a man who would let his wife support him.

No, he'd probably refuse to spend a dime of my money.

If you wed him, it will be his money. Have you forgotten a man owns everything of his wife's?

No, haven't forgotten.

That's why I can't marry a horse breeder. I'm not giving up everything I own to a man. My future husband has to be as wealthy as I am.

If you married the duke, he would own you. Your money would be his money. Wait a minute. If my memory serves correctly, you were willing to hand over all your inheritance to Douglas.

I was too young and Leslie would never allow that marriage.

You were willing to follow him to the Highlands.

I know.

"Well, you were lost in thought," Lacie said with a soft chuckle while looking at her as if she was half crazy. "Care to tell what you were thinking about? Maybe I can help."

"Just wondering if I'll ever fall in love. It was so easy for you and my brother."

Lacie fell in love when she was fifteen with Leslie. She didn't even know he was a duke, didn't care either. They didn't marry until she was almost eighteen. Her brother waited for her. She'd always thought that so romantic.

"The first part was easy, coming to trust a man was not. I'm glad now he convinced me to believe in him," Lacie said, her voice soft as it appeared she thought about her husband.

"My duke doesn't even know me. I don't even know if he's going to make an appearance."

Merry smoothed the skirt of her gown, thinking Devlin did have remarkable taste in women's clothing. She wondered more than once how that could come about. This was the most beautiful dress she'd ever owned as well as the most elaborate including everything she purchased to go with it, all at Devlin's suggestion.

Then, as if guessing her thoughts Lacie spoke, "The gown is beautiful but not as beautiful as the woman wearing it. Leslie said it's one of the most expensive he's ever purchased. All the intricate details from the five ruby clasps set in gold to the rows of white Persian roses along the border. Even your hair with the bows and blue and gold ribbons, he was astonished that you picked something like that out."

"You did tell him that Devlin selected the gown as well as the adornments," Merry said wondering how on earth a horse breeder would know about all the finery. As he'd told them, he did have remarkable taste.

"I did and all he did was wave a hand in the air then ask how on earth a horse breeder would know to purchase white kid gloves and medallion bracelets to go with everything," Lacie murmured. "Thought your Devlin said simple was best."

"He's not my Devlin."

"Perhaps more so than you care to admit," Lacie told her as her gaze roamed the dance floor.

"He did get rid of the roses going down the front as well as a froth of lace along the bodice," Merry laughed, gazing over the ballroom once more, searching for the duke she was enamored of.

"The gauze scarf and gold earrings along with the white satin shoes was definitely a nice touch also," Lacie finished on a breathy sigh moving back to take another long look at her. "You need to find willing dance partners or this time you are spending waiting for a man who might not show up will grow boring. Standing up here on this balcony will not get the man here sooner. If he doesn't come, I want you to have at least a little fun. You need to show off this beautiful dress. Put your mask on now then go dance. I'll stay here and watch for you since I've no care to dance with anyone except my husband."

Merry did as her sister-in-law bade her, leaving Lacie to stare at the dancers below. They agreed on a signal if she saw the Duke of Weston. Merry didn't have too much hope in that because Lacie didn't know what the man looked like. She was sure though that as soon as he showed up the murmurs through the room would escalate and she would know. Everyone there would understand he selected this ball out of his millions of invitations to attend.

At the bottom of the steps, she was met by not just one man but three, asking for a dance. She purposely left her dance card empty hoping to leave all the dances for the duke in case he would want them.

Merry wasn't quite sure what was expected of her. She couldn't very well pick one of these men and in the process leave the other two standing by themselves. Dancing with all three of them wasn't at all possible either. When it came to men, she didn't know what to do. Over the years she purposely stayed away from this type of entertainment. She tilted her head a bit sideways regarding the three men who were now vying for her attention. She wondered if it was because they knew who she was or if they were truly interested in her.

She looked to the balcony. Lacie was nodding her head in silent approval as if she was urging her to dance.

She caught her lip beneath her teeth. "I would like to dance. Should we take turns?"

"That's what your dance card is for," one laughed, quickly extending his hand in order to be her first choice.

The music was lively. The man danced her around the room until the music stopped. She was breathless and laughing. By the time she just barely caught her breath a second man stood beside her, his hand stretched toward her in invitation a wide grin on his face. She looked to the balcony. Lacie nodded her head.

This dance was slow. It seemed she glided around the room, wishing she could think of something witty to say. She couldn't. Thinking of the duke and what it would feel like to have his arms wrapped around her, she let out a slow breath of air.

"Would you like something to drink," the man asked as they danced by a table piled high with various foods and drink.

"Yes, I think I would."

She sipped the drink, alternately staring from the balcony to the door. Just as she expected a murmur began to ripple around the room. She rose on tiptoes hoping to see the man she was waiting for, the Duke of

Weston.

"It is the Duke of Southcliff just arrived," her partner said. "So, you know him?"

She grinned, wondering how they escaped introductions. "Yes, too well I suppose. He's my brother. I'm Merry Stewart."

The man flushed slightly. "I'm Cameron McInnis. Nice to meet you. Would like to dance again?"

"See you found someone to dance with, Merry," Leslie said as he stopped to greet her and receive an introduction to the man escorting her at the moment. "Where is Lacie?"

"Right here," she said, appearing seemingly from nowhere. "I didn't think you were coming."

"Change of plans," he murmured, searching the room.

Merry assumed for the same man she was looking for. In another second, Leslie claimed his wife for a dance. Merry was left sipping her drink while trying to find the man of her dreams. So far, he was nowhere to be found. You *ken* he forgets invitations, he has so many.

Feeling unsettled, Merry turned Cameron down then walked up the steps to the balcony above. She was ready to leave, depressed even though the evening had barely begun. Leaning on her elbows, she watched all the colors below whirl until they became a blur. She closed her eyes, breathing deeply, thinking about all her hopes for this evening. They were dashed before they barely began.

She felt the man before she turned to look at him. It had to be the duke, but why would he stop and stand by her?

"I'm the Duke of Weston. You're not dancing." His deep voice seemed to rumble from his chest, echoing in her ears. More than just this man's face was covered. His features were hidden from her. "A pretty girl like you should have her card filled, left with not even a moment to catch her breath."

"No, not at the moment." She wanted to ask him for the dance, just didn't quite have the nerve to do such a thing.

"You should dance with me." He too was leaning on the railing seeming to search the people below.

Her breath caught in her throat as she felt the heat he generated so close while the butterflies started dancing in her belly. "Are you looking for someone?" She needed to tell him the woman he searched for was standing beside him.

He placed her hand in his slowly raising it to his lips before kissing the top. Stepping back, he seemed to study her from the tips of her toes to her eyes, roving back to settle on her bosom. She stifled a small gasp, reaching to cover herself with her hand then her scarf.

"If you don't want a man to stare, you should not wear such a daring gown," he murmured softly.

"It's not daring," she protested as she all too well remembered Devlin's words when he encouraged the seamstress to make the corsage a bit higher. Had he known what the duke would think? Lacie assured her it was not cut too low. Perhaps she should have listened to Devlin instead.

He waved a hand in the air, "Of course not, but I've a nice view of the curve of your breasts. I do like the way they push up just the right amount."

Her sudden gasp startled her. The duke was grinning from ear to ear. *The lecherous cad.* She strove desperately to change the subject. "What should I call you?"

"My friends call me West and you?" Before she could answer, he pulled her into his arms, dancing with her on the balcony then finding the back steps. Taking her hand in his, he rushed her down the stairway then into the gardens.

"Stop, West, please." Breathing hard, she pulled back, unsure of what was happening.

"Sorry, I was in a hurry. Saw someone I know who I would rather not speak with."

The one word seemed to register with him as he slowed his pace still making no attempt at stopping. She was no longer tugged along but walked at his side now. A pathway he followed was lit with lanterns while stars twinkled in the night sky. The moon was very nearly full now. The air was warm, redolent with the scent of summer roses. Longingly, she remembered another time with Devlin when the moon was a narrow crescent.

"Where are we going?" Merry wanted to be alone with him but

then she also did not. A little tick of fear pulsed through her, settling in her mind as she recalled Devlin's words about this man. She didn't see anything at the end of the path where there seemed to be no end.

"There is a gazebo a little bit farther. We can talk where no one would think to disturb us. With what I've planned, I don't want anyone coming along to interrupt." He slipped an arm around her waist pulling her closer.

The heat from his body invaded her soul, touched her until her stomach filled with fluttering butterflies again. She was in love. She knew it for sure now. Still, Devlin's words touched her, giving her reason to pause. If he wasn't a bounder, didn't want something from her it was too soon to find privacy. Why were they walking in this secluded part of the garden headed for a private gazebo, far away from everyone?

Her steps faltered. She hesitated, setting both hands on his arm. "Maybe we should go back where there are other people."

He chuckled softly, "Pegged you for a bricky lass. Are you going to disappoint me now when I've just discovered you?"

At the moment, she didn't feel the least bit courageous. She was terrified, in love while the last thing she wanted was to disappoint him. "No. West, do you..." She ran her tongue across her lips before inhaling a quivering breath of air.

"Do I what?" he queried. "Ah, here we are. Sit down and you can tell me what has you so panicked."

She could hardly tell him she was afraid of him. One just didn't tell their future husband something like that. "I'm not afraid," she said stiffening her back.

"Good." He sat down, grinning then stretching his arms across the back of the couch.

She pulled one of the large pillows on to her lap, feeling a bit as if it would serve as armor.

You're acting like a ninny.

What would you have me do? Fall into his arms? Let him do with me whatever he wants?

Of course not, but you could at least pretend you like him and stop thinking about Devlin.

Can't help but think about Devlin.

He's not going to like playing second fiddle any more than Devlin does. Sometime you are going to have to make a decision. What are you going to do if he tries to kiss you? Slap his face?

No.

Then.

I'll kiss him. It's what I wanted and why I practiced with Devlin.

"You're still skittish as a newborn colt," the duke murmured, gently grazing his knuckles along her cheek then down the column of her neck.

He paused when she shivered. No more than a second later he continued his gentle investigation across the top of her gown, lazily exploring.

This was what she wanted. Good lord, it seemed too soon for him to pursue her so blatantly to touch her like he was doing. She moved away from him. "You shouldn't."

"I should." He smiled but stopped for a moment. "I should like to kiss you but you're going to have to meet me halfway."

Still, she just wasn't at all sure of herself and what she should and shouldn't do.

You never said no to Devlin or refused him anything, any touch.

No, I didn't. That was different.

How so?

I felt as if I knew him at least a little bit before he kissed me. I saw him nearly naked in the pond before he kissed me.

I see.

Of course, you don't.

You're going to let the man kiss you?

Yes.

With that thought prevalent in her head, she scooted closer, her eyes focused on his mouth that seemed to invite her to touch. His lips were beautiful, sensuous and full. She wondered if they were as soft as Devlin's or if he tasted as good as Devlin.

With his hand he cupped her chin. Leaning close, he brushed his lips across hers, once, twice. She swept her tongue across her mouth. For a second, he pulled back looking at her. He left her wondering if he didn't like what she did. A shiver quivered across her shoulders as one of his big hands wrapped around her back. Suddenly, she found herself sitting on his lap.

His lips molded on hers, his tongue parting them, stroking the inside. All confusion vanished as his hand skimmed her ribcage, settling beneath her breast. His other hand held her head still as he ravaged her, kissed her softly then hard, touched her inside while she reciprocated, meeting his tongue with hers. Tiny sounds of pleasure filled her throat.

Minutes later when he pulled back, he was smiling at her, a half smile she thought. It didn't reach his eyes. What she could see of him looked angry. She wondered if there wasn't something wrong with what she'd done. Devlin always swore after he kissed her. She never quite figured out what exactly that meant.

He was still staring at her, his eyes seeming to shimmer. Now his thumb was gently stroking over her clothed nipple. His lips found hers again, tugging with his teeth on the bottom one as his tongue soothed the tiny bites. He kissed her again and again before stroking her neck with his hand then following the exploratory caresses with his lips and teeth.

The ground seemed to float below her. He would think her easy if she continued in this vein. Marriage would be out of the question. She didn't want him to seduce her in this gazebo where anyone could find them. Didn't want to make love with him until after they were wed.

Merry shoved at him, putting all her weight behind the move. "We need to stop. Before I do something I know I'll regret."

"Why?"

"Because..." her voice quivered.

"I don't want to stop." His hand settled on her ankle. "It's very small," he murmured.

"You shouldn't touch me there."

His fingertips ran the length of her leg until he reached the top of her stockings. He squeezed gently then let her go.

"No, I suppose I shouldn't. Wondered when you would tell me no."

"We should get back to the others before my brother finds me missing and comes looking for me."

"Perhaps we should. Don't want an unwanted marriage now do we?" He laughed softly.

She wanted a marriage but not that way. "No, no we don't."

"Isn't that what you were bargaining for? Marriage?" His angry voice startled her out of any dreams she might harbor.

"Well..."

"The truth now."

She wasn't about to admit to anything of the sort as she was rapidly falling out of love with this man. He wasn't the gentleman she thought he should be. Nor was he falling head over heels in love with her. It seemed, to Merry, he just wanted something from her. She didn't intend to find out what that was.

"No, all I wanted was to meet you and now I have."

She struggled to get off his lap. He held her tight.

"I don't know you well enough at all. In fact, I believe I would like nothing better than to learn more about you," the duke murmured, his breath wafting across her neck as his lips took more liberties.

Regaining her sense, she inhaled a deep breath. "No!"

"Well." He touched her chin a small grin on his face. "Even though you don't kiss very well and could use some much-needed practice, I'd like you to become my next mistress."

~ * ~

The slap West felt across his face left him stunned, shocked, in disbelief. She struck out at him so quickly he didn't have time to react and stop her. He shook his head trying to clear the ringing. Closing his eyes, he held still for a few seconds.

"Your what?" Her anger seemed to simmer deep inside, her face flushing a brilliant shade or red. She struggled against his hold, appearing desperate to leave him behind. It was as he planned. It looked as if she didn't want the memory of this confrontation. "What did you just ask me?"

"I'd be honored if you would become my mistress," he repeated for her rubbing his cheek where her hand surely left a bold imprint. While he knew she would react to his proposal, he didn't believe the reaction would be so violent. "You had no cause..."

"No!" She rose to leave. He no longer restrained her. "Suffice it to say my answer is no. I would never humiliate myself in that manner or cause my family so much shame. They would disown me. A horse breeder I know is more of a gentleman than you."

He would let her go for now but sometime soon they would speak again. She smoothed her skirts before slanting him a scathing gaze, one that took all his fortitude not to grin at. She was bold as well as brazen. He would give her that nor did she hide her emotions. He knew that. It was part of what fascinated him about her.

"Hello, anyone out here."

West watched as she picked up her skirts, heading toward the voice he recognized all too well. Teddy, he sighed, wishing he dared go after her and teach her a few more lessons regarding the heart. A woman should not toy with a man's heart. A horse breeder she knew...

The devil but that was what he'd been after.

The man approaching must have realized he was here. Well, it was time for him to depart. He accomplished all he intended for now with the regal Miss Stewart. If he didn't want to end up facing his best friend in a duel, he would have to vanish into the night.

His grandmother had been right about this too. Attending this ball was not the smartest move on his part yet he found it necessary for his peace of mind. He slipped out the back between the hedge and the street. Strolling along the sidewalk, he found his carriage.

"To the Stewart residence please, quickly."

With vivid clarity his thoughts turned back to the ball and the lovely lady. Thoughts of Teddy dancing with her left his gut churning. Perhaps he shouldn't have been so blatant in his proposal. There might have been another way to discourage her pursuit of him. So why was he so jealous of Teddy dancing with her?

He sat back, trying to relax. He needed to let the steady beat of the carriage wheels soothe his rattled nerves. If she ever discovered the ruse he played, there would be hell to pay. He supposed when would be the more appropriate word than if, because he didn't doubt for one second sometime in her future she would recall the night vividly. At that time, she would know his truth even though he tried to change the tenor of his voice and nearly covered his entire face as well.

The arrival at the Stewart townhouse brought him back to his reality along with his role-playing. Now, he would have to figure out how exactly to carry on with his relationship with the duke's sister. He just burned a very important bridge. Now, he needed to demolish the second.

Well hell and damnation.

He sauntered up the steps then to his room where he changed from his formal evening attire into a pair of buckskins and a white shirt. A glass of brandy was in order so he made himself at home in the drawing room and waited, figuring it would not be long before she arrived in a huff.

True to form, only a few minutes later, Angelica whirled into the home, her eyes blazing a promise of retaliation. Her little fists were clenched tightly, her face flushed. When she saw him, she inhaled a long deep breath.

"Have a drink?" He lifted his glass to her grinning, understanding part of her story. He wanted to comprehend how she interpreted the happenings tonight. "Might soothe your fury. By the way, care to talk about it?"

"Nothing will do that."

She stormed to the brandy poring herself a nearly full glass before plopping into a wing chair near the fire. She inhaled several deep breaths, her bosom nearly popping from the low-cut dress.

"You'll tell this poor horse breeder what has you so mad? I'm a good listener. At least that is what I've been told."

His expression was pleasant, schooled to just the right touch of concern. He could barely wait to hear her rendition of the events. Relaxing back in the chair, he waited.

She drank a gulp, coughing and sputtering as the burning liquid slithered down her throat. "Don't know why you would want to know. Just to tell me you were right about the blasted man. If I don't ever see him again, I'll be the happiest woman alive."

He tried to hold back his grin, realizing his plan worked

splendidly. The duke did not disappoint. "Right? I was right about something."

"You know bloody well what you were right about." She drank another gulp. This time it seemed to go down a bit easier. "I'm going home. Now!" She rose, shaking out her skirts and frothy petticoats so she wouldn't stumble and started for the steps.

He'd been enjoying the view of her ankles when he suddenly realized what she said and where she was going. "The hell you are." He grabbed her by the arm turning her, incensed she would even think to ride all the way to Southcliff in the dark by herself. "What are you thinking? That you want me to turn you over my knee or forestall your riding habits for another week? I will, you know. Don't ever doubt it."

"I'm going. I don't care about all your bluster, all your threats. At the moment they don't mean anything to me." She tried to shake off his hold but failed. "I'd rather you turned me over your knee. I'm not riding. I'll take the carriage."

Her expression shouted out a challenge to him. One he wasn't going to let go of or forget.

"It's still dark, after hours. You're not going anywhere." He had not expected such complete and impulsive capitulation to the events of the evening. Had not expected her to be quite so angry either that or she would forestall any thought of caution.

"Don't try to stop me. Leslie keeps a driver on hand for all hours. He is a spy, you know. He has to be prepared."

She shook off his arm, heading out the door without even looking over her shoulder to see if he followed.

For a moment he stood back, watching her then with a heavy sigh he headed after her. He didn't relish her mood if he had to curtail her riding for another week, or his. While his thoughts had been on discovering her interpretation of this evening, he'd also been thinking about a good night's sleep. The latter wasn't going to happen. Perhaps during the carriage ride, he would get her to admit what happened.

In less than fifteen minutes the carriage was on its way to Southcliff. He sat opposite Angelica thinking he would just bide his time until she wanted to talk. He could be patient. Her initial sob caught his attention, had him swearing silently to himself. He could handle most anything a woman dished out except her tears. These weren't just tears. They were full blown sobs.

Feeling more than just a bit guilty, Devlin pulled her into his arms and onto his lap. She set her head against his shoulder, tears slipping down her cheeks, her breaths shallow. Her entire body seemed to tremble. He never wanted her to cry. Didn't expect his brat to cry when the Duke of Weston acted the cad. He couldn't help but realize he was responsible for the liquid rolling down her face.

She sniffed then wiped tears from her cheeks with the back of her hand. "I hate him." The whispered words shook him to the core. "He can go to the devil for all I care. You know him, don't you?"

"Maybe a little."

"You can tell him for me. Tell him I despise him. Not that he'll care a fig."

He didn't want her to hate the duke either. Didn't want her to believe herself in love with him just because he wore a title at the end of his name.

"Don't cry." He was at a loss as to what to do now. Soothing a woman was not listed among his better attributes. "That's a very strong word. Hate."

"I know. I hate the cad. You know what he did?" She sniffed again while he continued to stroke her back.

For a second, he found himself whispering nonsense words to her. This girl left him stranded in deep water. "That was what I was right about? The duke of Weston is a cad?" He kept his laughter behind his teeth since he really didn't think she would appreciate his good humor.

"Worse."

"What did he do?" Devlin wondered how much she would share with him, needed her perspective on what happened at the gazebo.

"Don't want you to get angry and call him out. His life isn't worth you taking a risk."

"So, you think I'd beat him." He fiddled with one of the curls adorning the top of her head. "Good God, what did you put in your hair? It's stiff as a board."

"I would think a horse breeder who has such impeccable taste in women's fashion would know a little bit about the hair. The curls won't stay unless you put something in it to hold them."

"It's bloody awful."

"I know," she sighed deeply reaching up to feel her hair. "I had to use the bandoline to keep it in place." She tugged at one of the bows then the ribbons.

"Let me help." With the removal of each bow and ribbon, he finger combed her hair until it fell in luxurious waves around her shoulders, all signs of the goop vanishing. Finally, after thinking about the question again, "What did he do?"

She looked at him waving her hand in the air. "I don't want to think about that man. He puts the title of duke to shame. Truly, I'd like to get out of this dress. Don't want to remember anything about this night."

He groaned low in his throat, thinking about holding her, feeling her silken flesh beneath his fingertips. "Can't get you out of this dress until I get you home."

"Can you just loosen it a little? The corset is too tight. I can't breathe, you know. You wouldn't want me fainting right here on top of you."

He drew in a shaky breath thinking about undoing the corset, thinking about her fainting on top of him. That tiny act could lead to things they would both regret. "No, you're going to have to wait. Doubt if it's that tight." He paused. "Now, what did he do?"

"You're not going to stop asking, are you?"

She sighed then leaned into him, fiddling with the buttons on his shirt. Before he could stop her two were loosened.

Finally, he put an end to her exploring fingers, holding her hand with his. "What did he do? Everything. Out with it or I might stop the carriage and have him turn around."

He thought she'd be more than willing to tell tales. He was wrong.

He touched her beneath the chin wanting to look at her when she spoke this time. "He," she swallowed hard, "he kissed me."

He did chuckle softly this time, not allowing the huge guffaw that threatened to leave his lips to do so. "Thought that was why we practiced, kissing. So, you wouldn't disappoint the man. You must have done an admirable job."

Pushing away from him, she stared at him for too many seconds, "You did a lousy job teaching me. He didn't like my kiss. Not at all."

"I did?" He looked at her skeptically, waiting for the rest of the things he did.

"He said I didn't kiss very well and I needed practice." Her earnest sigh buffeted his heart. Deep down he was glad the duke found her lacking in skills. So did he. That was part of her charm.

"We can certainly practice some more. If you want to that is." Devlin didn't completely understand why he challenged her again when he understood kissing her was the last thing he wanted do even though it was something he longed for.

"What good would it do now?"

As much as it pained him to say it, "For the next man you fall in love with?"

He arched a dark eyebrow looking at her speculatively. He didn't like the idea of her falling in love with another. He didn't like the idea of her practicing with him to use her skills on someone else either.

Yet his time here rusticating was rapidly drawing to an end. If he could hold himself in check another couple of months, he'd be safely away from his little temptress. Over half way done with the time allotted by his grandmother to hide away, he was ready to get back to work. Papers would have piled up at an alarming rate. Months, many months would pass before he could possibly feel caught up.

The woman snuggled in his arms, thought practicing was a waste of time. She didn't know how the soft curve of her cheek fit so perfectly close to his neck or that the pressure of her bottom against his groin left him reeling with desperate need.

"I'm not going to fall in love ever again. Men can just go rot for all I care. Don't want to kiss another man," she said petulantly.

She just issued a challenge he should ignore. For some reason he couldn't. Right now, would not be the best time to practice kissing. She might bite him. He smiled, thinking on chancing it anyway.

"Well, perhaps you're right. Who would want to fall in love?

However," he paused thinking, "I doubt if those words about your kissing capabilities would have put you in this frame of mind. So, what did the bounder really do?" He grimaced at his argument.

The Duke of Weston was not a bounder. Problem was, he wanted to know a person loved him for who he was not what he could give them. It just was not well done of the duke's ex-fiancée to start rumors about him. He'd come upon her with his carriage driver, stark naked and in an extremely compromising position. With that knowledge in hand, he ended the engagement.

They'd been promised to each other for five years. She put off the wedding time and again. Once, when a pressing appointment came up in conflict to their wedding date, he set the day aside. He supposed she enjoyed the title of fiancée more than she would have as wife or Duchess of Weston. When all this happened, he vowed to never fall in love again. A biddable woman would be nice to provide an heir, but he could wait. He was still young.

"Too embarrassed to say the words." She bit out angrily seeming to come out of the depressed stupor she'd been lingering in for the last half hour.

"You know you can trust me," he coaxed with a smile he was pretty sure would convince her to spill her secrets.

"How do I know that?"

Devlin thought on that for a while, needing to find the right incentive but falling far short of the mark. "Because I've never lied to you. I've always been straight with you."

"Oh." She sat up, pushing tangled hair from her eyes an indignant look on her face. "Like the time you told me you'd tan my backside and instead you took away my riding privileges? Like that time? Wasn't that a lie?"

He lifted his shoulders in surrender. "I didn't want to hurt you. So, I figured out a more fitting punishment." She had an uncanny way of changing the subject to something more to her liking. With a heavy sigh, "What did he do? I'm not going to let this rest until you tell me. So, you might as well do it now."

Anger rippling through her so hard her body shook. She crossed her arms over her chest. "I would have rather you spanked me. The pain would have vanished. Instead, you prolonged it for an entire week."

"Even if I tossed your skirts and hit your tender backside? I do believe I'll keep that in mind if you ever need help making the right decisions again." He watched the rise of color on her cheeks, realizing she thought the spanking would happen with her skirt as well as all the frothy lairs of petticoats and underthings she usually wore remaining in place. "What did he do?"

The creaking of the wheels echoed in the silence. He heard the neigh of one of the horses outside. His knuckles moving tenderly across her cheek he hoped would encourage her to trust him. In his arms she shivered then once again brushed moisture from her cheeks.

She didn't look at him, "He asked me to be his mistress."

His breath caught in his throat at the tone of her voice. He humiliated her more than he would have expected. He thought his words might have shocked her not demoralized her. Perhaps they did a little of both.

He didn't know what to say. Now it didn't seem she wanted to talk. While the carriage trundled on, he held her, listening to her breathe. The cadence of each shallow breath was soft, gradually slowing until he was sure she slept. He ran his finger through her hair, marveling in the silken strands and how easily they slid through his fingers. It wasn't hard for him to think about the length wrapped around his naked body while they slept.

Inhaling a draught of air, she would never allow anything of the sort. He wasn't going to make love to her, in the process ruining her future. Bloody hell, but he had only a short time to withstand her charms. She did entice him as no other woman ever had. She infuriated and worried him. Snuggling deeper her hand rested on his belly just above his waistband.

They needed to be home now before he acted on the emotions she was creating in him. Restraining himself was not an easy feat. He should have found a willing woman while he was in Glasgow. Instead, he found a new form of torment for himself.

A little while later he was thrilled to find the carriage turning into the long drive leading to Southcliff. He understood he would have to help Angelica from her dress but once that was done, he intended to hightail it to the stables and a bottle of brandy.

Angelica, once awake, seemed to have a different idea. The minute they stepped inside she turned her back to him. He half expected to follow her to the bedroom, undo all the tiny fasteners on her dress then leave.

"Have a drink with me," she said as her dress pooled on the floor.

His hands were on the silken laces of her corset when he said the word. "No."

"Please. I don't want to beg but I will if I have to." She turned around when the corset found the floor alongside her dress.

His lips brushed hers before he turned her again, moving her hair to the side. With his teeth and tongue, he tasted the slim line of her neck then across her shoulder. One drink shouldn't hurt. In this tenuous situation, he wasn't at all sure. He sucked in air, determined now to have one drink with her then leave. He didn't want to test his resolve. Tonight, her emotions were in a fragile state of vulnerability.

Dressed in her frilly underclothing then draping her shawl around her, she walked into the drawing room. She poured them both a drink. He didn't understand. This was way too far out of character for Angelica.

"Are you going to stand in the foyer or come in here?" she asked bringing the drink to him.

"Really, I should go. You need to go to bed."

He sipped the drink, his gaze focused on tight pink buds of her nipples he could so clearly see through the lightweight fabric of her chemise.

"I know," she murmured. "I shouldn't have asked. You must think," she looked at herself, "this is what would be expected of me wouldn't it?"

"What?"

"If I was his mistress. The duke would expect to see me wearing next to nothing. Just like I am now. He would take me to the bedroom and make love to me. Wouldn't he?"

Devlin raked a hand through his hair.

Well hell.

What the devil brought this on?

"Yes, I suppose he would expect that. He's not here and you're not my mistress so I believe you should go on up to bed."

She sipped again while she strode into the drawing room, her hips swaying. When she sat down, she pulled her legs up around her. He wasn't at all sure what was driving her but he needed out.

"I'm going now."

"Do you have a mistress?"

"That's none of your business," he muttered as he slammed the glass on the table by the door.

He heard the door shut as he walked down the steps toward the stables. His mind in a fog, he sat on his bed a bottle of brandy in hand. When the sun rose, he was still wide awake. The brandy in that bottle gone, he'd started on a new one.

~ * ~

Leslie helped Lacie with her shawl, setting it on the coat stand. He noticed the glass filled with brandy on the table as well as the eerie silence in the house. They would be asleep. There was no reason to expect either one to remain awake until they returned from the ball. The hour wasn't late though. He wanted to speak with Devlin.

Lacie told him when she saw the Duke of Weston leave with Merry. At least, she told him she thought it was the duke. Merry didn't look pleased.

"Where do you suppose they are?" Leslie asked as he picked up the brandy to swirl it around the glass.

Lacie shrugged, slanting him the delicate smile he loved and knew meant she thought lovemaking was in order. "Probably in bed." She paused then looking upwards. "In separate beds I pray."

"I'll check on Devlin. You can poke your head into Merry's room and see if she's awake. Don't want to worry about them if there is no reason," Leslie said slanting her a wry smile.

He had the distinct gut feeling no one except them were in the house.

"What do you know that you're not telling me?" She approached him, hands on her hips. "It's that spy in you. You know things or presume to know them before they happen. I don't like this. Not one bit."

He shrugged, lifting his shoulders slightly then to change the mood he ran his knuckles across her cheek. "Nothing. At least nothing I can share right now. The time isn't right. I promised."

He hated putting her off this way but a promise was a promise. Devlin had a lot to lose if the truth surfaced in Glasgow.

"You cannot trust me? Your wife?"

She appeared indignant, her eyes flashing, telling him he best make up something close to the truth to appease her curiosity.

"The Duke of Weston is very private. He wanted to speak with Merry alone and I gave him permission. What happened after that I've no idea? By your account the meeting did not go all that well. I didn't think he would take advantage and she did want to fall in love with the man. Simply put, I gave her the chance."

Leslie let out a long slow breath of air, wishing he was kissing his wife instead of checking on an employee who was not truly an employee of his at all. Well, for the time being he guessed the man was.

"Very well, I'll let it go for now."

Meeting in the drawing room a few minutes later they discovered both Devlin and Merry were missing. "He left his small valise in the room."

"As did Merry."

"They wouldn't have run off together, would they?" Lacie asked, sounding worried. "Did you look for a note of any kind?"

"Nothing in his room," Leslie said before starting for the door. "Going to check the stable. Stay here."

He was back almost before he left, "They've taken the carriage to Southcliff. My driver left a note saying as much and that he'd return in the morning in case I needed him."

"That's a relief," Lacie handed him a snifter of brandy.

"Shall we take this upstairs?" Leslie asked as he stared at her bosom.

"Why?" Lacie asked. "Don't get it why Merry would take off in the middle of the night."

"I'm just glad Devlin wouldn't allow her to go by herself. Also, glad he talked her into the carriage. I'm sure she would have taken off on her little mare if Devlin hadn't been here."

"Who is he really?"

"Who?"

"Devlin. I know one thing for sure. That man is not a horse breeder."

Chapter Six

Two weeks later, Devlin still tried to keep his distance from Angelica. He didn't trust himself to keep his hands off. She riled every sense he possessed. He was beginning to believe some he didn't possess. When he found himself close to her, he had a devil of a time keeping his mind and body from travelling dangerous places. One look at her and he wanted to pull her into his arm then kiss her senseless.

She came and went pretty much at any time she pleased. Except at night, he grinned. His little brat spent most of her time away from the house during the day, but she always made sure she was home before dusk. One morning he followed her to find her swimming in the pond a few miles away.

A couple of days later he watched storm clouds build on the horizon. He knew they would be in for one hell of a storm. By dusk the evening darkened more than normal. Less than an hour later the night exploded in lightning and thunder.

Buck-naked and wishing he could stop thinking of the way she felt in his arms, he sipped on another bottle of brandy watching the bolts split the sky. The storm echoed his most recent life. Ever since the ball, hell, ever since he arrived at Southcliff he'd been out of sorts, more restless than he'd ever been in his life.

What was it about her that tempted every ounce of strength he possessed?

When he wanted something, he either took it or bought it. Well, he wanted Angelica. He could do neither; take her nor buy her. Even the man of her dreams failed to buy her. She should have told the duke, yes. Of course, she wouldn't. She was too important to give her love in that way. A man would have to marry her to have her.

With a jaundiced eye, he stared at the brandy bottle, understanding he should dump the rest out. Unfortunately, he still had a case stashed in the corner of the room. He wasn't about to pour out all the expensive French brandy he purchased for his stay. He would just have to stop drinking the potion.

"To hell with stopping."

Devlin upended the bottle again, tried to recall how many glasses he drank before tossing the glass aside. Then he said to hell with it again, to hell with counting. He didn't want to think. He didn't want to feel. To get staggering drunk, that was his aim.

He closed his eyes, concentrating on the sounds of the night, the ruckus of the wind coupled with the rain pounding against his window. If he let his mind wander, the constant sound might lull him to sleep. The horses moved nervously in their stalls as another roar of thunder boomed against the turgid night air.

Restlessness seeped into his soul. He rose, bottle in hand, making his way from the small room he called home to the area where the horses were kept. Walking through the stable he stopped at Windwalker's stall. He soothed the huge horse, running his hand down the stallion's nose, whispering to him.

"No sugar or apples this evening," he murmured. "You're going to have to wait for the morning when Angelica comes to see you. Do you have that much patience?"

Bloody hell but where his little brat was concerned, he had no patience, no patience at all.

When he finished there, he turned his attentions to Sir Alistair as he remembered one of the first mornings and Angelica's whispered words to the horses. He thought she was talking to her lover. His grin widened at thoughts of her sticky buns as well as her remarkable innocence. She was wonderful. She would make any man a fine wife if he could shake some common sense into her. He guessed that feat would be left up to the man who did become her husband. Lucky bastard.

He'd wanted to tan her backside just so he would have an excuse to lift her skirt and look at her saucy butt. Well hell, he still wanted to do that very thing which was the reason he was walking around the stable naked as the day he was born talking to the horses all the while remembering what he didn't dare do. He wouldn't last until the end of the summer.

Insanity didn't run in his family; neither did cobwebs for brains. So, what was wrong with him? He found himself at the end of the stable. Opening one of the double doors he stood outside, rain sluicing his body soaking him. If she looked out the correct window right now, she would have quite the view. Would she be shocked? He rather doubted it. She did have two older brothers. Somehow, he thought it would take an awful lot to shock her. His nakedness would never do the trick. Even if she was embarrassed, she would most likely deny the emotion.

Two more streaks of lightning flashed across the velvet sky, the thunder nearly resounding at the same time. In all its glory the tempest was upon them. More lightning, the night was deafening. He was enthralled, invigorated by the tempest. Vibrant energy pulsed around him setting his blood pounding. Looking to the house and cursing softly, he turned and headed back to his room.

Soaking wet he slipped beneath the sheet. The brandy bottle in one hand, he swigged it before setting the container on the table, staring at the blasted thing. Placing his hands behind his head, he watched through the window as the rain plummeted in torrents. The water sluiced in continuous waves.

It was a god-awful night to be outside. He swiped at the water coating his chest, swearing again as he realized he had climbed into bed without drying off. He closed his eyes absorbing the sounds of the night. He must have napped. When he opened his eyes, Angelica was standing beside the bed staring at him. For a moment, he thought he might be dreaming.

Rain dripped from her cloak. Even covered from the top of her head to her toes, he could tell she was shaking. Her eyes in the meager light looked to be two huge pools of fear.

"What are you doing here?" he asked, his voice weak, either from the sight of her or his over indulgence. "You should not have been out in this weather. It wasn't safe."

She slipped the hood from her head then the rest of the cloak. She bent down in order to remove her shoes. Dressed in a thin nightgown he saw her curves, the sweet outline of her body. Without answering his question or asking, she climbed in bed with him. While the gown wasn't sheer lingerie, it didn't cover her completely. Now, even obscured by the sheet, he could see her fragile collarbone, her slim neck.

He groaned. This was probably his worst nightmare or best damn dream of his life. "What are you doing here?" he asked again this time hoping for an answer, realizing that an answer would not change his condition.

She placed her hand on his chest. "Please," she murmured, closing her eyes momentarily.

He caught the scent of lavender, felt the cold wet slide of her silken hair across his chest. His gut tightened with need for this slender precocious woman.

Well hell, what did she think she was doing tempting him so? Where a man was concerned, didn't she have any common sense?

"Please what?"

"Just hold me." Her head now rested on his chest, her silken hair falling across him. "That's all I want. Need to have you chase away the terror. I can't stay by myself."

The pulse at the base of her neck pounded. A flash lit up the sky. She pressed closer to him, her body quivering in terror against his. Sensing her fright, he wrapped his arm around her, pulling her closer. Enjoyed her body flush against his. Understood it wouldn't take much for him to get used to this.

"It's only a storm. It will pass," he murmured, stroking her hair, running his hand along her arm. Just lean into me, Angel. I won't let anything happen. You're safe here in my arms."

"I know. That's why I came to you."

Still, her slender, feminine body shook, his words not easing the terrible fear that seemed to encompass her.

Her lips where they pressed against his chest were cold, freezing as were her hands. He pulled a blanket up to cover them, hoping for warmth even while his body heated from the inside out.

"Tell me why or do you know?"

He felt the delicate flutter of her eyelashes against his chest. His body hardened with need. Well hell, just when he thought he had his body under control she jumped into bed with him.

Tonight, he had downed nearly a bottle of brandy. He tried desperately to clear his head, wishing he used common sense this evening. Who would have expected this? No one would think a young lady would walk into his bedroom then climb into bed with him.

"I'm just afraid," she murmured burrowing closer.

He didn't think she could get any closer. Somehow, she did. A curl of ebony hair tickled him brushing across his cheek. He picked it up, running it through his fingers. Her breast pushed against this chest. Once she accused him of torturing her. Couldn't have been anything compared to this.

He was damned.

Each time the sky flashed or thundered rolled she pushed against him. Her fingernails dug into his chest. He didn't know how much longer he could do this; hold her in his arms without stealing a kiss, or more.

"Do you want to talk?"

"No."

He certainly wasn't surprised by her answer. He didn't want to talk either. She wouldn't appreciate what he wanted to do.

Slowly, the storm passed on, her body relaxing into his. Her breathing grew easier, her heart not pounding quiet so hard. Even outside while the rain still fell the water didn't pelt the window with as much violence.

She would leave now. He waited. Nothing changed. The tempest outside was finished. Not the one beneath the covers on his bed.

Devlin sat up, bringing her with him, hoping to convince her it was safe to return to her bed. His intentions were noble or perhaps not so much. One look at her caused his breath to catch in his throat. Her nightgown slid low on her shoulder, held in place by three slender ribbons. In the lantern light her skin was as white as moonbeams, compelling him to sample to taste.

She was looking at him as if she wanted him, passion darkening her eyes. He touched a finger beneath her chin, lifting it. Lightly, unable to resist, he brushed his lips across hers, thinking she would tell him to stop. If he deepened the kiss, she would remember he was a horse breeder, not a duke.

Not a word.

He told himself he would kiss her and that would be that. He could stop with one kiss or perhaps two. She parted her lips, her moist tongue sweeping across her lips then into his waiting mouth. He didn't know if it was intentional or not, but the charge between them was like the tempest at its height. Her hands were behind his neck, her fingers threading desperately through his hair as if she searched for something she couldn't find.

She pulled him closer.

He discovered something different, a burning desire, so very feminine, charged with the energy of the storm. An unyielding thirst raced through him like the brandy he'd been drinking all night. The kiss began gently, meant to continue with a mild sweetness until she decided to leave. The passion quickly changed, becoming a hungry, searching prelude to the deeper joining he so longed for.

"Angel, we need to stop."

It was his first and only noble gesture of the night. The last thing he wanted at the moment was to pull away from her and end this dream. Damn the consequences. He would deal with that later.

"Not yet. I need you." Her voice was a sultry murmur in the passion-filled night.

"Don't know if I can stop if this goes much farther."

That was the truth. He didn't know if he could stop now. Devlin tried to rein in the wild need that had been driving his actions since he first set eyes on Angelica. Control vanished.

"I'll tell you to stop," she murmured.

He didn't believe her though. She had no idea what was going to happen once he allowed himself free reign. Perhaps she knew more than she let on. He just assumed she was a virgin. She sure as hell wasn't acting like one now nor had she acted like one the night he brought her home from the ball. She had all but flung herself at him. So, why did she take such umbrage at the Duke of Weston's suggestion?

"If you're sure," he murmured, touching the lobe of her ear with his tongue then teeth, worrying it gently until she responded sweetly, arching against him. This was heaven, definitely heaven. Tiny purring sounds rippled from the back of her throat. He absorbed the velvet heat of her mouth with deep repeated movements of his tongue, probing and stroking, needing her with a raw savage passion that was like nothing he'd ever known.

"I am."

"You're positive."

When Devlin finally forced himself to end the kiss, he was wholly, painfully stimulated. He braced himself on his elbows and closed his eyes, fighting for control. It was impossible. Every breath he inhaled was infused with the delicious scent of lavender and a woman's secret warmth. The scent overpowering, drove him to stroke and touch even more, discover new tender, sensitive places.

He nibbled kisses along her chin before sweeping his lips across hers for a tender encounter then down her neck as well as across her collarbone. His teeth grazed her shoulder once then twice. She was tying him to her with hot ribbons of pleasure. Using his chin he pushed at the sleeve of her gown, tugged on the border with his teeth. The ribbons bound it to her. Slowly he untied each one, watching as the front gaped open leaving her alabaster globes with soft pink nipples revealed to his avid gaze. Her belly was flat, tempting him to explore further to delve into her dark nest of hair at the apex of her thighs.

She was every man's dream; soft and curved, sultry in the way she moved coupled with the taste of her mouth he was doomed. He would be hard pressed to stop this as he coaxed the fabric slipping down her shoulders off her arms with his lips, stroking as he followed the fabric to her wrist before he tugged it free.

"Devlin?"

The huskiness in Angelica's voice was another caress, making him groan. He stroked her neck and jawline with fingers that weren't entirely steady.

"I hope you want me half as much as that kiss suggested," he said in a low voice.

She didn't answer with words but the way her body moved against his, the way her fingers stroked his back as she clung to him told him all he needed to know. Her hips rose to each soft caress, her sounds of pleasure continuous. For the moment she was his and damn anyone with a title who might want to claim otherwise.

He kissed her again, a slow lingering hot kiss then he pushed her lips open to take her with a harshness that she responded to. Her eagerness surprised him. With his teeth he tugged on her lower lip before gliding his tongue across the hard smooth surface of her teeth then exploring deeper.

Her fingers swept through his hair tugging on him, drawing him closer until the swell of her breast and taught nipples caressed him. He swept his hand across her shoulder before continuing down her other arm, dragging the soft fabric of her nightdress with the stroke. The gown pooled around her waist. He lifted her to push it off before tossing it to the floor. She set her hand on his chest, pulling away slightly, her eyes simmering in the night.

"You're naked?"

"As are you."

He paused, praying she was not on the verge of denying him. Stopping would be agony. He would end this sweet seduction the moment she spoke the word. Until then he meant to discover as much about his little angel as she would allow. Once he left for home, tonight would have to be a memory, one he would never forget.

Angelica took his hand and slowly moved it down to her breast. Devlin's breath broke when he felt the nipple changing at his touch, becoming a tight velvet peak. He rolled it with his fingers, tasted the sweetness then bit gently, listening for the response.

"I wish this moment would last forever," he murmured, turning his attention to the other nipple, flicking the bud with his tongue.

"Why?"

The answer was not forthcoming, Devlin bent and caught the tip of Angelica's breast between his lips then brought the delicate flesh deep into his mouth, pulling on her with hot, driving forces, until she cried out, her body moving in undulating rhythms.

His lips created a throaty purring sound as her back arched in passion, seeking more from him. He found himself irrefutably under her spell. Magic she alone seemed to be able to weave around him. This was like nothing he could conceive.

His hands slid beneath her butt, holding her while he drank on the soft skin she offered him. Her breasts were coaxed and shaped by his teeth and lips until they were swollen, glowing and topped by nipples that stood up high and proud. He slid up her body to her mouth, kissing her again, while his fingers danced, skimming her, stroking all the sensitive places he could find but leaving the most intimate place alone for now.

If he touched her there...

His groan rumbled up deep from his belly and chest telling him just how much he wanted his angel, needed her with an undeniable hunger. A fine sheen of sweat broke out on his skin as irrefutable possessiveness claimed him.

Devlin lifted his head, staring at the proof of Angelica's desire, her need evident in her swollen quivering lips and tight hard nipples. The sight did nothing to dampen the raw thirst she created so easily. He recalled all the times he saw her in next to nothing, all the minutes he wanted to lie with her just as he was doing now. She came to him tonight, needing and wanting him. He could no more deny her than deny himself.

"This is why I wish this would last forever," he said huskily pressing his thumb against her moist, soft lips. "I want to always see the pink buds swelling on top of your breasts. I need to bring you a woman's pleasure tonight. Will you allow it to happen?" He needed to be her first.

Her last as well.

He smiled, laughing softly when he felt the wave of heat climb noticeably up Angelica's body at his words. She seemed to mull over what he told her. He was sure of it.

"As well as the sweet blush that comes when I speak of what I plan on doing to your cheeky body. I like to see that also." He skimmed her neck with his fingertips stopping to feel the pulse beating so strongly at the base of her neck.

Angelica closed her eyes, making a sound he was sure was half embarrassment, the other half laughter. It certainly took very little to embarrass her. He wondered if she understood how endearing her shyness was to him. Most of the women he knew would never be sweetly shy, never embarrassed. They might pretend. His ex-fiancée was nothing like Angelica.

He touched the tight buds on her breasts with the tip of his tongue, spread her legs, as he slipped lower, flicking his tongue on her navel then lower against the softness of her belly. Devlin felt the tremor that swept through her as distinctly as she did, her eyes widening at the new invasion.

He flexed his hands deepening the arch of Angelica's back until her nipples just brushed against his lips. Sensations coursed through him straight to his rock-hard arousal, his smile full as he watched her shiver and twist restlessly, seeking a deeper caress.

"Angel," Devlin said thickly.

He would give her everything she sought. "So supple and graceful. Want me as much as I want you."

Devlin kissed her breasts, her throat, her lips, taking tiny bites of her in between each nuzzling caress. She ran her sharp little fingernails the length of his back, stopping at his buttocks to stroke him. He jerked with desperate need. Once again, he drew his mouth across each breast, flicking, nipping savoring her sweetness. She shivered and bit back a cry of pleasure. When the tip of his tongue fenced with her taut nipples, she arched again, wanting more than his teasing. She didn't know the end game. When the night ended, she would.

He gave her what she seemed to be asking for, his mouth both stroking and demanding down her body, seeking the sultry, delicate flesh that lay concealed between her legs. When he found her and caressed her once, very gently, she cried out again.

She quivered with her need, frantic for more. His body rested against her, between her legs as he gently parted the velvet petals guarding her entrance. He placed kisses along her legs to the sensitive spot behind her knee then on to her delicate tiny feet. When he finished there, he moved up her other leg, using teeth and tongue to wrack her body with shivers of raw passion.

She was crying out for him, arching and twisting in his hands. He needed to pleasure her, thought only of the way she would feel in his arms when she climaxed. He kissed her belly again, then the tight pink buds, wondering at the twisting and turning of her body against his. She was ready for him and all he could think of was the heat of her body linked with the velvet depth that would encompass him.

With his thumb he found the silken knot between her petals. Touching her there she flinched then as he continued to caress and stroke, her hips rose again and the tiny sounds rippling from her grew more intense. Aroused and anxious to ease inside her, he hesitated for a second as he watched the wonder on her face.

"Open your eyes, my impertinent angel." He stroked her again and again, was rewarded with more simmering passion, the fire in her eyes. Her body was crying for him, spilling more and more of its dewy moisture with each intimate caress.

"Please, Dev," she murmured as her hips twisted and arched against him.

Slowly, he slid inside her. The sultry warmth he found there encapsulated him, kissed the length of him. He touched the membrane just before he sheathed himself completely. She cried out, her nails biting into his shoulders, her body stiffening.

"Oh God, I'm sorry, Angel," he murmured, kissing her breasts, lips and neck while he waited for the pain to pass.

Her cry brought him temporarily back to the reality of the moment. His sanity precariously dangling on the edge. It was too late to stop or undo what had been done. She was supposed to tell him to stop.

Well hell.

He was so aroused ready to explode which was what he did, emptying his seed inside her before he could withdraw from her sultry heat. Sweat sheened, he braced himself on top of her. Her hips slowly started to arch and twist against him seeking fulfillment. She had yet to receive her pleasure. Had yet to realize she was no longer a virgin.

With his thumb he found the knot inside her swollen damp petals. Stroking her there, kissing the tips of her breast, he began to swell with his own need. He entered her again. Beneath him she quivered, her cries increasing as his strokes grew harder and faster. He had never realized he could become aroused again so quickly.

She did cry out then, her body clenching with the tremors he created. Crying out his name, her nails scored his flesh, her eyes wide with wonder. She met him stroke for stroke. She was beautiful in her pleasure as he drew the moment to last as long as he could make it. When she finally calmed, he lay beside her, stroking her arm.

He just did the unthinkable.

~ * ~

The silence in the stable room invaded the recesses of her thoughts. Slowly as she calmed, she began to realize what just happened. He blanketed her, his weight comfortable against her. A few seconds ago, he changed her life forever. She was no longer marriage material, at least not in the circles where she was expected to wed. Not to be selfish, she might have just changed his life forever too.

She told Devlin she would stop him, say the single word to keep this from happening. In truth she didn't understand anything.

"I'm sorry," she said stoically, realizing the words truly held little meaning.

"I'll marry you." He brushed damp tendrils of hair from her face, his smile vague, hinting at remorse. His breath blew out in a long breath.

"No, I was supposed to tell you to stop. No need to marry anyone because of this situation I got myself into," she murmured understanding now she had been so caught up in the magical sensations he created within her, the raging fire burning through her she could have never said the words. Didn't want to in any case.

"We will marry."

His words were throaty and insincere at best. No desire or anticipation of married bliss filtered through his mind, only dread.

"It's not necessary. I'm sure I'll recover just fine if you don't."

She knew she would never be the same again, knew she would want him for the rest of her life while she thought about this moment. Stonily, she fought the moisture threatening in the back of her throat determined not to cry in front of him.

Christine Young

"What will your future husband have to say when he discovers you aren't a virgin?" he bit out harshly, his voice tinged with anger yet the fury didn't feel directed at her.

"How will he know?" she asked feeling more than a little indignant. "I won't tell this imaginary man somewhere in my future. I'm sure you won't either."

She didn't want to think about any of this now. Didn't want to have this conversation with Devlin. She wanted to hide away where she wouldn't have to think about what she just did.

"You're not serious."

Now instead of anger she heard the hint of incredulity perhaps laughter as well.

"I am."

She stiffened not liking this turn yet it had to be better than before. It was just like a man to laugh at her inexperience. This wasn't all her fault.

He continued to rearrange damp strands of hair, gently touching her mouth with his thumb. "Your mother never talked about sex or marriage with you? You really don't know?"

"She never talked about anything with me." Merry didn't want to defend her mother. Somehow, she felt she needed to do just that. "Perhaps she didn't know."

"Bloody hell, she had three children."

"So?"

"Your brothers?" he asked still sounding amazed.

She was shaking her head feeling neglected, misinformed as well. "No."

"Well hell, the pain you felt when you cried out," he paused as if he tried to think of the words, the right words in any case.

"I never expected this. Never thought I would have to explain to a virgin how another man could tell she was no longer a virgin. "It was your..." he cleared his throat, "a thin membrane. I broke through it. It can only happen once. That's what hurt. That's how a man can tell if you'd slept with someone before him. I'm your first. Only one man in any woman's life can have that privilege."

141

"Oh my."

"What if you're pregnant?"

She caught her bottom lip between her teeth, a shiver of dread slithering through her. "Oh, my."

"At least you understand what we did together could get you pregnant. For that small fact, I'm thankful.

If you are, we will marry. I won't leave you alone to fend for yourself or explain things to Leslie. I won't leave a baby of mine without a father."

She couldn't tell by his voice if he was still angry. No man wanted to be forced into marriage. "You don't have to do that. I don't hold you responsible. As for the father business, I would let you see the baby anytime you wanted to."

"You can be damn sure your brothers will." He rolled off her, an arm over his eyes. "Anytime I want to see my child is not being a father."

He was angry furiously so. Of that she was now sure. "They don't have to know anything. I won't tell either one."

"I'm sure in a few months' time everyone will know what we did if you are pregnant."

"I'm not pregnant. It's just once. It can't happen the first time."

Could it? Once again, she felt ignorance explode inside her and silently cursed her mother for leaving her so incredibly naïve.

Fury and frustration eating at her she threw off the covers, searching for her nightgown so she could leave. Staying here any longer was out of the question. She had to get a way to think. He grabbed her arm, holding her in place. "Where are you going?"

"Back to the house. I have to figure something out." She didn't want to argue, didn't want to leave the warmth of his body. But...

"Stay. The harm is done. I'd like to hold you if you would like."

His husky voice sent spirals of heat flowing through her. He was soothing her rattled nerves, at the same time coaxing her into his arms. She knew it. He knew it. What to do about it?

Even the gentle touch on her arm reminded her how magical his fingers dancing on her body could be. "I shouldn't." She shouldn't have come here in the first place.

"You want to, don't you?"

Slowly, he ran his finger up her arm before he ventured across her collarbone, gently coaxing her to his way.

With that simple touch, her body heated, flamed. She shivered with desire. Giving forth a tiny sigh she nodded, "Yes."

He tugged. She tumbled to sprawl across his chest, the tips of her breasts still sensitized from his lovemaking, tightened even more. She nestled against him, absorbing his strength running her hand along his chest, wishing she understood the multitude of emotions sweeping through her.

"You should be angry with me," Devlin said, continuing to soothe and charm. "I understood more than you what was going to happen."

"I thought you were furious."

Her fingers explored his nipples, touching caressing, rubbing the tip with the flattened palm of her hand. She felt the sudden tightening of his muscles, heard the low growl of pleasure.

"Unless you want to make love again tonight, or this morning, you're playing with fire, Angel." He rested his hand on top of hers, stilling her exploration for a moment.

In reply, she pulled herself higher, touched his nipple with the tip of her tongue, flicking it once before setting her teeth there, nipping slightly, sipping gently. His hands settled on her buttocks, squeezing, stroking until she found herself twisting and turning against him, feeling his arousal pulse beneath her. She trailed kisses down his chest, following the line of dark hair to his sex. While she stared at him, she touched the tip with her tongue.

He rumbled deep in his throat. "I guess that's a yes," he said, flipping her so she straddled him. "Brazen hussy."

Merry blinked a few times, realizing his words held a tenderness she never expected. She felt the blunt tip of his rod, touching her, begging to enter inside. He was right about her. This was terribly brazen of her. He quenched her curiosity with the first encounter. Did he? Now while it wouldn't matter, she wanted to make love to him understanding what would happen. She wanted to experience that incredible pleasure one more time before she ran from him and the possible consequences of this night.

"I've always been shameless. Why stop now?"

She settled on him, sitting now, unmoving as she felt her body clench and quiver around him. This newfound intimacy amazed her, frightened her a bit, still she wanted to savor every new sensation.

"Why indeed?" he muttered, his hands on her hips guiding her. She bent over, let him take first one then the other breast into his mouth, sucking, tugging the tip as well as the sensitive flesh around it deep inside. Mindlessly, she rode his shaft until his thumb stroked her, bringing her even more pleasure.

Trembling, heat pulsing within, she closed her eyes, tossing her head back as the sensations he elicited in her grew to a crescendo. "Dev..."

She found herself engulfed with spasms as they pulsed through her into him. Finally exhausted, she collapsed against him.

He held her, stroking her back, murmuring words she didn't understand against her hair. Lightly, he kissed her forehead when she pushed up to look at him.

"Regrets?" he asked tenderly his voice husky with what she thought was desire.

"Not now. Not in this moment." She slumped against him, knowing there might well be regrets coming their way. Marriage was such a permanent, lasting endeavor. He didn't love her. She had no idea how she felt about him. Did she love him? How on earth could she hold him to a loveless marriage?

"Tomorrow?"

"Perhaps tomorrow. Dev, I should be embarrassed to be here like this with you."

"A horse breeder."

"I'm not. I'm afraid the embarrassment might come when I walk away, when I'm alone and realize what I've..."

"We've..."

"Done." She finished their thoughts.

"It's alright. We'll figure this out together. If you're carrying my child though, he or she will have my last name. There will be no arguments from you or your brothers. I promise you that."

"I understand. It's a nice last name. I suppose it could be a marriage in name only."

She needed to think before she spoke. After this night the last type of marriage she would ever want would be in name only. If they did wed, she wanted to be in his arms as well as his bed as much as possible.

"No," he said, staring at her as if she possessed sawdust for brains. "If I marry you, you will be my wife in every way. Don't ever think to deny what is between us." His words were dark, throaty with a threatening edge to them.

She shivered, thinking she might have thought she knew the man. She didn't, not really. He was a horse breeder. She didn't know where he lived or how he supported himself. Could he support a wife and a baby? She reminded herself her inheritance was more than enough to put food on the table as well as clothing. Hadn't her brother told her she couldn't spend her excessive groats all in her lifetime even if she tried.

With a shaky breath, she pushed away, "I need to get back to the house," she paused, "before Lucy starts looking for me."

"An excuse if I ever heard one," he murmured. "She never looks for you in the morning. You're always out riding."

"Maybe. I still need to go."

He held on to her wrist. "Don't run too far. I might decide to ask for your hand even if you aren't with child. It was my behavior that ruined you. No one else is to blame. Remember that, Brat."

"What? Now I'm back to brat? What happened to Angel?"

Not giving him time to answer, she dressed quickly then ran to the house. Once inside, she leaned against the door, inhaling long deep breaths of air. How on earth would she ever escape the memories and the things she did, the things he did. The way she felt. A flush rose to her face, in the process covering her body. Closing her eyes, she still felt the heat of his gaze, the texture of his fingertips, arousing, demanding, leaving her weak and trembling.

Her knees almost buckled.

She wondered if she had the strength to walk up the stairs. No time like the present to find out. Inhaling several times as if she needed extra oxygen, she pushed away from the door, heading to her room.

Once inside, she flung herself on the bed. She was almost nineteen-years-old with plenty of time before she would be considered on the shelf. Marrying just because she wasn't a virgin didn't make sense to her. Devlin wasn't a virgin last night. She wasn't his first.

Men are different you ninny.

Why? They shouldn't be. Makes no sense, no sense at all. I'm supposed to remain chaste so some man in my future, well not future any longer, will know I've never been with a man before?

You ken darn well why. It's the very reason he's going to wed you if you're with child. If his seed took then he has to do what is considered the right thing.

I certainly don't understand that difference.

Men can't get pregnant. It's solely up to them to make things right if something goes wrong.

An unwanted marriage is not making things right, only making things worse.

Maybe he does love you. Ever think of that? Perhaps he's just too big a coward to tell you so.

No, he doesn't love me. Like Douglas he probably just wants my money. I'm not going to run after him or make this easy. I don't want to see him again.

Of course, you do.

No.

It's a waste of time to argue with you today. You'll want to see him in a few minutes.

No. I'm not even going to go riding because I'll see him in the stable. If I see him there, it will bring up too many memories.

Suit yourself.

You know I will.

For several minutes, she lay on the bed, her arms spread wide across the mattress, staring at the ceiling. Sunlight began to filter through the curtains. She finally became aware of the birds singing. Their songs usually woke her in the mornings. Not this morning, she'd been lying in bed naked with the horse breeder in the stable.

Another flush swept through her, heating her, remembering all the ways he stroked her, created the enchantment inside she would never forget. He played her body as if he knew exactly what to do to make her give in to his ways. He coaxed and sweet-talked until he had her melting.

As much as she wanted to, she couldn't blame him for what she didn't say. The single word no or stop would have created the desired result. She trusted him. He would have ended what he was doing. Even if it was with reluctance.

An hour must have passed maybe two before she rang for a bath. She realized she was sticky, sweaty. Which brought on another round of memories as well as embarrassment, the way his bronzed body was so muscular, his chest broad, his legs long, his forearms corded. The Duke of Weston could never have been so incredibly beautiful as Devlin.

Her horse breeder.

If she wanted a man who could pass for a god, it was Devlin. The Duke of Weston simply could not have been built as well, could not live up to the solid good looks of Devlin.

What the devil was she thinking? This whole thing was an embarrassment. She should be thinking of what she was going to tell Leslie not what Devlin looked like without wearing a stich of clothing. Telling her brother anything was out of the question, unless she had to explain a condition she wasn't going to be in any way.

Lucy popped her head inside the room, "Your bath is ready."

A steaming hot bath was exactly what she needed. Hot, breathlessly hot, she could relax and forget about what happened after the thunderstorm. What happened after the tempest was of the most concern. She went to him for comfort because she was afraid, terrified. She trusted him.

Undressed and soaking in the hot water, she tried to keep her mind from drifting to Devlin. She saw the blood on her leg. She supposed that had something to do with her virginity. It was too bad Devlin didn't tell her about that. After all he told her about everything else. She was trying to figure out how exactly she would know if she carried his child. Lord, but she wished her mother had told her a few things before she left France over three years ago. She could hardly write a letter and ask her now. It would be too suspicious.

Merry knew she could talk to her sisters-in law but she was loathed to do that. Her questions might get back to Lacie. From there they were bound to reach Leslie. Her brother could not know unless absolutely necessary. She tried to swallow the lump in her throat.

Hope. Hope MacTavish.

She could ask Hope. Flynt's wife would help her out. Perhaps tell her without divulging anything to her brother. Hope lived in a harem once a long time ago. Well, not quite so long ago. She knew things most women had no idea about. Tomorrow, she would ride to Glasgow and seek her out. Any of her sisters except Lacie could be sworn to secrecy. If Hope couldn't tell her what she wanted to know, no one could.

Merry didn't care about disapproval or judgment. There would be none. Bliss, the oldest of the MacTavish sisters, nearly bore her twins before she married Brock. The ceremony took place only minutes before the birth. Chelsea tried to get Cam to make love to her before they were wed, but Cam tried very hard not to succumb to the seductions of his now wife. And Daryl, for the longest time, Daryl refused to marry ever.

Yes, she had possibilities besides taking her questions to Devlin who would undoubtedly have something to say about her lack of knowledge. She didn't want him to learn how ignorant she was. Seemed strikingly strange that a man knew more about womanly things than she did. Somehow, she never thought any of this would be important. Didn't believe she would ever be in this predicament, pregnant before wed. That just didn't happen. I'm not pregnant. She tried to think positive.

She finished with the bath then dressed. Looking out the window to the stables, she thought about riding. Couldn't because she didn't want to see him today. Didn't want to see him at all, knowing how he looked at her last night, knowing he'd seen her naked. She gulped down a huge bundle of air that settled in her stomach as a lump.

Thinking about last night, her body heated almost as if he caressed her. She saw him leave the stable. He was riding Windwalker and heading toward her pond. It wasn't fair.

Not fair at all.

What did Leslie always tell her? Life isn't fair. Get over it, Brat. No, that was Link who said such obnoxious things to her. Or was it,

Leslie? She supposed none of that mattered anymore. Both her brothers were probably that way.

Why did all the important men in her life call her brat?"

What would she do with a baby?

Merry had no idea. Her mother failed to teach her anything about children. Actually, she was always more interested in riding over the countryside than learning about children, or sewing or cooking or...

She always envied her brothers along with their freedom to do what they pleased when they pleased.

A few seconds later, Devlin vanished over the crest of a small hill. Perhaps today would be a good time to ride into Glasgow. She could find out a few things, information she needed to know then return home. More and more, Glasgow was looking like a good place to hide until she knew.

~ * ~

Lacie paced the small area in the parlor, wringing her hands, beside herself with worry. Merry had arrived over two weeks ago. The problem was not her arrival. No, the difficulty stemmed from the fact she barely left her room in all that time. She refused to see Devlin who came every day asking the same thing. She wasn't sick, at least that's what Merry told her.

If Merry didn't give in soon and talk to the man, she was going to make her. She would send Devlin to the girl's room then tell him he had to do something to shake her out of her pouting. Either that or she would send Leslie to interrogate the horse breeder. Something was going on here. It was high time to get to the bottom of it.

Leslie walked into the drawing room, grinning from ear to ear just in time to listen to her rant. "When are you going to find out what's going on between your sister and the horse breeder?" Lacie stood in front of her husband, hands on her hips as ferocious an expression she could muster.

"Well, good morning to you, lovely wife." Seeming preoccupied, he kissed her on the forehead. "It's not my business, neither is it yours as well you *ken*."

He sat down shaking out the newspaper to read.

Lacie sat down beside him staring at him. She wasn't about to let him get away with ignoring her. If she stared at his mouth long enough, she would get his undivided attention. Perhaps she should be blatant and loosen a few of the buttons on her day dress. He could never ignore her breasts. Once she had his undivided attention, she could talk to him again. Either that or he would pick her up and take her to bed and they would talk later.

She let out a long slow breath of air, "Leslie, please. There is something going on. I've never seen Merry so despondent, never seen her stay in her room all day. While it doesn't surprise me that she doesn't want to talk to Devlin, her reclusive behavior does surprise me. Your sister is usually bouncing from one place to another."

"You should go talk to her." Leslie set the paper on his lap long enough to respond and sip the coffee she brought for him. "Women have a way of conversing that leaves men muddled in the brain. I've no idea what is going on. When I think about her actions, quite frankly I'm terrified to find out."

"Now you're not talking sense. She isn't eating either." Lacie sat across from him in the other wing chair. "I'm not going to let you ignore me."

He grinned at her, a devilish look in his eyes. "Perhaps we can take this upstairs?"

"That's what I want you to do. You need to take this to Merry. Find out what she's pining about along with what she isn't telling us. This isn't healthy. It's been more than two weeks, the longest weeks of my life."

Lacie knew she couldn't sit by and watch these goings on for another day. The problem had to be solved today.

"I'm not going to get nosy. When she's ready to tell us what's bothering her, I'm sure she will. For now, we need to let her have some privacy."

"Well then, tell Devlin to stop coming here. Merry is not going to change her mind anytime soon. She doesn't want to talk to him. I tell you something happened between the two of them. It's not good. If we don't get to the bottom of this soon..."

"Lacy..."

She heaved a sigh then rising she strode to the bottom of the staircase. Looking from Leslie to Merry's room, she cast him a glance that she hoped told him what she thought of his cowardice then started up the steps.

Determined to discover Merry's problem she knocked on the door. With the slight pressure it swung open. "Merry, honey..."

She stopped eyes wide, watching her. Merry had one leg out the window, looking as if she was going to jump.

"Oh, it's only you." Merry's voice was weak, trembling. "I thought somehow Devlin got by you."

"No, as long as you tell us you don't want to see him, we'll make sure he doesn't. Don't you think jumping out the window is a bit drastic? You could hurt yourself. Is not talking to the man worth it?"

"Thank you, I just don't have the heart to talk to him. Haven't figured out what to say when he asks."

"Asks what?" Lacie sat down on the bed, patting a place beside her to encourage Merry to sit by her.

"Can't say. Not to you or my brother." Merry plopped down next to her. "It's not that I don't want to confide in you but if I do, I know Leslie will find out. Can't have that happening."

Lacie felt as if Merry had slapped her in the face. They'd been friends, good friends for such a long time. Three years to be exact. "I would never tell Leslie anything you said to me in confidence."

"I know you mean that but if Leslie thinks you're hiding something from him, then I know he'll find some way to pry the information from you."

"He's told me that whatever is bothering you isn't his business. That the two of you will work things out," Lacie tried to reassure Merry.

She realized in the few seconds her encouragements were doing nothing to alleviate Merry's problems.

Merry arched a dark eyebrow. "And you believe that?"

Lacie took some time to think about Merry's words. She wanted to believe what Leslie said was true but everything she knew about Leslie pointed in the opposite direction. "I did but I suppose I shouldn't. He always makes light of matters of the heart. I'm assuming this is a matter of the heart. By Devlin's persistence he is just as invested as you are," she said letting out a long slow breath of unfettered air.

"Of course, you shouldn't. Now, I do want to put my trust in you. I'll tell you soon if I have to do so."

Lacie couldn't read Merry's expression, wasn't sure if she wanted to understand what was behind the stress lines on the girl's sweet face. She would have to though.

"Very well." She set her hand on Merry's leg. "If you need anything, all you have to do is ask. Leslie and I will be gone for a few days. If Devlin shows up, I'll tell Westcott you don't want to see him."

Chapter Seven

Devlin counted down the days since the night of the thunderstorm. It had been sixteen days. Surely the woman knew if she was pregnant or not by now. He bit back several swear words as he curried Windwalker, wishing she would at least talk to him. If they were to wed, he had arrangements to make. Left in the dark was not a position he relished or was used to. For some reason he couldn't think of, Angelica was doing just that.

She wouldn't talk to him. Bloody hell, for the last fourteen days he'd ridden into Glasgow with the express purpose of speaking to his little brat turned angel at times. When he remembered her stretched out beside him, her white flesh pressing against him, he knew she was an angel.

He wanted her to understand how he felt about her. No matter what happened, whether she was pregnant or not, he intended to marry her. Somehow, she wormed her way into his heart. It was something he had a devil of a time admitting to himself but it was true. First though, she would have to get over her infatuation with the Duke of Weston. He was no longer intending to play second fiddle to the man.

He enjoyed the banter between them, the way her dark blue eyes twinkled when she saw or heard something amusing. Devlin even enjoyed the fact she dared disobey him. For a wife, he didn't want a woman who would bend down to his every whim. Angelica challenged him. That was exactly what he needed and wanted in a spouse. Without her his life would be just as it had been before he met her, boring and predictable.

There was so much he missed the last weeks. One was seeing her every day in the stable, sweet-talking all the horses, arguing with him while she sashayed her little fanny about. Since the breeding, she'd been especially interested in the mares, bringing them apples and carrots.

No matter what he decided as he saddled his stallion today, he wasn't about to take no for an answer. If he had to push his way through Leslie and Lacie as well as the butler, he would do that. He didn't think Leslie would put up much of a fight. If Westcott was the only one there, he would give way easily enough. This was no longer just about Angelica. He had a big stake in what happened between them.

A little over an hour later, he tied Windwalker to the hitching post in front of the Stewart townhouse in Glasgow. For several minutes he stared at the house, searching for the outside location of Merry's room. Bloody hell, if he had to, he'd shimmy up the tree located just outside what he assumed was her bedroom.

He wasn't sure why, but his hands shook, his nerves raw and on edge for the last weeks. His mission here was to remedy that. He didn't like the fact he didn't know what was happening to her. Had thought she would share with him her fears and thoughts about waiting. Instead, there had only been silence between them. His gut told him she was pregnant. His gut was never wrong.

Devlin knew she had been nervous, embarrassed at what they did together. He could have helped her sort out her feelings if she talked to him. Well hell, she didn't even want to look at him. How the devil could that kind of behavior hold up in a marriage?

Bracing himself for another rejection, he knocked on the door. It wasn't Westcott who answered as he'd expected. Instead, it must have been a maid. Perhaps his luck was changing. He grinned from ear to ear in anticipation of the long-awaited meeting.

"What can I do for you?" she asked seeming hesitant, unsure as well. Her arms were full of linens, as she looked upstairs then back to him.

"Came to see my fiancée," he brazened it out, hoping she wouldn't know better and let him in to the foyer.

"Oh," she said startled. "You must be talking about Miss Merry. She's in her room. Should I tell her you've come calling?"

He smiled, doffing his hat. "No, I'd like to surprise her. It's been a while since we've seen each other."

Indeed, his luck was changing. He heard a door upstairs slam shut, knowing immediately he jumped to his conclusion of changing luck a bit prematurely. He was now sure Angelica heard him, closing her door and most likely locking it to him. Well, hell would freeze over before a locked door would keep him from his intent.

All he wanted was to talk. First, he would have to charm her into compliance. His brat would never allow such a thing to occur. He was prepared for a battle.

Slowly Devlin strode up the steps, trying to form the words in his mind. All he wanted to know was if she carried his child or not. Sixteen days should be enough to know one way or the other. If she wasn't pregnant, they could plan a wedding. If she was, they would elope today.

When he finally reached the door, he paused, his hand lifted to knock. Sucking in a deep breath of air for courage or just to keep his anger from showing, his fist hit the door.

"Angelica?"

The hesitancy in his voice surprised him. He didn't understand the escalating nerves. Maybe it was because he was about to find out if he was going to be a father any time soon. Or the alternative, he was not. He wasn't sure which option he preferred.

"Go away."

He noticed a sob in her voice.

Or did he? "I'm not going anyplace until we talk. I'm going to stand right here until you let me in. Either that or I'm going to break the damn door down. You choose."

His fists tightened while anger simmered deep within. It galled him that she refused to meet him halfway.

The silence from the other side unnerved him even more. What the hell was she up to? Then he was sure he heard the opening of a window, the slide of wood against wood. She wouldn't jump, would she? In her possible condition? Bloody hell was he such an ogre that she would fling herself from a two-story window just to get away from him?

Devlin was glad he stood in front of the house for as long as he did, recalling now a large oak tree near where he thought her window might be. Still, he didn't like the idea she would have to resort to such drastic measures. She preferred shimmying down a tree than talking to him?

From the other side of the door, he heard a few grunts as well as some swear words, a few seconds later, a tiny shrill and a slightly muffled scream. She was headed out the window. Something went wrong. His breath caught in his throat as all the possibilities swept through him. Another scream. His heart rocked to a stop before it found the wherewithal to beat again.

Not wasting even one second, he raced down the steps taking them three at a time before jumping the last five feet to the floor below. He headed out the door and around the corner of the house images swirling through his head, sure he would find her sprawled on the ground.

He breathed a long sigh of relief at the sight greeting him. Perched on a swaying tree limb at least twelve feet above the ground was his Angelica. A delightful view of frothy petticoats enticed him. Frilly underwear along with legs that seemed to go on forever was all he could see. What he heard though terrified him. It was a scream that seemed to rip from her.

Devlin slowly surveyed the precarious scene, attempting to decide what he should do. Stopping so he could see her face, with hands on his hips, he looked at her. "What are you planning now, Brat?"

Her eyes sparked outrage as she glared down at him. "This is all your fault."

To his chagrin he was beginning to understand her convoluted way of thinking, "Ah, because I dared knock on your door you are stuck on a tree limb that doesn't want to hold your weight. When was the last time you escaped out that window?"

It seemed she didn't want to answer his questions. "Don't just stand there. Do something"

Placing his hands on his hips. "What would you like me to do, Brat?"

"Help me," she said indignantly.

"So, now you want my help."

"Well, I don't think I can get down without it."

"Then what? You will run from me and refuse to talk?"

He was trying to figure out how he was going to keep her from doing just that. Short of hog tying her or forcing her, he couldn't figure out one way to keep her from running the moment he set her tiny yet agile feet on the ground. Ah, but he was faster than she was. He also had more stamina. So, he was sure he could simply pursue her without breaking a sweat until she wore herself out and gave up.

"I don't want to talk," she gritted out in what he thought was a haughty voice. "Can't tell you something I don't know the answer to. Go away."

"Before or after I help you down?"

He grinned, seeing the humor right now. If the limb cracked, he would catch her. He could wait her out.

"After."

"Alright then. You should understand I'm not leaving until we talk. Also, you are coming down one way or the other." He groaned when the limb cracked again. Heard the scream of terror. "Swing your legs over and lower yourself down to me. I'll catch you."

He did prefer to catch her without the benefit of a tree branch in his face, taking consolation that now the only way from that room would be gone in a few minutes.

"Just because you are here doesn't mean words will come out of my mouth," she told him angrily. Then she turned away, refusing to look at him.

Well hell.

She was right about one thing. He couldn't make her talk to him if she didn't want to. Perhaps he would have to supply all the words in the conversation. He could always make verbal assumptions. Knowing her as well as he did, she would have to refute. First, he had to get her down from that tree. The need became more evident with the next crack linked with a terrified scream.

Her body flew up then down as the branch she was on dipped closer to the earth. "Drop your legs over. I'll catch you."

Angelica peered over the edge of the tree branch, her eyes wide blue pools of terror. "I," she swallowed, then nervously running her tongue across her lips "I can't. It's too far."

"You should have thought of that before you climbed out that window."

He tried to hide the smirk but found it nearly impossible. The view from here was indeed splendid.

"Don't make me feel worse than I do already. I can't move."

"Of course, you can, Brat. Just do it."

He grimaced when she tried, her dress catching on one of the extended branches. His breath caught in the back of his throat when the material ripped while her body lurched precariously on the branch. Breath didn't make its way into or out of his lungs.

"Dev..." There was a distinct sob in her voice.

Trying for a soothing calm voice, he held his hands in the air. "You're half way there. Swing your legs around and let go now."

She peered downward. He knew it looked like a long way. His hands almost reached her ankles but not quite. Trust, he thought. It was an elusive proposition. What were her alternatives? For Angelica there were no other alternatives at this point.

"I-I'm letting go now."

He heard the thin wail. His hands closed over her ankles then legs as she slowly settled into his waiting arms. Burying his face in her hair when she was finally secured, his knees nearly buckled with the relief he felt. Now all he wanted was to shake her. He would too if it would lodge a modicum of sense into her female brain.

"What the hell did you think you were doing? That was almost as foolish as riding at night." His bone deep anger was not something he was in control of at the moment. Sucking in several deep breaths of air, he waited striving to remember she was unharmed. She squirmed in his arms trying to make him let go. A few seconds later, he strode along the brick walkway to the gazebo in the back of the gardens. They would have it out now.

It seemed she knew he wasn't going to set her on her feet. She didn't say a word. Instead of arguing or trying to wriggle free, Angelica buried her face in his shoulder. He felt moisture wet his shirt. Understood she was crying. Her tears were useless in this case. He made up his mind. She would have to come to terms with what he decided. In the end, she would have no say in the matter of their upcoming nuptials. As soon as he told her brother what happened between them in his stable room as well as how he felt about her, Leslie would agree with him.

Angelica had been a willing participant the night of the storm albeit an innocent. She never told him to stop. If that had been the case, he would not pursue this quite so diligently. Bottom line was he wanted her. He was going to have her. He always got what he wanted.

Loved her.

Well hell. Where did that thought come from? She would come to love him as soon as she figured out marriage to a horse breeder wasn't a fate worse than death.

In the gazebo, he sat keeping her in his arms. She tried to squirm off his lap but he held tight. "Not yet," he whispered, brushing flyaway strands of hair away from her ear. "First you have to tell me what you were doing. You've had a few minutes to think about my question and come up with some passable excuse for the reckless behavior."

Stiffening in his arms, "I had to get away from you. Didn't want to talk."

"See how far that got you. You could have put yourself as well as the baby at risk if you'd fallen." He couldn't help the last sentence, cringing as he thought about what might have happened if he had not been able to catch her. Since he'd come to know miss Angelica Louise, his thoughts had been a passel of what ifs.

"I would have landed on my feet," she protested weakly.

His smile didn't reach very far and he made sure she didn't see the smirk. She wasn't a cat. She didn't have nine lives. "You might have." He didn't have an argument for her. Anything was possible. "Why were you calling for me?" he asked realizing he didn't want to dwell on this business.

"I didn't."

"Really." One eyebrow arched. "Little liar."

"Devlin, I don't want to talk about you know what." Her voice was whisper thin, soft, compelling.

He felt a moment of pain for her. "You can't run from this, Angel. Are you increasing?"

He needed to know, wanted to begin making arrangements one way or the other. It was time for him to get on with his life. He'd had enough rusticating at Southcliff to last for several years.

For the longest time she didn't answer. He pushed hair from her face, needing to see her eyes when she told him yes or no.

When she didn't answer him, "Angel."

She pushed away from him. A stifled sob followed then a gulp of air. She coughed sucking the air into her lungs as if she was drowning. "I don't know."

"How can you not know? It's almost been three weeks." His gut turned. No woman her age could be that naïve, could she?

She lifted her tiny delicate shoulders to shrug, her face drawn tight. "I just don't."

He breathed in then again, closing his eyes before studying the tiny face in front of him, a face that was quickly becoming dearer to him than he could have ever imagined. "Why?"

"Why what?"

"Why don't you know if you are pregnant?"

She was shaking her head then, tears slipping down her cheeks. As she wiped them away with the backs of her hands, "I asked Hope. I asked her how I could tell but I still don't know."

It seemed he was missing some very intricate pieces of the puzzle. "I didn't understand a single word of what you just told me. You do know when your last woman's time was?"

She inhaled a swift deep breath of air, her face flushing a deep shade of red before she could turn away from him.

"Angel? Tell me."

"No."

"Why ever not?" His frustration never before had reached such a level where he was very nearly speechless.

There was no other way to explain it. She was holding her breath, turned away from him. He wondered if she was going to breathe anytime soon.

"Let me go. I told you I didn't want to talk with you today. I've nothing to tell you."

"Not until I get some answers." His grip tightened on her waist, his determination to get to the bottom of this problem as well as the solution growing more intense with every passing second. "I'm also not letting you run away from me or the questions."

"It's not your business." Once again red tinged her cheeks.

He didn't think her last statement warranted a reply. He saw the problem in a different perspective. This was not just about her. Whether or not he sired a child was not his business? "When did you bleed last?"

She sucked air again. In a weak voice he had to bend close to hear. "I don't know."

"What kind of an answer is that?"

"The kind that's true. I don't know. So, I can't say. That's why I don't know." Her sobs as well as the embarrassment turned to anger. She was yelling at him now.

He relished that more than when only tears streaked her face. "Calm down. Now that the question is out and I've a partial answer perhaps we can proceed in a different way. Can't say why I believe you but I do. So, I'm going to get this clear. You have no idea when you bled last."

She turned away but this time she didn't yell. Her answer was barely audible. "No."

"I always thought women kept track of their monthly flows."

She stiffened again. "I don't. Didn't."

"Perhaps you should."

"Perhaps I will in the future. Won't do me any good now."

"Maybe if we try, we can get some idea in respect to the night you came to me, the night of the tempest. Can you try to do that?"

She nodded, seeming to become a bit more agreeable. "Yes."

"Good, think back. Can you recall how many days it was before the tempest that you bled?"

He knew he was talking to an innocent. Had no idea how he would have handled things if he had a little sister but this was insane. Angelica had no clue about sex, no clue about anything concerning sex. Where the hell had her mother been when she was growing up?

Looking around the yard, Devlin was sure hours passed before she finally said something. He was cognizant of the wind as well as the ever-changing light on the leaves. He watched the squirrels and the birds. Then, "Not really sure. It might have been a week and a half to two weeks."

His heart constricted, the realization exploding in his gut. She had to be pregnant. It had been nearly five weeks since her menses. He would have a devil of a time explaining away the wedding date along with the early delivery of their child. Arrangements would have to be made and soon to rectify the situation. He decided he needed to allow her to come to the conclusion herself.

"Now," he paused, gently rubbing her back as the soothing gesture began to relax her, "that wasn't very hard. Why don't you speak with Hope again, hmm? Don't talk to anyone else. Promise me? We don't want any gossip."

She nodded, gulping air. He brushed hair from her face, his thumb lingering on her soft lips. Wanting to kiss her he decided to wait. She didn't appear receptive to him. Her face still flushed, her breathing heavy. It appeared she'd rather cosh him over the head with that tree limb she'd been dangling from than allow him one kiss.

"Angelica, listen to me. I'm going to be gone for several days. When I return, I want to see you privately. Not here, or at Southcliff. Is there anywhere we can go to decide what we're going to do with the rest of our lives? I also want you to tell Hope everything you told me. When you do that, she will help you decide if you carry my child. Will you do that?"

She nodded again. "Where are you going?"

"Nothing you need to worry about. Just know I'll be back. Now, where should we meet?" In his mind, plans were beginning to unfold at a rapid pace.

"We could go to my brother's hunting lodge or maybe Chelsea will let me use the beach house."

"Where are they?"

The hunting lodge is north of Edinburgh and the beach house is on the Firth of Clyde."

"In five days, shall we meet at the beach house?"

~ * ~

Merry stood on the balcony overlooking the Firth of Clyde. It was dusk, the sun falling beneath the horizon. Salt spray stung her nostrils as seagulls swooped then hovered on the currents of air. A myriad of silken colors spread across the sky in picturesque ribbons. She wanted to smile, needed to be happy. Truth be told she was terrified of seeing Devlin again. Placing her hand on her stomach she tried to swallow the nonexistent moisture in her throat, nearly choking in the process.

A tear slipped from her eyes as she angrily brushed it away with the back of her hand, cursing Devlin Mathews at the same time. This was not how she planned her life. She never meant to marry a horse breeder even if she did love him. The way she planned her life had been a dismal catastrophe. Thinking the Duke of Weston would be a suitable husband.

The cad.

Now this.

She wasn't going to dwell on that. As her brother would tell her, she made her bed. Now she would have to sleep in it. Still, Leslie promised albeit when she was only fifteen that he would not make her marry any man unless she wanted to even if she carried that man's child. That was when he'd been talking about the man who pursued her for her inheritance. Devlin wasn't like that. At first glance, he didn't seem to care anything about her money.

Leslie wasn't making her marry. She hadn't even told her brother about her condition. Bloody eyes, after talking to Hope and narrowing everything down she was now almost four weeks pregnant. She didn't feel anything, didn't look any different. Hope had terrible morning sickness. So much so that the butler had a bowl in every room in case she lost her breakfast. She hadn't felt even a twinge of queasiness.

Devlin would be here soon. Today was the day they agreed to talk. Although she was never sure she did any agreeing, just listening and feeling as if she had no choices left. She would have to tell him he was about to be a father. He didn't want to marry, didn't love her. She didn't want a marriage without love. He was hell bent on doing right by her.

So noble.

He would probably drag her from one stable to another all over the English and Scottish countryside while he went about his business of breeding horses. She didn't want to sleep in tiny stable rooms. Didn't want to wake up every morning in a stable as much as she loved horses. With her inheritance perhaps they could rent a room nearby his work. The scent of leather and horses, coupled with his own manly scent would always linger on his person. That would not be difficult to deal with.

She found herself shaking her head over the idea of renting a room. He would undoubtedly want to be close to the mares. He was like that, caring. Thirsty, actually needing a drink, she rummaged in Cam's stock of wine. Finding one and opening the bottle she poured herself a full glass of the red Bordeaux. Once again, she turned her attention to the ocean as well as the road leading to the house. So far, the road was empty. No one was coming. Thoughts of abandonment pulsed through her at an alarming rate.

If he hadn't changed his mind, he should be here any minute. She didn't know what to say to him having guessed he already figured it out. He must have known before her that she was pregnant.

Sipping the wine when she wanted to toss the contents down her throat then pour herself more, she stared blankly at the ocean. The colors of the sunset were dimming as the night began to grow darker. Mist from the incoming tide hitting the boulders, shot into the sky.

Where the devil was he?

Twisting her hands on the railing, she thought to go inside. Was sure now he wasn't coming. He was going to abandon her. More minutes ticked by then the sound of horse's hooves echoed across the grasses around the house. Looking down the road, she saw the rider and Windwalker. She held her breath, waiting for him, terrified yet longing to see him and feel his arms around her. A strangled breath of air rushed through her.

When he reached the house, he dismounted before tying the horse on the porch railing and vaulting inside. She could have yelled at him so he would know where she was, but no sound came from her lips. Her heart in her throat she continued to wait. For the last weeks, ever since the night of the storm, it seemed all she'd been doing was waiting. Nearly a month passed since the tempest that sent her into his bed, since she lost her virginity to a man completely unsuitable to be her husband, to the man she loved with all her heart.

Devlin was outside now, his hand to his eyes searching for her. He would have known she was at the beach house. Her things were all over the house. Perhaps he didn't know about the stargazing balcony Cam built so he could watch the stars and the planets. She tried to call out his name again. This time the wind picked up her feint words, blowing them away.

He must have noticed her, a movement of sorts. She pointed to the side of the house as she watched him race toward the stairway leading above. He stopped when he reached the top, a smile forming on his handsome face, his brilliantly blue eyes alight with a hint of amusement. Her feet wouldn't move despite the fact she wanted to race to him and throw her arms around him, feel his body flush against hers. A fading ray of sunlight caught his face as he stood on the balcony staring at her.

"You're here. Leslie told me about the balcony. I could have never guessed it was quite this seductive."

Slowly, he walked toward her, seeming to take an eternity to reach her. When he stood in front of her, his knuckles gently touched her cheek.

"Where would I be?" she questioned. "You told me to be here."

"Running from yourself. I was afraid I'd have to search for you. Couldn't believe you actually did what I asked."

"Wine?" She held up her glass, her breaths coming in ragged little gulps as her heart sped.

"Not until I have the answer I've been waiting for," he murmured, standing beside her. He clasped his hands on the railing while he ignored her to stare out at the ocean. The incoming waves crested a frothy white. She so wanted to know what he was thinking.

"I'm sure you already *ken* it." She couldn't look at him, didn't want to either. Yet she felt his heat so close to her.

"I'm sure I don't know. I have to hear it from you."

Silence hovered between them. Nothing else seemed to matter. All she could think of was the man as well as the fact she was forcing him to do something he didn't want, a marriage he never bargained for when she came to him in the middle of the night frightened by the lightning and thunder. The roar of waves crashed against the rocks as she wondered about the wisdom of waiting him out.

Finally giving up, realizing waiting for him to leave was foolish. "I'm pregnant," She suddenly blurted.

He touched her chin with a fingertip, turning her to look at him. "How far along? Were you able to figure that out too?"

He asked the question. She was also sure he already knew the answer to it. "I'm thinking nearly a month maybe more."

His nod left her wondering why even though she was sure she would discover his reasoning soon enough. He poured himself a glass of wine. Saluting her with it, he said, "We are getting married tonight. I brought you a dress to wear if you like. If not wear what you have on. I thought it would be nice if you had a wedding dress."

That was indeed thoughtful of him. She finally noticed he carried his saddlebags and that a carriage was even now pulling up in front of the house. Her heart heaved beneath her ribs. She didn't want to marry him tonight. He could have given her a little time to get used to the idea of a baby without insisting on an immediate marriage. Now she had no time to come to grips with a husband, a real husband.

"You are thoughtful indeed," she murmured trying to think of something, anything else to say to him. She looked at his saddlebag then to him, "Are you expecting me to dress up here?"

He laughed softly, touching her nose, "These are my clothes. Thought I should wear something a little finer than what I would ride a horse in. The dress is downstairs. Lucy is in the carriage along with the minister and his wife. She will help you dress."

The lump in her throat seemed to grow. No one in her family or extended family would be there to witness the hasty ceremony. She supposed it was what she deserved for her lack of moral judgment. Nodding her head, she gulped the remaining wine then started for the stairs. She stopped then to look at him, "Thank you for Lucy," she murmured then raced away from him, wishing she could continue down the road and back to France.

He would only follow.

Today was her wedding day. Leaning against the side of the house at the bottom of the steps, she closed her eyes tight as she held her breath. She didn't know what she expected after she told him. Not this.

Inside her room, someone had set out a tray of meats and cheeses another of bread. An open bottle of wine with glasses she supposed one was for Lucy on a nearby table. There were more than two glasses.

A puzzle.

Lucy hung the pure white wedding dress on the armoire. It was beautiful. She assumed Madame Chantel made it. She was sure the gown would hug her beautifully. How did he pay for it on a horse breeder's salary? Suddenly, she found she was shivering, her body trembling and she didn't understand so very much.

"You will look so beautiful in this dress," Lucy told her smoothing the skirts.

The dress was made of satin and it was very plain by the standards of the time. There was no adornment, no lace, no frills, nothing. When she put it on, the dress hugged her perfectly emphasizing every curve she possessed. She wore nothing beneath. If she did, the lines would show as the dress fit so snuggly against her. The only adornment was a row of tiny pearl buttons down the back. The neckline was scooped low, accentuating the tops of her breasts. The back molded closely against her derrière, seeming to outline every part of her.

Suddenly, Lacie burst into the room, seeming to fill it completely with her nonstop chatter. Too her surprise Lacie was followed by her sisters-in-law, Bliss, Chelsea, Hope and Daryl, Sophie too. She wasn't going to be wed alone and with no family. Merry nearly cried with joy, realizing if the women had come then Leslie was here too and maybe Link. She swallowed back the wave of moisture hovering in her throat.

"Don't cry," Lacie dabbed tears away as she grinned. "Devlin told me he doesn't want you to wear makeup but I see you have some on already. We will leave what you have, no other enhancements. Now," Lacie set a package on a nearby table before pouring herself a glass of wine as well as one for Merry. "I have a few wedding traditions for you along with this necklace Devlin would like you to wear."

While Lacy rummaged through the packages, Lucy fixed her hair arranging the locks in soft curls around her face with the bulk of her hair on top her head. The other ladies, chatted, telling her what a beautiful bride she was. Daryl poured her a second glass of wine. Merry was sure she needed it for fortitude. Yet the room seemed to spin. Suddenly, she wasn't at all sure the wine was a good idea.

"I don't know what to say. I didn't think anyone would be here. Until a few minutes ago, I didn't know I was getting married today. Thank you, all of you for coming here. I know it couldn't have been easy."

"Devlin went to Leslie and asked for your hand in marriage. He told him it was the proper thing to do. You should have a proper wedding also." Lacy looked as if she wanted answers. "Leslie might know why the sudden haste but I can only guess. Care to tell me?"

"Tell all of us."

Hope blushed but kept her lips sealed when Merry cast her gaze in that direction, a warning in her eyes.

"Leslie wouldn't say?" Merry plucked at her skirts putting little creases in the fabric. "I'm not going to either. It's between Devlin and me. He felt it was most urgent."

"No, you just stop that fiddling, Miss Merry," Lucy told her brushing her hand away from the fabric. "You don't want to ruin this perfect dress before the wedding takes place. As to answering all the questions, you don't have to do that either. They are all just curious. That's all."

"No, he didn't tell me," Lacie said sounding a bit annoyed. "But I'm sure he approves, haste and all. Devlin said in a month or two there would be a celebration of the wedding. That's all I know about any of this. Now," Lacie held up a necklace of diamonds and sapphires. There were eight small daisies. Each daisy was fashioned with one sapphire surrounded by six diamonds. The chain was fashioned from white gold. It was delicate, almost fragile looking. "He wants you to wear this and to know this is a wedding gift from him as well as something new for you to wear. If no one else brought something blue it will do for that as well. He said he had the piece fashioned especially for you. It's exquisite just as you are."

Merry found herself backing up, her hands extended. This was all happening way too fast. "No, I can't except this. He can't afford..." her voice trailed away as her stomach knotted. She never wanted expensive gifts, especially ones that would put him in debt.

"Devlin told me he thought you would say as much. He wants me to reassure you that as a bachelor, he never had time to spend most of his earning from horse breeding. He also made a lot of money at the racetrack betting on his horses as well as other investments."

He was a gambling man? Merry nearly panicked at that thought. What if he gambled all his money as well as hers away? "I can't wear that." She was shaking her head backing away all the while pointing at the piece of jewelry Lacie was holding out.

"Nonsense," Lacie said smiling as she stepped closer. "Wear it then convince him to sell it or return it. We both know the money could be spent in a better way. Don't we? Don't put a damper on your wedding day by insulting your new husband with your refusal."

Merry thought Lacie might have a good point. She let her fasten the necklace. "It is beautiful."

Hope handed her a small handkerchief she could place between her breasts for something borrowed. Bliss gave her one blue garter to replace one of the white ones that would hold up her up her silk stockings.

"Now, all we need to finish here are your shoes and stockings. He did want you to wear these sheer white stocking with the white garters as well as these white slippers. You are beautiful, Merry. Are you ready to say your vows and become Devlin's wife? If not, you only have a few minutes to change your mind."

She heaved in a full draught of air before nodding her head, as it seemed the room turned. "As ready as I'll ever be."

"Leslie is waiting to give you away. Link is upstairs as best man. I'll be your matron of honor. I'm going to leave you here. Follow in about two minutes. Your sisters as well as their husbands will be witnesses."

As Lacie and the others left the room, Lucy adorned her hair with a few flowers brought along with her then handed her a beautiful bouquet of white daisies. For a moment she thought she might be sick. That was all she needed was to get sick on her wedding day.

When she opened the door, Leslie waited for her, his hands

clasped behind his back, a grin on his face. She wondered if he was truly pleased, she was marrying a horse breeder combined with the notion her brother gave his permission without asking how she felt. In any case, none of that made a difference now. Devlin was determined nothing would stand in the way of this marriage. He had been resolute in this from the night of the storm, even though the courtship had been nonexistent at best.

He held out his arm for her, "You ready, Brat?"

She cringed at his pet name for her but nodded, accepting his arm. Lucy followed behind holding the train of her gown from the floor. By the time they reached the balcony overlooking the ocean, she thought surely she could not take another step, her body shaking violently. She wasn't sure her knees would continue to hold her up.

When she saw Devlin standing by the preacher, Link on the other side, her heart stopped for a second. In his waistcoat and perfectly shined hessians, Devlin looked like a noble. His cravat was snowy white and perfectly tied, the material expensive. She always took Leslie's appearance for granted but not Devlin's. His shoulders seemed broader his legs longer than she ever noticed before. The heat of his eyes as he stared at her reached all the way to her soul. She understood there was no turning back.

She was going to be his wife. What lay in store for her she didn't know because she was beginning to believe she really didn't know him at all? She wondered if he had family. He never spoke of anyone he might be close to.

Leslie paused at the top as if he understood she needed time to compose herself. She gripped her bouquet tighter than she thought possible. She swallowed hard hoping for courage as she looked from Devlin to her brother then back again.

"It's okay. You're going to be just fine. Devlin will be a good husband. Trust me in that. I couldn't have chosen a better man for you," Leslie whispered close to her ear.

She nodded, swallowing the fear rising in her throat, trying to believe her brother along with the fact he just told her that he had her best interests at heart. Slowly, they began the march toward the minister and her husband to be.

The time seemed to last an eternity while she listened and responded in all the proper places. Before she knew it, a beautiful sapphire ring was on her finger and Devlin held her in his arms, kissing her passionately. She thought he would just brush her lips lightly with his own. Instead, he parted her mouth, seemed to touch every single dark crevice within until she was breathless and needed his arms around her to stand. All she could think of was the way her naked flesh would feel against his tonight after they were alone.

Leslie popped the cork on a bottle of champagne, bubbles overflowing. After pouring everyone a glass, he held his high. "Here's to our newlyweds. May they have a long happy life with lots of children."

Merry was sure if she had liquid in her mouth, she would have embarrassed herself and spewed it all over Devlin. He slanted her a mocking, all-knowing look after the toast. Gingerly, she sipped, her gaze riveted on her new husband. His eyes sparkled with amusement as he returned her regard. Quickly, she looked away not wanting him to see her humiliation or perhaps embarrassment that Leslie might have guessed at her condition.

The unborn babe was between the two of them, no one else needed to know. In about eight months all would know the reason for the hasty marriage.

Link gave her a quick hug as did Sophie, his wife, "Congratulations, Merry. I'm sure you'll be happy. He looks like a fine man," Sophie told her sincerely.

"Behave yourself, Brat," Link tweaked her nose before giving her a quick kiss on the forehead.

The others congratulated her, giving her hugs and wishing her the best. She felt as if she was living in a dream world. If she blinked, she was afraid all would disappear. She'd be left alone again.

The wine and the food flowed. More servants than she could count seemed to come and go constantly refilling and exchanging the various trays. Thankfully, Devlin didn't hire musicians. She cringed at the additional costs. She needed to tell herself this was not her concern. If it had been Leslie who paid for this, she would have no cares.

The minister brought them the papers to sign. They both wrote out their names. It seemed to take Devlin an inordinately long time to sign. When she looked at the lengthy signature, she bent for a closer look but the papers were whisked away before she could read what he wrote.

One more thing to wonder about.

The lanterns surrounding the balcony were aglow with light. The evening was growing darker. A bold, silvery moon shone in a cloudless sky. Sometime when she wasn't looking, more food and wine had been brought upstairs. It seemed a veritable armada of servants were rushing around downstairs as well as on the balcony to see to their needs.

Leslie and Link must have had more to do with this than she previously assumed. Once again, her fears of Devlin overspending rushed through her in a raging current of doubt. He had to learn to be careful with his money. When she looked around, no one else seemed concern. She assured herself once more, Leslie must have paid for this celebration of their wedding. It was his place to do so since she was the bride and the bride's family usually paid for these things. That still didn't explain the costly necklace and ring. She stared at the ring. The sapphire was huge, diamonds surrounding it. She didn't need a ring or if she did a simple gold band would suffice. She would have to talk to him about her feelings, let him know she didn't need costly jewelry or anything expensive. Simple things had always been fine by her standards.

"How are you doing?" Lacie stood by her side, slanting her a puzzled look. "You look awfully pale."

"Just worried about so many things. Please tell me Leslie paid for all this." She waved her hand around the balcony taking in everything. By the look on Lacie's face even before she had a chance to answer, Merry knew the stark truth.

Lacie shook her head in apparent confusion, her features schooled as if she sought to answer her in a way that would alleviate her worst fears. "Neither Leslie or Link spent any money on your wedding, including that beautiful dress you're wearing. It's so unique. I've never seen anything like it. The gown looks as if it was painted on you. Only a man would have ever designed something like this for his appreciation. I didn't realize Devlin had such amazing taste in women's fashion."

Merry felt her stomach roll with unease. She wiped sweaty hands down the length of her dress. Needing some reassurances, she looked for Devlin who was talking with Leslie. Deciding she should wait until all left before she confronted him, she grabbed another glass of champagne.

Before she could accomplish what she set out to do, Devlin was beside her, holding her elbow and smiling down at her. "How are you, Mrs. Mathews?" he queried softly his lips brushing lightly against her cheek. "Are you ready for the wedding night?"

Merry had been so concerned about the money spent on this affair she forgot about the night to come. He would expect her to be more at ease with him she supposed. Thinking of his body pressed against her, her nerves kicked in. She didn't know if her body was responding to fear or passion.

"Nervous," she murmured as she leaned into him. "Very nervous."

"You don't need to be." He bent, whispering close to her ear. "It's not as if you're a virgin. Not as if we haven't known each other intimately. I've kissed and touched every part of you."

She jerked in his arms at the implication of his words. Turning from him she waited trying to think of some reply. Until this moment everything seemed to be going well. "You don't have to be rude."

"One should never overlook the truth." Possessively, he pulled her close, wrapping his arm around her waist. "I did not mean to be rude, just stating the facts and reminding my new bride. I can't wait for everyone to leave."

In his arms she stiffened, "They will all be downstairs, below us. They will know. You can't possibly expect me to..."

"Of course I will. Now, it's too bad I couldn't find musicians on such short notice. I would love to dance with my wife. Perhaps when we celebrate our nuptials with my family and friends, we will have music."

~ * ~

Downstairs after the cake cutting everyone sensed the couple wanted time alone. After Devlin led Merry outside then upstairs, Leslie brought his wife into their room. He pulled Lacie into his arms for a tender kiss. He turned her, deftly unfastening her gown. As he let it slide to the floor his hands cupped her breasts, thumbs stroking the tight hard buds he loved so well.

"Leslie, I need to talk to you."

She was sighing softly leaning into him as he intended.

The last of his intentions right now was talk. "Hmm...later. We can talk as soon as..."

She pulled away from him. He allowed it knowing the questions simmering in his wife's head were put there by Merry. He expelled a heavy breath of air, resigned to this.

"No, I want to talk now." Her hands were on her hips, her breasts pushing from the corset she wore.

He groaned wishing he could convince her to talk later. "Very well."

He sat on the bed, slipping off his boots then shrugging out of his shirt.

"Who is Devlin Mathews?"

The question certainly didn't surprise him. He had a hard time keeping secrets from his wife. This was one he promised not to divulge until Devlin gave him the go ahead. So far that had not happened. Leslie assumed it would be long past the wedding night before Devlin would want anyone to know. A few days of wedded bliss would be appreciated, he was sure.

Another heavy breath of air rushed out. "I can't say. At least not until Devlin tells me it's all right. I don't like keeping things from you. Honestly, you have to understand this is not my choice."

"You know he's not who he is pretending to be." She accused him stepping forward, lightly touching his lower lip, enticing, flirting. She lowered her lashes provocatively. When she looked at him again, "This can't be good for Merry. Don't you think she deserves to know who her husband is?"

Leslie patted a place beside him on the bed, wishing she would forget. "I know he is a horse breeder," he told her honestly. "What else he is, I'm not at liberty to say. It's not a bad thing. It's just that, well..." he paused trying to clarify his thoughts, placing Lacie's hand in his, continuing the seduction she began. "Devlin has burned a few bridges since he met Merry. She won't be pleased to discover the truth about him. In the end though, once she adjusts, she will be happy."

"Merry is worried about the money he spent tonight. Should she be? That gown was not inexpensive and the necklace must have cost a small fortune. It's something you could afford but Devlin?" In question, she arched a perfectly shaped eyebrow.

"All true," Leslie said with a masculine grin he hoped would coax his wife to forego more questions.

His knuckles brushed the top of her breasts. He delighted in the tiny sound of pleasure he created with the simple gesture. Quickly, he kissed her, parted her lips with his, explored and delved the soft intimate recesses.

Having nothing to do with his advances for the moment, she pulled away. "Did you see just how long it took him to write out his name?" Her eyes blinked a few times. Then, "He's a lord of some sort, isn't he? Just like you he has at least a hundred names."

Leslie schooled his features, unwilling to confirm or deny Lacie's sudden conclusion. With more indignation in his tone, he said, "Lacie, please. You're putting me in an uncomfortable position. One I'd rather not be in right now when all I want to do is love you. Can't you just let it go for now and make love to your husband? I've been looking at the tops of your breasts all night and I'm dying to taste them, stroke your silken flesh. I've been a patient man."

He was close enough to reach out to her. He wasn't going to deny himself a moment longer deciding tonight might be as good a time as any to begin working on another child.

He pulled her close, spreading his legs so she stood between them her hands resting on his shoulders. Her breasts were eye level, just where he wanted them. Expertly he loosened her corset, letting it fall to the rug below. A few more seconds and her petticoats joined the rest of her clothing on the floor. His lips closed over a veiled nipple. Once more a tiny mew of pleasure rippled from her throat.

"You don't play fair, Leslie Stewart."

"Never intended to."

Chapter Eight

Devlin didn't think Angelica had ever appeared more beautiful than she did tonight. The wedding gown he had fashioned for her was everything he wanted it to be. His only regret was that he wasn't the only one to see her wearing it. Just looking at her caused every muscle and sinew of his body to harden with need. Lightning bolts shooting through him could not have aroused and tempted him more thoroughly than the sight of his wife in the form-fitting gown.

Ever since that night four weeks ago, he'd wanted her with a hunger, a pulsing throbbing need he didn't understand. She provoked thoughts that had never crossed his mind. Until his angel came into his life, he'd never felt this kind of passion or hunger for a woman. He'd been a saint to wait so long to taste her, to feel her move beneath him, arch her back to press closer to him. If the tempest had not arrived when it did, they might not be wed now. If he were true to himself, he would admit he wanted her from the first time he saw her.

He knew she was worried about the expense of the wedding. Would undoubtedly press him for answers, for information he wasn't ready to divulge. She needn't worry about money though. He possessed more than he could spend in a lifetime, was making more as they stood on the balcony watching the ocean blast the rocks below. He wasn't going to explain anything tonight. For tonight all he wanted was peace and loving between them, passion and desire that would result in another tempest of craving that would burn them alive. He knew how easily one look from her exotic blue eyes inflamed his passion for her. He knew how they darkened when he pleasured her.

If he told her the truth about him, he had every reason to believe she would be angry with him for the deception, furiously so. He only hoped that when the information was revealed she would listen to his explanation. Knowing his angel, she would react first and listen later.

Not tonight.

This evening there would be nothing but magic and passion between them. The enchantment building with the heated looks they cast toward each other.

And the fire.

Tonight, the scent of lavender swirled around her, encompassed her hair as well as her body. She would taste of the sweet Sauterne she drank. He'd already tasted the icing from the cake on her moist lips. Leslie's contribution to the wedding was a case of Sauterne as well as one of Bordeaux. Devlin had no doubts the couples downstairs were enjoying his hospitality as well as Stewart wine.

"You're not afraid, are you?"

Slowly he undid the pins from her hair letting the ebony waves fall to her waist. He ran his fingers through the length, feeling the heat, the sweet fire of the silken locks. A ragged pulse beat in his groin as well as in his mind. The thunder ragged throughout his fingers in his limbs and in all of his body.

She turned to him, her small sweet tongue tracing a path across her lips, one he would mimic soon. "I'm nervous. We've only done this once. It seems so long ago."

"Twice," he corrected searching through his mind for the right words. From his experiences, there were most likely no right things to say. "There should be no virgin's fears tonight. Nothing to frighten you." Her waist was small, her hips flaring beautifully, her legs were long. He remembered them as they wrapped around him in her throes of passion, the way her body trembled when she reached the crescendo of their lovemaking.

He could not tell her how he felt about her, could not leave himself vulnerable. Once before, he laid everything on the line. Had been betrayed, vowing then he would never give a woman that type of ammunition to hold over him.

"Twice," she murmured, turning her face to look at him, running her finger along his bottom lip.

"Your nerves have vanished or were they ever there in the first place?" he asked, his thoughts alive with amusement. She would always puzzle him, confuse and bedevil, an enigma in his brain. He wanted the nerves gone. He didn't care if they'd been an act in the first place.

He ran his hands along her sides, traveling across her hips to move to her back, keeping them placed on her rear. Squeezing, he felt her move against him. She would feel his sex. There was little between her and his pulsing rod, only a thin layer of bridal satin then his pants.

Tonight, he wanted to take his time, needed her to be so hungry for him she would beg. He meant to tease her until she could think of nothing else except the length of him inside her. He wanted to bury himself in her velvet warmth, becoming one with her, a part of her.

Letting her go for the moment, he walked away. Poured each another glass of champagne. A bottle of Sauterne was chilling in a bucket of ice brought up from the ice house. When he reached her side, he placed his hand in hers then drew her to the railing to watch the stars and the moon. A slight breeze ruffled her hair, sending silken strands against his face and hands.

"Drink up," he murmured hoping she would relax completely in his arms this evening. He wondered if making love to a wife was very different than making love with any woman. "We've another bottle waiting for us. We have all night, you know."

They both sipped the champagne as she leaned into him. His hand for a time was settled on her hip. He couldn't resist the sirens call of her slender body against the hardness of his larger one. Slowly, he ran his hand along her delicately feminine form until he cupped her breast in his hand. Only one layer of fabric separated them. Her nipple pushed hard and erect against the satin of her gown. It was so simple and nearly sheer. The gown might have passed for provocative lingerie only it wasn't. The dressmaker had done an excellent job. Expertly fashioned, the gown concealed as well as revealed.

A sudden intake of breath on her part was his reward for the subtle play of his fingers. With only one layer of fabric between them, he stroked the taut peak of her breast, toyed and tantalized. Her hand holding her champagne trembled yet she didn't set it down but continued to sip the drink. He released her breast, exploring her side again, stopping at her hip.

"Are you cold?" he asked as he still felt the shivering of her body against his, hoped it was from the gentle coaxing of his hand and fingers.

"You make me hot. So hot I can barely breathe," she whispered then shivered anew as he pushed her hair aside and his teeth grazed her neck.

"That was my intention," he murmured, sipping her flesh, nipping and teasing. He finished his glass then set it on the table. "We could go for a ride. I noticed a place where we could spread a blanket and make love with the waves crashing around us."

"In the sand?" She sounded appalled by his idea.

He laughed. "What, you don't like sand?" He set her empty glass beside his before turning her in his arms. "Perhaps tomorrow then. A ride in the morning, make sweet tender love on the beach where no one can find us."

His lips found hers, parted them, bathing them with his tongue before exploring the dark softness within. She was pliable in his hands, her curves molding hot and provocative against him. He felt her swelled breasts against his chest and nearly growled with delight. Yet he wanted to prolong this joining for as long as possible.

He could not keep his eyes from hers watching her all the while. She didn't close her eyes. That pleased him. It seemed she returned his gaze with heat and passion, hunger too. He wondered how he'd ever lived without her. How he waited so long to touch her, hold her in his arms, make love to her. What happened between them that lead to this had not been planned, he reminded himself. He'd done everything in his power to stay away from her. Told himself he should not touch her. It would be folly to give in to his hunger.

Here they were. It was not idiocy. Marriage to Angelica was the rightest thing he'd ever done. He'd been a fool for waiting so long.

"Sand can end up in all the wrong places," she told him her voice soft, whispery in the silver moonlight that played against the whiteness of her flesh.

He chuckled at her words knowing them to be true. "Maybe tomorrow. We have all day, you know. The others will leave in the morning. Before the dawn, I hope."

She turned in his arms. Her hands clasped around his neck, fingers playing with his hair. He bent low to kiss her again, to touch inside her and feel her warmth. She did want him. He needed her love. He was afraid she would always feel as if she did not have a choice in this marriage.

She didn't.

The only choice was to wed him. He would never have accepted anything less.

He poured them both some wine then taking her hand in his, he led her to the huge bed and silently thanked Cam for his foresight, for the lover's retreat, wondering how many women had been seduced here into their lover's waiting arms.

The number didn't matter. The only woman he cared about seducing here was in his arms. He turned her so her back was to him, undoing the first of many pearl buttons. When he ordered this, he had in mind kissing each uncovered portion of her skin one fastener at a time.

One button, one kiss, one nip before he trailed kisses along her neck to find her ear. He worried the tender lobe with his teeth, his palm flat surrounding the tip of her breast then the other one. Tiny sounds of pleasure rippled through her in hungry waves of desire. Handing her glass to her he bade her drink again.

"Devlin..."

His name on her lips was pure heaven the sigh afterward telling him his persuasive sweet-talking was working well.

He wanted to hear the sounds over and over again tonight and every time they made love. His teeth closed gently on her lower lip, tugged softly before letting her go. Her back was to him again.

Two buttons, two kisses, two nips this time he followed with a third and fourth button. More tender kisses, enticements. Her shivers followed the passage of his kisses.

"*S'il te plait*, Devlin," she murmured in her native language, softly as she tried to turn in his arms.

He would have none of it.

Tonight, would be his way. "My way, Angel, my rules."

A portion of her back was visible. Her flesh was perfect, white, silken to his touch, more tantalizing than the satin her gown was made from. The scent of lavender filled him. Lord, but if this was torture to her it was sheer hell to him. He wanted tonight to be remembered by her forever.

He ran his hands along the satin of her arms. Here too the material was a perfect match for her body. She set the back of her head against his shoulders, bearing her neck to his kisses, the potent coaxing of his lips, the erotic stroking of his tongue, the heady enticing of his teeth.

More pearls were undone down her back. He was nearly at her small waist. He pushed the fabric from her shoulders, once again exploring her softness. His arousal was hard, thrusting against his pants. Quickly, he untied his neckcloth tossing it on the ground.

His throat was parched, his body on fire yet he still needed to seduce and coax, sweet-talk and charm with all the persuasive powers within. He found her glass, holding it to her lips until she drank then he sipped the wine. Sliding the gown down her arms until her breasts were bared and free from restraints, he watched, mesmerized. Her skin was as white as her gown but her aureoles were rosy, the tips a dark pink.

"You are so beautiful."

Slowly, keeping his gaze riveted on her, he sipped one breast, the taste exquisite reminding him of strawberries and cream. With the sensual touch she cried out, whimpering with her mounting need. He looked up grinning at her, knowing the passion simmering within was building. He wanted her to be desperate, hungry with her desire. He needed her to want him as much as he needed her.

"Please, Devlin," she sighed softly, her voice whisper thin a tiny mewling sound emanating from the back of her throat. Her hands were imprisoned at her sides.

He understood she wanted to touch to stroke him. He couldn't allow that, not yet. She would have to wait until he decided she was ready for him. He sucked her other breast deep into his mouth. They were soft and firm, potently arousing. He grazed his tongue around the tip as she tossed her head back. Moving from one breast to the other, he paused to watch her eyes but she closed them.

"Open your eyes, sweet angel," he said as he bit gently.

Her eyes were open now, wide and so very dark, a blue, passion simmering in silver waves as the light from the moon seemed to reflect from them. The beautiful flush of rose came to her cheeks as his fingertips trailed up the naked flesh of her back.

He paused to memorize the way she appeared flushed and wanton, a woman desperate in her passion and desire. Her thirst and hunger were for him, only him. He turned her again so his lips trailed the length of her spine to her waist. The dress open, nearly uncovering all of her back, he continued his onslaught with her buttons until the last pearl was unfastened. Still the gown clung to her curves, held tight by the sleeves.

Her buttocks were round and smooth. The muscles firm, the flesh soft, silken to his touch. When his teeth grazed her, she quivered, her body trembling. She sank against him no longer able to stand on her own. Lifting her, he brought her to the bed. Laid her upon the covers with gentle care before coming down beside her.

Devlin straddled her then, drawing the sleeves one by one from her arms. He lifted a hand, kissed the palm then bit gently on each fingertip. He did the same with her other hand.

When he let go, her hands moved upward to his shoulders, her fingers clutching him. "It's not fair you are still dressed."

"As you are," he chuckled softly. He allowed her to unfasten his shirt until the front hung open. She stroked his chest, her fingers caressing, stopping to splay her hands across his tight nipples.

He created a desperate hunger in her but none so great as the thirst and desire she created in him. He moved upward seizing her lips again, kissing her until her breaths came raggedly and her breasts rose and fell heatedly in his hands, until she quivered wherever he touched her. He lowered himself against her, near blinded by his need. The tips of her breasts touched upon his chest. She was still clothed, too much so.

Devlin moved back, his fingers between her belly and the gown. At his touch, she gasped in a sharp breath of air. He rose from her enough so he could strip her of the remaining fabric. In the moonlight, her alabaster skin reflected the silver beams from the moon. His hands were dark next to her, his skin bronzed from the time he spent outside. The contrast struck him with awe and reverence, reminding him of the amazingly dramatic differences between the two of them.

Slowly, he slipped the gown from her. Her hips flared from a tiny waist, her legs were long and the ebony nest of hair at the apex of her thighs was damp with her honey. He rose from her, folding the gown and putting it in a trunk. Quickly, he divested himself of his clothing, letting everything fall haphazardly on the floor near the bed.

She watched him, her eyes wide. He touched one foot, placing a tender kiss on the bottom before kissing and nipping his way up her leg, stopping at her knee then repeating the process with the other leg. He moved higher, kissed her inner thighs, stroked her legs then rose to dip his tongue into her bellybutton before feathering kisses across her belly and lower. Her fingers dug into his hair as her hips arched to meet him. He stroked, kissed, touched every part of her, leaving nothing unclaimed.

"Are you hungry, sweet Angel?" he asked as his mouth explored her intimately, touched and caressed the velvet bud as he watched her hips move in response. "I need you very hungry. Hungry for me."

She cried out for him but didn't seem to be able to answer. Small whimpers escalated into harsher cries of passion and desire. He slipped a finger inside, feeling the moist cream within along with the clenching of her velvet damp walls around him welcoming him.

He withdrew his finger then carefully lowered himself over her and pushed within. She was arching, anticipating what she knew would come. Her eyes were wide, staring at him. Her hips were moving, bringing him deeper inside, so deep he touched her womb. She was still small, still innocent and he vowed to be careful, not to hurt her yet she was so very hot, wet, enticing him deeper while her body pulsed around him.

Devlin caught hold of her chin. Her eyes widened, so large and dark with passion, then they fluttered closed again as he kissed her lips and caressed her with long slow leisurely strokes—taking all of her mouth, exploring, tasting, savoring. As he kissed her, he began to move within her, strokes as soft as velvet, slow and evocative, coercive. It was enchanting, magical and he didn't think he could ever get enough of her, of loving her. She was his now, despite all her protests and the weeks of elusiveness.

She was his.

Her long enchanting legs wound tightly around his hips, bringing him ever deeper. Her fingertips grazed his shoulders, the nails lightly creasing his skin. Continuous soft sounds of passion rippled from her in enchanting ribbons. He thrust hard then releasing the hunger that had grown and simmered and become explosive within him. While he moved, found the driving force to reach the culmination he sought, he whispered words to her, reassuring words, words that truly meant nothing, lover's words. Their lips met again and again, fused and sealed as did their bodies. He fought the climax that would soon explode from him, fought it until he felt the tremors that would consume her body taking her ever higher.

Then he felt it.

Felt the stiffening of her body just before she trembled beneath him in huge, violent shudders that seemed to go on and on. Spasms of pleasure flowed from her into him, giving him consent to find his release.

He cast back his head. He felt a groan rumbling in the back of his throat just as the heat and fever and excitement within him drew to a massive pitch. The sound escaped him, the life and energy and heat of his body shot from him, filling her. Again, and again shudders seized him, traveled into her, filled her. He gave a last shudder then wrapped his arms around her, held her very tightly, cherished her. After several seconds, he eased off her, removing his weight from her all the while keeping his arms around her so she fell atop him.

She sighed softly, her breath floating warmly across his chest. Damp tendrils of her hair curled around him. He touched them. Wound them around his fingers, remembering how once before they felt against his skin.

Like silk... They felt like...silk. She felt like silk, her body so slick with all that had been between them. Her face lay against his chest, her fingers roaming across his body. She still struggled for air as he felt the still pounding rhythm of her heart.

For minutes they lay together, stroking each other softly, enjoying the moment. Cherishing her, he ran his fingers along her arm, absently wondering if there was anything so beautiful in life than what they just did together.

"Are you hungry or thirsty?" He brushed damp hair from her face, touched the tip of her nose. "I'm parched but I doubt if I could eat anything."

He pulled her to a sitting position, placed a pillow behind her before gently touching the tip of her breast to watch it come to a tight little bud again. He was jaded. Had slept with too many women to count. This was all new to him.

The tray of food was close by so he drew it to the bed. She sat up cross-legged, the sheet wrapped around her breasts, secured beneath her arms and sampled a piece of cheese and bread. He poured them each another glass of Sauterne. She cleared her throat, looking at him and he was sure she was about to ask questions he didn't want to answer. He didn't want to answer anything, wanted to continue with the magic and enchantment of the night.

~ * ~

He leaned back, closing his eyes, his hands behind his head. To Merry he looked pleased with himself, content, a man well satisfied with himself and the world. It seemed he was putting something off, probably her questions. She was surprised when he changed his position, fixing himself a snack then sipping the wine, expecting her to do the same.

She listened to the crashing of the waves to the west. It was dark now, the moon hanging low in the sky, stars twinkling on the black velvet of the night. When she looked at him, he was staring at her, a crooked smile of amusement painting his handsome face. She didn't know if he was mocking her or anticipating the questions yet to come.

Devlin was patiently waiting for her to say something, she was sure. She didn't want to change the mood of the moment, knowing her inquiries would most likely do that. With wisdom Merry didn't credit her maid with, Lucy did tell her she should not embarrass her groom on the wedding night by speaking of money. Women were not supposed to be concerned with financial situations. It was just that she had so many unanswered questions. He spent so much money, money she didn't think he possessed.

Merry had never been known for her patience, waiting was not in her blood. She was curious. She needed her curiosity assuaged. When she wanted something, well, she usually went after it with a vengeance. She understood that was not something she should do now.

Still...

"Devlin?" she began as she sampled the small bites of the cheese she picked up to help her over her nerves.

Nervous energy, that was what she told herself this was. If she didn't say something soon, she'd be a bundle of ragged anxieties ready to explode.

The breath she inhaled was ragged and weak, her heart pounding nearly as fast as it had when he was deep inside her. It wasn't what she needed to fill her lungs.

"What?" he asked as he ran a fingertip along her spine then back to her neck. "I was going to look and see if you had two little dimples at the base of your spine. I forgot. Suppose it will have to wait until next time. There will be a next time. Tonight, as a matter of fact. In the morning. Tomorrow afternoon."

Inhaling sharply, she guessed as much. For now, she didn't want to tell him what the 'what' was she had in mind. Finding out how he could afford the gown, the necklace, the ring the food. In addition, where had all the servants come from was uppermost in her head.

"Okay, Brat," he grinned knowingly. "I'll allow you one question then it will be my turn to ask something. Of course, I'll want a kiss or two in between."

"Promise you'll answer honestly and not prevaricate?" she asked, wondering which one of the myriad of questions she would present him with that were circling in her head.

"I won't evade your question if that's what you're asking me. I'll answer to the best of my meager knowledge. I am going to stipulate though if it has been asked previously, you will have to think of something else to query me about. Either that or you will forfeit a question."

She closed her eyes seeing the hands on a clock slowly tick by as she tried to make up her mind. One question, how could she ever decide? There were so many. "I'm not sure where to start," she finally murmured.

"I would tell you at the beginning. However, I'm not sure that is what's on your mind."

He picked up a lock of her hair, rubbing it between his fingers before bringing it to his cheek.

For fortitude, she downed the wine left in her glass closing her eyes while she did. "I'm going to tell you a few things before I ask my question."

"Yes?"

He cocked a dark brow in a perfect arch his grin still filled with amusement, his eyes seeming to focus on her mouth.

At his not-so-subtle suggestion, she passed her tongue across her lips. "I don't like being called Brat and my name is Merry not Angelica. No one calls me Angelica, not even my mother who named me." She let the air she'd been holding out in a satisfied whoosh before she looked to Devlin who was still grinning.

"Hmm... I like your given name, Angelica Louise. Merry is a pet name given to you by your brothers, I assume. I don't like it. I'm not going to call you Merry because as I see you the name doesn't suit. As for brat..." There was a long pause and a slight lifting of his shoulders before he finished his thoughts. "I call it as I see it."

"So, you won't change."

Of course, you ninny. You knew it before you told him. Devlin Mathews changes for no man or woman.

I could hope. I don't like the name Angelica. No one calls me that.

I suppose you could hope. Maybe he wants to call you Angelica because no one else does. By the way, why haven't you talked to me for a while?

I didn't have anything useful to say.

Oh.

"So," she paused for a few more seconds, "since I can't change that, I want to know why it took you so long to write your name on the marriage certificate. There were almost a hundred names."

He grinned and with a soft chuckle. "That's an exaggeration."

"People just don't have that many names. My brother does but he's a duke. He has to have that many names." Her gaze rose to meet his, the question challenging him. She didn't like the tenor of her thoughts. Truly did hope he would appease her worries with a reasonable explanation. "Why so many names?"

He popped a piece of cheese in his mouth before sipping the Sauterne. With a soft chuckle and a wry smile, "My mother couldn't make up her mind. Then my grandmother wanted to put in her wishes so my mother gave up and named me for everyone's suggestions. She didn't have the heart to disappoint. Hence, nearly one hundred names."

"Your mother. You never..."

He placed a finger on her lips. "One question at a time. Now it's my turn. Don't you think? Hmm...what should I ask you?"

"I'm an open book. You know everything about me." He actually did know everything.

"Why did you let me make love to you that night a month ago?" His voice was deep, throaty his look of amusement vanishing.

She guessed he was wondering if she thought to trap him into marriage. Her spine stiffened, the mood changing. "I..." She cleared her throat trying to speak, to tell him it wasn't what he was thinking.

"You what?" He caught her chin between his fingers, forcing her to meet his gaze, challenging her.

"I don't see how you can ask that. You sweet-talked me. Caressed parts of me I didn't know existed until then. I couldn't breathe. I couldn't think. How could I have ever told you to stop? I didn't even think to say the words because my brain was mindless, filled with nothingness. I had no thoughts except what you were so expertly doing to me."

"It was my fault then."

She thought perhaps he was leading her and didn't like it. "No. I promised I would tell you when to stop. Everything happened so fast and was so..." she couldn't think of the right words. "Magical maybe?"

"You never spoke the words," he prompted gently. "Did you know I felt the same way you just said you were feeling? A brain filled with nothing?"

"But you're experienced." She countered unwilling to except all of the blame. "What are you getting at?"

"Ah, is that a second question?"

"No. I already think I know the answer to that." She wasn't enjoying this game of question and answer he was playing with her. Answering his questions was not comfortable.

He bent to kiss her again, sipped gently on her lower lip. Kissed her thoroughly and deeply, his hand on her now bared breast, moving lower to flick the tip with his tongue across the tight bud before he kissed her again. Pulling away, he handed her the glass of wine she'd been drinking before leaning against the headboard again.

"What's your next question?"

His voice took on a harsh note. Clearly, he didn't like this game either. Still, he seemed determined to carry through with what they started.

"This isn't a question. I just want you to understand a simple gold band would have been good enough for me. I don't need an expensive wedding ring."

She hoped he'd be pleased when she told him she didn't care about the jewelry, but his brows creased together, the lines of his mouth harsh. He was clearly not pleased.

"You don't like sapphires? I can get you something else," he said, holding her hand while he stared at the ring then her.

"That's just the point, well, not exactly the point. The ring and the necklace are beautiful. I've never owned anything so expensive or... I don't have the words to describe them. I'm just trying to tell you I don't need expensive things. I'm a very simple person."

"Even if I want to give them to you?" he asked. "That's not my question either."

It's more of a question than my questions that weren't supposed to be questions.

Do you really want to argue with him?

No, arguing was never my intent. Finding out the truth is.

You're not very subtle about it.

Perhaps that's why he looks so angry.

Perhaps it is.

She looked away, wishing she had something to wear. Standing at the railing looking at the waves crash against the rocks would be preferable to sitting naked in the bed with this man sparring about things that were incomprehensible to her.

Sucking in a huge expanse of air. "I don't want you to give expensive things to me."

"It pleases me to do so."

"You can't afford it." She spit it out now.

He would retaliate if she guessed right about the expression on his face.

"I assure you I can."

This isn't getting us anywhere. Mayhap you should ask a question instead of arguing with your husband about something you don't understand Maybe horse breeders, good ones make a lot of money.

"I understand you spent a great deal of money on a wedding. None of this was necessary." Her hands were fiddling with the clasp of the necklace intending to take it off. When Devlin undressed her, he left the jewelry around her neck.

"No." His hands stopped her, brought hers down. "You will leave it where it is. It is yours. Forever. I enjoy seeing it on you, with clothing or without."

Defeated, she leaned back, resting against the pillows he so thoughtfully gave her when they first started this discussion. She didn't know what else she could say. He was impractical. All she needed was his love, not things.

Then you should tell him that. The sooner the better. He'll like what you have to say if you say it that way.

Not until he tells me he loves me.

Doesn't seem like you're telling him you love him.

He'll make assumptions.

Ah, yes, he probably will and would that be so bad?

Yes.

"Then," she paused, "since you don't want to talk about money, where are you taking me?"

He laughed softly, "It's about time you asked a question I don't mind answering. I'm taking you home."

"Where is that?" She thought he could give her a better answer so she wouldn't have to keep asking him things. It didn't seem to be his intention.

"Angel, you only get one question at a time." He pulled her on top of him, her legs straddling his. Beneath her she felt the hard muscles of his legs and abs as he moved, adjusted her so she rested on top of his sex.

The sheet slipped to her waist; her breasts bared for his viewing enjoyment. Amusement sparkled in his eyes as he slowly lowered his head to take one tip into his mouth. He flicked the tight bud with his tongue then grazed it with his teeth before sucking it deeply.

"You don't play fair, Dev..." She leaned into him, her fingers running through the length of his hair. "Don't I get another question?"

"When I'm finished here and after you answer one of mine."

His attention switched to the other breast as he stroked and nipped the tender sensitive bud. She tried not to respond, tried not to let the tiny sound of pleasure ripple from the back of her throat.

"Dev..."

Before she understood what he was intending he slipped inside her. "Don't move, Angel. Don't move a muscle."

Her body clenched around him, pulsing with the need she knew he wanted to feel. She tossed her head back, trying to do his bidding. Holding still was impossible. When his fingers caressed her intimately, found that spot that made her lose all inhibitions she cried out again and again.

"Don't move."

His hands settled on her waist, holding her still when all she wanted was to move on him, feel the pleasure and the magic. He found her mouth again, kissed her deeply and hard, lingering there second after second. She felt her body begin to pulse, feeling his rod so deep inside. The heady rush of desire kissed her so thoroughly she was moving despite his orders.

He laughed softly watching her and knowing how hard his request was. This time the kiss was wild and reckless, his tongue ravaging the inner recesses. His attempts to keep her still abandoned as they rode the tempest together, crying out each other's name.

Once again, she lay replete in his arms knowing he played her, used the sensual play between them to keep her from asking probing questions. He would never allow her to discover the truth about him. He did a splendid job of evading her queries. Despite her deepest fears about his true identity, it seemed he meant to keep everything important and personal from her.

She was getting used to the roar of the ocean, used to the man and the tempest that rose within her every time he touched her, stroked her with the callused fingertips of a horse breeder. She wanted to rail at him, make him understand her feelings, but it didn't seem he cared, at least not tonight.

Tonight, was his.

Merry nestled her head against his shoulder, getting used to his serene calmness that seemed to invade him. Now that they were away from the stables, he seemed different. She couldn't put a finger on it but she didn't think she was wrong.

He ran his hands through her hair before resting his hand on top of her head. The gesture was intimate in a different way, protective and reassuring too, comfortable. Merry felt as if she could stay in his arms forever. Her hand rested on his muscled abs, his scent masculine and heady.

"Well, you do have a way of getting a man provoked," he murmured gruffly. With one hand he gave her the glass of wine she had yet to finish.

She lowered her lashes, unsure of how to respond to his teasing. Provoked? "I don't mean to."

"I'm not complaining."

"Oh."

He chuckled softly, sipping at his wine before setting it on the table again. His back was against the headboard still, his eyes closed when she peeked beneath her lashes to look at him.

Then he spoke. "It's my turn for a question, don't you think?" Even with his eyes closed he was smiling. That subtle hint of amusement she was growing used to seeing hinted from the corner of his eyes.

"I don't remember," she murmured deciding it was becoming devilishly hard to keep her eyes open. She yawned.

"Trust me it is."

"You should ask before I fall asleep," she murmured, relaxing even more against his chest.

"Oh, I won't let that happen." He kissed her neck, softly at first then with more urgency, finding her ear, swirling his tongue inside.

With a heavy sigh, "Go ahead then. I'll do my best." She didn't know what was left to ask. Although, she supposed he could come up with something.

"Why are you afraid of storms?" he queried, turning her so she had to look at him.

Her eyes opened wide when she felt him move closer. He was watching her concerned, apprehensive. She lifted her shoulders slightly, knowing that was not a good enough response for him. "Have been since I was about ten. When I tell you, you will say I was doing something foolish and call me brat. I wasn't though. The thunderstorm came unexpectedly. Maybe I shouldn't have been out riding by myself, but I wasn't far from home. Mother never told me no. So, I left without telling anyone."

"Did you have permission?"

"That's two questions," she reminded with a half grin. Finally, she was able to toss his attitude back in his face. "Should I go on?"

"Please."

"No, I didn't have permission. However, it was only because no one was home at the time. It was assumed that I would be out riding. As I said before, Mother never told me no. There was no one else to grant permission or withhold it."

His hold tightened on her as if he suddenly realized that perhaps this was more serious than just a little girl afraid of loud noises. "What happened?" His voice was soft, gentle, filled with kindness.

The trembling in her body always seemed to encompass her when she thought of that afternoon. "I was so terrified. Didn't know what to do. The noise and bright flashes closed in around me."

With a gentle hand he placed her head on his shoulder. She felt the even rise and fall of his breathing, understood he was listening. He cared as well. He didn't say anything, just waited for her to finish. She felt the same gut-wrenching fear when she spoke of that day.

Shivering she began again. "The rain started falling then pouring so hard I could not get away from it. I was soaked through to my skin. The thunder was all around me, bolts of lightning hitting the ground as I raced my mare home."

She swallowed hard, wiping tears from her eyes with her hands. Devlin caught some of the moisture with his fingers. "Hush, Angel. You don't have to tell me if you don't want to. I understand more now. It cannot be easy for you to speak of this."

Looking at him, she recognized the tenderness in his eyes. "I want to. Never told anyone before this. All anyone knew was the fact I was caught in the storm. Had to explain why the mare came home without me. Mother never thought to ask even when I would crawl in bed and hide under all my covers whenever another storm passed by."

"Was Leslie or Link there?"

"No, only mother. She never asked. I never told."

He pulled her close, kissed the top of her head. "Go on then. Know you can stop anytime you wish."

She nodded. "You understand this was Bordeaux. The land was filled mostly with grape vines. There was no shelter. I ran through the rain to a tree, taking cover." She paused, thinking remembering, wishing she could forget. Every time there was a storm, a thunderstorm she would remember. "A bolt of lightning hit the tree. I think I was lucky to be alive. You see, it hit me too. Went right through me." She showed him the two tiny scars that were a reminder of that day.

The ensuing silence echoed around them. His hands tightened. The sound of the wind and the birds floated all around them. Summer was here and they could possibly have a thunderstorm.

"I will always give you shelter from your storms, Angel." He ran his hands through her hair, kissed her again.

He kissed her so gently she nearly swooned. His actions were slow and deliberate. He lured every ounce of passion from her. When he was deep inside her once more, she realized how tender and caring he was.

194

The man of her dreams.

Yet she knew he was lying to her.

~ * ~

The next morning Devlin walked into the drawing room just in time to see his new in-laws getting ready to leave. He left Angelica in bed, having kept her up most of the night. Lacie's arm was linked in Leslie's. She was giving him a look that didn't bode well for his secret. He understood Angelica must have confided in her about the wedding and possibly other things. All the doubts would be cast aside in the next few days. He only needed to gain the courage to reveal his truths to his new wife before they arrived at his home.

It seemed Lacie wanted to know now. Devlin cast his attention Leslie's way and was greeted with a shrug of his shoulders, "As promised I told her nothing. If Merry is still sleeping, you could tell her now."

"No, I'll let you do that on your way home. With my luck Angelica could be standing just outside the front door listening to everything we say." Devlin chuckled softly thinking of his new wife along with the tender night they shared. He was a man truly pleased.

While she had been sound asleep when he dressed and left the balcony, she could wake up any time, understanding it would take her a few minutes to shake the sleep from her eyes and a few more to dress. Lacie shot him a quelling glance before looking to Leslie with the same expression. Devlin almost felt sorry for the man having kept his secret so well.

"You will tell me," Lacie said, the command in her voice sending the message loud and clear that there would be no getting around it once they left.

"Your plans?" Leslie asked, drawing his wife close, his arm around her, clearly sending a message of his own.

"Travelling home, to the country home in the north of England. I'll have to head into London within the first few weeks. My grandmother will undoubtedly make more plans once she discovers what I've been up to."

"She knows Merry?" Leslie asked.

"I understand, or at least I assumed so. Angelica did tell me where they bought Sir Alistair. It was at my stables."

"Now the two of you are just talking around the truth. You, Devlin, have almost slipped up. If I didn't know better, I would think you were the..."

Leslie put her hand to her lips before she could get the rest out. Thank God. He already said too much and he wasn't joking when he told them Angelica could be listening. She wouldn't have any qualms when it came to discovering this secret of his. So many hints came from her questions last night for him to have any doubts this morning.

"Hush darling, we'll speak in the carriage. We should stop at Southcliff. We'll have it all to ourselves."

"You're incorrigible since I *ken* what you have in mind. Doesn't make any difference though, we've the townhouse to ourselves too."

"If we don't count the little one, Westcott, the nanny, and all the servants." He kissed her soundly on the lips despite the audience of one.

"Have a safe trip wherever you end up. It will take us a few days. Think we'll make two stops, the last being at my great aunt's home in Scotland just this side of the border. She'll enjoy knowing about the wedding before her sister."

Devlin laughed knowing that was one of his mother's greatest displeasures. His great aunt always, beyond a shadow of a doubt, knew all the latest gossip first.

This would indeed be gossip. The ton would be ripe with the news once they learned of the marriage. There had been no pending engagement a scant few months ago. He extended his hand to Leslie. They shook. Devlin watched them leave then headed for the kitchen.

Breakfast for his wife would be in order. It was time she woke. The morning wouldn't last forever.

Chapter Nine

Devlin changed his plans midway to the kitchen. He had correspondence that needed his attention. He wanted to finish the work before his wife woke to ask more questions as well as hinder his concentration. When she was with him, he seemed to forget everything except her. She was an aphrodisiac to his soul, an enchantress he could not resist. He didn't feel so old when she was near him. Pulling out his satchel containing the most important missives as well as documents, he set to his business.

An hour later, he sent his secretary on his way to London with several letters and documents. Also, he sent messages to his home as well as an inn along the way as to when they would arrive. He wanted all accommodations perfect. After watching the man leave, he once again stepped to the kitchen where the cook put a fresh pot of tea on a tray along with a huge breakfast of eggs, potatoes and bacon along with a few scones and strawberry preserves. His stomach rumbled at the marvelous scents, anticipating a leisurely breakfast with his new wife, the first of many.

"Have one of the servants bring this up in about ten minutes," he said, immediately heading for the balcony and his sleeping wife.

He did keep her up most the night. He intended to keep her up the rest of the day and well into the evening hours today. They would leave at dawn, so he would have to put an earlier end to his lovemaking than the night before.

He grinned, remembering the sweet so very soft curves she possessed as well as her innate beauty, the feisty young woman he needed to know better.

When he reached the bed, he pulled the curtains surrounding it apart, letting in the brilliant sunshine. There wasn't a cloud in the sky. The breeze from the ocean was light, the day promising to be beautiful, perfect for his intentions. The clothing he wanted her to wear was set out on the opposite side of the bed. Before he left Glasgow, he had an entire new wardrobe made for her.

She would protest.

He didn't have one doubt.

Too bad.

As her husband, it was his duty to see she was properly clothed. He sat down beside her, pulling the covers off. God's teeth but she was beautiful, still sound asleep, still curled on her side. The rounded curve of her back as well as her buttocks was displayed for him to see. Thoughts of sticky buns swept through him. He ran his hand along the curve of her tiny waist then the flare of her hips, bent to kiss her tenderly. Felt a sudden and very strong surge of passion. He was hungry for her, not breakfast. If he didn't stop now another hour or so would pass before they got to the ride along the coastline he planned.

He gave her a gentle pat then one a bit harder to her bottom. She gasped awake, turning. Her eyes were wide with anger if he didn't miss his guess. Her breasts, her soft belly, the dark hair at the apex of her thighs, so visible in the bright light of the morning sunshine, a grumble of pleasure left his chest.

They didn't need to go for a ride, at least not yet.

They should spend a few hours at least outside this bed.

Her eyes blinked a few times as she sat up, pushing the length of her hair away from her face, her breasts swaying with the movement. "That was not very nice, Devlin."

"Perhaps not." He reached out to her, touched a nipple with the flat of his hand, grinned as the tip grew taut, begging him for more attention. He needed control. "Breakfast is coming in about ten minutes. There is a steaming bath waiting for you if you would like." He nodded his head in the direction of the tub.

"On the balcony?" Her eyes widened. "Someone would see."

"Not unless you are still bathing when breakfast comes. I suggest you get up and get on with it since the ten minutes you once had now has turned to nine. Clothes for you are on the bed. If you like, I will stand guard at the top of the steps."

He wouldn't want any of the servants to see her naked either.

She rushed off the bed, throwing a quilt around her as she hustled toward the waiting tub. He made sure lavender scented soap was nearby as well as a huge bath sheet for her when she finished. There was extra water to rinse her hair if she wished to wash it.

When the servant arrived with their breakfast tray, he took it from her. Setting it on the table near the bed, he watched his wife finish her bath. Bloody eyes but he could watch her forever. Even now after a night with her in the most intimate endeavors, he still wanted her. How he resisted her for so many months was beyond him.

"You're staring at me," she said as she rose, the water sluicing down her back, rippling across her buttocks.

He swallowed hard, resisting the urge to carry her back to the big bed and spend the rest of the day enjoying her. "Can't seem to keep from looking at you, Brat."

She turned looking over her shoulder, one dark brow arched in question. "Brat? So, I've become that again."

"You've no idea," he murmured, striding to her, enfolding her in his arms to kiss her soundly. "I'm hungry." While it was true, he needed sustenance, he needed her more.

She pushed on his chest, "Not now."

"Now."

Still damp from her bath they made love again. Afterward, fully sated, he pulled on his pants before pouring tea for both of them. They ate. Silence seemed right for the moment even though he was waiting for the questions to resume.

She watched him from below lowered lashes. He saw the humor in the situation but only a little, certainly not enough to ruin the tranquility he felt around her now. He needed a few more days if possible, having the feeling today and tomorrow would be the last days of serenity. When they reached his great aunt's home in southern Scotland, he was sure the truth would be told. Perhaps during the boring miles from here to there he could tell her. Perhaps explain the reasons why he remained silent.

"You look pensive," she finally said, as she drank the last of her tea. "Care to tell me what you're thinking about?"

She set the cup on the table; her beautiful blue eyes focused on his lips.

"About making love to my wife," he told her, not a complete lie as he looked from her to the bed. All she wore at the moment was the towel. It would not take much to unwrap her then set her on the bed.

"Is that all you think about?"

The smile on her face told him she might well be thinking about the same things. Her gaze travelled from his lips to his chest then lower.

Clearing his throat, he said with a nonchalance he didn't feel, "Would you like to go for a ride this morning. There's a spot just south of here where we can have a picnic lunch. A place where we can do inexplicable things to each other."

He waggled his eyebrows at her, hoping to keep her attention diverted from last night's questions and resuming them again.

She tossed her napkin at him. "Sir Alistair is not here. What would I ride?"

You could ride me, but he kept that thought to himself. No, he had Sir Alistair taken to his stables so the mare would be there for her when they arrived. "With me, on Windwalker."

Her eyes lit up with pleasure. "Truly?"

He nodded. "As soon as you dress, we can go." He nodded to the clothing on the bed.

"There are things missing," she murmured, a slight flush to her cheeks as she shuffled through the items.

"As in your underwear?" he asked, having made that omission on purpose.

He wanted her with nothing on beneath her outer garments.

Her blush grew deeper in color as she nodded her head. "I can't possibly. Is my trunk downstairs? I'll retrieve what I need."

Inwardly he was laughing, enjoying the rise of color even though they spent the night together wearing nothing at all. For her, the thought of no drawers or corset or chemise was beyond the pale. "No one but the two of us will know you've nothing on beneath your skirts. If you put something on, I don't approve of, I'll simply remove it."

She lowered her head hiding her face from him. When she looked at him again, "Daryl told me I should wear nothing beneath my skirts for the first two months of our marriage. After that I should keep you guessing as to whether I'm naked or not."

He tossed his head back laughing uncontrollably, "Then I've played right into your hands, Brat."

"Couldn't I be angel this time?"

"No, this is delightfully wicked, sinful, nothing an angel would conspire."

"I suppose so. Is..." It seemed she noticed the clothes, her brows pinched together as she pursed her lips. "You bought more new clothing? I don't need anything new to wear. My clothing is just fine." Still, despite her protest, she looked momentarily pleased.

Then as her eyes darkened, Devlin knew she was thinking once more about the expenditure. Before she could query him again, "I've sufficient funds to keep my wife clothed. I don't intend to talk about my finances with you now or ever."

"This fabric is so expensive." Her fingers roamed over the riding habit. When she looked up, realization in her eyes, "Did you have Lucy pack any of my old clothes for our trip?"

"No, your old things were for a maiden not a wife," he told her, for a moment looking away from her, sensing he should not be so autocratic.

She was traveling to a new life in a new country. He shrugged his shoulders as he watched her again. Getting used to this was an absolute necessity.

What was done was done. He would have it no other way.

"I should have been given a choice," she told him showing more than just a hint of anger. "You had no right."

"The right of a husband," he said before thinking that might not be the wisest thing to say to her.

He seemed to be making one gaff after another in his quest to please his wife.

"It's going to be like that is it?"

"No, I promise from now on I'll ask first. I just assumed you would enjoy having new things. Was I wrong? Be honest now."

With a reluctant letting go of her breath, she said, "No, but there are things I would have liked to bring with me."

"When we reach my home, you can write and have anything you want sent to you there." He hoped this gesture would do a bit to alleviate her concerns.

"Thank you." She dressed quickly. With only a few items to put on, not even a chemise, dressing herself did not take more than a minute or two. She slipped on the new stockings and riding shoes then stood.

He could tell she was pleased with his offer but resentful too. "I should not have to ask but Angel, please talk to me, allow me to know what you're feeling." He stood, extending his hand, "Now, shall we ride?"

Angelica was sitting in front of him, his hands circling her as he held the reins to Windwalker. They were riding bareback, just as he imagined, just as they had done once before. He raced the stallion down the narrow trail following the water. Her head was tossed back, her hair streaming around him. He reveled in her laughter along with the simple enjoyment of the ride.

After a few minutes he slowed the horse to an easy gait. Earlier her hands gripped his forearms, now she loosened her hold, relaxed as she leaned on him. Against his arms, her breasts caressed him with the subtle play of the movement, her nipples hardening.

"What, did you like the ride?" he queried, as he kissed her ear then the side of her face. She turned into him. He found her lips, pliant and damp, soft. To tease, not intending to make this more than a coaxing caress, he swept his tongue across her bottom lip.

"Hmm...yes," she murmured as his nimble fingers unbuttoned the jacket then the blouse beneath. "What are you doing?" her voice whispered softly as she gasped for a breath of air. He was sure she knew full well what he was about.

"I think you know, at least you should by now."

With his words, his other hand ran the length of her leg, stroking as he moved higher until he found intimate wet petals waiting for him beneath her skirt.

Windwalker drew to a stop. They arrived. The trail to the beach below was narrow, twisty also, but he was sure it would be easy enough to navigate as it was bordered by sea grass and sand. Earlier this morning he had found a flat grassy area. He sent two of his servants with a lunch for them. The surf was mild here, gently flowing in and out. They could wade here, play in the water, make love. If this was to be the last day of their miniature honeymoon, he wanted to make the most of it. Once he caught up with his business, he meant to take her to Paris. After than on to Bordeaux as he wanted to meet her mother.

Yet at the moment, he could not bring himself to leave the inviting depths he just discovered, the moist warmth hidden between her thighs. She moaned softly then again as he stroked her intimately, one hand teasing the tight pink bud at the tip of her breast. She was arching for him, making tiny little sounds that thrilled him. He found she responded so quickly to his caresses. He could stroke her to a point of ecstasy in a matter of minutes. For now, that would have to be enough. Later this afternoon he would take longer spend time teasing and provoking until she begged.

She cried out. He swallowed the sound with a kiss. She was arching against him as he stroked her again and again. Her climax was hard and fast. Soon, she was limp in his arms as he soothed her.

"I think I've a sex slave in my midst," he murmured, nipping her ear with his teeth while he waited until he thought she could stand by herself.

Her eyes were closed now. For several seconds, he heard the rapid breathing, listening for it to slow. When it finally did, "How do you do that to me? Never mind." She waved a hand in the air.

"Should we go down the trail? See if there is a surprise for us? Windwalker will stay here." He dismounted before helping her from the stallion. "Do you think you can walk?"

For a moment, she appeared indignant then nodded, seeming to understand his concern. "You have this way of making me feel as if I've no muscle whatsoever or bones. You've rendered me very nearly spineless."

Devlin placed a quick kiss to her lips. "I like it when you tell me what an amazing lover I am."

"Did I say that?"

Flirtatiously, Angelica lowered her dark sooty lashes, peeking at him from beneath.

He tossed his head back, boisterous with laughter, thrilled with his new wife as well as how easy she was becoming with sex between them. "You did, Brat."

He placed her hand in his, enjoying the feel of her tiny hand encompassed in his. Slowly, he massaged circles on her wrists. Her eyes darkened once more with the pleasure coupled with the hunger just for him. They would do fine together as soon as he got his lies out of the way.

In time she would forgive him.

"I don't think I would like to make love on the sand," she told him, her voice prim as she looked around the beach.

"Neither would I," he told her as he showed her the secluded area behind several large boulders.

The space was covered in a thick layer of grass. A blanket as well as a basket had been set nearby. "Will this do?" he asked, wondering now if there might be other reasons for her slight hesitancy in answering.

"I suppose," she told him and he heard the reluctance in her voice.

"Are you sore?" he blurted without thinking.

They had made love numerous times in less than twenty-four hours. She must be feeling...well hell. He was an inconsiderate lout.

With his question, she turned a brilliant shade of red. "Dev..."

He waved his hand in the air, his brows drawn together. "Forget I said that." Perhaps they would not be making love here. Mayhap he should hold back on his ardent endeavors for tonight. "It's alright, Angel. We can take this one step at a time," he said as he thought of other delightful ways to fill the time for them.

After all, he just brought her to pleasure without any discomfort. If she was amenable, he could teach her how to pleasure him with her mouth and fingers. For this afternoon, now that he realized what was going on, he meant to tease and entice, show her things that could be done.

Now she was standing near the blanket looking a bit forlorn, her gaze moving from him to the water, to the blanket. Her thoughts seeming to travel in circles, he kept his smile behind his teeth as he watched her suddenly becoming shy.

"Are we staying here for a while?" she suddenly asked.

"We are. Now, why don't you sit down?" He gestured toward the blanket, his gaze riveted on her.

She stood in front of him looking at the water. He didn't want to command her to do so but he wanted her to sit so he could remove her shoes and stockings. Instead, he sat down, tugging at his boots to remove them then his socks. He dug his toes into the warmth of the sand thinking how absolutely frigid the water would be.

It seemed she realized what he wanted. With a hesitant smile, she sat down. Before she could do it herself, his hands were brushing hers away. Seductively, he slid each shoe from her feet. Treating each foot individually he held them in his hands. Slipping his fingers the length of her leg, he found the garters to her stockings. His touch was intimate, his strokes bringing her to an aroused state if the darkening of her eyes was any indication.

"You can stand now." He told her when everything except her skirt and blouse were removed. His mind leaned toward removing all her clothing to watch her frolic naked in the Firth of Clyde. Deftly, he tucked the bottom of her skirt into her waistband. Standing back, feeling pleased with himself, "Now you can play in the waves without getting wet, or at least not too wet."

"I used to play in the surf in France," she told him thoughtfully. "The water was probably warmer," she began as her toes felt the first onslaught of the chilled water in the Firth of Clyde. "Very much so."

He joined her, his pants rolled up nearly to his knees. "How far do you want to go?" Sand washed away by the outgoing tide sucked at his feet. The waves swirled against him, threatening to drag him into deeper water. He watched as her arms whirled to keep her balance.

They played for hours in the water as if they were children, laughing and splashing each other. By the time they were hungry enough to eat, the top of her gown was plastered to her skin, her nipples tight buds against the fabric. It was all he could do to keep from tossing her skirts and having her here on the beach, as was his fantasy. His air let out in a long fluid rush through gritted teeth. He supposed he had a lifetime to fulfill all his dreams.

On land, he dried her feet and legs with a towel he put in the basket, making sure all the sand was gone. He opened a bottle of Bordeaux pouring each a glass of wine. She leaned against him, her back to his chest as she sat between his legs, one of her slender hands on his thigh. He felt her even breathing, watched the pulse beat at the base of her neck.

"Who am I going to meet when we get to your home? Anyone?" she asked, turning slightly so she could look into his eyes yet her gaze seemed fixed on his mouth.

At least her questions had switched from his finances to his family. The truth here would serve him well. He had nothing to hide from her except the pet name for his grandmother. He would have to make sure he didn't slip up and call her Duchy. She had to learn the truth sometime. Now was not the right time to turn their lives upside down.

"Well," he began running one hand up her arm, teasing her with the caress, delighting in the tiny shudder of pleasure she gifted him with. "My mother and father both passed away but my grandmother is still living. She has a sister we might encounter when we pass through Scotland on our way home. I've planned on staying one night, sent word ahead of us so they will be expecting our arrival in two days." He twined his fingers through hers.

"Are they nice?"

"If you're asking if they will like you, I know both my grandmother and great aunt will love you. Are you nervous?"

"Wouldn't you be?" she queried softly, looking over the rim of her glass at him. She'd turned so she was staring at him again. He saw the question in her eyes, the hesitation and insecurity.

"You shouldn't be worried. People like you, genuinely like you." He tweaked her nose unsure what else to do to. Kissing her was out of the question. He did want to make love to her tonight but in bed not on the beach where she was still insecure.

"You didn't like me when we met," she told him bluntly her voice sounding way too serious. "You started calling me brat from the very beginning. You were always yelling at me. There was the time you kept me from riding...”

“Discipline was done because I cared what happened to you. I liked you well enough. Truth is, I was afraid I wouldn’t be able to keep my hands off you,” he paused, “and I can’t.”

~ * ~

More than an hour passed before they returned to the house. Truth be told Merry longed to spend more time at the beach yet storm clouds on the horizon drove them to seek shelter before the skies opened in a possible deluge. By the time they gathered the blanket and packed the basket the servants brought to their secluded bit of paradise, a strong wind whipped around the boulder, blowing her skirt against her legs. She rubbed her hands along her arms, warding off the sudden chill, wishing they were anywhere but here. The clouds were huge. She was positive thunder and lightning would follow.

“Do you think you can carry the basket?” Devlin asked, holding it out to her. “Don’t want to send someone back if this storm hits before we can get home. What do you think?”

“Yes. Of course, I would not want to have to go outside.”

“Good, you’re a bricky lass.” He grinned running his hand down her arm. “Take my hand.” He led her up the path to Windwalker.

By the time they reached home, the first bolt of lightning and roar of thunder rolled from the water inland. She shivered, wishing she was as courageous as he just told her she was. Where storms came into play, she was anything but bricky.

With the first boom, she felt the same terrifying sensation that swept through her every time she heard the noise. She always felt the strongest need to bury her face somewhere and not look out until all the noise and bright lights ceased. He rode Windwalker directly to the stable where the lad who took care of the horses met them.

“Thanks.” After dismounting he handed the reins to the boy before helping her down. “Let’s get you inside and warm. Everything you’re wearing is damp. Don’t want to take a chill now do we?”

She didn't have words at the moment. All she could do was let him sweep her into his arms and race to the house trying to stay as dry as possible. Not until they reached the master chamber on the second floor did he set her down. He found a towel. Taking her pins form her hair, he toweled the length then went searching through the trunk in the corner of the room.

Startled by the next rumbling wave of noise, she jumped, clutching her arms around her body, frozen in place. He returned a few minutes later, clothing in his hands. Gently, he began disrobing her. When he was done, she was dressed in a silken nightdress and warm robe.

He followed suit. A few more minutes passed. Now he wore a dressing gown. She didn't think there was anything beneath, didn't remember seeing him put anything else on.

"Are you up to watching the storm? I know you're afraid. If you allow yourself to enjoy the tempest, it can be quite exhilarating. Perhaps together and in my arms some of your fears can be eased, hmm..." One dark brow arched speculatively as he waited for an answer.

Merry didn't think anything would assuage her fears, however, she was willing to give it a try. "No but..." She inhaled a swift deep lung full of air. "Alright."

Once more he swooped her into his arms, carrying her as far as the drawing room where one of his servants waited. He gave orders then continued on to the front porch heading for the swing. She eyed it critically, grasping him around the neck when more lightning speared the earth.

A quilt was folded neatly against the back. After setting her down he shook it open then wrapped it around them. Another bolt of blue-white lightning flashed in the darkening sky followed by the roar.

She shivered, closing her eyes while leaning into his hard body, searching for the protection she craved. All she wanted was to soak up the courage he possessed. She needed not to jump and cower at every turn the storm took. He sought to rid her of her fears. She didn't think that feat was possible.

He pointed to the flash above them, "See, out there it is truly an amazing part of nature. While you sit inside, the tempest cannot touch you. You are safe here my angel."

Her voice was shaking, "I can't forget when it did more than touch the earth, it seared through me. With each flash it's as though I feel the fire again and again."

"Breathe deeply, try to relax. Know I will protect you. Don't close your eyes. Don't hide. Accept the energy of the storm into you."

Devlin held her close, brought her to him, his hands warm, his arms circling her. A servant arrived with a tray of food and a bottle of wine along with a pot of tea. She found that she was hungry. Indeed, she didn't want to leave his arms. He took the matter into his hands, leaving her for as long as it took him to pour the wine.

She stuck her hand from the wrappings of the quilt to accept the glass and grace him with a hesitant smile before shuddering when another roar passed by them. "I don't know about this," she told him honestly.

"Would it be any better if you were hidden beneath the sheets and blankets in the bed upstairs? Don't you think confronting the storm with your bravery is better than hiding? You can't hide forever."

"Yes, no, I don't know." Her voice was whisper thin.

Still, she felt the need to admit if only to herself this was better than burrowing under covers as long as he sat next to her.

He laughed then. "Your shivers are not as strong as when the first flash lit up the sky. You are sipping your wine as well as speaking to me. There is food waiting. Don't forget you are now eating for two." He paused thoughtfully. "I still remember the night you came to me. That moment changed our lives. For the better, I might add. To the point though, that night you spent in my arms you were shivering, your eyes were closed, your face buried against my shoulder. I doubt you could have moved for the fear let alone watch the tempest as you're doing now."

She didn't want to be afraid, didn't want to hide every time there was a thunderstorm. "Perhaps you are right," she murmured.

Together they watched until the storm passed them by. She felt better, the terror not as stark and unforgiving as usual. After the wine was finished followed by a cup of tea, he carried her upstairs.

"This is our last night here," he spoke softly then gently showed her how much he cared for her.

She wanted to tell him she loved him, had yearned to do just that for the longest time. She didn't though. She was afraid he would not return the sentiment. The morning came too quickly, yet it was a beautiful day. The tempest having passed left the air fresh and clean. They were treated to a large breakfast. Once again, he picked out a traveling dress for her. Again, she wondered if she would ever have a say in what she wore. He told her it was only because he knew where all her new things were packed. She wasn't at all sure about any of what he said.

By the time the sun had barely risen they were ensconced in the carriage left by Leslie. It carried her family's coat of arms on the side, proudly proclaiming it belonged to the Duke of Southcliff.

A few hours down the road, Merry knew she was in dire trouble. Ever since breakfast, her stomach had been rolling, telling her it wasn't happy. Now she was sure she was going to lose everything she ate. The thought was mortifying, humiliating in the extreme. She didn't want Devlin to know. His discovering the truth was inevitable. In a few seconds he would see for himself.

At the moment, he was sitting back against the cushioned seat, his long legs stretched out in front of him. His eyes were closed. Merry didn't think he was sleeping. If he was, it might take too long for the coach to stop. She prayed she would not do this inside the carriage.

"Dev..." she began in a tight voice, bile seeming to rise from the pit of her stomach as she spoke. Merry leaned over, lightly touching his thigh in hopes of getting his eyes to open. "Devlin," she said in a louder voice.

One eye opened then the other. "Yes?"

He didn't look concerned. Why should he? He slanted her an amused grin as if she was waking him to talk or perhaps his mind was traveling to other places. This morning while eating he, spoke of the delights that could be found by making love in a carriage.

She wouldn't do that.

"I need you to stop the carriage," she spoke frantically, looking out the window then back to him.

His amused grin vanished as he sat up. "Something wrong?"

She licked her lips, her fingers on the handle of the vehicle. "I'm," she paused swallowing, "I'm going to lose my..."

Before she could finish, he was pounding on the roof, calling for the carriage to stop. While it was slowing, he opened his door. The moment the vehicle rolled to a stop, he helped her outside.

While she lost the contents of her stomach on the grass near the road, he soothed her back with the hands that had so gently made love to her. She was mortified beyond anything that had ever happened to her before.

"I'm never sick," she said her voice hushed as she looked at him.

He handed her a flagon of water, "Rinse your mouth out then take a long drink. You'll feel better. I promise."

But she didn't, "I can't believe..." she quit speaking because she was suddenly losing the water she had sipped seconds before.

This was not happening, could not be happening. She moaned softly, the sound seeming to come from the back of her throat. Then she was heaving again only this time there was nothing to lose.

He gave her the flagon again, "Just rinse your mouth out, Angel. That should do the trick for now." He watched and waited for her to finish. "Don't believe you're sick."

Devlin placed her limp body in his arms before finding a shady spot to sit. He held her soothing her, stroking her back, murmuring syllables that didn't make much sense to her.

"Not sick?"

"No, Angel." He wasn't bothering to hide his masculine grin of amusement, "We'll just stay here for an hour or so. You can rest. I suppose I shouldn't be rushing you here and there given your delicate condition. When you're feeling better, we can continue. We'll make sure we begin our trip later tomorrow."

Merry didn't understand why he could appear so bemused, nor did she want to play guessing games with him. "What are you talking about?" If she had the strength, she'd punch him, but right now she was squirming against his hold trying to get him to let her go before she embarrassed herself again this time on his shoes.

Over an hour later they were back on the road. Merry now knew exactly why she was experiencing the stomach problems. She blamed him for it. He laughed, clearly pleased. Then he had the nerve to tell her he wasn't happy she was sick, just pleased that she was going to have his child and together they would enjoy all the symptoms that went along with pregnancy.

She punched him in the arm. He grinned even more. She didn't find anything enjoyable about morning sickness. She knew when she couldn't see her feet, that would not be much fun either.

They rolled into the first inn, way past their estimated arrival time. Devlin told her they would plan on leaving later. Told her she could sleep late, sleep as long as she wanted. She should have nothing more than tea and perhaps a few pieces of toast for her morning meal. He would arrange to have a filling lunch made for them to eat half way. They would reach his great aunt's home by the evening meal. Merry didn't believe any of it even though he looked pleased with himself.

The next day Devlin's plan turned out to be a good one except that he rode on Windwalker most of the way, leaving her alone to ruminate about the upcoming meeting with his aunt. Her mind created a myriad of scenarios about the meeting, none of which she liked.

When they stopped for lunch, she had questions. He poured wine before handing her a sandwich of ham. "We need to talk."

"I know. I'm surprised it's taken you this long to broach the subject." He chewed thoughtfully before washing the food down with his wine. "What do you want to know?"

"We could have talked if you would have joined me in the carriage," she told him indignantly as she sipped the cold tea.

"Sorry, Brat, needed the air."

"You just didn't want to talk. You were putting it off as long as possible. I want to know," she paused thinking, "at least the name or your great aunt."

"That's easy enough. Her name is Mary. You shouldn't have any trouble remembering it."

"Mary." She smiled thinking about his aversion to her name, assuming his great aunt's name was spelled in the conventional manner.

"Yes."

"So that's why you don't want to call me Merry." She was

astounded by the obvious. He made up names for her because his great
aunt's name was Mary. "Does she have a last name?"

"McNeel."

"Mary McNeel."

"Yes, anything else? I'm an open book."

"I don't know. I guess I need to know what to expect. Does she
know we are married? That I'm pregnant? How am I to behave?"

"With all the grace I know has been bred into you over the last
nineteen-years, Brat." He grinned. "You need to eat up. Unless we have
to stop again, I don't intend to."

She set the half-eaten sandwich down. "Not hungry." She was
looking at the serious face Devlin was presenting her with. "I can eat later
in the carriage if I get hungry. I'm not really eating for two, you know."

He nodded finishing his meal then packing the basket. "Very well.
I'll ride with you for a while."

That decision proved to be more disconcerting than she
anticipated. By the time they reached the destination, she was a bundle of
nervous energy, ready to explode at any given time.

When they pulled up in front of the mansion, she knew then he
deceived her in more ways than one. He could not be related to someone
who owned this fine a home. She didn't understand why he couldn't just
tell her the truth. He was her horse breeder. She loved him and didn't care
about anything else.

Then you should tell the poor man that.

He doesn't want to know.

*Every man wants to know the woman he married is in love with
him. Maybe if you were a little nicer, he would return the favor.*

I'm pregnant.

What does that have to do with anything?

*I can't keep any food down. I'm so hungry all the time it makes
me angry and not very nice. It's his fault by the way.*

*You can eat now. Half your lunch is still in the basket. You could
even have a glass of wine.*

Maybe I should.

Yeah, I shouldn't have said that. You don't want to give the wrong impression when you meet the relatives.

I should swig the rest of the bottle.

You'll regret it if you do.

I don't doubt that.

Before she could think past the voice in her head, Devlin was assisting her from the carriage. His hand was around her waist, helping her up the steps. He lifted the gigantic knocker on the door before pounding the brass on the hard wood surface several times.

"No one is home. Perhaps we should find somewhere else to stay," Merry said starting to back away.

Her heart was lodged in her throat while all the nerves she possessed seemed to be unraveling at a furious pace.

"Of course there is someone home. All the servants."

After what seemed like the longest wait, the door opened. A tall thin man answered. His hair was white, his smile broad and infectious.

"Master Devlin," he greeted seeming to be very pleased to see her husband. "Welcome. The countess is away. She might be home in the afternoon tomorrow. I did, however, make sure she knew you were coming. I'm sure she will do her best to arrive here before your scheduled departure."

Countess? Merry shook her head a few times sure she heard wrong. Perhaps she heard something untoward in her ears. She was half asleep. It was late. The pregnancy seeming to make her more exhausted than ever before. So, of course she wasn't thinking straight.

Countess?

"This is my wife, Angelica," Devlin introduced her. "Angelica Louise Stewart now Mathews, her brother is the Duke of Southcliff."

She nodded graciously having realized she never heard her husband quite so regal and precise, "Nice to meet you."

Not knowing what else to do at the moment, she curtsied.

"I'll show you to your room," he said, turning and heading for the stairs.

Wearily, she followed behind Devlin who seeming to sense her fatigue swept her into his arms again. When they arrived at a lavish bedchamber, "Here you are. Hope everything is suitable. I will see you all in the morning. Ring if you need anything."

"Perhaps a bath for my wife would be nice and something to eat and drink. It's been a long day for both of us."

"As you wish," Hasting said before turning on a heel and disappearing out the door.

Merry sat down on a wing chair near the fire. It was comfortable. She didn't have one urge to stand up. However, the thought of a bath gave her a reason to smile. Devlin wandered the sitting room then into the bedroom. The suite of rooms was large and well appointed.

A countess? His great aunt was a countess.

She watched his back for several minutes as he roamed through the rooms. Asking questions again would undoubtedly ruffle his feathers more than she wanted. Another night of ignorance would not be difficult. Several times Devlin implied she would be angry when she knew the truth. Well, at this moment, she was too damn tired for that emotion, for any emotion for that matter. She wasn't even sure if she could get up from the chair to take that bath when it arrived.

She would force herself.

Servants began entering the rooms. All manner of items were brought to them. Food, a tub, wine, tea, and eventually hot water. She watched fascinated by the parade of men and women all bent on making their stay as comfortable as possible.

His great aunt was a countess. She couldn't seem to get that terrifying notion from her head. What did that make him?

Devlin was standing by the fire, his back to her, one arm resting on the mantle, one foot on the hearth. If she could see his face, she might be able to read something there. It didn't seem to her he meant to turn around. A fistful of air slipped quietly from her lips.

"Devlin?" she asked unsure what she wanted to say.

"What is it?"

"Is your great aunt really a countess? What does that make you?"

"She married a count. I've heard it was love at first sight." He turned a smile of amusement in his eyes. "Just like us, Angel, love at first sight," he said dryly.

His expression changed almost as if he said something he didn't want to say.

He doesn't love me. That was a mistake, she thought, even though she wanted his words to be true more than anything.

"What does that make you?" she repeated.

"It doesn't make me anything. You understand lines of heritage along with how titles are passed down. Just because my great aunt is a countess that doesn't give me a title."

"No, I suppose it doesn't."

She was nothing, Link was nothing, even though Leslie the oldest was the duke. Neither younger brother nor sister bore a title. Her thoughts were convoluted at best. Why she thought he might be other than a horse breeder was absurd.

The last of the servants bringing hot water closed the door behind them. Her bath was ready. With great effort she pushed from the chair.

"You're tired."

"Exhausted."

"Would you like me to leave you alone tonight?"

Her head was shaking thinking all she wanted after their baths was for him to hold her, perhaps make love to her. "No, can we just spend the night together? I know I'd like that."

He smiled, helping her to the tub in a special bathing chamber beyond the bedroom. She set her head against the rim, soaking up the steamy liquid, her hands on her belly, wondering when she would start to show.

The knock at the door surprised her, as did the murmuring of voices. When she opened her eyes, Devlin stood by the tub. "Mary is home. I'd like to see her. You can meet her in the morning. Is that alright with you?" he asked. "Do you need any help? I can send someone."

"I can manage."

She watched him leave the room. Oh, how she'd like to be a fly on the wall at their meeting. He hid so much from her. This omission of truth was just another example.

~ * ~

Devlin strode into the drawing room grinning broadly. Too many years passed since he'd seen his great aunt. She didn't look a day older yet time had gone by. If he'd not rusticated in Scotland over a lie from his best friend's little sister, he would not see Mary now. Admitting there were good things that came out of this situation was not difficult.

She welcomed him with open arms. "I hear you are wed. Will I approve?" she asked, her smile endearing. "You know this is fairly sudden. It's not Teddy's little sister, is it?"

"Bite your tongue," Devlin laughed as he enveloped Mary in his arms, hugging her tightly. "It was a lie all along. I've disliked that young woman since she was a little girl. Teddy should know by now his sister's baby is not mine or that his sister was never pregnant."

"The duchy doesn't know about your marriage?" she asked even though it sounded more like a statement.

"Not yet. I thought I would wait until I arrived home and could tell her in person. Doesn't seem something to spring on your grandmother via messenger."

"When am I going to meet the young lady? You said she is the Duke of Southcliff's little sister?"

"She is. Tomorrow morning. She was exhausted from the days of travel, the lack of sleep as well," Devlin beamed, vividly recalling the evenings alone with her.

"Oh," she winked knowingly. "You've kept the poor little thing awake at nights. You should be ashamed of yourself. You must want an heir sooner than later."

"No, Aunty, it's not so much that but the fact I can't keep my hands off her. I'm hoping she'll be asleep when I get back to the room tonight."

He did hope for that only so he could have the enjoyment of waking her with kisses in certain spots he couldn't deny himself.

Mary waved a hand in the air. "Don't believe one thing out of that mouth of yours, young man. I can see it in your eyes. Once you return, she won't get much sleep tonight either. So, tell me something about your new wife."

Mary poured them each a healthy glass of brandy then sat down, motioning for him to join her in a chair near the fire.

Truly, he didn't know where to begin. "Let's just say she's a tiny spitfire hell bent on behaving like a man. She scares me to death half the time and entices me to throttle her the other half. As I said, I can't keep my hands off her."

Mary laughed, her eyes twinkling with mischief. "Someone who will keep you from being too stodgy, I hope. Your father got to be a stodgy old man in his later years. Wasn't a bit of fun. Too obsessed with the duties of his title as well as his role in the House of Lords to pay your mother much attention. She wouldn't have anything to do with that."

"I don't remember much about either of my parents. They died way too young. I barely remember my mother's face. What I recall of my father..." he paused thoughtfully. "He was always working. Sometimes I thought he worked himself to death."

"After your mother died in childbirth, he might have done just that. Blamed himself. The duchy raised you. I hope she taught you that life is not all work. She doesn't want the same thing to happen to her grandson."

Devlin sat back, his legs stretched comfortably in front of him. Until he met Angelica, he did spend too much time working. Perhaps that's why his fiancée lost interest in him seeking pleasures elsewhere. "Rusticating in the Scottish countryside did more for me that way than the duchy could ever have expected. However, we both know when I return to London, I'll be bombarded with overlooked work. I promise you, I'll try not to work myself into an early grave. I'm sure Angelica will keep me on my toes, forever challenged by her antics. She does have a penchant for getting herself into trouble."

Mary leaned forward for a moment before sitting back and eyeing him critically. "She doesn't know who you are, does she?"

Shocked by Mary's acute sense of the situation, he grimaced. "Don't know how to tell her she's married a duke. Thinks I'm a horse breeder."

Devlin felt walls closing in on him more so today than ever before. He meant to tell her this morning while they were traveling here. Knowing that once she started seeing him in a different environment it would not be long before she started adding up everything. Couldn't put the right words together to form a coherent sentence. Oh, by the way, you're married to the Duke of Weston. You know the man you decided you'd marry when you first saw him in Paris as a little girl, the man who asked you to be his mistress, the man you slapped. Well, she slapped her horse breeder too. He deserved it both times.

"Just say the words. It's better late than never. Tell her when you wake her up tonight before you do anything else. Surprising her in front of other people will not do. A surprise such as that would not sit well with her. She will resent the untenable position you put her in. If you do something like that, it might be a very long time before she forgives you."

"I'll give it some thought."

He knew Mary was right in her assessment of the situation he found himself in. Still, it would ruin the evening as well as the next day. He swallowed the remaining brandy, thinking perhaps the time was right now. "I'll see you in the morning."

He set his glass on the table determined to tell her the truth.

As he left the room, he felt his great aunt's gaze on the back of his neck. Steeled himself for Angelica's anger, perhaps even disappointment. She might be pleased. No, he lied to her. Married her under false promises. He could now give her more than ever before. She would be a duchess. He reminded himself she didn't care about titles or money. That fact alone should please him.

Why on earth would she be angry?

Well hell.

He just knew she would be.

Chapter Ten

As it turned out, Devlin didn't tell her that night. She was sound asleep when he pulled back the covers to the bed. Her exhaustion was evident in the muted light from the silver beams slanting through the window. Dark circles painted the hollows beneath her eyes.

When he knelt beside the bed, she was curled on one side, her hands under her cheek. Her breathing was soft and light. He kissed her on the forehead before he shed his clothing and climbed in beside her taking her into his arms. Her soft supple body molded to his.

They were nestled together spoon fashion, her bottom cupped between his belly and his thighs. Hours passed before he finally closed his eyes, knowing he had lost his last opportunity to tell her what she should know about him. The truth would come out as it always did. He would have to bear the fruits of what he'd done for good or bad.

He felt the cad that he'd been when he asked her to be his mistress and she slapped his face.

She would inevitably feel wronged. He never meant to hurt her. Sometime during the hours before dawn he must have found sleep. When he opened his eyes, she was kissing him, light nipping kisses across his chest, her fingers playing with the hair on his chest.

His groan rumbled up from his lungs. This was how he wanted to wake up every morning for the rest of his life. Her tongue found one of his nipples, laved and licked until more groans resounded from his chest. Sometime before she began this heady exploration, she removed the silken nightdress she'd been wearing. Now, her naked breasts pushed against him, swayed and teased every sense he possessed. His breath caught in his throat.

"Good morning," she whispered as her attention found its way lower, then lower still until the tip of her tongue embraced the tip of his rod.

He closed his eyes. A shudder of pure male arousal pounded through him. This was not how he expected to wake up this morning. Actually, he never thought she would take this type of initiative. Never believed he would wake up to something so sensual and delicious.

She was passionate and daring.

Angelica was all his.

"Bloody eyes!" He nearly jumped from the bed.

Her lips closed over him, sucked and nipped, enticed and stimulated to a fever pitch. She ran one hand along his length.

She rose, staring at him, an angelic smile on her beautiful mouth, her lips parted and moist. "Is that an I like what you're doing or the opposite?"

He needed to taste every part of her beginning with her mouth. "Neither, it's an I love what you're doing curse. Don't stop." Yet he pulled her away, witnessed the tiny mew of confusion on her face as her lips pursed. "I'll explode before I give you your pleasure if you keep that up."

"Oh." She blinked a few times, digesting his words, attempting to figure out what he wanted her to do.

He pulled her over him. She straddled him, his rod touching soft swollen petals of her femininity. "You can sit on me." He massaged and stroked the tiny swollen knot he found in her damp folds. More sounds of desire erupted from her. "Are you hungry for me?"

"I woke up hungry," she murmured.

His hand rested on the back of her head as he pulled her close.

His lips found hers in a passionate dance between them. Their tongues dueled and played. "You are an angel in disguise," he murmured. "I don't think I'll ever get enough of you."

He kissed her again and again. She settled on him, moving slowly as her body tightened around him, the walls of her sultry core kissing and licking him. So far inside it seemed she pulled him deeper and deeper. The climax was fast and hard. He covered her screams with his mouth molded tightly on hers.

When they finished, she lay on top of him, her skin sweat sheened and beautiful. He could not tell her now. He shuddered with the fear of what was yet to come between them. The rocky road they were about to embark upon was all his doing. Before they wed, he should have informed her who she was marrying. It had been her right to know, his duty to tell her. He'd been afraid she would refuse to exchange vows of commitment with him. All of his fears stemmed from that one moment at the ball when he went directly for the jugular and asked her to be his mistress. Showing up there had been a big mistake, asking her that question possibly the biggest mistake of his life.

"How is your stomach?" he asked thinking in this position perhaps he should have a basin close by.

"I've not eaten yet. Don't fear. I'm not going to lose my breakfast on your belly." She giggled, running a delicate finger along his jaw then down to tease a nipple. "You might deserve it though. You did cause this predicament I find myself in."

"Thank God. Are you ready to meet the countess?" He brushed damp hair from her eyes. "Or would you like to do this again?"

"Did you want to leave this morning? It's already past ten o'clock. I'm surprised you slept so long."

He looked at the clock and was also surprised. The stress of the last few days was getting to him. He supposed that if Angelica was tired from sleepless nights he would be also.

A couple of hours later, they stood in front of the carriage that would take them home. The meeting between his great aunt and Angelica went well. Windwalker was being led from the stable. This carriage was much the same as the other one except for the insignia proclaiming it to be the Duke of Weston's. He inhaled, watching her closely.

During the light repast at noon, she and Mary spoke of so many things. Mary asking about her life in France along with the wineries her family owned. Angelica promising to have the manager of both wineries send her a crate of each a red Bordeaux as well as a Sauterne, the sweetest of course, because she discovered Mary had a sweet tooth.

So far, his wife did not know. Now, he could, would, tell her during their ride today. He was beginning to breathe more easily.

"West! Oh, West, darling it's been so long." A young lady ran down the road from the home nearby. She was waving her hands. "I thought it was your carriage." She threw her arms around him. "Can't you stay another day so we can visit? I've so much to tell you."

"West?" Angelica queried, looking from the woman to Mary to him then back to him, her eyes wide, sprinkled with confusion as well as a spark of anger.

It seemed she noticed the emblem on the carriage. He knew the moment recognition set in as he was still trying to dislodge Margret's arms from around his neck.

"I-I can explain," he said as Margret's lips found his. To no avail, he was attempting to push her away. Lord, but she was stronger than he remembered.

"I don't want to hear anything, no excuses from you."

Angelica ran to Windwalker, leapt on his back. Without thought, she raced away, her skirts flying as her hair unwound itself from its pins.

Devlin's heart caught in his throat, terror for her rushed through him. He broke lose from Margret and whistled. The stallion reared, coming to a complete stop but not before Angelica slid from his back. His heart twisted as he ran toward her. *Angelica.* Sweat broke out on his forehead, sliding down his face.

Terror for her swamped him. When he reached her, he cradled her head in his lap, smoothing his hands over her arms and legs, checking for injuries. Her eyes were closed, a small moan of pain making its way to his ears.

"Angelica, tell me where it hurts."

He smoothed her hair, stroked her cheek with the back of his knuckles. Mary was there as was Hasting, Margret too.

"Who is she?" Margret's strident voice penetrated his fears for long enough to answer.

"My wife," he murmured softly never taking his gaze from Angelica, his wife, his life, his heart.

Angelica opened her eyes, staring into his. "West?"

At this moment, she didn't appear angry but she raced off when she learned the truth. Perhaps she was more furious about the woman than the knowledge of his identity.

The baby?

Bloody eyes, her fall could have hurt the child. He should have never whistled for Windwalker. The horse would have stopped sooner than later when he discovered the rider was not him. He scooped her into his arms, striding toward the house.

"We aren't leaving yet," he spoke to Mary then to Hasting, "Have someone fetch the doctor. She needs to be examined."

"Why?" Margret asked hands on her hips, her voice strident. "She looks fine to me."

Devlin continued into the house then up the stairs to his room, Mary behind him. In his arms, Angelica moaned softly. "It's alright, Angel. Everything is fine. You're fine."

"What has you so concerned?" Mary asked, hovering over the two of them, trying to soak in what was happening. "She looks alright."

"She's..." He cleared his throat, his voice husky with distress. He had not wanted any of this information to come to light so soon. In a few months when there was no choice as to whether or not he would say anything was different. "She's increasing." His voice was a hushed whisper. "The fall, she could lose our child."

Mary's hand was on her chest. Devlin realized she was schooling her features. It wouldn't matter what she told him.

"Now, don't you worry, Dev. I'm sure your sweet wife will be well, up and about by tomorrow morning so the two of you can go home. The doctor will come and examine her and you'll see. Everything will be as it should be, just as you told her," Mary said as she watched him.

"No," Angelica said, trying to push upward so she could sit, her eyes dulled with pain, alarming to Devlin. "No one is examining me. I won't have it. I mean it, Devlin. Don't you dare bring a man in here to look at me."

"We need to see if you're alright then the child. It's important." Devlin knew they would have more children. What he wanted from all this was to know if there was anything he needed to do to take care of Angelica.

"No. Truly I'm fine, Devlin. Actually, I don't need or want a man looking at me."

She was shaking, yet her words were indeed strong, her face flushed to a soft pink. A change from the paleness of death she wore when he first reached her lying on the ground.

Devlin didn't want to force her but... He would do anything to make sure of her health as well as the child's. "Now, Angel," he began, his tone meant to placate, wishing he could convince her this was for her good.

Bloody eyes but he didn't want another man looking at her either. However, this was important and the man was a doctor for Christ's sakes.

Well hell.

"Don't Angel me when you want to get something from me or talk me into doing something I don't want to do. No man besides you..." She was adamant, her voice strong and sounding more determined than ever. "No other man is going to see me."

"I understand."

"No, you don't. I know you don't." She was pushing against the backboard shaking her head, her hair in wild disarray around her shoulders.

She was stunningly beautiful, evocative. He cursed his wayward thought. "Angelica," he began but had no further words.

"Devlin." Mary placed a hand on his shoulder, "Allow me talk to her, woman to woman. I believe I understand better than you how she feels. Plus, I think I can remedy this before the two of you start fighting. She doesn't need more stress, poor child. Why don't you leave until the doctor arrives? You can bring him upstairs with you. Have a brandy while you wait to show him in. Take Margret with you."

"I don't want..." Angelica began to protest once more.

"Hush, child." Mary rearranged the blankets, pulling them up to cover her more thoroughly. We'll humor your husband for a while. It will make him feel better. If you have no cramping, there is no reason for anyone to look at you, in the process embarrassing you. I'll make sure Devlin understands that. Is that all right? I suffered a miscarriage once. Of course, it was a long time ago. I will know the symptoms. I also *ken* how to treat you if the very worst happens and you start bleeding. Now, shall we think of something more pleasant to talk about while we wait?"

"Truly? I don't have to let some strange man look at me?"

"*Dinna fash* yourself. I saw how you fell. Your back took the brunt of the landing. You should be fine. How is your head?" She placed her hand on Angelica's forehead. "A headache? Any aches and pains anywhere?"

"My back is sore as is my head. I'm angry with Devlin, too, furiously so. He has no right to bring someone in here to look at me without asking. He has no right to pretend to be a horse breeder when he is really a duke. He was wrong to lie to me."

"Unfortunately for you, he does have all those rights and more. He is your husband, you know. Now tell me about this child no one knows you are carrying."

"There is little to tell. The babe is the reason we married. It's the reason he asked me anyway, no demanded. He would not have asked me otherwise. He doesn't love me. Just felt an obligation to do the right thing."

"I see," Mary said thoughtfully, drumming her fingers on the side table next to where she sat. "I think I see more than you, dear child, but time will tell."

"I forced him," Angelica whispered softly. "This marriage should not have happened."

"So, you held a gun to Devlin's head and made him bring a preacher because of your condition."

"No, it was nothing like that."

"I didn't think so."

A few minutes later, Devlin brought the doctor into the bedchamber. He was pleased to see Angelica had more color in her face. She was still sitting up talking with Mary, covers arranged around her as if they were armor, "Now, the doctor here will take a look at you. He will then tell me what to do. In this matter you will do as I say."

His voice held the command of a husband as well as a duke as if he expected no argument from her.

"There is nothing to do. I've no cramping." Shaking her head,

Angelica looked to his great aunt as if seeking advice. "Mary knows what to do if there is. If I begin to bleed. You see, sir, no disrespect, but I don't need you here. Nor do I want you in this room. There will be no examination today or any day for that matter. Do you understand?"

"It's true," Mary agreed with her then to Devlin, she spoke softly, "I will take care of your wife. She needs rest, nothing more. You will not be returning home today. We need to make sure nothing bad will happen to the babe or Angelica. If you leave her alone tonight and she feels sufficiently rested in the morning, you have my permission to leave here knowing she will be as good as new."

~ * ~

Devlin felt a momentary rush of heat to his face. Mary's stern expression reminded him too much of his grandmother. He knew Mary had questions about the hasty marriage as well as the child that would need answering. He wasn't at all sure how to explain the situation other than he knew he had to have her, the child giving him the reason to marry in haste.

"I don't like this," Devlin said, jamming his fingers through his hair. "Perhaps he should check her heart or her lungs."

"Yours needs checking more than mine," Angelica shot out, her lips pursed together in apparent frustration. "For now, I don't want to see you. I don't forgive you either."

"You're just saying that," Devlin said as he turned to the doctor, "I'm sorry for bringing you here. I suppose..."

"She seems fine. However, I would like to check on her condition tomorrow before you leave just in case," he said turning to Mary. "I would feel better."

Mary blushed and Devlin wondered what exactly was going on here. Perhaps he wasn't the only one who had a confession to make. "I will see to some refreshment for you before I send you on your way."

Mary linked her arm in the doctors as they walked from the bedroom in avid conversation.

Devlin used the next few seconds to get his emotions under

control. He was worried and furious all at the same time. "What the devil were you thinking taking Windwalker?"

"Why did you lie to me?" she shot back, quickly her eyes flashing retribution.

"By omission only, I planned on telling you today on the last stage of our journey." He sounded remarkably calm to himself, belying his seething emotions as well as his fear for her.

"Why did you lie? Why did you insult me at that ball? I would have never married you if I'd known who you are."

"Now who's lying?" he queried despite the seriousness of her injuries he couldn't keep a smile of amusement hidden from her.

She crossed her arms in front of her a mutinous expression on her face. "This wasn't well done of you, West or is it Devlin. What is your name? I wasn't wrong was I when I saw that long list of names. It wasn't because your mother couldn't decide on a name. Why, West?"

He let out a deep rumble of air, staring out the window as if he could escape the questioning. There was no dodging this. "My friends call me West. No one, well very few call me Devlin which is my middle name."

"You never thought to inform me of that. What? Am I not your friend? Oh, I suppose a wife can't be a friend," she said clearly miffed at all his answers. "Or if you asked me to call you West, I might guess at the game you were playing. What is your name?"

He deserved every bit of her sarcasm. "Lord Alistair Devlin Mathews, Duke of Weston. If there are more, I don't recall them."

"You wrote more on the wedding certificate," she shot back still angry, still seeming to breathe fire at his expense. "Is that why you were so upset with my naming the sweet mare I purchased at your stables, Sir Alistair?"

He nodded briefly. "Now why are you being so stubborn at having the doctor examine you?"

"I thought you understood. Who was that woman? Margret?"

"She is no one. Someone I met a few years back. I was engaged then, and, well, I'm sure she heard about my breakup. She was always interested in becoming a duke's wife. Never me."

"But not your marriage. She didn't hear about your marriage. Does she always throw herself at you?"

She was jealous. Perhaps that was a good sign for their marriage. If there weren't more weighty problems in their lives, he might enjoy the possessiveness she was displaying. "We've only been wed a matter of days. Few know about our marriage except your family and now Mary. Not even my grandmother will know until we get there."

"Which will be in another couple of days."

"Tomorrow if all goes well in the morning."

~ * ~

After the evening meal, Merry locked the door to the bedchamber. She was angry with Devlin. Needed him to beg for forgiveness. So far, he didn't seem repentant at all. Well, he could sleep somewhere else tonight and every night after that if he refused to say the right words. What he did was unconscionable.

The banging on the door didn't make her feel any better. His yelling from beyond didn't help either. She didn't even want to talk to him long enough to tell him to find a couch. So, she rolled over in the bed then pulled the covers over her head to drown out the noise. When all she heard was the ruffle of the curtains as the wind whispered through the window, she began to relax, closing her eyes in a belated effort to sleep.

Merry must have slept. Slowly, she woke to hands roaming across her body, touching, exploring, seducing. She was naked. "Devlin!"

"Don't ever lock me out again. I won't allow it," he murmured his voice hard. "Thought you learned that lesson at the townhouse."

A soft puff of air whispered from the back of her throat as the palm of his hand slid across her nipple, her waist then her hips only to probe lower, resting between her thighs. "You don't play fair."

"Neither do you. I'm sorry, Brat," He murmured, his breath whispering against her ear. "That's the only apology you're going to get from me."

She squirmed. Felt her body begin to move to the dance of his fingers. "Are you really sorry."

"Yes, and not just because you kept me out of my bed. I knew from the very beginning I should have told you, struggled with how and when. Well, almost the beginning. My secret was important. I didn't want to..." He paused then. "If I didn't pretend to be someone else, I would have had to marry someone completely unsuitable."

She flinched, feeling as if she was exactly that person even though she wasn't, not really. Her family was titled and what more did a duke want than to be married to a woman whose brother was a duke? Perhaps a woman he loved.

Merry understood how she forced his hand.

Devlin was honorable. He would always do the right thing.

The night of the storm she should have been able to say the right words, should have told him no, demanded that he stop.

Merry felt his regrets then wondered if some of that disappointment didn't center around their marriage. Once it was announced he could not ask for an annulment. A duke did not divorce his wife. They were bound to each other through eternity.

When the doctor arrived, their breakfast was finished. She was declared fit and ready for travel by both great aunt, Mary, as well as the doctor. Unsure if she wanted to go further than this home, a little bit later she found herself seated next to Devlin on her way to England along with the reality of a marriage that was more inevitable now than ever.

The only way she could see to free Devlin of his obligation to her was to tell him she lost the child. She didn't think she had the courage for such a falsehood. If she did, if he ever discovered the fabrication, he would never forgive her. Would most likely take his child from her. He'd have every right to do so.

The hour was nearing six o'clock when the carriage rolled down the long drive toward Weston's Corner. She began to shake, her body trembling with the very real fear of the unknown. With a swift intake of air, she struggled to waylay her nerves.

Devlin set his hand on hers. "The duchy won't eat you alive. I promise," he told her, a wry curl of amusement on his face.

"That's not funny," she mumbled, taking her hand from his. "You should know you're not completely forgiven. Even though I allowed you to make love to me last night."

The ensuing bark of laughter surprised her. "Allowed me? You were begging for each and every stroke of my hands."

Silence followed her statement along with his declaration. It seemed to her they spent hours saying nothing. Now would likely be no different. Even her voice in her head abandoned her, leaving her in solitary desolation.

It seemed, here they were. How all the servants knew when they would arrive was beyond her, unless Devlin sent a message ahead. He would do just that she surmised. They were lined up on the steps of the front porch. Devlin didn't even get a chance to open the door for her before a footman was beside the carriage placing the stairs for her.

Eventually, Devlin did end up at her side. Between the carriage and the house, she heard more Your Graces than ever before. Heard more than she could count. The arrival of the Duke of Weston put any arrival of her brothers to shame. She reminded herself that Leslie abhorred scenes such as this. Preferred, at least in his Scottish home to have as few servants as possible. He had just enough for simple necessities. Lacie didn't object. So, there was not a lot of fanfare. The home in Bordeaux was a different story however.

Once they entered the mammoth entry hall, more servants arrived to give them their greetings, welcoming him home. Devlin finally got around to her introduction then more Your Graces started all over again. It seemed everyone wanted to welcome home the master and when they discovered he was married, his new wife.

Merry wasn't at all sure how she survived. She knew now the last thing she expected was this type of welcoming. In the short time since she learned of her title, she never thought of herself as a duchess. Whenever they had guests at home in France, she found a way to make herself inconspicuous. The fanfare truthfully wasn't something she felt comfortable with.

It seemed the butler along with the housekeeper was determined to give her the name of everyone present. What they didn't know about her was that she was terrible with names and would never remember. They were at best wasting their time.

Devlin didn't appear to be any help. It seemed he allowed her to flounder making a fool of herself as she tried desperately not to do just that. The sister of a duke should not be out of her element when confronted this way. Incredibly, she was trying to do her best with no thanks to the duke, her husband. If it killed her and it probably would, she was determined to conduct herself like a proper lady. Nothing like this had ever been expected of her at home. So, she wasn't at all sure how to act.

She hoped to hear something from her husband, some word of encouragement as she tried to behave in a regal manner, like a perfectly bred lady as her mother would say. She didn't want to be seen as the brat her brothers and husband often called her. This was, after all, the beginning of a new life for her. She did want to make the most of it. A good first impression was invaluable. She was after all the Duchess of Weston.

Suddenly and without the least provocation, Devlin was speaking. His voice was one of total disbelief coupled with a slight tinge of amusement. His bark of amused laughter startled her. "Good God, where did my brat go?"

All the air in her lungs rushed out at once. She looked to him in disbelief. Shock as well as unbearable degradation pummeled her from all sides. She was mortified to the very depth of her soul. All her blood drained from her face. For a moment her heart stopped before it began a frantic race.

It seemed he knew the folly of the words as soon as they left the space behind his teeth. His eyes grew dark as he stuffed his fingers through his hair, a look of chagrin on his face even as his dark brows drew together.

Merry turned to him, stunned by the unthinking but probably true words. She was crushed beyond belief, humiliated by her husband, the duke, of only a few days. What else could go wrong? Giving him no warning, and without thinking past the moment, she kicked him as hard as she could. Once again, she was devastated at what she did as well as at what he provoked with his unkind words. Tears slid down her cheeks as she sped out of the hall.

The direction she ran was of no consequence to her. She had no idea where she was racing off to except that it was away from the source of her humiliation and shame. If she never saw the Duke of Weston again, it would be too soon. Tomorrow she would find some way to get herself home.

She found herself in the yard behind the house, where the lawn was immaculately taken care of and where a path led farther away. Flowers lined the walkway. She gave them little notice bent on putting as much distance from the house as she could.

She ran until she could run no longer.

A stitch in her side made her slow to a walk as she struggled for each breath of air, wishing the maid this morning had not laced her corset so tightly. She couldn't go back there. Couldn't face his grandmother or even the servants after what he said, after what she did. His dreadful words were compounded by her deed. She proved herself to be exactly what he called her, a brat. For now, she decided she would keep walking. She would walk until she could walk no farther. The path had to lead somewhere. She stumbled upon a lake, a large lake that put her tiny pond to shame.

Shame.

Disgrace.

Dishonor at her stupidity bolted through her. She would never be able to look at his people again, never step back into the house. They would all see her kicking him, hurting His Grace. They would probably put her in the Tower of London. She would have her baby there. He would take the child from her, all because she lived up to his expectations. She sniffed, wiping away the moisture from her face. Southcliff called to her. She wanted to go home where there were no expectations, where she could be herself.

He owed her a serious apology. He'd probably expect one from her too. She heard him calling her name. She didn't want to see him, refused to acknowledge him. Thankfully, it was still summer and the chill of the night wouldn't descend until later. If she could think of a way she would stay here, would pray he wouldn't find her.

Unfortunately, that was not to be the case. It wasn't too many more minutes before she heard the tread of his boots along the pathway. Even before he knelt down beside her, she felt the heat of his body begin to warm her. His hand on her back caused her to flinch away.

"Don't touch me."

"I'm sorry. That was not well done of me."

He sat back, seeming to give her the space she craved. He didn't speak again, seemed to be waiting for her to say something.

Well, she didn't have one intention of apologizing to him. He would have to do better. It was the second time in the same number of days that he did something to apologize for. She wanted to lock him out of her room. Needed to find a way to keep distance between them or she would be in his arms again. He had that effect on her.

"It was a terrible thing to do."

She sniffed again, keeping her gaze focused on the swan to the left of her. Tiny ripples spread from the bird through the water. The bird had no cares, no responsibilities. Its life was its own.

"I apologized to everyone, all the servants, Duchy too. They all agreed the whole fiasco was my fault. They thought I deserved the kick in the shin and a hell of a lot more."

"Of course, it was your fault."

She was surprised others would agree with her. She sniffed, wiped tears away as she leaned into him. Her heart seemed to be bending already. He didn't have to do anything to weave her into the seductive spell he so easily created.

His hand once more on her back preceded his soft chuckle. He was lifting her now. If she didn't take care, she would be in his arms. He would kiss her. She would return his kiss because she could never resist him.

"Do forgive me. It's getting cold out here. Neither one of us is dressed for the evening's chilled air."

He pulled her to him, his hands cupping her rear squeezing, stroking so diligently, slowly lifting her dress, cold air caressing her legs.

She felt his heavy arousal against her belly, recalled vividly how it would feel deep inside her, desire rippled through her. "I don't want to make love to you, Devlin Mathews. I'm a long way from forgiving you."

"I know but your body does. If I touched you intimately, your woman's flesh would be weeping for me. I intend to collect after dinner tonight." He whispered kisses across her chin, down her neck.

He knew exactly what to do so she wouldn't or couldn't refuse him. He was experienced, a rake, a cad, her husband. She drug in a deep breath of air hoping to fill her lungs. "You would force me then?"

"Never." His body tensed, his frown more evident. "It's clear I wronged you, Angel. I do want to make amends." He set her on her feet then held out his hand. "Let's go back to the house where it's warm. Since it's late, Duchy is having a tray sent to my...sent to our rooms. You can have a bath and relax. We can talk."

"We had all afternoon to talk. You chose not to say a word."

She meant to challenge him, needed to understand why. She paused in thought, needed to know everything from the moment he made the decision to talk to Leslie and live at Southcliff.

"I know. The words were always on the tip of my tongue. Even so, I couldn't bring myself to set a conversation in motion. I was afraid."

He was afraid?

"You will talk to me tonight?"

"You must also be truthful with me," he told her as if he believed she was the one with lies and half-truths as well as omissions of fact.

He had always known who she was. There had never been any pretense on that matter.

All she was guilty of was not telling him how much she loved him. She wouldn't demean herself to give him fuel to laugh at her. Finally, she extended her hand, letting his fingers close around hers. She wasn't sure if it was merely to help her up or if the gesture meant something more, mayhap a truce of some sort.

They walked back, their steps slow and measured. Once again, he didn't speak, leaving her wondering if the overtures just made were simply to bring her in from the encroaching darkness and cold or if they might indeed have some other deeper meaning. Was marriage always this confusing and frustrating. She'd thought the first night she was in heaven. Now, it seemed she'd fallen to the deepest darkest part of hell.

Devlin seemed oblivious to her seething emotions. His thumb

pressed lightly to her wrist traveled in lazy circles, coaxing circles, seducing and binding her to him. He could wheedle all he wanted. She wouldn't fall victim to his charms so easily, not this time, not like she did just this morning. She winced at the thought even while a rush of heated desire shivered through her.

The house was amazingly empty when they walked through the back doors then up the stairs to his rooms. Inside, she smelled the delicious aroma of roast beef as well as other scents of fresh baked bread. Her stomach growled. She couldn't quite recall exactly when they ate last. It must have been hours past. Of course, she had little at breakfast.

"Do sit and relax," Devlin said, watching her with his dark brown eyes. "I'll serve."

She laughed softly, "I'm sure I can dish up my plate without help. If you must to keep from talking, then be my guest." She gestured to the trays of food. "It all smells and looks delicious."

He poured her a cup of tea, handing it to her before finding a crystal glass and giving himself a generous amount of brandy. When they were both served, she ate and waited, watching through half-slitted eyes. Still, it didn't seem as though he wished to speak with her.

Merry finished, setting her fork and plate on the serving tray. Devlin followed suit before ringing for the maid. When everything was cleared and the servants gone from the room, he sat back in his chair, stretching his feet in front of him. His eyes closed briefly.

"Don't know where to start," he sighed as he spoke softly.

"How about the pertinent information. Things I should know. So I won't be surprised, of course."

"Have I spoken of anything in my past? Truly, I'm not sure of anything."

"I know you had a fiancée who betrayed you." She knew little of this part of his life and wondered if it was any of her business. "Is it pertinent?"

"Not really," he murmured. "I didn't love her. She was always there, beside me. The relationship was comfortable. We liked each other well enough. I suppose she didn't love me either. She stopped the wedding three times."

"Comfortable," she murmured, "That's the farthest cry from our relationship. No one who saw us would describe us as comfortable."

"True. Couldn't we change that?"

"She liked the thought of being your fiancée but didn't want the title? Why does that surprise me?"

Most women would have rushed the duke to the alter to possess the wealth as well as the coveted title. This woman did not.

"After the fact it surprised me too. She cheated on me with one of my footmen. Probably more men too."

He sipped his brandy until he downed the last drop then he poured himself more. She watched and wondered. "That didn't bring you to be a horse breeder or to the stables at Southcliff now did it?"

"No. It was shortly after I broke off the engagement that my best friend came to me. His anger was seething and unsettling. He accused me of bedding his little sister and getting her pregnant. It was so far from the truth I laughed at him. One cannot get someone with child if you haven't had sex with them."

"Did you?"

"Good God, no! I could barely stand the chit. When we were younger, she barely left Teddy's side. He had to lock her in the house to get away from her. She was a constant nuisance."

"Little girls grow up. Is she pretty?"

"I suppose in her freckle faced sort of way. I don't find her attractive," he mumbled. "I never bedded her. So, I never got her pregnant. Duchy suggested I rusticate for as many months as needed to prove she was not in a delicate way or until she gave up the ruse and named the real man who got her with child."

"Why Southcliff?"

His breath heaved, his chest filling with air before he let it go with a long sigh. "Duchy suggested the place. I met Leslie once a few years ago. Knew he bred horses. It was logical. Plus, we became friends. So, Duchy got a hold of your brother, apprising him of the situation and asking if I could hide away there for a few months. She did not want me to have to meet Teddy with seconds named."

"Who would have won?" she almost laughed at the distress on

Devlin's face. Truly, she didn't need to ask the question to know the answer.

"My shot would have grazed him. Teddy couldn't hit the broadside of a barn on a sunny day," Devlin said.

"Of course, you felt duty bound to marry me because you did get me pregnant. When I fell from Windwalker if I lost the child, would you have cried out for an annulment?"

His glass landed on the table with a resounding thump, brandy sloshing onto the table. His eyes alert now. "No! Good God no!" he said with a force that startled her.

"No? Then why? You waited until I knew if I was increasing."

"You would not see me or talk to me," he said. "I was adamant about marriage from the moment I broke through your maidenhead. Had nothing to do with a possible pregnancy. I wanted you. Was going to have you."

"Oh."

~ * ~

"You are going to London? Now? The two of you have only been here a few days," Duchy said, fiddling with her teacup, dismayed at her grandson's words. "You owe it to your wife to stay here. From what I've seen and heard this has been a huge upheaval for her. It seems she still doesn't know how you feel about her. Leaving will not help your marriage."

"I've work to do."

His back was stiff, reminding Duchy of his grandfather as well as his father and their insistence on working all hours of the day. One way or the other, he would do what he wanted.

"The ball is only a few weeks away. Can I assume you will return to attend the celebration of your marriage?" she asked, disgusted with Devlin who was moping around the house, his young wife in not much better condition.

It seemed to her they were planning a funeral not a celebration of a marriage. "My God, Devlin you're as stuffy as your grandfather was when he was seventy. When I first saw how you reacted to Merry, I was sure she was exactly what you needed. Still am, for that matter."

"I won't disappoint," Devlin said softly. "I know what my duties are."

"Duties," she said disgustedly. "Duties, we aren't talking about duties. It's a marriage you need to make sure thrives that we're speaking of."

"Yes, things that keep a roof over our heads and food on the table. Those are also my duties."

"You don't have to earn another penny for the rest of your life to do that. Don't you think it would be nice to enjoy life once in a while? Spend time with Merry. She is beautiful, your wife. Unless you are more talkative in the privacy of your rooms, you've barely spoken to or seen Angelica, or is it Merry, since the two of you arrived days ago?"

"Her name is Angelica. I prefer that to the nickname that makes her sound like a little girl. You're right. We've barely spoken to each other. She hasn't forgiven the deception or anything else for that matter. I don't have the foggiest clue what to say to her. The best thing for the continuation of our marriage is for me to leave until her anger cools and she can forgive me."

"I believe she might need for you to grovel."

"You and I both know that won't happen."

"You haven't slept with her either, I take it." Duchy wondered about asking him such private things but she needed to know because she meant to discuss her grandson with Angelica.

"No, as if to avoid me she goes to bed early and locks the door. She knows I can't keep my hands off her. In return, she won't ever say no. I lust after that woman night and day. I want her right now, this instant. That's because we are talking about her. If I'm going to get any work done, I have to leave."

"You, on the other hand, I've seen right here drinking way past midnight. I'm not at all surprised she is asleep when you finally come to her bed. That doesn't sound as if you can't keep your hands off her. Why don't you go find her now?"

"I don't go to her bed. I go to mine."

With that said, Duchy's heart caught in her throat. Things were worse than she thought. Even now he was avoiding his wife and running away to London where he could immerse himself in his work. In such a short time, things indeed had gone from bad to worse. If they could just sort out their feelings for each other, all would be solved. She didn't have one doubt they both loved each other.

"What on earth for? The girl is obviously crazy about you."

"Why did you pick Southcliff?" Devlin asked, turning to watch her.

"Ah, you are finally asking about that. When Leslie brought her to Weston's Corner, she was only fifteen but strikingly beautiful, full of life as well. She took interest in everything. Her curiosity outshone her physical abilities. I was certain if the right man came along," she paused smiling as she thought on those days. "I thought she would be just the woman to pull you out of your doldrums, to teach you how to play, that there were wondrous things in this life besides work."

"When she bought Sir Alistair?"

"It was a mare she bought," Duchy said, a twinkle of amusement surging through her. "You say she named her mare Sir Alistair?"

"She did."

"Why don't you go to her right now, take her in your arms, make love to her as if it's the first time? Grovel if need be. Don't leave until the two of you have made up. Tell her you love her."

"I'm leaving for London."

"Now?"

"She told me she lost the child. Duchy, I don't know what to do. She doesn't love me. Perhaps you should not have the ball."

"Nonsense." She waved a hand in the air, terrified this would not end well. "The two of you are married now. I'm sure you will figure this all out. How did she lose the child?"

"She didn't say."

Chapter Eleven

It was the day before the ball. Guests were arriving at the inns around Weston's Corner. The establishments were filling at an amazing pace. The dressmaker was here. The last fitting of the stunning ball gown West requested specifically for her was being finished. Merry had never owned anything this magnificent except the wedding dress and the earlier ball gown Devlin designed for her. Unlike her wedding gown, this one did not sensuously hug every curve of her body. It was cinched in tight beneath her breasts displaying just the right amount of her breasts. The small puff sleeves sat daringly on the edges of her shoulders, begging to be pulled down.

Merry smiled when she thought about Devlin looking at her in the dress and hoped he would like the gown. His grandmother assured her he would except for the provocative and very sophisticated display of her breasts. That was her doing. He would have to get used to it, Duchy told her. She was in the height of fashion. Since she was a married woman now, she could display a little more of herself. She was the Duchess of Weston. She needed to present herself this way.

Merry remembered the gown she wore to the ball, the first gown he specifically designed for her. He didn't want that one cut lower. Still, with Lacie's encouragement the corsage was lower than he wanted. She wondered how much say he actually had in this gown, probably everything but the cut of the bodice. He was too far away to protest the neckline.

"Do you think he will get here before the ball is over?" Merry asked as she watched Duchy drink her tea.

Her gaze was now focused on the clock, which seemed to move

exceedingly fast.

Duchy supervised the ball every step of the way. She meticulously went over the guest list explaining who each person was as well as why they had been invited. She stopped at Teddy and his sister enlightening her as to the reason why she sent her grandson to rusticate at Southcliff even telling her she'd been taken with her when she met her when she was fifteen. Her brother and his wife would arrive soon, at least she hoped they would. Lacie would give her someone to confide in.

"What I believe is that Devlin will do his duty. He always does. However, it is up to you to coax him out of his melancholy. Why did you tell him you lost the child when it is obvious to me you did not?" Duchy set her cup on the table, clearly and impatiently expecting an answer. "You should never tell a man something like that. Your callused and unthinking words will come back to haunt you."

"There, it is finished." The seamstress said as she stepped back to peruse her handiwork.

"You are lovely, my dear, and don't answer that question just yet." Duchy waited for the dress to be put away until the ball then for Merry to dress. When all was taken care of, they were alone in the room. She repeated the question.

Merry poured herself a generous portion of brandy then sat down, head in her hands. When she finally looked up, "There was no other way. You see he doesn't love me. I thought I would set him free. If he didn't have the baby to make him stay with me, he could go on with his life. I would have never said the words if I had any hope at all that he loved me."

"Didn't work, did it?" Duchy asked softly.

"No, we are still planning this ridiculous celebration. He is still in London. I'm not trying to feel sorry for myself, but he should have taken the out I handed to him. If he had, I'd be home at Southcliff where I wouldn't be haunted by my feelings for him. He'd be free to spend the rest of his life the way he planned. Instead, here we are, immersed in this mire of falsehoods that don't suit anyone."

"What would you have done when he found out you lied? He would discover the truth. If you returned to Southcliff pregnant, I know your brother well enough to understand he would waste no time in informing my grandson. You know that don't you? You have to face the facts then explain why you did something so very stupid. Perhaps this time you owe him an apology."

"Well, he did make love to me before he left. I would just say I was pregnant again."

Duchy didn't say anything to that bit of nonsense. Merry could almost hear her words coupled with the stupidity that went along with them. All he would have to do is count backward from the date of her admission. If he did that which, she knew he would, he would know she never lost the baby. I'm gathering, you would have lost the child after your minor accident on Windwalker. How many times does it happen the first time you make love? Most couples have to wait for a time before conception.

"You expected he would believe your tall tale?" Duchy asked, a wry look of amusement on her face. "You don't give him much credit for common sense or intelligence."

"No, but..."

"You go on up to your room and get some rest. Land sakes but you will need it tomorrow. Already the guests have been arriving. A nap now and hopefully you will be able to greet your husband properly when he arrives later tonight." Duchy patted her on the hand a wry look of amusement painting her face.

"He will be here then? For some reason I've a hard time believing it."

"Yes, don't worry yourself. Devlin will arrive before nine. He sent a message that I received just this morning. He always keeps his word."

Relief washed through Merry. She half expected Devlin to shirk this appearance. Humiliated one more time by her husband, she believed nothing would surprise her. He was supposed to have arrived this afternoon. She anticipated his arrival, hoping she could talk to him before the festivities of tomorrow, deciding she should tell him two things. One that she loved him, the other that she really didn't lose the child. He would wonder why the lie. He would be furious at first, perhaps even unforgiving.

Duchy was right. It was her turn to apologize.

When she reached their rooms, they seemed surprisingly empty, more so than the last few weeks. For some reason she couldn't explain to herself, she didn't think he would arrive tonight. Everything seemed so empty. A few tears welled in the corners of her eyes. She fought them thinking she should prepare herself for the denouncement of their marriage tomorrow night. Instead of an introduction as the new duchess, she would be shamed. After all she sowed the seeds. If he asked for an annulment, it was what she expected when she claimed the loss of the child.

You made a terrible mistake. I would have told you so if you bothered to talk to me.

I wasn't talking to anyone.

That's why you're in so much trouble now.

Perhaps not if I tell him I love him.

Should have told him weeks ago.

I know.

Why didn't you?

I was too afraid.

Even so, she prayed he would not go that route. That he might decide he loved her and wanted her. Her hands rested on her stomach, still flat although she sensed a quickening she could not explain.

Servants arrived with food and drink, enough for two. Devlin wasn't here though. She didn't expect him despite the message he sent Duchy not her. Aimlessly, she roamed the sitting room then into her room. A few minutes later she wandered into Devlin's room. While they had been living here, he only came to her one time, nor did he invite her into his lair. Once, he told her he could not keep his hands off her.

It seemed he lied or he no longer felt that way. She ached for him in ways she would have never thought possible if he had not been such a kind, tender lover. What was she to do now?

You should have thought of all the possibilities before you lied to your husband.

I thought I had.

No, you only thought of yourself and the fact you did not tell him no. You wanted to absolve yourself of any wrongdoing.

I did.

So how are you going to fix this before he does cry foul and ask for an annulment?

I've no idea.

You could try telling him you love him?

We've been over that before.

Yes, and I was right then just as I am right now and I'll be right the next time you decide to ask me for advice. The man might love you. If you have the courage to admit the fact then he might confess his love.

At this point I don't see how anything could hurt.

Then you will do it?

As soon as I see him.

Promise?

Really? Of course I will.

She swallowed the breath into her lungs, praying for the courage to tell him how she felt. It would have to be the first moment she got the chance or surely, she would have too many misgivings to go through with the telling. She would have to do it without stopping to think.

No, you won't.

I will.

She decided to wait for him in his room.

~ * ~

Devlin raced from London, understanding he would be late. If the weather held though, he might be able to spend the night in an inn close by then rising early he could be home before dawn and Angelica wouldn't know.

Over the past weeks he'd taken his grandmother's advice to heart and decided to tell her he loved her, had probably loved her from that first time he saw her. That seemed eons ago. He'd been butt naked in her pond. She'd watched. She'd been seemingly unable to take her eyes off him. He grinned.

Good breeding or fear, he was never sure which caused her to turn her face away just before he took the last step that would have revealed everything to her. Bloody eyes, he wanted to wrap his arms around her right now and kiss her senseless. He needed to sleep with her through the night and wake up next to her in the morning.

Well hell.

He'd been such a stupid, blind fool. This was not what he expected from himself. How had he ever let his emotions rule his mind? How had he not? This hell was of his making. He had no one to blame except himself.

Mile after mile fell away, still he understood luck was not with him. Finally, around midnight, he tried to find a place to spend the night. The ball, the damn ball had every inn from London to Weston's Corner filled to overflowing. Eventually, he was offered a place in the stable. How ironic, he was sleeping in a stable again this time without the benefit of a bed or his wife. He curled up in a corner of an empty stall.

Sunshine woke him. He knew he wouldn't make it to his home before dawn. It was dawn already. He had at least another couple of hours of hard riding ahead of him. In hindsight, he should have counted the lost hours of sleep and ridden through the night. At least he would be in his bed now then he could have slept until noon or later.

Angelica and even Duchy would be grinding their teeth in worry that he wasn't coming. As he expected, he rode into the stable at Weston's Corner slightly after the noon hour so exhausted he could barely walk the distance to his rooms. If he were to make it through the ball this evening, he would have to sleep. He wanted to see his wife. She wasn't in their rooms. He didn't have the strength to search for her. There would be time for that later.

Kicking off his boots, he slipped from his shirt and cravat, letting everything fall on the floor as he toppled onto the bed. It seemed to him that only a few seconds passed before servants woke him. Steaming water, food and clothing were all brought into the room. His head aching, he groaned as he sat up realizing this was all for him.

When he could open his eyes far enough to see, he found the clock in the corner of the room. The time was nearing six. He hadn't even seen to his wife. He supposed she was dressing in her room. His untimely arrival would probably not be appreciated. As he moved from the bed to the tub, he stretched stiff muscles. He was so bloody tired he couldn't think straight.

When Devlin made his way down the stairs to one of the two ballrooms, the place was filled with lively chatter as well as delightful music. More than anything he wanted to see his wife then greet her with a long slow mind-drugging kiss before whisking her upstairs to his bedroom. Bloody eyes but he missed her. He wasn't in the mood for this.

He supposed he should curtail the kiss in lieu of a scandal. Well hell, this was his ball, his celebration. He was the duke. They were married. He would do what he wanted when he wanted and he wanted to kiss his wife properly. If she'd come to his room first, he would have the privacy needed for what he had planned.

Standing in the middle of the steps, he searched the first room for his wife, his Angelica. He saw Teddy and his sister then his grandmother but there was no sign of the new Duchess of Weston. Striding with purpose to his grandmother, he greeted her with a very proper kiss to her hand.

"Where is Angelica?" he asked, knowing his grandmother would have something to do with the fact he couldn't find her right now.

It would be some kind of penance he would have to pay for not making it home on time. His tardiness was his fault. He thought he could do one more thing then one more until he realized his mistake.

"She is mingling as you should be. I've left her alone to discover all your invited friends, enemies as well. Seems, as is always the case, there are a few uninvited guests," Duchy looked to Teddy when she spoke the last words. "Is Teddy friend or enemy?" she asked. "Then there is your ex-fiancée. You didn't invite her, did you?"

Devlin turned to look at his longtime friend who seemed to be grinning, unlike the last time he saw him at another ball. Teddy had his hand around his little sister's wrist and was tugging her along with him. He supposed an apology was forthcoming. From both of them he hoped. However, if he'd not been forced into hiding, he would have never met Angelica. He grinned.

When they stopped in front of him, he ran his gaze the length of

Emma's body but didn't say anything. He stared at her, a slight tilt to his head and watched as she squirmed. When nothing was said, he arched a brow in question as Teddy nudged her once then a second time a bit harder.

"Emma," Teddy said.

Devlin watched her swallow while her lashes lowered. "I'm dreadfully sorry. I lied about the baby and you."

"You almost caused two friends to duel in your behalf when you could have stopped it." Devlin's tone was curter than he intended but what could the chit expect?

"I know," she murmured. "I'm dreadfully sorry. It won't happen again."

"Were you ever pregnant?"

Devlin was sure he knew the answer to that. Emma was immature, difficult to get along with simply because she was headstrong and didn't take direction well. He paused thinking those words could describe Angelica too. The grin was slow and directed to the ballroom as he once more looked for his wife.

"No," she said. "I wanted the title and you were the only duke I knew who wasn't a doddering old man."

"The title," he paused recalling his wife never coveted his title or anyone else's.

He supposed she would be happier if he was indeed a horse breeder even though she had difficulty coming to terms with that too. "Excuse me, I'm going to find my wife." He turned to Duchy, "What color is her dress?" It seemed he couldn't remember what he ordered.

"The palest blue with silver threads running throughout just as you ordered. She is wearing the sapphire and diamond necklace you bought her," Duchy said grinning. "Your wife is really quite beautiful. I also believe she is quite irritated with you too."

"Because I was late."

"Because you were more than late. You made both of us a promise, which you did not keep."

"Well, I mean to make it up to her," he said dryly, thinking if given the chance, he might tell her he loved her tonight. It would be as good a time as any. "In every way possible."

"Keep your hands off her."

Duchy's words left no imprint in his head as he strode to the other room searching for the woman he loved.

"I'm going to find her first."

"Do something, Teddy," Duchy whispered as Devlin's long strides carried him into the second room in search of Angelica.

Devlin passed friends and acquaintances alike as he made his way through the throngs of people probing the room for his wife, his angel. He passed the Duke of Southcliff and his wife. He was greeted with polite hellos and Your Grace as well. Single minded in his purpose, he finally spotted her surrounded by several young men seeming to fawn over her. She was animated, laughing at what they said. Jealousy left a searing trail from his head to his toes.

His heart raced at the sight, anger boiling inside. What the hell was she doing flirting with men. Didn't she know she was married now? She had no business flirting with anyone but him.

He reached them with clenched fists, his feelings blazing. "Duchess," he said his voice curt. The men surrounding her backed away. "You are stunning tonight. Why didn't you wait for me to escort you?" Her crystal blue eyes were wide, confused.

"Your grandmother told me you were sleeping and you would come when you were rested. She told me..."

The rest of her sentence was cut short. Devlin wrapped his hand around her waist dragging her to him. She let out a startled gasp then his lips found hers. He swept his tongue across her lower lip then into her mouth, delving into the honeyed depth, tasting champagne. With a tiny mew of pleasure, she opened for him, her fingers winding around his neck then into his hair.

This was not enough of her. He knew it. She knew it. He hadn't seen her or been with her for the longest time. His hands cupped her buttocks bringing her to his hard arousal, caressing her. He groaned into her mouth. Sweeping her into his arms, her legs around his hips, he headed for the stairway and his bedroom intent on seeing his wife most thoroughly, every naked inch of her and to hell with the ball. Bloody eyes but he hadn't been with her in two weeks. If she lost the baby, he needed to put another one inside her.

With purpose he was striding through the people, his teeth and tongue making tender forays on her neck, his hand cupping her breast, floating over her taut nipple. He was vaguely aware of the ooh's and ah's, the oh my's in the room as well as the I nevers. She was his duchess and he was going to make love to his wife now not later tonight or in the morning.

Before he reached the foot of the stairs, Teddy stepped in front of him. "Do you have any idea what you are doing, old chap? Duchy doesn't want a scandal on her hands but I'm afraid, well, let's just say if you go up there, it could be worse than it already is. Right now, you and Angelica will be the talk of London for months to come."

"He's right you know." Leslie stood beside them a strange expression on his face, Lacie slightly behind him, her hand on his arm, "Though faced with a similar situation with Lacie I would have done the same. Not sure I could have been talked out of it."

Devlin rested his forehead on hers for several seconds while a restless commotion continued in the background.

Well hell.

Slowly, he let her slide the length of his body, attempting to tuck a few wayward locks of hair back into place. Now, he kept his hands on her waist. She clung to him. He heard her breaths, long and deep. Saw the rapid beat of her pulse at her neck, wanted to kiss her there, taste the silken flesh, feel her fire burn him.

"I say, why don't you let her dance with me while you mingle. I'll hand her off to another friend. You should dance with some women too," Teddy said.

The ragged breath he inhaled did little to ease him. He'd known what he was about, never thought of Angelica or the repercussions. Lord, but she was so innocent. She would have let him take her upstairs despite the gossip that would have ensued. She probably didn't understand any of that. Duchy did and her timely intervention saved his wife's reputation when this was all his fault. Once again, he needed to take the blame. Who in the ton would see it that way?

He watched as Teddy took her into his arms to dance. Jealousy flared. He found Emma and danced with her then his grandmother, always keeping an eye on Angelica. He danced with Lacie when Leslie did the same with his little sister. He could not stop wanting her, needing her. By the time she joined him and Duchy for a glass of champagne, her cheeks were flushed. Her lips were moist, pink begging him for the kisses he wanted to give. He turned away, wishing he could touch her again, kiss her, take her to his room.

"The ball will be over in another two hours or so then you can have your wicked way with your wife. Until then behave yourself," Duchy told him, tapping his shoulder with her fan. "In more ways than one, you will regret it if you don't."

Where Angelica was concerned, he didn't have one breath of common sense inside his fevered body. Held tightly in the circle of his arms, she was the fire he needed to live. "I will certainly try," Devlin said as he pulled her close before wrapping his arm around her waist. "Is this alright?"

"Just see that you do nothing more," Duchy told him watching closely for any improprieties.

"What? You don't trust me?" he asked laughing as he ran his hand up Angelica's side, stopping just shy of her breast.

"Not with your wife I don't. Everything else, yes."

"I don't either. It does seem as if I gave you fair warning. Not only can't I but I don't want to keep my hands off her. Don't expect to see us in the morning tomorrow, perhaps not even until the late afternoon. I plan on keeping her very, very busy."

"We should make the formal introduction before you lose what little hold you have on decorum," Duchy said with one slanted eyebrow coupled with a decided sparkle in her eyes. It seemed she read his mind. "Once everyone has had too much to drink, they will forget you and your wife. If you are discreet, you might be able to slip away then."

"Perhaps we should make the introduction," Devlin agreed his voice soft. "What about you, Angel? Do you think we should introduce you then escape to my room?"

"I think we need to spend a few more hours here." Still, she leaned into him belying her words while secretly agreeing with him. "I have things to tell you, important things."

He liked the way she moistened her lips, the way her eyes darkened with desire. "I have things to tell you, Angel."

Chapter Twelve

Introductions were completed but the night was far from at an end. She was now besieged by all types of men, some not so nice as before, lechers might be a preferable word. The time was doing anything but fly by. She meant to endure the hours simply because she knew now just how much her husband wanted her. A soft shiver of happiness rushed through her.

She was sure when he found her and kissed her, he was about to drag her away to make love to her. That very act would create a scandal far and above anything the nobility had seen in England for quite some time. She heard the whispers from the matronly ladies who all but swooned one moment then swore how horrible it was the next. All the younger women wished they caught the Duke of Weston's eye as she did. Strangely, Duchy looked pleased even though she reprimanded her grandson.

Even while he danced with lady after lady, she couldn't hold back the smiles. She would hear them giggling, watch his grimace before searching the room for her. He would wink then grin shamelessly. She knew first hand he didn't like giggling women. Clearly, he was not enjoying himself, would rather be with her. That fact gave her more confidence than she felt before. She meant to use each moment to her advantage. Her only problem was the confession about the baby she meant to make to him tonight. She had lied to him. That very fact might take some groveling on her part to make amends.

Well, she had two confessions but who was counting? The first and foremost declaration was to tell him she loved him. She prayed he would return the sentiment and would forgive her the lie about his child.

Duchy seemed to think he would, hence the ensuing courage. She hoped it wasn't false courage. Hoped she wouldn't regret the confessions.

"I suppose you're pleased with yourself, the congratulation on winning Devlin's hand. All the attention. The accolades." Laced with venom, the voice spouted pure poison.

Merry whirled surprised by the underlying malice in the lady's words. The woman was beautiful, blond hair and dark brown eyes, a smile that promised retribution that belied the kind words. Merry wondered what the woman wanted. Clearly, she had an agenda. "That does seem to be the reason for the ball don't you think?"

"Then you don't know the kind of man you married." More hatred in her tone came from generously painted lips.

"Excuse me?" Merry questioned realizing this lady must be one of the uninvited Duchy spoke of when they were making the guest list. Duchy told her there would be a few who would come with reasons of their own, usually enemies of her grandson. Merry didn't think Devlin could have any enemies. Apparently, she was wrong.

The woman laughed, a brittle sound floating on the music. "You have no idea who I am, do you?"

"No, I don't suppose I've any idea. Obviously, you're not a fan of the duke. So, why are you here?"

"How could I be? I'm Starr Robertson. The woman he jilted at the altar."

Merry watched dumfounded as the scene continued to unfold while she tried to remember everything Devlin told her about the relationship. One of the gentlemen nearby said, "I say, Miss Robertson, you never got to the altar, did you? Recall Mathews breaking it off before it got as far as that. Wonder why that was?"

"Then do you also recall he kept me waiting years and years?" Starr snarled at the man. "Years wasted. It's all his fault. This could have been our ball." She waved her hand in the air, encompassing the scene.

Merry was appalled at the woman's words. She had no idea they had been engaged that long. However, what was clear to her was that it was not Devlin's fault. He did not make her fall into the arms of his footman. That much she did know. This was outrageous. She wasn't sure at all what she should do about this. What she did know was that Duchy would not want an ensuing scandal having narrowly avoided one earlier.

"You were amazingly lucky, my dear," Starr remarked to Merry with less heat, but with no less bitterness. "You got him to the altar before his interest grew less, or did you get pregnant first? Did he have to do his duty by you? His interest will diminish with time. His work you know. Don't expect his declarations of love to continue much longer."

Pregnant?

It's too close to the truth if you ask me.

What declaration of love? He hasn't spoken a word to me of love. He still calls me Brat when he thinks it suits.

I doubt if he ever told that snake he loved her.

What do you know?

More than you. Best you tell that husband of yours how you feel. Seems he's been mistreated by that viper and you as well. You wouldn't want to find yourself in the same category as that nasty woman.

You're right of course.

"Why was your engagement so long?"

That was something Devlin never told her. He'd been in such a hurry to wed her. Merry understood his haste was because of the child. How did he go years and years without siring a child on Starr? Unless they never... Well, she didn't see how any right-minded person would want to sleep with her let alone Devlin.

"Because every time we set a date, he figured out some reason he couldn't attend. He would have a meeting or a commitment in London or some other place. He was always too busy too much work to make time for us. When I finally refused to put the ceremony off one more time, he broke it off completely."

"But...why would he do that if he asked you to marry him in the first place?" Merry asked, confused now by everything Starr told her as well as the subtle things that seemed to be left out. A lot of information was not said.

"Why else, little innocent. He didn't want a wife. Liked being engaged so he wouldn't become the most sought-after bachelor in the ton. Mothers were no longer introducing their simpering daughters, just as your mother must have introduced you. As it was, he didn't have any obligations to fulfill."

Merry felt the sudden drop of her stomach. She wanted to yell at her that she never simpered in her entire life. Yet everything she knew about Devlin belied the story Starr wove around the two of them. She couldn't help but go over Starr's words that obviously Devlin didn't want a wife. He didn't want Starr. Perhaps he didn't want her as well. It was just the babe growing in her womb that brought him to the altar. If she needed any proof her marriage was a mistake, here it was handed to her on a silver platter.

Starr was no longer young. She would not have it easy finding a man who wanted someone such as she, used and put on the shelf. Still, information, knowledge of Devlin, niggled at her brain. Some of the things Duchy told her didn't refute Starr's words.

She had nothing to say to Starr Robertson. She understood the bitterness too. Merry felt sorry for her.

"Spreading your vicious lies again, dear Starr?" Teddy said, suddenly appearing at Merry's side.

"Just telling the young bride how things happened," Starr replied stiffly, though with apparent unease. "Your duke is a bounder of the worst sort."

"Keep your claws sheathed," Teddy smiled agreeably. "Shall we get the other side of the story before Merry passes judgment on her new husband? What do you say? The truth perhaps?"

"Stay out of it, Teddy," Devlin said, standing at Merry's side. "In time, Angelica will know everything. Already understands most of what went on between the two of us."

"However, I feel the need to atone for my past sins, especially since I've seen that green eyed fiend jealousy in your eyes when I danced with your wife," Teddy said with a wry humor Merry didn't understand.

When she tossed her glance Devlin's way, she saw that Teddy hit some nerve.

"You should keep your mouth shut about what you know so little," Devlin said pitching his friend a look of utter disgust before taking Merry's arm and leading her away. She allowed it for all of three seconds before she jerked her arm back. "You, sir, are despicable."

Devlin didn't pretend not to know what she was talking about. "Condemned before I can speak my side of the story. Before you pass judgment, you should hear all the facts, Angel. But then Starr is very good at weaving tall tales and putting herself in the best light possible. She doesn't deserve your sympathy. I do, however, deserve your trust."

No, perhaps she didn't. Over the few minutes of Starr's story, she forgot the woman cheated on her husband and the fact she was very glad it happened. "She waited years for you."

"Indeed, she enjoyed every one of those years as my fiancée. I told you about the footman. Did I not?"

Merry could only nod, her eyes narrowing as she thought. "You never postponed the wedding over and over again as she said?"

His heavy sigh surprised her as did the narrowing of his eyebrows. "We were to wed eight years ago. It was her decision. She postponed the big event. In all that time, I set the date back only once. Every other time was her doing."

Merry was shaking her head, intrigued by the new set of facts placed in front of her. The matter was obvious to her now, "Starr didn't want to marry you, did she?"

"No, I don't believe she did. Perhaps later, sometime in the future she might have gone about the business of a wedding. I don't know. We bore no love for each other. Together, it seemed we were comfortable."

"She had other lovers..."

"I believe so. Once I discovered the footman, I never asked. It was over, done. How many she had over the years didn't make a difference."

Merry didn't understand why Devlin was so calm and reserved. No anger crossed his face. Starr lied to her, tried to stir up trouble. At this moment, he seemed to be ignoring the fact of it all. She prayed he would never consider her disloyal to him. The thought of telling Devlin she loved him set her courage back several notches creating more self-doubt than she wanted to think about.

Merry was furious at herself, but more so at Starr Robertson. Starr should pay for the lies she shed about Devlin. The woman tried to cause trouble between them. She should be made to pay and the ton should know why Devlin broke it off after more than eight years of engagement rather than blaming him.

She was appalled that Devlin let all of Starr's lies stand. "Why the devil didn't you defend yourself?"

He shrugged his broad shoulders, stretching the perfectly fit waistcoat across them. "My friends, the people who I care most about, know the truth. In my mind, that is all that is necessary."

Her back stiffened dramatically. She drew in a swift breath realizing she wasn't in the category he just described. She wasn't a friend. He didn't care about her enough to tell her the truth. "I'm sorry," she said curtly, hurt beyond anything she'd felt before.

He let out a heavy sigh seeming to realize what he said, his hands on her elbow as if he meant to reassure at least a bit. "Merry, even though we are married you don't know me well enough to jump to my defense when something like that is told. I really don't care what others think. I also regret not telling you everything the other day when it was brought up. It never occurred to me she would show up today, at the ball. I actually thought I had time to tell you."

Distressed she waved a hand in the air. "No, I should have known. You're nothing like she said. I had no reason to believe her. You should defend yourself. The fact you don't is something I don't understand."

"When the truth would ruin her? I can't do that, even to Starr."

"Which is more reason why I should not have believed her. You're a man of principles. I more than anyone understand that." She felt more than ever the only reason they were married was because of her pregnancy as well as his principles. She decided then and there she would be the best wife possible.

Without further thought, she whipped about searching for Starr and called out quite clearly through the crowd, "Lady Robertson, you are a liar."

Beside her Devlin let out a low groan as a path was cleared so Starr could see her accuser as well as hear her. Conversation as well as the music came to a complete halt. Silence spread in a wave throughout both ballrooms.

"What did you say?" Starr asked in seeming disbelief.

"You do not speak the truth."

In the ensuing silence Duchy's voice could be heard, "Bloody eyes, what has he done now?"

"Merry, stop before you do something you'll regret," Leslie said from across the room, loud enough for her to hear but not take heed.

A few twitters followed that, a few coughs and a great deal of foot shuffling as the crowd moved closer to catch every word.

Devlin cleared his throat before placing a hand on her shoulder, seeming to guess her intent but he had no idea. "Listen to your brother. Don't do it," he said.

Merry turned to him and smiled not at all unaware of the commotion she was causing yet intent on her mission to at least in some small way clear Devlin's name. "You know I don't take injustice lightly. One must pay at least in a small measure for the rotten seeds they sow. For Lady Robertson to slander your good name without cause is an injustice to you and your family as well as to the dukedom. I won't tolerate the dishonesty at your expense. Had I known she was lying to me about you—well, you know my impulsiveness. There is no telling what I might have said before I had time to think about any repercussions. This time I've thought."

"You do know you aren't just talking to me and that every ear in this room is hearing every word. You are aware of that, right?" Devlin asked with another low rumble of a groan following when she nodded her head, fully aware of the attention they were receiving.

She was deliberately making her warning as public as possible without ruining the lady as Devlin requested of her, actually the request was more of a command. When she looked at Devlin, it seemed he was now appreciative of the drama she was creating which wasn't nearly as damaging as it could have been. Of course, she wasn't finished yet.

"I think you've made your point, Angel."

It seemed he was attempting to stop her from going any farther in her castigation of Miss Robertson. That wasn't going to happen. She had every intention of ruining her with as few words as possible.

"No, not even half way," she replied with just enough true anger to warn him that the scene for the assemblage wasn't over. It was now clear that despite what he told her, she was going to say her piece no matter what. "You might be too much the gentleman to stop her slander, but I'm not."

Over her last statement, she heard a few outright chuckles. However, nothing potent enough to stop her from facing a very humiliated Starr again and saying, "They say truth will prevail in the end, that it will even come back to haunt you or perhaps bite you in the arse. In this case, I hope it does. Would you care to discuss the real reason my husband ended his engagement to you, Starr—or were you leaving? If you recall you were never invited in the first place. I can tell everyone why he, not you, called off the engagement, including why he ended the engagement."

It seemed to take Starr a few seconds to realize she was being given an opportunity to escape complete ruination. She didn't answer. She took the out Merry had graciously given her and left abruptly, appearing mortified, labeled a liar but no more than that.

"Are you finished?" Devlin asked at Merry's back, his hand resting gently on her waist.

She turned to him, a brilliant smile, "Yes, I do believe all has been said. At least what is necessary. What happened to the music? Perhaps we can dance this one."

She needed to talk with him. For the first time in what seemed like forever, she felt as if she could speak freely with him. Clearing the air about her pregnancy as well her love for him was uppermost in her mind. Now might be the perfect time to begin.

When the music began, Devlin pulled her into his arms, grinning. "I've always wanted to do something like that. With all my responsibilities hanging around my neck, I didn't dare. Thank you." They whirled through the room in complete synchronization, her heart a flutter with joy. He was proud of her.

"It was my pleasure."

She smiled, thinking things were finally as they should be between them. The man she loved with all her heart was now acting like the man she thought she knew.

"Of course, it was. It was very well done of you. It will drive the ton crazy trying to figure out what you hinted at. Unless Starr tries to press her point further, a course I doubt she will take, no one will ever know the truth."

He drew her closer than appropriate. Merry just didn't care any longer. Neither Duchy or Leslie said anything.

"They have better things to do than worry about such things." She smiled up at him, content, wishing they dare leave the ball.

"Did you enjoy causing such a ruckus? I was afraid you'd do something we would both regret," he asked seeming to read her mind as their dance led them closer and closer to the stairs.

Her thoughts of leaving must parallel his.

"You know I don't. It was all in your defense. She is a horrible woman. I couldn't let her get away with dragging your good name into the mud while she played games pretending you are a cad. I would have done more than just embarrass her if you hadn't asked me not to do just that. I hope you realize I stopped just for you."

"Indeed, I do as does everyone else in the room. You showed remarkable restraint just now. So don't be surprised if it doesn't come back to haunt you after a while. Everyone will be terrified of causing you the tiniest insult for fear of a like retribution. You have made your stance clear."

"I haven't noticed you having that problem," Merry said.

"Nor will you. I won't allow you to terrify me into silence."

"I believe I've yet to find courage to speak out to you. There are some important things I do need to tell you."

"No courage? You can say that after what you just did?" Devlin asked sounding a bit confused.

She shrugged that off. "That was temper coupled with injustice, not courage. You see, I've been meaning to tell you something, actually a couple of somethings but I keep putting it off. That's not courage that's fear. I'm afraid to say anything."

Devlin grunted. She heard the noise. She knew he was thinking about the last time she put off telling him something. Put it off until she almost fell from a tree and he had to pry the information from her. At least that time he had a pretty good idea what it was she wasn't telling him. This time was very different.

"I don't think I want to hear your secrets. Just want to take you to bed. In the process forget about the ball," he told her emphatically. "I've missed you in my bed."

"You don't?" she sputtered, clearly taken aback by his words. If he didn't want to hear her confessions she didn't quite know where to go from here. "Well, you don't have a choice. I'm having a baby." She blurted the secret she meant to keep to the last, after she told him she loved him.

He stopped, his feet sliding against each other as he seemed to trip over them. "I thought you told me when we made love last time another pregnancy wasn't likely to happen twice in a row. You know the first time."

"Well, how should I know? You're the one with experience not me, but this isn't the same as what you're talking about. This is the first baby. The one I didn't lose."

"You lied to me. Lied about the loss of a child. I don't..." His hands tightened on her just before falling away. Frown lines formed across his forehead as he thought about what she just told him.

"For your own good. I didn't think you wanted to be married to me. I wanted to give you an out. You didn't take it."

She tried to make the lies right but her words tumbled awkwardly. He wasn't listening in any case. Everything about him screamed at her just how furious he was.

"Angelica, you think too much and always come to the wrong conclusion. I know what you were thinking so now I suppose you changed your mind. You wanted me to get an annulment while you were still carrying my child." His anger seemed to be building, his face turning red. "You actually would have left me while you still carried my child. I find that incomprehensible. I can't be with you right now."

She flinched at the fury of his words. She tried for all softness, needed to explain her thought process. "I wasn't thinking along the same lines. All I understood from watching you was that you were miserable. You hated being married to me. I couldn't stand for that to go on for the rest of our lives. You didn't even come to my bed anymore nor did you want me in yours. What was I supposed to do?"

"Don't you mean the opposite? No, I don't want you to answer that. One more word, just one more and the scandal Duchy has been trying to avoid all night will crash down around us. Well hell, I need a bloody drink."

He turned then stomped from the ballroom. She watched as he strode up the steps, effectively distancing himself from her.

She wanted to run after him, she really did, but she saw the anger in his eyes, the darkening that seemed to reach all the way to his soul. Terror engulfed her, a blinding seething terror. She was going to lose him, forfeit the man she loved out of sheer stupidity. Even if she wanted to, she couldn't move her feet. A few of the guests were staring at her then gazing to the man who was striding from her a black rage painted on his face.

That didn't go well.

No, it didn't. You should have told him you loved him first. The fact about the baby could have waited you know. Perhaps you could have waited a few more weeks to make sure he loved you too.

I know. I'm always messing up.

You know what it must seem to a proud man to be told you didn't want to be married to him on the very same night he introduces you as his duchess?

It wasn't well done of me.

No, and you've got more groveling to do than you thought earlier.

I just never thought he'd get angry about the baby. Thought he would be overjoyed.

You've got a lot to learn about men.

Apparently so.

He was angry you were willing to lie about the pregnancy to avoid marriage.

I'm confused.

For the rest of the ball, Merry wandered aimlessly hoping to see Devlin but he didn't make another appearance. He didn't even show up for the conclusion and the departure of his guests.

It was nearly dawn before Merry was able to retire herself. She hoped to find him awake and sitting by the fire. When she entered their suite of rooms, she found the main chamber empty so she wandered into his bedroom.

She found him in his bed after all, a great lump with the covers pulled over his head. She sat down beside him. Her hand rested on his back while she hoped he would turn over. He didn't. He was sound asleep. Of course, he was. When she pulled the covers away, she saw he was on his stomach, his head turned away, his arms circled around his pillow.

His back was bare. She had the most urgent desire to crawl under the covers with him and wait until a decent hour to tell him the second part of her confessions, the part that should have been the first, the part where she told him she loved him. Courage eluded her.

She fought to uncover a tiny bit of the bravery she possessed only a few hours ago. Merry shook his shoulder trying to wake him. "Devlin?" He groaned and mumbled. She shook him again. "Devlin? Wake up please. I only told you one of the things that needed to be said."

He reared up before spinning around to peer at her through slitted eyes then dropped back to the bed. "What do you want?"

"To talk."

"Haven't you said enough already?"

"No, not yet. You walked away before I could tell you the rest, the most important part of my confession. I didn't think the first part would make you angry. I'm sorry for that. I want you know that I really did have the best intentions. It's just that I always mess everything up. Suppose you know that though."

Her hands began to shake. She wasn't sure she could go through with this. He wasn't cooperating at all. In fact, he was making this exceedingly difficult. She caressed his back and shoulders for a moment before moving up to brush a lock of dark hair from his face.

He had not cut it as Duchy asked. She liked him this way, this rugged look appealed to her. He was more like her horse breeder this way. She couldn't put the words off any longer.

Merry inhaled a deep breath then quickly said the words that had been on the tip of her tongue all evening. "I love you, Alistair Devlin Mathews." She waited breathlessly, but he said nothing, causing a sharpness to enter her voice. "Did you hear?"

Her voice must have startled him. He jerked awake. His eyes wide open for a second only. "What?"

"I said did you hear me?"

"Yes," he brushed at her hand, "Now leave me alone."

Her heart stopped as did her breathing. She had no idea he would be so callous. All joy rushed from her. Now she knew how he felt about her.

~ * ~

Devlin woke with this vague feeling he should remember something that happened earlier. Something that might be important. He did remember Angelica by the side of his bed. Knew he didn't want anything to do with talking to her at least not until he could get his seething emotions under control. He'd given her no indication he loved her. He did. He loved her more than life. She was his heart. In her position, he almost couldn't blame her for lying to him.

Almost.

Sitting in the drawing room with a cup of hot tea as well as a variety of other foods, he nursed the pounding in his head with food. The scones were delicious. He knew that for a fact having had them before. Today, this morning, they tasted like sawdust. Even had the delicious strawberry preserves made early summer did little to help.

He kept thinking there was something he needed to remember about last night.

The memory was so close.

Decided at least for the moment to stop thinking so hard. He just picked up the London Times and was looking over the front page for any news from the House of Lords when he saw her. The paper fell to his knees as he watched Angelica walk from the house. Her head held high, her back stiff, she gave no indication she saw him.

His breath caught in his throat at the site of his wife, valise in hand, leaving the foyer and walking down the steps. What the devil happened last night in their bedroom that would cause her to leave this morning? He wouldn't have it. She would talk to him now. They would come to terms with the baby fiasco. He rose striding quickly to the door as he watched her head to the stables. She was leaving him. God no! She wouldn't do something like that. Would she?

What the devil was she about?

Duchy stood behind him now. He was sure his grandmother would have something to say about the apparent state of their marriage. Last night had been a near debacle, a scandal in the making that was quenched, just barely by Teddy. He had no idea what transpired after he left to drown himself in his best French brandy. Except that was what he tried to remember. Something happened. He knew it just couldn't put a finger on it.

"What do you expect?" Duchy murmured blandly in her best prim voice, "After the way you treated her last night at your wedding celebration, your duchess. I'm surprised she didn't leave earlier this morning. I certainly would have done just that. You've given her no reason to want to continue with the marriage. If what you've done to her so far is any indication of how you intend to proceed...well...she has every right to seek a better life than the one you seem intent on giving her. You left her to send your guests home all by herself. How do you think that made her feel?"

"Are you implying I've treated her badly?" he asked turning then and wondering what the devil he was supposed to do now. He remembered her telling him that she didn't actually lose the first baby. Also remembered she had two confessions. What the devil was the second one? It couldn't possibly be as bad as the first.

"This doesn't bear repeating. For your sake in hopes the words will find a way through your thick skull, I'm going to do it anyway. You left her in the middle of the dance floor and never returned," Duchy said accusingly. "Can you even begin to imagine how she must feel?"

Bloody eyes but that was the way she made him feel when she admitted lying to him as he began to believe all women were treacherous liars. "She lied to me."

"I know," Duchy said softly, reaching out a hand to give comfort before pulling it back. "You can't find a way to forgive her? After all you do love her. Don't forget you also lied to her. Kept a secret from her that she should have known from the beginning. Perhaps not the beginning but after you slept with her."

"How much do you know?" He was angry now thinking she talked to everyone but him, her husband.

"Undoubtedly more than you. Why don't you go tell her you love her? The girl is head over heels in love with you. Anyone can see that."

"She told you she loves me?" He was incredulous, astounded. It was what he'd wanted. He should hear the words from his wife not his grandmother.

"No, she didn't."

If he didn't know better, he'd swear Duchy was laughing. "Then why...?"

"Because of the way she looks at you. It's a bit reminiscent of the way you look at her, the way you nearly created a scandal last night because you wanted her in your bed. You wouldn't have done that with just any lady. Wouldn't have done that if you didn't love her. Where women are concerned, you've never been impulsive."

"I do love her. Damn it. She lied to me about a precious baby."

"Get over it. I hope it's the last time either of you lie to each other but..." Duchy shrugged. "She thought you didn't want her. That the baby was the only reason..."

"I never gave her any indication that was why we married."

"Didn't you?" One haughty silver eyebrow rose a fraction. "You didn't tell her anything else. If you told her your feelings, none of this would have occurred. You're aware of that fact, right?"

"No!" he whirled, "I'm going to find out what is going on here. She's not going to leave unless I say she can."

"That's a bit autocratic even for you."

"I'm her husband, damn it!" he said his body shaking with the need to throttle her then make love to her until she understood how he felt.

"Then act like it."

"I thought I had. I've done, well, I've given her things..."

"Things she doesn't want or need. You truly don't know her very well if you believe she craves...things or your title. What she wants and needs is your love. Have you given that to her or have you always held just a little bit of that from her? Love is more than sex you know."

Devlin was sure it was but so far, he couldn't get past the lust he felt for her and the way he burned with just the suggestion of her touch. His teeth gritted together. How the devil did one know the difference?

At this point, he was sure he didn't understand anything. Love, he didn't understand any of it. All he did understand was how he felt when she stood next to him, when he heard her laughter or watched her smile. She was everything to him. He was sure he told her that he wanted to marry her with or without the child.

Now he wasn't sure of anything.

"You should probably go to her before she takes a buggy to London or Glasgow."

"She wouldn't."

"I thought you knew your wife better than that," Duchy laughed softly. "You know she would."

"It's dangerous. It would take more than one day to go to either city. She wouldn't dare." He knew she would. What he did know was that Angelica had no common sense. If she took a notion to do something, she would do so without hesitating or thinking. It was still broad daylight. She wouldn't get far. He was ready to chase her down, tell her how he felt. The guessing had gone on long enough, too long.

He broke off the conversation, Angelica's status the most pressing on his mind and started running. Inside the huge stables the workers glanced at him. One nodded toward the back. The others watched him with intense interest.

"Did anyone get the duchess a buggy?" He asked looking over the space.

"Were we supposed to? She never asked, just headed to the back there. No one wanted to interrupt her or ask any questions. She looked so grim as well as determined." He pushed his hat back leaving a smidge on his forehead. "Figured sooner or later you'd be here to sort things out with your wife."

Devlin nodded then waving his hand in the air, he called out, "You all have the day off. I want to be alone with my duchess."

He needed privacy for what he had planned. The men left. When everyone was gone, he slid the bar across the door, locking him in with Angelica and everyone else out.

Several deep breaths later he was as ready as he could ever be to find his wife. She would tell him this second confession. If she didn't, he'd throttle her. He searched throughout. Finally, he found her standing in the middle of a horse stall. Her bag was set on the ground. It seemed she placed a blanket over a nice pile of hay.

"Your stable doesn't have a room for the horse breeder," she said, her eyes wide, her body shaking visibly. "I looked for a room. I wanted to find the room." She was rambling. "Why don't you have one? I need one now. One with as nice a bed as you had."

He found her repetitious words endearing. She wanted to relive their summer. He could go along with that at least for a little while.

"There are too many employees at this stable. They all have places of their own nearby." He stepped closer wanting to take her into his arms now and talk later. "There is no bedroom here."

"I see. That's why I made one. In the future you need to make sure there is one." The pulse at the base of her neck told him she was frantic either with desire or fear.

Perhaps a little of both.

"What the devil do you think you're doing?" He only understood part of this. She was such a perplexing little piece of baggage. His baggage. He meant to enjoy this side of her until he cocked up his toes.

This time when he stepped closer, she stepped back. He needed to know more than his suppositions. He wanted her to admit to her intentions instead of leaving him speculating.

That was part of her charm. She always left him confused and guessing at her intentions.

His wife shouldn't run from him. When he left her last night, he didn't want anything to do with her until his anger was under control. Problem was he was still out of control. This time it wasn't anger that had him sweating. No, the emotion he couldn't control now was his lust.

"You have that ducal mien I'm beginning to tire of. I'm moving into this horse stall since there is no bedroom and I'm going to stay here in the stable until I get my horse breeder back, until I get the man I married back," she spoke so softly he leaned forward to hear.

"You're doing what?"

"You heard me the first time."

She looked so mutinous he didn't doubt she meant every word. Even her small hands were fisted, determined. He just couldn't figure out why she meant it. His terrified rage was receding. She wasn't leaving him. Not that he would allow her to do so. With time he could figure out the rest. She had this way of doing things without a thought or care that unnerved him.

Bewildered for the moment, "Thought you couldn't stand the horse breeder."

"You thought wrong."

He ran his hands through his hair then carefully tried to explain, "He doesn't exist."

"You're wrong about that. He does," she insisted her eyes flashing. "You're just keeping him buried beneath all that ducal haughtiness and impeccable, expensive clothes. I'm giving you fair warning right now. I'm not leaving here until I have him back. If I can't have your love then I want Devlin Mathews back, my horse breeder. Perhaps he will love me at least a little even though you do not."

Her words sparked a flame inside Devlin. He moved forward, so close he could feel her soft breath whisper against his cheek. "Are you telling me you want me to love you?"

"That is the most stupid question I've ever heard. I've been agonizing for weeks over telling you that I love you. I don't want that torture any longer. If you don't love me, I'll settle for having my horse breeder back. You will build a room for him, one at the back of the stable. We can live there. My horse breeder can visit me when he feels like doing so."

This was all craziness to Devlin. Of course, he loved her. Didn't she understand that? He married her. He wouldn't have if he didn't love her, child or no child. He wasn't sure he completely and thoroughly understood that fact either until this moment. "The devil you will. If you want to talk about agonizing..."

"I don't!"

"Then let's discuss you. I would have been very interested if you had ever found the courage to tell me you loved me, so if you agonized so much why didn't you?"

"I did."

"You did not! I bloody well would have remembered if you said those words."

"You wretch, you did hear me say them last night in your bed. Don't try and tell me..."

So that was what he couldn't remember. "Angelica." He cut in with the very real need to shake some sense into her then realizing what he needed more was patience, which was draining from him more than rapidly. "It wasn't well done of me. I went to bed with a bottle last night thinking about your lie. I bloody well don't remember a thing let alone hearing you tell me you love me."

She looked at him, eyes wide, her breath seemingly caught in her throat for a few seconds. "You truly don't remember anything that happened last night. Well, this morning when I came into your room, you told me to leave you alone." He saw the moisture in her eyes, knew he put it there.

"No, I don't. I don't remember anything."

"Truly?"

"Would you mind telling me again what you said? What I didn't hear? It would mean the world to me."

She turned away from him for a few seconds, her hands clasped tightly in front of her while her breasts caught the brunt of her ragged breathing. "No."

He cursed, poking his hands through his already disheveled hair, wishing she wasn't being such a stubborn little brat. He wanted his angel back. At least at this moment, it didn't seem she was willing to come back to him. Pacing, he kicked straw, swore again until he noticed his wife staring open mouthed at him. Her bottom lip was moist, parted from the top, even white teeth clamped down sweetly. He knew that was exactly where he wanted his teeth. He stopped suddenly and burst out laughing.

"No one on this earth can provoke me more than you. I love it.

Have missed the pleasure of arguing with you. Missed how you set my blood boiling. Even more missed making up with you and having your sweetness beneath me."

For a moment, he thought himself a bit irrational. Everything he told her was the truth.

Her eyes darkened and grew wider with what appeared to be apprehension. He'd seen that look so often it was singed in his brain. He started removing his jacket as she said, "Does it?"

"You're no longer a wide eyed innocent if you ever were one. You've practiced riling your brothers for years. You do it with ease. Now, you've turned that talent on me, your husband." He wouldn't have it any other way. "If you want a bedroom in this stable, you've got it."

"Of course, I don't. Don't *ken* what you're talking about. What are you doing?" Her eyes widened.

"Exactly what you want me to do." The white lawn shirt came off and was dropped to the floor. "What does it look like I'm doing. What I wanted to do last night before the ball barely got started and you managed to put your foot in your mouth. That is something we should work on avoiding from now on. That foot in the mouth thing you do with so much ease."

She stepped back, though her eyes seemed to be caressing every inch of his chest he was displaying for her. "It's the middle of the day."

"You know that would never stop me. Perhaps I want a taste of your sticky buns for lunch or a midafternoon snack."

"We can't, not here, the stable hands. Someone might...one of your employees might...my sticky buns?"

"Thought you wanted the duke on the shelf and your horse breeder back. It's what I'm giving you. Don't complain now that you've got what you want. You've need of a bit of courage. While your horse breeder needs another taste of your buns."

"I did, but—but—" She ended with a shriek as she went over backward into the straw, her train tripping her up when she'd stepped back one more time.

"Falling for me again," Devlin grinned broadly. "I like you this way, on your back, legs spread, waiting for me. It's every man's fantasy.

You're mine, my fantasy though, Angelica. Now I've managed to put you exactly where I want you."

He fell upon her, his fingers dancing over the fastenings on her dress. She was protesting even though she was laughing so hard she was having trouble catching her breath. "Devlin, please," she finally breathed out softly as his lips closed over hers in a deep drugging kiss he didn't want to end. When his lips left hers, it was to finish ridding her of her clothing.

"Please what?" he asked, his lips teasing a bared breast, prowling across one tip to tease it then back to the other.

She ran her fingers along his shoulders. "We made love in the stable at Southcliff. I suppose it would be only fair to make love in your stable."

"There is nothing fair about it. I thought you wanted the duke on the shelf." His voice was rough with passion. "Thought you wanted your horse breeder."

"I do. I love it when you forget all the formalities and you're just yourself." Her voice was soft, enticing, her fingers trailing down his back. "You are indeed my horse breeder now. Will you build that room? I can go there instead of taking a midnight ride on Sir Alistair every time you let the duke take over your persona."

"Yes, if only to keep you from trouble. What else do you love?" He nipped her bottom lip.

"You," she gasped as his fingers found the softness between her legs, touching exploring. "Do you think someday you might come to love me?"

He forgot what he was about, gazing at her, smiling, "What makes you think I don't?"

He watched the swift motion of her tongue across her lips. "Do you?"

"I'll have to think about it."

"You beast." She hit him, pounded his shoulder with her fist.

He tossed his head back laughing, "You know I'm not a beast. You love me."

"And you?"

"I'm thinking about it."

"You like to torture and tease, Devlin Mathews. Are you going to leave me waiting so long I grow old and gray before I hear the words? Duchy says you love me?"

"No." He continued his exploration of her body, his fingers dancing across her, probing her sweetness until she moaned, tiny ribbons of sound continuing with each new caress. "No, not until you are old and gray, never that but I will say the words when we are both old and gray."

"I haven't heard them yet."

"I love you, Brat. You're my angel, Devlin's Angel."

"I love you too, whether you are my horse breeder or my duke. I love you with all my heart."

For the time being, there was no need for more words. They made love on the hay, slept then repeated the process. Night fell on them. He cradled her in his arms vowing he would never keep secrets from her. Telling her he would not assume she understood his feelings without telling her.

With her love, Devlin felt as if his life suddenly came together. He would rather be the horse breeder than the duke. His life suddenly seemed more bearable when he understood when necessary, he could escape all the ducal responsibilities he had with his angel. She sparked something inside he left dormant all these years. She was his salvation from a life of work and drudgery. He was sure she would never allow him to go back to what he once was.

"How long should we stay here?" he asked as he lay beside her stroking her arm.

"Duchy will worry."

"No, I don't think she will," he said kissing her nose. "How much food did you bring with you?"

"Probably not enough," he inhaled the soft sigh.

"We should go to the house, to my bed where it's warmer and softer."

"You're not reverting back, are you?"

"No, never, Brat. I love both my angel as well as my brat with all my heart."

"Promise me you'll keep telling me that. If you ever change, I'll make sure I go riding at night."

"You won't."

"I most certainly will. Now, will you keep telling me?"

"As long as you keep reassuring me."

"Very well, I love you, Devlin. Make love to me again then we can go back to the house. Do you think Duchy will be waiting up for us?"

"No."

Coming Soon by the Author
at
Rogue Phoenix Press

Needing Gill
Bad Boys Book Eleven

Bordeaux countryside 1826

What little was left of Jenna Bonnet's luck ran out at the bottom of *Colline du Cimaron,* the hill leading to a past she'd rather forget. Now, the *Cimaron* vineyard and the chateau sitting at the top was a place of demons she had to confront for the sake of her son, the heir to the vast land. The holdings, now that Jacques was gone from this world, should be in the will with Brice's name. When she shielded her eyes from the hot rays of the sun, she clearly saw the chateau she lived in two years ago with her husband the Count of *Cimaron.*

For herself she didn't mind the walk up the mile long road to the front entrance. Both her son Brice and the aged horse that stopped pulling the small cart containing all her belongings exactly in front of the gatehouse would not be able to make the distance to the place she once called home. The ancient mare balked at taking one more step. Now the old lady was contentedly munching grass.

Jenna wasn't at all sure why she returned. All along she understood her return could be foolhardy with nothing to gain and so very much to lose. There were valid reasons though. None of which made sense at the moment when she wanted nothing more than to turn tail and run in the other direction. She let out a long slow breath of air deciphering the facts in front of her as she tried to put reality in the front of her mind.

One could call this attempt to regain what had been lost a disaster. It wasn't, not truly. She had such convoluted emotions. Somehow, she would find a way to get her belongings to the chateau. It was, after all, hers now that her husband passed away. Well, legally, as the only heir to the Bonnet fortune it was Brice who inherited.

Fortune, she mused, if there was anything of monetary value except the jewels she left behind when she fled. The money was in the grapes then the wine. She didn't have the means to take care of the vineyard, to hire the hands needed for harvest along with making the wine. After more than a year of neglect, much would have to be done to make a profit.

"Mama?"

Her son's tiny voice shook her from her reverie. Brice was the reason she was reminiscing. "What my *petit rayon de soleil*?"

She had used up the last of her spare francs in a shabby hotel in the town of Bordeaux; possessed enough for a couple days of food but naught else.

"Do we have to walk up that road? It looks so far." Brice was always so well-behaved. He never complained even when she knew he was hungry or tired. To get here she pushed them too hard. Even the horse protested.

"Not today, *mon petit chere*. We'll stay in the gate house tonight or in the cart as we have before if the door is locked." She did pray the old cottage would be open to them, as she wasn't looking forward to spending another night sleeping in the cart. A soft bed would certainly be nice.

"I don't like staying in the cart," Brice said with his little boy voice that always managed to make Jenna feel guilty about the life she forced on him. If she hadn't run from his father. If said father wasn't abusive to both of them. While he never hit her, he made them both feel as if they were useless. He treated her as if she possessed no brain. After she gave him his heir, he ignored her. She was thankful for that. She could not believe how a woman would ever want to be with that man in his bed.

Staying with her husband along with his family who moved unannounced into the chateau a year after Brice was born had not been a choice she could live with. Every moment she spent in their midst she feared for Brice as well as herself. Her aged husband was unable to defend them even if he'd wanted to. Jenna had never been certain the man cared. His brother was after the land, resented the fact he was the second son and would never inherit.

Jacque Bonnet was a selfish man, a greedy man who had feelings for no one other than himself. The night she fled, she took her son along with a few meager possessions vowing to never return. She sewed coin into her cloak. The money was gone now. To feed them she worked wherever she could find a job. In the threadbare pocket of her frock, she had twenty-five silver francs. Before she left the village below the chateau, she bought bread and cheese. They had food tonight. If she rationed the meager fare, Brice would be able to eat in the morning.

"We should go on up the hill to the house up there." Brice stared up the long drive pointing a tiny finger in that direction. He was saying the words she wanted to hear. "Did I used to live there?"

"Yes, you did. Maybe tomorrow we will have enough energy to walk the distance." She patted her son on the head, wishing she could give him everything his little heart desired. She was afraid for the boy. He'd been terribly sick a few months ago. Even now, he still showed signs of the ailment. He was weak and thin and coughed too much. Of course, he'd never been a large boy, never actually strong as many others his age.

"Are we going to die?"

At the question Jenna's heart lurched. Too many times to count she asked herself that same question. Day-in and day-out, life for them had been precarious. "*Non mon petit chou.*" *Not today.*

"Mama! Don't call me a little cabbage." He stared at her with his deep blue eyes a tiny, little boy frown creasing his forehead. "I don't like it when you do."

No, now that they were back at the chateau, their lives would be different, better. At least she prayed their lives would be better. She smiled, supposing he'd outgrown the endearment.

"We just have to find a way to change our luck, that's all. Why don't you get down from the cart, perhaps run around a bit, stretch your legs? Don't go very far. Make sure you can see me." With a half-hearted sigh, she watched him leave.

While he struck off in the direction of the gatehouse, she

rummaged through their limited belongings. After that, she saw to the horse hoping the old girl would be up to the trek to the chateau in the morning. One more night in the cart would be survivable.

She cringed.

A carriage whipped by her on the road behind them much too fast in her estimation. The horses would be winded, exhausted by the time the people reached their destination. Jenna looked down at her dress, smoothed the worn skirt. It seemed to hang shapeless from her bony shoulders. Her hair was lank. Once she had clothes that fit, a body that was not all skin and bones. Her hair had been shiny and thick. While she'd never been considered a beauty, she was passable fair.

Jenna fought back the tear that wanted to slide down her cheek. She sniffed a few times pushing all thoughts of self-pity behind her where they should be. She didn't have time to wade around in despair. At least she'd not been forced to sell her body to put food in Brice's stomach along with clothes on his back. Drawing in a long drink of air, she held it inside. She let it go with a gasp when she heard the deep rumble of a man's voice.

As she turned, thinking she needed to check on her son, she saw Brice held fast by the collar of his shirt. A large man, hair as dark as midnight, eyes cold as ice, carried him along, his toes barely touching as he tried to walk. Anger flared inside her. At her sides her fists tightened. The urge to swing her knuckles at this man simmered deep in her gut. How dare that man misuse her boy? Only prudence stopped her from her foolishness.

"Get him out of here." The voice emanating toward her was gravely and harsh with bitterness.

"Why? What has he done that could possibly merit this anger toward a little boy?" Her back stiffened as all motherly instincts to protect her child rallied inside her. "I'm sure he's done nothing wrong."

"He peed on my vines," the man seemed to grit out as he let go of Brice.

Brice scampered away. Jenna wasn't sure she'd ever seen her boy move so quickly.

When he stumbled toward her, she met him half way pulling him protectively into the shelter of her arms. "That can't possibly be a crime that would cause a grown man to treat a little boy so scathingly. Haven't you ever peed on a plant?" she shot out without thinking, her body shaking with the anger simmering deep inside. She wanted to lash out. Give that boorish man something to think about besides harming children.

He didn't blink. Kept coming. With a wave of his large hand, he spoke again, "Get out of here. Both of you. Don't want you on my land. Don't want anyone especially not little boys anywhere near." His eyes glistened with the anger that seemed to be boiling over as he strode closer. His brows were drawn together, frown lines marring what could have been a handsome face with eyes nearly as dark as his hair. His forearms were thickly corded with muscle, his legs long as his loose-limbed strides seemed to eat up the ground.

Well, she would leave if she could but she couldn't. This wasn't his land. The little boy he terrorized owned this little piece of Bordeaux. "It's my land. You get off! You leave!"

His grin turned feral, "My land. Bought it at auction two weeks ago. What makes you think it's yours? You've a sizeable number of francs in your pocket from the sale. Can go anywhere."

The shiver erupting within swept cold waves into her belly. No, oh god, no... "Whoever sold the land to you had no right. It wasn't theirs to sell. You will have to give it back. In this, the law will be on my side." Foolishly a small measure of courage erupted. This was Brice's inheritance, his legacy left to him by his father. For her, she didn't care about the chateau, the grapes or the wine. All the memories she had of this place left a sour taste in her mouth, curdled in her belly. She needed the income though. Wished to find the jewels that were hers by right. Wasn't going to give it up for this arrogant man.

"All the papers were in order." His broad shoulders stiffened as he spoke while his voice deepened. "Nothing you can do about this person who sold it. Wasn't truly a sale though. Man lost it because of back taxes due. So, suppose you wouldn't have francs in your pocket."

"That can't be." At the moment, she was all bluster. "My husband would never let his land..."

"Rumor has it the old Count Bonnet was bankrupt. Owed back taxes from several years. When I paid them, the land was mine. No one actually knew how the family was able to maintain the land after the revolution. Should have lost his head to madam Guillotine. Somehow, he managed to elude the madam. Kept the land for a while. Now it's mine."

His relatives, the same ones who succeeded in chasing her away caused this. Still, she meant to stand firm, fight for what was rightfully her son's. "I'll pay you back."

Haughtily he sauntered around the tiny cart, ran a hand over the weary ancient horse. He pulled out the small basket holding all their possession. He looked inside then to her, as he seemed to peruse everything. The odious man even allowed his gaze to travel the length of her then back up to settle on her bosom. Instinctively, she placed a hand where he was staring.

His grin didn't reach his eyes, eyes that were cold, frigid.

"Stop that! You've no right to go through my things." To look at me as you just did. She grabbed at his thick forearms understanding she would not be able to deter him from his quest. He would choose what he was about.

"You're trespassing, Madam. Seems I don't need permission to toss you off my property on your scrawny arse. Don't need consent to go through this bundle of nothing." If his eyes were indeed frigid, they didn't come close to the coldness seeping from his dark, despairing words.

She choked back the not-so-subtle reply she had to this man. Jenna didn't mean to let him get the better of her patience. Tried to think of some way to soothe the icy fury that was so evident in his eyes. Eyes that seemed to turn from dark brown to black the farther the conversation proceeded. She did nothing to be the recipient of this hatred.

"Mama?" Brice tugged on her gown, fabric slipping. With more insistence, "Mama."

She pulled the gown back onto her shoulder. His steely-eyed glare followed her movements. He found her lacking. She didn't care. She found him equally as lacking.

"*Oui, mon chere?*" She pulled Brice's hand into hers hoping the gesture would give some measure of reassurance.

"Is the bad man going to make us leave? He's not nice. You tell me to always be nice to people." His little boy voice melted her heart. He had such a tiny hand. His limbs thin and frail. He would not survive another sickness. She wanted to bundle him in her arms, keep him safe from the world as well as men such as this one. She realized long ago, despite her best efforts, she could not do so.

The man did want her to leave. Was certain there was no way she would give up ground, at least not tonight. No matter what he told her, tonight she was going to sleep on a bed within the cottage. They had nowhere to go. Even if they did, they had no way to get there. She was going to do everything in her power to remain here.

"Could we stay in the gatekeeper's cottage for the night. I would pay you in work tomorrow if you'd allow it. I'm a hard worker."

"What would you do with the boy? Don't want him around," he asked leaning back on the cart, his huge arms crossed in front of him while he glared from the boy back to her. Fear for her child crawled up her spine.

If he didn't have a perpetual scowl on his face, he might have arresting features. His dark brows tightly drawn together did nothing for his appearance except make him look threatening. She would give him that. He was intimidating.

"Brice would have to stay with me. There is...he's too young to leave him here by himself. He would never get in the way. You won't even know he's around." She was pleading, begging him. They both understood the fact. It seemed her words weren't swaying him.

The man waved one hand in the air. "It won't work then. Don't want the boy anywhere near me. Don't want the boy on my property. Don't want to see him."

That was more than obvious. She wasn't stupid. She got the picture he painted. "I know the chateau. Know what needs to be done. You won't find anyone more competent than me to help clean."

"No." He turned his back on her stomping up the trail to the house. He looked over his shoulder. "There is nothing for a woman to do. Don't plan on hiring women."

Especially not you, she heard the words he didn't say.

She ran after him, tugging on his arm to stop him. "I will do anything." It was true. She would do anything to put food and clothes on Brice. "Anything at all."

One of his eyebrows slanted upward in question. "Anything? I'll keep that in mind."

She understood she just offered herself to this man. Knew what she told him was true. Desperation had been a solid part of her life for so long now. "Yes, I've no other choice. I'll work twice as hard as anyone, as any man. Do the chores no one else will want. The place must be a mess. How long since anyone lived there?"

Several seconds passed while he stared at her. For a moment she noticed a partial smile then it vanished replaced by the frown she was getting used to seeing. "I want you and the boy gone tomorrow morning. Stay in the cottage if you wish. Vacate the place by six. If you aren't gone in the morning, I just might take you up on your offer. If I see you again, be prepared to let me see more of you."

The breath she'd been holding rushed out in a loud whoosh. Thank god, for one night. Instead of leaving she intended to be at work at six. Perhaps her luck changed a tiny bit. She would work so hard he wouldn't be able to turn her out. Tonight, they had shelter as well as food. With the francs he would pay her when he discovered she was working for him, she could walk into town. She was certain Brice could ride the mare.

His long-legged stride took him quickly up the hill. He didn't look back. Jenna found she was once more holding her breath.

"*Tete de butt*," she mumbled under her breath before realizing she didn't want Brice to hear the words. She made sure he knew swearing was wrong. However, this was apropos. He was exactly as she said. Her muttered words were not a lie.

"I thought I wasn't supposed to say bad things."

She whirled. Embarrassed, she let the man blind her to the fact her son heard her frustration. "You aren't." This time she didn't know how to get out of the conversation that was certain to follow. How was she ever going to explain herself? She knelt so she could be eyelevel searching for the right words. She didn't believe she could think of any.

"How come you can?" He sounded a little indignant as well as curious.

Tenderly, she pushed an unruly lock of hair from his eyes. He was so precious, his question so innocent and pure. She wished she could simply tell him it was because she was an adult. Being older didn't make it right. "I'm not supposed to either. It's just that he was acting like a butthead. I'm sure he is not that way most of the time."

"*Tete de butt*," Brice murmured seeming to agree with her. "He's a bad man. I don't like him. You shouldn't want to work for a man like that. We need to find somewhere else to go."

Jenna was sure he was right. Knew she shouldn't have offered herself to the loathsome man. In any case the coldness in his eyes when he looked her over told her he wouldn't want her. She didn't have to worry about him taking her up on the offer of her body. "Don't say the words in front of him. Can't lose this opportunity. Shall we see what the gatekeeper's house looks like?"

"He told you we had to leave. Told you he didn't want to see us. How are you going to work for him?"

"I'm hoping that if I'm already in the house working, he won't send me away." Well, he most likely would.

"We really don't have to sleep in the cart tonight? Will I have a real bed?" For the first time in weeks, Brice sounded eager to see what would happen next.

"Yes, and probably not. I would want to make sure all the linens are clean before you sleep on them. Maybe things inside are just dusty. What do you think?" Her hand settled on his shoulder as they walked.

"If they are not too bad? Wouldn't be any worse than the bottom of the cart and our old blankets," Brice said looking up as if to see into her eyes.

"No, it probably would not. Let's see if I remember this place."

The heavy wood door creaked on its hinges when she opened it. Before she did anything else, she pulled all the draperies wide to let the sunshine inside the dreary room. Dust flew as the fabric was swept aside. Muted light from a setting sun filled the drawing room. Particles of grime left by years of unuse swirled in the warming rays of the sun.

Hope filled her.

"Shall we look at the bedrooms? If I remember correctly, there are two. Do you want to sleep with me tonight or in your own room?" She understood he would start in one before he came to her later in the night. He did like to snuggle. They were a team. Had been so, for a very long time.

"My own." He looked at her sheepishly through lowered lashes while he clung to his wooden pony. One time in his life he had an entire army of ponies and soldiers. Now he had the one. Their lives had been reduced to nearly nothing.

She did have her love for her son. One could not sneeze at something so valuable as love.

If the ill-humored man allowed her to stay and work, would he pay her? How much, was the next question. She knew she was getting ahead of herself. Feeding and sheltering Brice was now her sole concern. In his present mood if he allowed her to work, he would most likely pay her next to nothing. She needed to save so she could pay the back taxes.

That thought did not put a smile on her face. The taxes were paid. It didn't seem the man would sell the land to her. He probably didn't even need this place. He had the markings of wealth about him.

He could possibly make her work for the food and shelter without paying her. As a man in another village did, he could ask her for other services. She fled that place. The man was ghastly. He stunk of garlic, his teeth rotten. Even for food she couldn't let him touch her. Couldn't sleep with him. During the month to reach the chateau, there were times she thought she should have closed her eyes and spread her legs for him. In doing so she could have kept Brice healthy. Could have fed him. He might not have taken sick. She pushed those thoughts to the back of her mind. The past was just that, the past.

Jenna thought of this man, the man in her future. Would it be so bad if she shut out all sounds and thought of other things? She knew women who did just that in order to survive. For a brief time, she worked as a maid for Angelique in her bordello in the city of Bordeaux. She saved. Eventually she had enough francs to move on.

Now, she was here. She offered herself to the man. Jenna realized she didn't even know his name.

Brice disappeared into the smaller bedroom. When he returned, he was grinning. "It's dusty like everything else."

"We'll take the bedding outside. Give it a good beating. You can sleep there. First, however, we are going to have dinner. Are you hungry?"

After Brice ate, they took the bedding outside. The beating didn't take long. Before she knew it, she was tucking Brice into bed, his wooden horse under his arm. She hugged him then kissed his forehead. "Sleep tight."

"When are you going to eat? You never eat anything, Mama. Your clothes are going to…"

"I'm not hungry," she whispered then gave him another tender kiss on his forehead. "I'll have something as soon as my tummy tells me it's time."

No, she wasn't hungry. She'd gone so long without eating she barely recognized hunger pains. Keeping Brice healthy was all that mattered to her. Once every couple of days if there was extra bread, she would have a piece.

With everything done for the evening, she didn't want to sit inside the stuffiness of the house. Needed to feel the fresh air on her face. The old rocking chair still sat on the porch. She remembered sitting on the porch steps while Oliver told her stories. He was ancient. Seemed as old as the hills. He must have been forced to move on when the chateau was sold. Often, he spoke of the revolution along with the terror.

The scent of ripe grapes hung on the air. Harvest season was upon them. If the vineyard was in working order, there would be people from the village tomorrow milling around waiting for orders as to what they should do.

Lost in thought, Jenna didn't hear the soft tread of booted feet on the grass as she hummed a French lullaby she used to sing to Brice. Those days were a very long time ago, the memories nostalgic.

She jumped when the man cleared his throat. "Thought you and the kid might be hungry. Didn't see a lot of food in the basket. Also brought the two of you clean linens. My cook suggested I bring this to you."

At the bristling of her back, the man's eyes narrowed. "Are you asking for favors in return?" While only a few minutes ago she thought she could give herself to this man she now understood it wasn't what she wanted. Even though when he let his guard down for a second, he was handsome as sin.

When her question registered, it seemed the words also burrowed under his skin. "Didn't come down here looking for sex. Just making sure you understand you can't stay longer than tonight." His gaze once again roamed over her, heating her from the inside out with what appeared to be raw hunger. She didn't understand. "Thought a bit of ham might go with the cheese and bread coupled with a bottle of *Cimaron's* finer Boudreaux. A vintage from two years ago."

That was when she fled the *Cimaron*. "You don't want anything from me?" Her pulse pounded as her breath caught deep in the back recesses of her throat. If she offered herself more blatantly...

Turning her head, she watched him walk into the cottage to return with two glasses and an open bottle. He set the sack of meat on a tray, emptied it. "Eat. Don't want sex at this moment if that's what you're asking. Maybe later. Just want to make sure you have enough stamina to get your skinny butt off my land tomorrow morning. No offense intended, but you don't appear to be very strong. Appear as if you could just faint dead away any second."

"Stronger than I look," she muttered as she set aside most of the meat for later, for Brice. She didn't remember the last time they had meat. He still wanted her to leave. Well, she wasn't about to do something so stupid.

"It's not all for your kid. Want to see you eat and drink then I'll leave. Not a second before." He poured two glasses of the wine.

She accepted when he handed her one. She sipped closing her eyes as the liquid warmth slid down her throat. The wine was delicious, a reminder of another, better time.

"So, you used to live up there on the hill? Jacques Bonnet is your boy's papa? You know, the people around here, in the village, the ones who worked for him, didn't like him."

He wasn't telling her anything she didn't already know. "Jacques wasn't a nice man." Seemed to run with the territory. He certainly wasn't a very nice man either.

"I didn't know him. Been away for a long time."

"Who are you besides the man who stole my son's inheritance," she asked as she watched him close his eyes almost as if he tried to ward off immense pain. When he opened them he was staring at the rows of vines as if they didn't exist.

"Look...if I didn't pay the government what was owed on the land and chateau someone else would have."

"That doesn't answer my question."

"Gill Allemand."

"What do you need these vineyards for? I recognize the name. Your family owns several a little north of here."

Silence stretched across the small distance separating the two people. "Haven't seen you eat anything. If you don't, I'm taking this with me so the kid won't get any of it. Is that what you want? No, I don't suppose it is. Eat."

His one word sounded as a command. She didn't want to eat anything she could save for Brice. He'd been so wrong about not seeing her eat. To appease Gil, she did have a piece of ham along with a slice of cheese. If she didn't eat anything more, there was enough left for breakfast as well as lunch for Brice. She wasn't going to allow her son to go without.

After eating two pieces of ham and cheese she looked at him. "I'm Jenna," she told him as she watched his taut features smooth slowly. For a fraction of a second, his eyes warmed, golden flecks dancing in them.

It didn't seem he meant to stay that long. "Jenna, finish the wine. Save the rest of the food for the boy, breakfast for both of you. Make sure you eat something before you leave in the morning."

"I'm not leaving tomorrow. We're too tired. You're going to have to give me another couple of days to recover." She rose. Must have been too quickly. She swayed slightly. Trying to hide what just happened she sat down.

"See that you eat." His command didn't go unnoticed.

As Jenna watched Gil walk up the hill she understood she hid nothing from him. He had this way of looking at her, one that seemed to burrow into her soul.

~ * ~

Gil sat in the darkness of his room. His body trembled as a seething darkness encompassed him. Seeing the boy, who would have been the same age as his son when his child died along with the boy's mother, sent ice pouring into his veins. He didn't even know about the two of them until his son was four. They shared one year together. After Etienne Dubois wed the woman he thought to be in love with, Elisa Moreau, he aimlessly wandered France visiting old haunts. He didn't go back to his work for the French government. Didn't function with the same lethal nonchalance as he had previously. He discovered he yearned for a family along with peace and quiet of a rural life.

That was when he discovered his child. Unlike Jenna's boy, his son was robust, big for his age. The boy could run and climb. He laughed easily. For that one year, he slept with Chantel, played at having a family. Unlike his son, he didn't truly love the woman. When she died though...

When she died, he found himself haunted by thoughts of her. Found there was a hole left in his heart that needed filling. It seemed he would look into a room and he would sense their presence. At times in bed, he felt sure Chantel slept beside him. He might have made a life with her, just to be close to his son. Had been thinking of marriage even while he knew wedding a woman he didn't love would be a mistake.

Elisa disturbed his nights. Still, he missed Chantel simply because she came with his son who he adored. Now, alone with his memories, the emptiness in his life bled into his soul. Too many times to count, he didn't see a reason to live. Without his son, thinking of his son, he could not breathe. Air refused to enter into his lungs.

The room he slept in was black, pitch black. He reached for the pistol beside his bed. Turned it over in his hands, thinking to end his misery. If he did, too many people would be hurt; his family, his friend Etienne along with Etienne's wife, Elisa. Every step he took each day was filled with pain, not the physical variety but the mental. No one dared mention the boy or his wife. They were terrified he would collapse. Perhaps they were correct in their assumptions. Without them he felt broken.

Jenna...

Her son Brice...

Gil couldn't manage to swallow the lump in his throat. Couldn't condemn himself more when he wished it was Brice and not his son, Lance, who perished in that fire. He should have been there, perhaps made a difference. If he'd been able to get him out, Lance would still be alive.

Head in his hands, he sobbed. Copious tears rolled down his cheeks in an unbroken flow. His head pounded painfully with each new breath of salted tears slipping between his lips.

He didn't want to see Jenna or her son in the morning. Prayed they would be gone when he checked on them. Didn't know what got into him when he allowed her to offer herself to him. Lord but the woman was all skin and bones. The soles of her shoes were coming lose from the tops. Her threadbare dress might be ripped to strands if threatened with a stiff wind. When he looked into her basket of possessions, she owned one more dress, which was in just as bad shape as the one she wore. While the little boy didn't have much, he possessed a great deal more than his mother. Clothing that was new, a shirt plus another one, two pairs of shoes that were not falling apart. He had a warm coat tucked away at the bottom of the basket.

It wasn't his place to improve her life. The reasons for her leaving the winery years ago were unknown to him. Though they must have been very real and valid. Now, with the passing of her husband she returned thinking to take up where she left off, believing her son would inherit.

He wouldn't.

It was almost dawn. He told her to be gone at six. Not knowing why, he expected her to stiffen her shoulders then beg him for another night. She'd already done just that. Perhaps his expectation had something to do with the boy. She would have to get him ready, feed him before she could leave. He hoped she didn't give all the food he brought her last night to her son. He wanted her to be able to put that old mare to the cart and leave. If she couldn't, he wasn't positive how he could get her to leave. A sick woman to care for was not high on his list of priorities. If she continued in this vein, she would be sick. If she meant to take care of her son, she needed to take care of herself first.

The next morning when he made his way to the first floor, it was five thirty. He needed to make certain the cleaning supplies were out and available to the workers he meant to retrieve from the nearby village. Striding through the kitchen, he grabbed a slice of bread hot from the oven. He would eat later or perhaps while he worked.

"She's out there working her skinny derrière off." The woman, Gabby, who cooked for him all his adult life, pointed toward the main hall. "Seemed to know where everything was located. Got herself a rag and some soapy water, says she's going to use the lemon oil when she finishes to make the wood shine. Been working since I started baking bread this morning around five o'clock. You tell her she could work for you?" Gabby asked sounding skeptical.

"The devil you say. No, told her to leave by six. Apparently, she didn't listen." That didn't surprise him. Where Jenna Bonnet was concerned, it seemed she had a mind of her own.

He stabbed his hands in his hair as he strode the distance into the entrance. She was humming softly, working on the staircase with what smelled like lemon oil. She must have found the cleaning supplies. When she heard him, she looked up. Smiled softly.

"Where's the boy?"

The soft smile vanished at the penetrating sound of his gruff voice. Despite his feelings about this woman and her child, he found he wanted to see the soft curve of her lips again. Cursed himself for the weakness. He didn't like feeling vulnerable. When he asked about her son, her entire demeanor changed.

Her shoulders squared while her back stiffened. "He's not in the way," she told him, her voice curt, her eyes icy. "He's playing with his toy horse."

"Eating, I see." He turned his attention back to her. "Did you eat?" He couldn't help asking even though he knew the answer.

"What do you think?" she spoke softly as she continued stroking the wood, making it gleam more with each swipe of the soft rag. The transformation was vividly apparent.

"You were supposed to be gone by six. Instead, I find you working. Told you I wouldn't hire you. Haven't changed my mind." His voice was harsh, gruffer than he intended, but her visible grimace was the effect he wanted. He knew she didn't eat. Saw her hang on to the railing as she pushed hair from her face. Didn't expect her to so blatantly defy him.

"I never thought it was a bad thing to be early to work," she spoke as she watched Brice completely ignoring the fact she wasn't authorized to do anything she was doing. "Hope it was alright that your cook, Gabby, gave Brice a glass of milk."

"You need the nourishment more than your boy. You're all skin and bones. When are you going to leave?"

At his words she flinched, red suffusing her cheeks. He supposed that wasn't candid of him. Candid was not something he sought. If his disposition was nasty enough, he prayed she would decide on her own to leave. No job could possibly be worth the belittling he'd already directed her way. As her lips moved, he was positive she was calling him a *tete du butt*. Well, she had him pegged right, a butthead. That's exactly the way he intended to carry out this relationship of theirs that was going to be extremely short-lived.

"Do you need some help leaving?" He strode toward her ready to do whatever was necessary. Pick her up then carry her if she continued the defiance.

She stiffened then, her shoulders squaring as it seemed to him she prepared to talk. "Not leaving. Can take care of myself. Besides..." she paused sipping air just to keep herself standing as she once again wavered.

"Besides?" he queried as he started up the stairs. If she was going to fall someone needed to be there to catch her. While he wanted her and the boy to vanish, he didn't wish anyone harmed.

"What I do is none of your business." She finished on a whisper.

"It is when it seems I'm paying your wages. Wages I didn't intend to pay you since you were never hired. You will be gone first thing tomorrow."

"Please, let us stay. I'll do anything." She paused looking as if she just heard his words. "You're actually going to pay me?" Now, she sounded wistful, a bit of apprehension thrown into the mix.

"I'm not that big an ogre that I expect you to work for nothing. Today at least but if you turn up tomorrow unexpected, I'll send you on your way."

"Oh."

"Oh?" He lifted an eyebrow as he studied the expression on her face. "What did you think?"

"I hoped." She ran her tongue across her bottom lip, leaving it dewy with moisture.

A feminine ploy to entice him, he just might take her up on the blatant offer before sending her on her way. It had been a long time since he had a woman beneath him. "Well, your fondest wish just came true. Not paying you if you faint and I have to rush to Gabby for the smelling salts."

"Wouldn't expect you to do anything like that. We can stay then?"

She sounded so hopeful and sincere.

"Madam, look here." His voice was stern but it didn't seem she listened.

"We can stay."

"I'm not hiring you."

"Of course, you are. You need this chateau cleaned up from top to bottom. You need to harvest your grapes so you can do what this place does best, make wine. Don't see anyone lining up to get rid of the dirt and grime in the house. If you want to live here..."

All this talk of food was making him hungry. Her arguments were having the same effect on his stomach while managing to make his head throb. *Tete du butt.* "Carry on." He strode back to the kitchen ignoring her question as well as her statements about his needs. He didn't want her to stay or to ever see her again. Gabby set a plate of food on the table that she took from the warming oven. "You going to bring the little lady here to eat. It's the least you can do. She needs some more meat on her bones. If she filled out a mite, she'd be quite attractive."

"You're meddling in what doesn't concern you. Save the matchmaking for your mama. She's not staying."

Gabby huffed as if she was indignant. "I'm the better matchmaker, besides just looking at her one would know she's not eating enough."

"Says she's eaten."

"Well, I'm sure she is lying."

"So am I. Jenna gives all her food to her son. Doesn't eat a thing. I sat at the cottage last night until she ate two small slices of ham and cheese. She did sip a glass of wine."

"Doesn't need wine. The girl needs food, good French cooking would put some well-needed meat on her bones. Then you'd want her stay around for more than just the cleaning."

"Give her anything at all and Brice will have the food."

"If you give her more than the little tyke can eat, she'll have to eat some of the leftovers. Won't she?"

"One would think." He did sit down to eat. As always whatever Gabby cooked was delicious. Before she left for her home, she set about making sandwiches leaving them wrapped and on the table. Gabby would be back in time to cook dinner.

In the meantime, he had to oversee the collecting of the grapes. Harvesting was one of the most important parts of the vineyard. He wanted wine this year. While the grapes had been neglected, it was only for a year and a half. They would do fine. The harvest might not be as bountiful this year as in the past, but his manager assured him this year's crop would produce a wonderful red Bordeaux.

Gil spent the remainder of the morning and well into the afternoon talking with the manager about his vines as the man gave him a tour of the property. He brought help with him from his family's vineyard closer to St. Emilion. The men and women had over a hundred years of experience in wine making. All would go well. Yes, it would go well if Jenna Bonnet would leave as he instructed. He didn't want a woman in his life nor did he want anything to do with the child.

By the time he finished, he was dusty and dirty which suited his mood. When he walked into the entrance, Jenna was finished with the stair railings. The wood was smooth and polished. The lemon scent of the oil she used filled the air. He breathed in deeply.

When he found her, she was sitting on the floor, scrubbing the stones with skim milk. Where she cleaned, everything reflected the sunlight. He looked around for Brice. Finally catching sight of him, he was sitting beneath the piano, playing with his toy horse as if he didn't have a care in the world. The boy didn't. His mother certainly did. His heart lurched. Gil didn't appreciate the protective feeling toward Jenna that surfaced blindsiding him. He doused that feeling with a cold dose of realism. The pain in his gut was too raw and deep. All he wanted was to be left alone.

He pushed the sensation away with an angry nod toward the boy. "Has he done nothing today but play and eat?"

She stopped mid-scrub, lines in her forehead deepening as her eyes seemed to draw together with a pointed scowl. They flashed blue ice shards at him. He didn't care.

"He's just a little boy. What is it you want him to do? Get down on his hands and knees? Scrub the stones?" Sarcastic venom filtered through the air severing his mind with the ridiculousness of his words.

Her question was valid even though it reeked of disrespect. She should quell her unruly thoughts if she wanted to get paid. Gil didn't have an answer for her. Children were supposed to play. Why would he want him to work? *To ease her burden.*

Jenna shouldn't have Jacques Bonnet's child to look after. She should have had better than a man who was despised by almost everyone who knew him or worked for him. All he heard was rumors. He had not been around to know the man first-hand. Gil had been in Paris most of the years since he turned twenty. Even before that, he'd spent a great deal of time there. Most of what he knew he'd heard since his arrival a month ago. At the time he didn't care what was said. He bought the winery. It was his now. Eventually, the land his family owned adjoining this one would be merged.

He couldn't bear to be such a burden on his family. That was why he moved out. Thought he could work so hard it would take his mind off his losses. Since the death of his boy, he didn't want to be around people who cared about him. Saying he was morose would be understated. The people he cared most for sidestepped the issue that overcame his mind. Never spoke of Chantel or Lance. He liked it that way. Needed his thoughts to be bleak and dark, desolate was best.

He didn't want to think about these two either. Just looking at the woman and her child brought painful memories to the surface. Seeing her love shine so clearly for the little boy brought him to his knees.

"Hell if I know. Just don't want to see him when I'm in my house. If you expect to work for me, keep him somewhere I don't have to look at him."

He didn't miss the tiny look of relief that crossed her face to be changed when she spoke. "Can't leave him by himself in the cottage. What do you propose I do with my son?"

"Maybe you should quit. Move on. Find some other means of employment. *Some other man to torment.* "A place that will welcome you with open arms." Angrily he fisted his hands while his gut coiled then soured. He didn't know what else he could say to her.

"There is no place like that," she gritted out through teeth that were clenched hard together.

"It isn't here either, Madam."

Blinking a few times, she then ran her tongue across her bottom lip. At the sight he hardened, his arousal blatantly evident to anyone who looked. He knew he was looking at her with raw hunger in his eyes. He didn't like his reaction, despised what the sight of her automatically did to his body. She told him she would do anything.

Jenna Bonnet wasn't a virgin. So, what did he care? He should take what was offered and enjoy it.

If he took what she blatantly proposed, he'd be no better than dirt, lower than dirt. He understood her desperation to some extent. They were both dying inside but for different reasons. She wanted to keep her son alive while he mourned the death of his.

If he'd only had the chance to try to keep Lance alive, to rescue him from the fire that consumed his tiny body. Lance would be seven now. The boy had been strong and vital, so different from Brice. Gil hated the comparison.

What he did know was that he'd never again put himself in the position to love so thoroughly that the loss of that love would devastate him. He couldn't go through anything like that another time.

Not ever.

"You should understand. I'm not going anywhere," she spoke softly as she slowly pushed herself off the floor.

Her foot caught on the threadbare dress she wore. He heard the fabric tear. Quickly, she moved her foot before rearranging her skirt.

"What time do you put your boy to bed?" he asked as he studied her swaying form. Her body was small. She was skinny but what curves she possessed were womanly, tempting even to a hard-edged, jaded man who'd been through hell and back. Her blue eyes were warm when she looked at her boy, turned to ice when she directed them to him. If she eased some of his pain, he didn't care if ice flowed in her veins as it did his. Perhaps together they could thaw. One time with her would never melt the ice that was so much a part of him now.

"Why?" Her question didn't surprise him even when he saw the immediate change from blue to frozen silver. Her lips trembled as if she guessed the answer to his question.

She might propose giving her body to him. He had no doubt giving herself to him to use was not something she wanted. What she didn't know was that he would never take something from her she wasn't willing to give. All he wanted at the moment was to scare her out of his life. She didn't seem to catch onto any of the clues.

"Come, eat. Gabby left sandwiches. Enough so you don't have to give yours to your son."

A whisper of air left her lips as she wiped her hands down the front of her dress. As if he could see into her mind, he knew she was trying to figure out how to save one for Brice's dinner.

"Don't get me wrong but I'm a bit skeptical that you're asking us to eat with you." Her voice held a wealth of censure while the summer-sky blue eyes sparkled with bits of sharp, silver-ice.

"We all need to eat. If you're going to insist you have a job, I don't want to be picking you up off the floor when you faint dead away."

"Truth be told I'm not hungry. I'll give Brice his. He can keep playing while he eats. I need to start on the wall paper."

"No, you don't. Since you defied my order of leaving this morning, this employer wants to get a full day's of work out of you. The only way that can happen is for you to finish off that ham sandwich. Won't take no for an answer."

"If you insist."

Her quick answer surprised him. He expected some half-witted argument. It seemed she capitulated too easily. "I do."

"Gil." The male voice coming from behind him caught his attention.

"What is it?" Gil asked as he turned to see Stephan striding toward them, a grim look on his face. "Something wrong?"

"No, not at all. Need for you to check out the vats in the cellar. There are years of wine kept in a second cellar. You should take a look there. Figure out what you want to do with everything."

He turned to Jenna. "You can relax now. Looks like I'll be gone for a couple of hours." Gil didn't leave though. He waited for Jenna to head to the kitchen with her little boy in tow.

When she didn't move, he nodded in the direction of the waiting food. "Take the boy with you. I won't be there."

She nodded, grimacing as she tried to stand. He knew she was feeling the pain of working all day, part of it on her hands and knees. Wondered too if she ate any of the meat and cheese he left the night before. He doubted it. Now that he wasn't going to watch her down the sandwich, he was sure she would wrap the food up and save it for Brice tonight.

More food could be brought to her tonight. Food she would hand over to the boy. It wasn't as if Brice didn't also need meat on his bones. Jenna, however, appeared to be starving herself to death.

Why did he seem to harbor a soft spot for this woman? The faster she moved on the better. *Enfer!* He smashed a fist into his palm. All he wanted was to see her leave the chateau behind. Would do just about anything including intimidating her to succeed. He couldn't keep up the pretense despite how hard he tried.

Gil grabbed his lunch on the way out the back with Stephan. "What is it you wanted me to see?"

"Viens."

Once inside the building housing the cellars, they made their way down a flight of steps to the area where the vats were located. The cellars smelled of darkness and wine. Hoses ran the length of the floors leading to each huge vat.

"They all seem to be in working order. If we go on through this hall, we'll see the real interesting part of the estate."

The cellar was cool, dark as well. He remembered playing inside the family cellars with Etienne. Wondered if his son would have enjoyed some of the same pastimes.

"What is it?"

"Wines going back to the early seventeen hundreds. They are all labeled and dated. Just thought you should see this. If you want, we can sell some of the bottles for hefty prices. Buy more vines to plant on some of the unused land."

He thought of bringing one of the vintage bottles with him tonight when he visited Jenna.

He should bring food too.

Make sure she ate.

~ * ~

"Tomorrow I should visit Gil. Don't want to leave him by himself too long. He might do something we'd all regret."

"Not sure what he'll do," Elisa spoke softly as she watched Etienne sip his wine. They were all afraid for Gil. The desolate and sometimes desperate look in his eyes was so different from the jovial man she first met. The man who helped her get over the loss of Etienne those first years as well as played with her son, Masson, when she had no one except the boy's grandfather to help her.

Masson played with their little girl, Margo. A blanket was spread out on the floor, toys scattered haphazardly. Margo turned one a month ago. She was a precocious little thing. She had her big brother wrapped around her tiny little finger. Masson would do anything for the child.

"Gil doesn't like to visit. Don't think he enjoys watching Mason. Brings back memories he'd rather forget. Lance and Masson were the same age. Don't want to push the man to do something too soon."

"Makes him remember all he lost," Elisa agreed with her husband as she watched their children. "At least to some degree, he shouldn't hide from the memories. Sometime he needs to embrace what he once had as well as except the fact it is gone. It would be nice if he could learn to live again."

Etienne missed the first four years of Masson's life simply because she kept the truth about his son from him. It wasn't well done of her. Now, she regretted keeping the facts from him with all her heart. None of that time could be made up to the man she loved since she was a little girl.

Her husband would feel some of the pain Gil felt but it wasn't the same. He didn't lose his child forever. They'd both been so happy for Gil when he discovered he had a boy. Elisa knew Gil thought for a time to be in love with her. She never could return the sentiment. Now, Gil loved that boy with all his heart. Gave everything he was to him. Wound up devastated when Lance died. At the moment, everyone tiptoed around the man whose mean temperament was so different than the light-hearted, loving man she once knew. They all wanted to hear him laugh again.

Elisa didn't think there was anything Gil loved more than playing with Mason until he was reunited with Lance. The joy carried over to his son. She was certain Gil was meaning to ask for Chantal's hand in marriage. She didn't think Gil loved Chantal though.

Now they were both gone, leaving Gil a shattered man who

seemed to barely live in the shell of his body. In Elisa's mind the man she once knew so well needed a swift kick to his backside. Etienne continued to tell her he just needed to be handled with care. If everyone left him alone, he would eventually come out of his melancholy. When they were around him, she was warned not to speak of her children and especially not Lance.

"He shouldn't be coddled," she told her husband who scowled at her. "You know he has to find a way to adjust to this, to learn to live again. He needs to find a woman to love, one who can give him more children."

"Gil doesn't need the thoughts brought to the forefront. Whenever they are, he withdraws farther away."

"Every time we see him he is worse. You know it's true. Coddling does not work. He needs to be confronted."

Etienne wrapped her in his arms. "What we need is to start another child," he told her nuzzling her neck. She shivered.

Trying to ignore him, she spoke again, "Remember the children."

"Always do. Isn't that what I just intimated?"

"We should go see him." Elisa had reasons her husband would not agree with but she intended to visit soon. It would be fun. The weather was nice. Fresh air and new scenery would do her good. Masson would love to spend time with his grandfather. A sleep over would be wonderful for him.

"We're not traveling that distance. Not with the kids or without them. I know what you're trying to do, Elisa, but it won't work." Etienne picked up Margo, cuddling her for a few seconds. "I'm putting her to bed then Masson. After that I'm going to put you to bed. No arguments."

"Why would I argue?" She smiled softly, lowering her lashes. Elisa let her fingers hover over the fastenings to her dress. "I'll get a bottle of wine and something to eat. We can sit on the balcony."

"Watch the stars?" he queried, his voice husky, his eyes warm with the desire she hoped would never waver.

"The moon as well." The laces to her gown were unfastened far enough she knew he could see the swell of her breasts.

"I'll hurry," he told her.

"Make sure that you do."

Other Books by Christine Young
Available at Rogue Phoenix Press

Connal's Eternal Love
Sweet McKenna Book One

A few days shy of All Hallows' Eve Connal McKenna, Laird of Clan Chattan stands on the parapets of his castle. Bonfires line the hillsides while his clan prepares for the upcoming festivities. Drawn by the whispering of the wind, Connal McKenna feels a strange restlessness in his soul. Setting out to discover the wickedness that is calling to him, he discovers his mate. With gentle words and sensuous kisses, the auburn-eyed highlander conquers his mate, the beautiful, defiant Wynnie Adair who he comes upon during an evening ride. She must ultimately put her trust in the only man who can save her from the ruthless plans of her father and succumb to his gentle coaxing.

In Brady's Arms
Sweet McKenna Book Two

Forced to run from the only home she knows, beautiful, headstrong Lillian Townsends seeks shelter in the wild highlands where the McKenna clan live. Trying to avoid a betrothal contract signed by her stepfather to an aging lord, she is desperate to find a means to sidestep the inevitable, including a marriage to the oldest son of the laird. Lilly is enamored of the young lord who pursues her with unrelenting determination flashing his devilishly handsome charms. She is hard pressed to resist.

Besotted from the first moment Brady McKenna sees Lilly, he is determined to find a means to coax her into his arms and bed. With only the promise of carnal pleasure as his mistress, Brady relentlessly pursues the woman who has unwittingly forged a place in his heart. She is like no other woman, proud, defiant and enchanting. Despite his father's advice to stay away from her, he cannot. He boldly seeks her out and makes her his own.

Nobody but Walker
Sweet McKenna Book Three

The Highland Lass...

She was brought up, adored and loved by a doting mother and father ardently protected by her brothers. She was everything sweet and innocent until she was faced with betrayal and an unexpected and out of wedlock pregnancy. When she gave her love to a man who couldn't return her passion and commitment, she was left devastated and furious. Faced with the loss of her child if she didn't comply to his demands, Crissie McKenna followed him to Belfast then on to his country home to discover he was already married.

...The Irishman

Stunned to find out his one and only encounter with the woman he wanted to love forever created a child, Walker Endicott, Earl of Briarwood, claimed his child as his only heir. Walker threatened all her previously held values even while he thrilled her senses. From the moment he first saw her to the second she ran after him begging him to make love to her, his captivating masculinity held her fascinated. In his arms she would know tempestuous passion, bitter despair, and a soaring joy that would humble them both before the power of love.

My Sweet Broc
Bad Boys Book One

He's a bad bad boy...

Broc Wallace is a fun-loving rake who never thought any beautiful woman could melt his heart. He lives life in the present enjoying the camaraderie of his friends and the pleasures of his mistress. When Bliss races into his life, he is ill prepared to deal with her secrets or give up the tenor of his life. When the truth is revealed, he finds himself unable to forgive and forget the betrayal.

...but she's sweet for him

Bliss MacTavish knows she's playing with fire when she refuses to tell this bad boy her name. He tempts her with sweet whispers of seduction knowing her innocent nature will be unable to refuse all he yearns to give her. Deciding to follow her heart, she finds the repercussions more than she bargains for when she gives herself to this bad boy.

Crazy for Cam
Bad Boys Book Two

He's a bad bad boy...

Lord Cam MacEwen, Viscount of Rosehill, tries his best to be proper and court the lady of his dreams in the acceptable way. The feat proves impossible when the lady in question uses every means at her disposal to tempt him. He fights his jealousy for another man as well as the need to make her his own, finally giving in to her irresistible passion.

...but she's crazy for him.

Chelsea MacTavish wants the bad boy she fell in love with and kissed just before her eighteenth birthday. With feminine wiles and irresistible allure, the sensuous lady plans to best Cam at his game of hearts and make him forget his need to court her properly.

Falling for Flynt
Bad Boys Book Three

He's a bad, bad boy...

Fascinated by Hope's loss of memory yet haunted by her sultry beauty, Flynt is irresistibly drawn to the stoic miss—and into her troubles with the sultan who wants her for himself. When he discovers she is the sister of his best friend, his pride keeps him from pursuing her and making her his.

...but she's falling for him.

Raised in a harem but now penniless, alone and without her memory, Hope must discover a way to remember all that she has lost. She finds a way to continue with her life as a servant in Flynt's home. The first sight of Flynt steals Hope's breath as well as her heart. Can she overcome her fears and give herself to the man she fell in love with.

Dancing With Donal
Bad Boys Book Four

He's a bad bad boy...

Once a bad boy always a bad boy, Donal Chamberlin's carefree ways come crashing down around him when he meets the ravishingly beautiful Daryl MacTavish, the innocent little sister of one of his best friends. He is determined to win her heart as he sets his sights on marriage and an heir. His past gets in the way of his quest when a woman he once loved threatens Daryl's life.

...but she's dancing with him.

Daryl has seen the control her sister's husbands hold over them. She yearns for a life where she makes decisions for herself. No man will have power over her. But no man kisses her the way Donal does. No man can make her forget all her goals leaving her helpless to give up her dreams. Yet Donal is determined to dance through all the barriers she thrust in front of him, pursuing her until she says yes.

Loving Leslie
Bad Boys Book Five

He's a bad bad boy...

Leslie Stewart, Duke of Southcliff is stoic, set in his ways, a spy who is used to having his life well ordered. He expects life to continue on in this perfectly conventional fashion. He assumes his bad boy status while keeping mamas and debutantes at arm's length. An heir is needed but Leslie has every intention of finding a woman who doesn't covet his wealth and tittle. He is irresistibly drawn to the headstrong young lady who becomes more beautiful as she develops into a woman.

...but she is loving him.

When Leslie kisses Lacie MacTavish, she knows even at the tender age of fifteen this is the man of her dreams. Forced to wait until she comes of age, Lacie withdraws into herself. Now she is eighteen and Leslie has returned from a mission for the British Government ready to claim her as his bride. She refuses him and he must find a way to seduce her and in the process create a burning passion within her, which she cannot deny.

Pleasing Arie
Bad Boys Book Six

He's a bad bad boy...

Arie Demir has never been denied anything in his life. He takes what he wants. What he undeniably yearns for is the beautiful redheaded spitfire he sees in a restaurant in Glasgow. At every turn, she confuses him by disputing his power over her. Alison refuses to accept the fact he owns her. While Arie tries desperately with patience and tenderness to drive her wild with new sensations, his scorching kisses ignite the fires of her very soul to make her understand he is all she will ever want.

...but is she pleasing him?

Alison Fletcher never expected to find herself kidnapped and sold to a whorehouse then bought by a Turkish sultan to become his slave. She vows to never surrender to the arrogant man who believes he owns her. She is stunned by the magnificently handsome man who awaits her compliance. Unexpectedly, she finds Arie the lesser of all the evils. The hidden depths of his mesmerizing dark brown eyes hold her into their power; his muscular embrace makes her weak with desire. She is his to do with as he wishes.

Graham's Wicked Kiss
Bad Boys Book Seven

He's a bad bad boy...

Graham Chamberlin is stunned to find three young boys dangling from the trees lining the drive to Runningmead Manner. On further inspection, he is astonished at their obsession to protect a young woman who has been brutalized by her pimp. The woman he discovers hiding in a third-floor attic room is gravely injured. He takes the silver haired stowaway under his wing. Clearly, Graham's new guest is a lady with many secrets. He is determined to unlock all the mysteries surrounding her.

...But she can't resist his wicked kiss.

The years since Ria left the convent where she was raised have been a nightmare. Her secrets are dangerous—as is the powerful man determined to find her. Handsome Graham Chamberlin is clearly a gentleman with secrets of his own, but staying with him could mean the difference between life and death for Ria. With each passing day, her handsome host turns Ria's convalescence into an increasingly sensual escape. Now her greatest challenge may be imagining anything less than a future in his arms.

Feeling Etienne's Love
Bad Boys Book Eight

He's a bad bad boy...

Etienne Dubois is the son of a wealthy vineyard owner who craves the excitement of putting his life on the line. Working with the French government and as a confidant of King Charles X give him reasons for living. An encounter with a beautiful young woman in a plush bordello in Paris has him rethinking his roguish ways. Etienne never expects to become a father especially from one encounter with an innocent prostitute who whispers his name and has him rethinking his well-ordered life.

...But she can't help feeling his love.

Elisa Moreau, the only daughter of Angelique Moreau, the owner of an exclusive bordello in Bordeaux, France, has loved Etienne Dubois since she was six. Unfortunately, until an unexpected encounter at a brothel in Paris puts the two of them in the same room, Etienne doesn't even know she exists. Confused but wanting Etienne and this chance meeting to never end, Elisa gives herself to the man who has held her heart in hands for what seems like her entire life.

Al I Want is Link
Bad Boys Book Nine

He's a bad bad boy...

Link Stewart is an incorrigible rake, a woman's man who knows his way around the bedroom. When he travels to Virginia to solve the mysterious happenings on the Stewart tobacco plantation, he discovers there is more than one mystery that needs to be solved. A beautiful seemingly sophisticated young woman, Sophia Carter-Brown, sets her sights on him. She makes it abundantly clear she wants him for her next lover.

...but she's a desperate woman

Sophia has learned about men. She knows them. Has controlled them. When she discovers she cannot control Link, she is terrified. This man is different from every other man she's known. She finds herself out of her element, reeling in self-doubt, even afraid for her life. Link, confident as only a carefree, successful rake can be when it comes to understanding women, sets out to teach her who exactly is in charge.

Foolish for Piper

The pickpocket...

Piper has spent her life surviving the streets of St. Giles Parish in London, a den of iniquity and crime. Masquerading as a boy she escapes the whorehouses the young girls are sent to as they come of age. The day she encounters Brett MacLachlan begins the same as every other one. When she picks his pocket, she has no idea her life is going to change irreversibly.

...and the mark

Handsome aristocrat Brett MacLachlan has come to London for his amusement only to find his world turned upside down by a thief and her dog. From the moment he spots her, Brett knows there is something intrinsically wrong. In his arms, Piper discovers passion and joy. Yet secrets of her past haunt her, and a scar will tell the true tale as well as her identity.

Taylor's Destiny

She traveled to another time and place to change destiny...

Enjoying a day of sailing, Taylor Maxwell never expected after a suffering a concussion she would wake up in another century. A resilient independent woman in the twenty-first century, the blond beauty is ill prepared for life in the 1800s. Her first sight of the naval captain who rescues her makes her heart stop, giving her hope for her future.

His life is transformed by a woman who appears from nowhere...

Born to a life of ease, Reid Stewart defies the dictates of those born to aristocracy and chooses a life of adventure in the navy and as a spy for the crown. When he discovers a nearly naked woman on the bow of small sailing ship, his heart warms. His love for Taylor and his need to protect her from a man who pursues her might cost him his life as well as hers.

Caitlin's Duke

She played a fiddle in an Irish pub...

Caitlin O'Shea Is the most beautiful woman Roc Leighton has ever seen. With her blue violet eyes and long black hair she captivates him. In turn he mesmerizes Caitlin. Caught in the power of his gaze as he watches her, she is wise enough to know he desires her but will never give his heart to her. Caitlin has vowed to never be any man's mistress.

And fell in love with an English Lord...

Roc knows the first time he watches her play the fiddle and dance around the pub, she will be his next mistress. Despite her protest, he will find a way to convince her that her place is with him. While Caitlin's determination to keep her vows, fate takes a cruel turn and she is forced to seek refuge with Roc.

Catching Meara
Book One in the McKenna Clan Series

Meara Thorton was a feisty, world-class computer hacker—cornered by the FBI and shockingly given the chance to be their newly acquired technical analyst. Brilliant and intuitive, yet aching with the loss of everyone she has cared about, her restless heart led her to discover a love she fought and a world she didn't know could possibly exist.

Sweet Sexy Sadie
Book Two in the McKenna Clan Series

From the first time Sadie's eyes met those of Brody McKenna in the hot Sierra Madre Mountains, theirs was a potent attraction—not gentle, slow, and easy, but hot, hard, and all-consuming. The daughter of a dysfunctional family, Sadie had dreams no man could wrench from her with hot sex and an all-consuming passion. She'd challenge this alpha male with all the strength she possessed. But her red hair, fiery temperament, and indomitable spirit obsessed Brody...and he knew he had to find a way to show her he was more than he appeared and convince her to make a life with him.

Sweet Misbehavin'
Book Three in the McKenna Clan Series

Cast adrift after fleeing the home of Jokul, the ice demon, Atantsi, a firestarter, grew to womanhood as she moved through time to keep the demon from finding her. Though stubborn and courageous, she was ill prepared to use powers she had not been taught. Her first sight of the intoxicating Carr McKenna left her breathless, and her second encounter gave her hope for a future she never thought she had.

A playboy, a second son and a shifter, a man who thought his life would be carefree, Carr McKenna was shocked to discover the woman he'd paid as an escort is a firestarter who is running for her life. He is the leader of all the McKennas around the world and that he has multiple powers. His passion for Margo and the need to defend her might cost him his life as well as hers.

Sweet Talkin' Sugar
Book Four in the McKenna Clan Series

Lyonesse McKenna, was dreaming, or was she? From the instant Lyn saw Deacon McClain across a black jack table in a crowed Las Vegas casino the unmistakable attraction sent Lyn's senses flying into overdrive. Her family of shapeshifters believed in soul mates. She'd always been skeptical yet she couldn't help but question the way her heart sped when he looked at her.

When Deacon appeared in Las Vegas he knew his first job was to save Lyn from a Sea Demon, but the next order of business was to convince her he would someday mean more to her than she'd ever expected. But her stubborn nature and unbendable spirit consumed Deacon...and he had to chase away all the demons real and imagined in order to win her heart.

Sweet Surrender
Book Five in the McKenna Clan Series

Ripped from her family at the top of Infinity Cliff, Kimi McKenna finds herself thrust somewhere into the future. Dark elements threaten to destroy the earth unless Kimi can work together with the white witch to stop the destruction. Confused by her mate's role in the conspiracy, she refuses to acknowledge the connection. But amidst raging fire and attacks on the people she is coming to hold dear, she allows Maska O'keefe into her heart.

Maska O'keefe has loved the beautiful shapeshifter for years. Unable to save her life years ago, he vows to watch over her as he is given a second chance to convince her that even though he is a witch and not a shifter, they are indeed soul mates. Kimi's divided loyalties between her family and the cause she is now a part of will determine their relationship. Only the part she plays as the messiah can bring this to a conclusion in the final battle.

Dakota's Bride
The first book in the Lakota/Pinkerton Series

When Emma St. John received her brother's letter imploring her to escape her stepfather's vengeful scheme and to trust Dakota Barringer with her life, she was willing to chance it. But the handsome, brooding riverboat owner Emma found in Natchez a danger of another kind. For Emma soon found herself surrendering to an unrelenting desire.

Raised by the Sioux when his parents were killed, Dakota had been betrayed once before by a white woman. He wasn't about to trust another, especially one claiming that her stepfather, a powerful U.S. senator, had framed her as a murderess. But he couldn't let Emma's intoxicating effect on him. Now Dakota would risk his very life to protect the innocent beauty who had seduced him with her tender love.

My Angel
The second book in the Lakota/Pinkerton Series

A BEAUTY IN BUCKSKINS
When her father decided to send her to a finishing school back East, Angela Chamberlain refused to be confined to stuffy drawing rooms. Instead, the daring spitfire who could shoot like a man and ride like the wind longed for a life of adventure and romance—and she knew exactly who could give it to her. Devil Blackmoor was a hired gun with a dangerous reputation. But Angela was willing to go to the ends of the earth to capture the handsome devil's heart.

A DEVIL IN DISGUISE
He'd come to America looking for excitement, but Devil Blackmoor got more than he bargained for when he encountered a beautiful rebel who answered his kisses with a wild innocence that touched his very soul. Yet standing between them were more obstacles than either ever dreamed. For Devil had strapped on a gun for the wrong man. And that made Angela his enemy. Now he'll have to choose between his duty and the woman he loves more than life.

The Locket
The third book in the Lakota/Pinkerton Series

The year is 1894. Seeking revenge for crimes against his family, Misha Petrovich follows a path that leads straight to Ariel Cameron's boarding house in Mist Harbor, Oregon. A family heirloom in Ariel's possession leads Misha to believe she is guilty. The locket has been handed down to the oldest girl in the Petrovich family for generations.

Ariel is innocent of wrong doing, but her father is not. Misha is torn by his feelings for Ariel and his need for restitution against her father. Knowing that the relationship between them is fragile, Misha does everything in his power to protect Ariel's father. His efforts are to no avail when her father is shot. Ariel comes to realize Misha's steadfast courage and determination to protect her and her father despite what has happened to his family. Ariel's love and devotion heals Misha's heart.

The Talisman
The fourth book in the Lakota/Pinkerton Series

Running from a marriage that lasted one night, Dr. Moriah McKeown discovers the land she has settled on is coveted by determined and lawless men. Yet the proud young woman who once vowed never to abandon her home has second thoughts when her adopted children are threatened. Her only recourse is to enlist the aid of a dark, dangerous gun for hire.

Haunted by the past and a betrayal he will never forgive, Ian Civanovich uses his fast gun and his reckless courage to forget the faithlessness of a woman in his past. He will trust no female—nor will he rest until the threat hovering over Moriah McKeown is put to rest.

Forever His
The fifth book in the Lakota/Pinkerton Series

Struggling to come to terms with the part she played in Jacob St. John's death, Etta Barringer resigns from Pinkerton Agency and seeks peace and solace in a Rocky Mountain Cabin.

Jacob has vowed to discover the reason Etta has betrayed him, sold him out to his enemy and left him for dead.

Isolated in their cabin, they discover their love for each other and learn to trust. But the trust is shattered when Jacob learns she is married to his sworn enemy; the man who left him in the desert to die.

Allura's Secret
Twelve Dancing Princesses Book One

Allura McClellan is horrified by her father's decision to take out an ad in the Times awarding her to the man strong enough and smart enough to win her hand and uncover her secrets. She's an intelligent young woman who takes great delight in the freedom allotted to her by her father. She's well aware that marriage would effectively curtail the adventures she's shared with her sisters and cousins.

Hunter Gray is nothing like the other men who've arrived to vie for Allura's hand in marriage and everything that goes along with it. However, he is the first to refuse to concede defeat and pursue her despite her attempts to disguise her true appearance. It's her temperament that is of more concern to him than her looks. Hunter has worked all his life with the hope of someday owning his own land. Now that it looks like there's a very real possibility that everything he's ever wanted is within reach nothing is going to deter him – including Miss Allura's disagreeable disposition.

Amorica's Wager
Twelve Dancing Princesses Book Two

Amorica Hepburn was sent to London to find a husband. Finding a man was the last item on her agenda. With her two cousins, Amorica wagers she can dissuade her suitor before the others. Despite her efforts she discovers a chemistry that cannot be denied. Suddenly she is the arrogant man's wife, pledged to a marriage neither desire. But swept off to his ancestral home above the Dover cliffs and into his strong embrace, Amorica is soon possessed by a raging passion for the husband she had vowed to despise...

Damian Andrews couldn't afford to trust the emerald-eyed spitfire who happened upon his secret. Amorica's hatred of all men of his kind only inflames the war that rages between them. Still, he can not control the intense desire his stubborn bride inspires, or make her surrender to his will until he has conquered the headstrong beauty on the battlefield of love...

Ravyn's Marriage of Inconvenience
Twelve Dancing Princesses Book Three

A REGAL BEAUTY

When the duchess decides to wed her to a wastrel and a fop, Ravyn Grahm takes matters into her own hands and declares her engagement to another man. Instead of fessing up and telling her great aunt what she has done, she goes through with the pretense. Ariec Lakeland is the bastard son of an earl and has a dangerous reputation. But Ravyn is willing to do most anything to keep the duchess from discovering the lie.

A DEVIL-MAY-CARE SMUGGLER

He'd bought land in America, looking to put down roots and end his life of adventure, but Ariec Lakeland got more than he bargained for when he encountered a beautiful heiress who made a promise she didn't want to keep. But the promise could not be undone and standing between them were more obstacles than either ever dreamed. Ariec had made plans to spend the rest of his life in America and that was at odds with Ravyn's plan of living in England and running her father's estate. Now, he'll have to choose between his dreams and the woman he loves more than life.

Christel's Sunrise
Twelve Dancing Princesses Book Four

He Made Her An Offer...

Life has thrown Christel McClellan some experiences that could have devastated a less determined woman. Beautiful, self-assured and fiercely independent, she is trying to forget the loss of her stillborn child. But is the child alive?

She Couldn't Deny...

Life is carefree for Ryder MacLaren who loves to see what is on the other side of the sunrise. Laird of Clan MacLaren, he is wealthy, handsome and happily unencumbered...until stunning Christel McClellan enters his life. When he hears her story, he believes the child she thought dead has been sold to a wealthy buyer.

Storm's Passion
Twelve Dancing Princesses Book Five

SHE MADE A PROPOSAL...

Life strikes Storm Graham a shattering blow when she learns her father has bartered her to a man she detests. Storm is beautiful, self–assured and fiercely independent, and refuses to be a pawn in her father's schemes, yet she can find no way out of this bargain made in hell. Going on the offensive she asks the wealthiest man on the eastern coast of England to marry her, never believing she might fall in love.

HE TRIED TO REFUSE...

For Hadden Johnston life has provided everything he ever wanted, including a sanctuary for homeless children. He is wealthy, handsome and happily unencumbered...until stunning Storm Graham marches into his life and proposes a marriage of convenience. Yet this type of marriage to a woman who inflames his senses is far from acceptable. If he's going to be tied down, he will move heaven and earth to have this woman warming his bed.

Gotta Have Fayth
Twelve Dancing Princesses Book Six

A regal beauty with raven hair and piercing blue eyes, Fayth Graham is unwilling to parade herself in front of the wealthy Lords of England during the season. Seeking a means to dissuade any man wishing to wed her, she seeks a way to ruin herself for marriage. When she unexpectedly meets a man with sparkling gray eyes and an infectious grin, she decides this is the man who will keep her from agreeing to obey.

He returned from six months at sea, looking for a few nights of pleasure with a willing lass, but Jarret Kinsley got more than he bargained for when he met a beautiful debutant who responded to his kisses with a wild innocence that touched his heart. Yet the obstacles looming between them might rip them apart. Both had vowed never to marry, so when consequences of their dalliances got in the way, Jarret would have to choose between the life he's always desired and the woman he loves more than life.

Ella's Pleasure
Twelve Dancing Princesses Book Seven

A WHISPER OF PLEASURE
Ella Hepburn was an auburn haired debutant from the harsh Scottish coastline—a wild innocent to be seduced and tamed. A spirited beauty, she captivated Drake Montgomerie's jaded heart—while succumbing to the smoldering desire she felt for her unyielding suitor.

A WHISPER OF DANGER
In Drake Montgomerie's glittering world of money and privilege, young Ella discovered passion and desire could overcome everything she'd been taught to resist—entangling Drake, the heir apparent, in a lethal coil of aristocratic family intrigue. But grave peril would only nurse the sparks of a love that knew no limits and a magnificent ecstasy that would not be denied.

Eveleen's Seduction
Twelve Dancing Princesses Book Eight

A WHISPER OF SEDUCTION
A brutal attack on Eveleen Hepburn's cherished island off the Scottish coastline leaves her shattered and bewildered. Learning a man she once trusted can kill as easily as he can breathe even though the deed

saves her life, creates questions that need answers. An innocent beauty, she enchants Logan Maxwell's cynical heart—giving in to the raging passion she feels for her mysterious suitor.

A WHISPER OF INTRIGUE

In Logan's Maxwell's world of espionage and privilege, young Eveleen discovers truths about herself she never expected, and a need for passion and love can overcome all her fears if she learns to accept certain truths. She finds herself entangled in a lethal battle for land that was once owned by French nobility, taken from them during the revolution and sold to Maxwell. But grave peril would unleash the flames of love that simmers, creating a magical union that cannot be refuted.

Tavia's Deception
Twelve Dancing Princesses Book Nine

WHISPERS OF DECEPTION

When her father decides to send her to London for her season, Tavia Hepburn resolves to see the world instead. The raven haired beauty decides to disguise herself as a lad and find employment on a ship bound for Barcelona as a cabin boy. But she never bargains on finding passion and love to a red haired sea captain who rescues her from certain death.

WHISPERS OF MURDER

For James Macmurra, the world is black and white until he meets a young debutante, who turns his world upside down. He's unable to deny Tavia's intoxicating effect on him. In a match tense with obstacles, unwillingness to divulge secrets, and unforeseen peril, irresistible desire and passion grows into undeniable love. James would risk his life to shelter and protect the innocent debutante who seduces him with her sweet love.

Larena's Fascination
Twelve Dancing Princesses Book Ten

WHISPERS OF FASCINATION
Fiery, free spirited Larena Graham never wanted to marry a duke. She is thrilled to be in love with the fourth son of an aristocrat, Gavin Broon. But when it seems Gavin ignores her, she set her sights on politics and bettering human life. Unsuspecting intrigue and a plot against her, she continues her dangerous plans despite Gavin's wishes.

WHISPERS OF TRUST
Gavin has every intention of properly courting the beautiful Larena until he must leave the city in order to put his affairs in order. Returning to London, he finds the woman he means to make his own is embroiled in political protests that could lead to a prison ship. Larena must learn to trust the handsome Scotsman whose most pressing mission is to protect her and keep her from harm.

Tira's Education
Twelve Dancing Princesses Book Eleven

WHISPERS OF EDUCATION
Learning how to build ships is Tira Hepburn's only dream until she meets Jamie Lundin and her world is turned upside down. With her raven black hair and vivid green eyes, she tempts Jamie and pushes him to defy his vows. She never bargains on finding an irrevocable love and a passion to a man who cannot fulfill her dreams despite his burning desire for her.

WHISPERS OF A BARGAIN
Arrogant and self-assured Jamie is brought up short when Tira captures his heart. All his carefully made plans are put to the test when he decides to teach her the art of ship building if she will spend a week with him alone on his ship. He is unable to deny Tira's intoxicating effect on him. When Tira leaves him behind unwilling to live with him without the benefit of marriage, he races after her. Jamie will risk everything to shelter and protect the innocent debutante who seduces him with her sweet love.

Aidan's Love
Twelve Dancing Princesses Book Twelve

Whispers of Love
Aidan McLellan has loved since she first set eyes on him as a young girl. Spontaneous, wild and eager to grow up, Aidan haunts his waking thoughts day and night, insinuating herself into his life. With her fiery red hair and sparkling sapphire eyes, she seizes Blade's heart even while he tries to resist the innocent child until she becomes a woman.

Whispers of Courage
Blade has waited what seems a lifetime to claim the woman who captures his heart as a little girl. Claiming his inheritance before his younger brother takes what is rightfully his, Blade must convince Aidan of his sincerity after years of avoidance and wed her before his father dies so he can return home, securing his rightful place. Everything is put to the test when his life as well as Aidan's is threatened by the man who once called him brother.

Twelve Days to Love

When Archer Steele shows up at Calanthe Durand's failing plantation with an alligator over his shoulder, Cali thinks she's never seen a more handsome man. During the war she had to defend herself and her servants from both union and confederate soldiers. Independent and self-sufficient, she vows to never marry.

But Archer Steele has different ideas. The first time Archer sees Cali in town, he feels an instant attraction. He decides he will do everything and anything to convince the beautiful Miss Durand he is worthy of her love. During the weeks leading up to Christmas, he gives her twelve gifts in hopes she will fall in love with him. Yet they are faced with challenges they must overcome before Cali can commit to a marriage.

Door to Heaven

Jessica Lawrence is the stepdaughter of a woman born in the twentieth century transported back in time to the year 1868. An acclaimed suffragette, she raises Jessica to believe in the equality of women. Jess Law believes everything she was taught, and when the time is right she becomes a private investigator. Courageous and impetuous, Jess finds danger in her quest to save all women from white slavery. Her passionate mission results in a wedding to Roc Newman, a man she knows can steal her heart...

Roc can't trust the sapphire-eyed spitfire who invades his home in search of secret papers and knocks him flat with her karate moves. Jessica's refusal to obey his wishes serves to inflame the war between them. Still, he cannot control the intense desire his reluctant bride inspires, or make her surrender her independence, until he has conquered the headstrong beauty on the battlefield of love...

Rebel Heart

HER REBEL SPIRIT DEFIED HIS OUTSIDERS SOUL...She was velvet and silk, eyes the color of a summer storm and amber hair. Victoria DeMontville, because of a promise and a codicil to her father's will, was forced to marry one man to protect her from another. She hated Cameron Savage with a fierce passion. But to hold on to her genetic research and find a cure for the deadly Signe virus, she must pretend to love the enemy at her door, come with weapons of fire to melt her icy heart...

HIS OUTSIDERS TOUCH IGNITED RAGING PASSIONS...· He wore a mask, disguised as the Phantom, a true legend come to life. Even as war and debate over new genetic research engulfed them all, he would find his greatest adversary in the beauty who'd branded him an outsider and barbarian, the woman he was born to possess, his soul mate.

Safari Moon

Solo St. John, a wildlife photographer, is preparing for a trip to Alaska. Suddenly, Solo finds women of all sorts invading his privacy, his home and his office, all cooing nonsense words and blatantly throwing themselves at him. Solo doesn't know why, and he has no idea how to rid himself of the persistent women. He finally decides to beg a favor of his best buddy Nyssa Harrington.

In love with Solo for the past ten years and knowing he doesn't return her feelings Nyssa doesn't want to talk to Solo. She knows if she accepts his phone call, she will not be able to resist the temptation to hope again.

Straight to Heaven

Running from demons, Alexandra McMurdie stumbles into Forbidden Ground where up is down and elements of nature are contested. Though a strong independent woman in the twenty-first century' she is unprepared for life in the 1800s. Her first site of the formidable James Lawrence makes her heart skip a beat, giving her cause to reconsider her desperate need to find a way home.

Born with a silver spoon, James' life was torn apart during the War Between the States. Moving west he vows to put the life he once knew in the past. When he discovers a half-frozen woman near Gold Hill, his heart begins to thaw. His love for Alexandra and his need to keep her from a man who has pursued her through time might cost him his life as well as hers.

A Valentine's Anthology

The Lending Library-a fantasy by Christie L. Kraemer
Faeries try to fit into the human world when the forest where they make their home is destroyed by a mysterious enemy.

Chasing Rainbows-a contemporary romance by Genene Valleau

An eccentric aunt, an inventive uncle, a mother who wears poodle skirts, and a brother who wears pearls provide a hilarious backdrop for the courtship of a young woman who yearns for a "normal" family.

The Gift-an historical romance by Christine Young

A man and a woman on opposite sides of the Civil War get a second chance at love after one final battle returns soldiers to their war-torn homes to rebuild their lives.

A St. Patrick's Day Tale
Christine Young, C. L. Kraemer, Genene Valleau

Tumble through time...

...to Ireland in 1817, when tensions are high between Protestants and Catholics and fae people guide the fate of villagers. A lovely Catholic lass stumbles upon the weakly ritual fisticuffing between Irish lads. She falls into the lap of a handsome young Protestant. Family ties, grudges, and two conniving faeries threaten their budding love. But the faeries outsmart themselves when they hijack a time machine that has mysteriously appeared in their forest and are whisked to...

...Eugene, Oregon in the 20th century, amid a property feud between the local faeries and night elves. The conniving faeries from Olde Ireland try to stir up more mischief. However, a warrior gnome convinces the magic folk to control their own destiny, and forces the intruding faeries to take refuge in the time machine again, spinning their way toward...

...A modern day castle in western Oregon. An eccentric inventor is determined to reclaim his wayward time machine and save his beloved wife from her latest misadventure. If only they can travel safely past the black hole...

a May Day Anthology
Christine Young, C. L. Kraemer, Rosemary Indra, Genene Valleau

Highland Miracle — Christine Young

HURTLED THROUGH TIME, Sean Michael Sterling, landed in the midst of a May Day celebration he didn't understand, assuming the role of Laird Sterling.

ILLIGITAMATE CHILD OF NOBILITY, Reagan Douglas searches for a way out of her half brother's house.

Defying the Odds — C.L. Kraemer

The night elves on the hill aren't happy without their magic. They concoct a plan to punish those who were involved in the act that rendered them almost human. Meanwhile, Uther, the rogue night elf, has returned to woo the Librarian to be his eternal mate.

Love in Bloom — Rosemary Indra

When childhood friends reunite it takes two fairies and a matchmaking daughter to help them admit their true love for each other.

No More Poodle Skirts — Genie Gabriel

After drifting for years in the innocent age of the 1950s, a woman struggles to join today's world by finding a career and a new love, with some help from her zany family.

Once Upon a Christmas Moon
Christine Young, C. L. Kraemer, Genene Valleau

TWELVE DAYS TO LOVE

When Archer Steele shows up at Calanthe Durand's failing plantation with an alligator over his shoulder, Cali thinks she's never seen a more handsome man. During the war she had to defend herself and her servants from both union and confederate soldiers. Independent and self-sufficient, she vows to never marry. But Archer Steele has different ideas. The first time Archer sees Cali in town, he feels an instant attraction. He decides he will do everything and anything to convince the beautiful Miss Durand he is worthy of her love. During the weeks leading up to

Christmas, he gives her twelve gifts in hopes she will fall in love with him.

BOOTS AND BLADES
An ancient evil from the old country has arrived in the high desert of Oregon. Gnome children are vanishing then re-appearing, showing various stages of traumatization. Tiamoon, warrior gnome, will put her skills to use alongside Killian, a handsome warrior, also in need of a cause.

CHRISTMAS PAWSIBILITIES
With their world destroyed and their space ship malfunctioning, the dogizens of Planet Canid have little choice but to crash land on Earth. They face tortuous experiments at the hands of the Geeks in Green...or they can trust an eccentric inventor and his zany family to deliver the Canine Queen's puppies and help them celebrate new lives.

www.ingramcontent.com/pod-product-compliance
Lightning Source LLC
Chambersburg PA
CBHW070646180626
46817CB00006B/2254